A VAMPIRE'S VENGEANCE

Ella Kindred

Kindle Direct Publishing 2024

ISBN- 9798373218344

Cover design by: Ella Kindred
Library of Congress Control Number: 2018675309
Printed in the United States of America

*For the readers who fall into the book's universe and
go on the adventure alongside the characters.
May you find peace in your existence.*

"Be the change you wish to see in the world."

MAHATMA GANDHI

CONTENTS

CONTENT WARNING

This book may include explicit material, including depictions of drug use, mildly sexual content, and use of profanity. Reader discretion is advised. This book explores themes of veganism and vampirism, delving into real-world conflicts of morality alongside fantasy content, with the goal of encouraging kindness and courage in readers. Recommended for ages 16 and up.

PROLOGUE

Flashing lights. Booming bass. Sweaty bodies brushing up against their peers. It was heaven to me. I headbanged at the front rail to Rezz's song, Edge, next to some of the greatest people I'd ever met. A slower song came on then and we headed back to the center of the crowd so we could take a hit without getting caught. I turned to my best guy friend as he passed the blunt to me. A clearly drunken man stumbled over to my group and gave everyone a high five. When he got to me, he gave me a flirtatious smile, complimenting my outfit. I replied with thanks and gave him my kaleidoscope glasses to try on. He practically fell over in awe and the group laughed. I was wearing a blue mesh crop top with glitzy pasties underneath and a matching bottom with a thin skirt. I also had cloth wings that were attached to my ring fingers so when I raised my arms it looked like I grew beautiful blue wings. My female friends were wearing similar costumes but the guys in the group just wore shorts and tanks, and we all had many coordinating Kandi bracelets. It wasn't the first time we had gone to a rave together, but it was the first time with the whole group at the same show at the same time.

The music transitioned to Melancholy, and I waved my arm to the beat of the music. The crowd started singing in unison and I was reminded why I love going to shows more than anything else. The unity, the friendships, the music, the lights, the sounds, the smells, all of it made for one exhilarating experience. The only downside: some shows were on weekdays, and I had to be up and ready for school in 6 hours.

I lived in a suburb just south of Kansas City. It was what many of my fellow students called a rich neighborhood, and I suppose they're right. Both my parents were crazy hard workers and they made pretty good money because of it.

My cell phone vibrated in the morning, waking me up in a groggy state. I wasn't hungover, but I was still a bit hazy from copious amounts of weed. I did my best to put on a smile and go about my morning routine as usual. This day's look consisted of athletic leggings and a pink blouse with matching sneakers. I accessorized and applied my makeup, only combing through my hair to style. I suppose to most I would be considered pretty, I rarely had acne and I enjoy sports, so my body type is desired by most of the males at my school. Sometimes I wished I had more exciting features, but usually I didn't hate the way I looked.

I smiled at myself in the mirror, checking my teeth for imperfections. At one point in my life, I had had braces, so my teeth were straight, but not perfectly white. The only thing I was truly unsatisfied with was my fangs. My canines were unusually large and sharp, which is ironic considering my herbivorous nature.

I then jogged downstairs to the kitchen where my mother was eating some cereal. We hugged each other good morning, and she slid the box over to me. I poured myself some soy milk on top of organic cinnamon crunch and bit into the savory breakfast.

"You look tired," Mom smiled.

"So do you," I teased.

"Yeah, long night at work. Sometimes I wonder why I ever decided to quit traveling the world as a day job."

"Cause you had us," I rolled my eyes.

"OH, that's right," she laughed.

She and my father were teens in the '70s, both hippies, which explains my unique name, Purple Haze Miller, although most people just call me Haze. In their youth my parents learned all about kindness and equality for all and it was the one thing they wanted to make sure they passed on to their children. I have an older brother, but he's away at college.

"How was your show?" She inquired. My mom was my best friend, I told her everything, we had always been big on honesty.

"It was amazing! Probably one of the best I've gone to yet!"

I showed her some videos and photos of the show and she responded with excitement. After that I finished my breakfast and rinsed out my bowl then headed off to the bus stop. It was my senior year, and I couldn't be more excited to abandon high school forever. The only teacher I truly liked was my English teacher, who let me come sit in her classroom and read whenever I had a free period or if I wasn't feeling up to eating during lunch hour. Most of my classmates were awesome, so I was grateful to have such amazing friends to end my high-school experience with. On Thursdays I volunteered with the school's recycling program. I would go around to each classroom during my aide hour and pick up all the recycled papers and bottles. After school I ran with the track team, it was exhausting, but at least it helped me sleep at night. I wouldn't get home till nearly 6, carpooling with other students on the team, and was always starving by then. That night my parents worked together on a nice organic meal: zucchini spaghetti with a tomato-basil sauce and a tomato-basil salad to go with it. As we sat down to eat, my father asked how my day went. It was something we made tradition in the family; we always had dinner together, and we always put our cell phones away and smartwatches off so we could converse without interruption.

I repeated my day's events to them and shared that I had a lot of homework to catch up on. After that I helped clean the kitchen then ran up to my room to get started. By the time I was done with the homework it was already 9, so I showered and went straight to bed, collapsing in exhaustion. With all the extracurriculars it was hard to also have a social life, but I always tried to make it a priority, as I usually had time to work on homework in the morning before my second class of the day.

I anticipated the next social event, a vegfest over the weekend. A group of gals that I volunteered with would be meeting me there and I was super excited because it was only an annual festival. Upon arrival I found my friend Serenity, an older woman who had the biggest heart. She had silver hair and green eyes, and somehow had energy for days. She and I walked around until we found the rest of our group, and all together we paraded the festival, stopping at every booth, meeting each owner and volunteer working them. There were t-shirt companies, jewelry makers, corporate businesses, and my favorite, food stands. I was big on plant-based cheese: cashew cheese to be exact. It was so creamy and smooth with some spices thrown in for that kick. We sampled all the food vendors that we could, then bought jackfruit tamales and seitan nachos for lunch. A speaker came on stage in the center of the festival, and we set up in the grass to watch. We only stayed for two speakers, but they were both so inspiring, sharing their story of how a plant-based diet changed their lives, and the lives of others, for the better.

Once we had seen everything at the festival, we crossed the street to the local farmers market, the biggest one in the area. There wasn't a single fruit or veggie they didn't have. Lastly, we crossed the next street over to a strip mall that had a cute little flower and decor shop. A few members of the group had broken off by then, so it was at that point just me and Taylor and Tiffany, package-deal twins from a few towns over, whom I also knew from volunteer work. They were always super sweet and always put others first. They also volunteered and did activism much more often than I. Activism was something I was interested in, but due to my many other activities, wasn't something I got to do very often. Although there's an opportunity coming up this next weekend that I was ready for, a rodeo protest.

Taylor pointed to a cute little frog statue, and we laughed at his odd position.

"Oh, happy little frog!" I exclaimed,

"I think I need to buy him," Taylor replied.

"I'll get the one that's lying down then we'll have two!" Tiffany added.

The girls made their purchases, and we headed out to meet the trolley. We didn't usually have too many weirdos in the area, it wasn't New York, but while on the trolley I noticed a man in a dark hood staring me down. I wasn't typically one to get scared easily, as I pride myself on being non-judgmental, but something about the man set me off. He gave me the creeps, the way his dark eyes scanned me, the way his stiff shoulders slumped, even his smell. Something about him told me to stay away, but me being me-I decided to give him the benefit of the doubt and we carpooled the rest of the way through the city with no incidents.

School for the next week was as bleak and bland as usual, the only exciting thing being that I received an English achievement award for my dedication to my favorite subject and the readers club. I was super proud of myself and even my parents came to cheer me on.

Senior year was coming to its end and as I prepared for finals, I started getting stressed, more stressed than I'd ever been in my life. My mom and dad had always raised me to work hard, and just try my best, and as long as I remained kind and selfless, great things would come to me, but it was times like these I wished I could be a bit conceited. I didn't stop my volunteer work or my extracurriculars just because of finals. Instead, I stayed up late, and just went about my days tired as hell. I just hoped it would all be worth it.

The weekend finally arrived and that Friday night I spent 12 hours catching up on sleep. Waking up on Saturday with nothing to do but the protest was my favorite kind of Saturday. Since my parents both worked stable 9-5 jobs, they were both free and more than willing to help with the protest, and we spent the morning making posters and signs. It was a fun activity for the three of us, and we got quite a few laughs out of it. Not about the animal cruelty of course, in our family we had a lot of inside jokes that we liked to reminisce about. My dad drove us downtown and we met up with the other protestors outside the venue. We were a peaceful group so all we did was stand there and hold signs up. The organizer of the protest stood front and center handing out flyers and talking to the people that were willing to listen. It was a mildly successful event, with a few people realizing how cruel the show was and deciding to enjoy their weekend elsewhere.

Towards the end I was people-watching more than anything and someone in my peripheral caught my attention. It was almost like a 6th sense. Something told me I needed to look in that direction; a man stood across the street, loitering. Something seemed familiar about him, but also something seemed off. Maybe it was that they were wearing a hoodie when it was early May and 75 degrees. I couldn't put my finger on it, but I decided my gut must've been wrong as occasionally it is, and turned back to my group as we made plans to meet up the following week.

My parents and I waved to the group, and we sped off to go grab lunch at our favorite vegan coffee house, Mud Pie. I recognized some of the employees but didn't really know them by name. The coffee shop was a cute little yellow, Victorian-style house in the middle of downtown, white picket fence and all. It was very out of place and that was one of the things I loved so much about it. We got our drinks and pastries and found a spot outside to eat. It was a gorgeous day, and we were excited to enjoy it outdoors.

"So Purple, are you ready for finals?"

I shrugged, "getting there."

"Only two weeks left until you're a free woman!" My mom smiled, "you still haven't mentioned anything about college sweetie, have you thought about what you want to do yet?"

"Yeah, I'm starting to think about that... honestly what I really want to do is travel like you guys did! I want to go on adventures, I want to go to EDC and volunteer in Africa, and build houses in Mexico, and tutor in France. I don't want to go to the boring college in the boring town I've been stuck in for almost 20 years... and... sorry, I didn't mean to go on a rant there."

I sighed and my mom reached for my hand across the table.

"Honey... that sounds wonderful. If that's what you want to do, we will support you."

Dad rested his hand on my shoulder, "I miss the days we used to travel all the time, but we settled down because we thought stability would be good for you. If you're ready to venture out and do your own thing, that's okay, just know that we love you and we are so, so proud of you and the young woman you've become."

"I love you guys," I smiled and hugged them both. I was so lucky to have such supportive parents, "there is something else I've been wanting to talk to someone about though."

"What is it babe?" My mom looked concerned.

"I'm sure it's nothing... but I've been getting this weird feeling, like last weekend I saw this guy, and then today at the protest. I don't know, I saw this person and I just got bad vibes. His aura was way off."

"What color was it?"

"I don't know... I wanna say like black. Maybe grayish, but I could be wrong," I was never good at reading auras.

"Tell me everything."

I shared the story in detail and my parents hadn't a clue either. They believed me though and made sure I knew that if I ever felt that way again to call them and tell them. They wanted to keep me safe, and I was grateful for that.

CHAPTER 1

Graduation

The next couple weeks at school were mostly stressful, but a few of my classes had finished early and there were now free periods for me to study in other areas, which was helpful to say the least. I hadn't gotten any negative vibes other than anxiety, so the curiosity of the hooded man was belittled and pushed aside in my thoughts. I focused on my studies and my track team to finish out the year strong, meanwhile searching for ways to expand my volunteer opportunities after graduation. Upon my searches I found an organization that pays for your travel expenses in exchange for the volunteer work and it sounded perfect to me, so I worked on my application in what little free time I had.

Finally, the weekend arrived, and I was just as nervous as I was excited. Like most of my peers, I was worried about tripping on stage and making a fool of myself, but I stayed strong and reminded myself that I don't need to worry about what others think of me, and if anything did happen, that it's best to laugh with them and move on. I only have to step foot inside my school one more time and then never again.

The door opened without a knock, and I ran to it knowing I would find my older brother in the entryway.

I gave him a big hug and helped him carry his bags in. There was a man with him who I assumed must've been his new boyfriend that he recently told me about. I said hello and Jerry introduced me to Luke.

"It's nice to meet you, Luke." My parents and I exclaimed.

"It's good to be here, congrats grad!" He cheered.

I smiled, trying to test my aura reading skills, but again, wasn't sure what I was looking for, no matter how many times I did research. I guess it just wasn't a skill for me to acquire. He smiled nicely though, and as long as he treats my brother right, I'm content.

Mom steered us in for dinner, "Luke, I hope you don't mind but as I'm sure Jerry has told you, we eat all organic, plant-based foods in this house, so for dinner we have spaghetti squash with eggplant and a side of garlic toast."

"Sounds delicious, thank you Mrs. Miller."

"Oh please, call me Cindy, and you're welcome, do you eat vegan as well?"

Jerry spoke then, "he's vegetarian, but I have yet to take him to a vigil so maybe one day."

"Well, no judgment here, come have a seat."

The boys settled in and took their seats next to me. We caught up throughout the meal, everyone with phones stowed away. It was nice to see my brother again; the last time I saw him was during winter break. It was good to have him there to cheer me on at graduation.

"So, Haze, have you got a boyfriend yet?" Jerry asked me.

"No Kush, I don't." We both liked to use each other's middle names as nicknames, especially to tease each other.

"Hold up, you forgot to ask if she has a girlfriend," Luke snickered.

I rolled my eyes, "no I don't have a girlfriend or boyfriend, I'm too busy for a committed relationship, thank you."

They laughed and finished their meal. We chatted throughout the night, staying up way later than I would normally when I have something important the next day, but it was worth it.

Luke caught our Roomba doing its job and shrieked, "oh my gosh you guys have one of these?"

My dad laughed, patting the Roomba like a dog, "ain't she a beaut?"

"You guys name her?" He joked.

"Nah, we only name living beings."

"Do you guys have any pets?"

"We've helped rescue some cats and dogs, and a few chickens and pigs but we don't adopt any just because we work so much, we don't really have enough time for devotion. It just wouldn't be fair to them, you know?"

"Of course, so you guys take them to shelters and stuff?"

"Yes, we'll help we're we can, most recently we helped the transportation of a group of chickens from a tipped truck, many died but with help we were able to save almost 100 of them."

"Wow, that's awesome! You guys are like superheroes or something."

Mom shook her head, "not superheroes, just people, doing the right thing. If situations were reversed, it's what I would want someone to do for me."

Luke wasn't sure how to respond so he nodded and changed the subject. Sometimes our conversations make people uncomfortable, but it's going out of your comfort zone that creates change. We wouldn't have all the amazing inventions of today's world without a little uncertainty.

The next day began with a rush as I had slept in a little later than I'd have liked and knew I would be behind on getting ready. The ceremony was in the evening but before that we had family and friends over to celebrate early, so I had to be ready by noon. Luckily, I had already set out everything I needed the night before, a shimmery rose-gold dress, matching pumps, and a faux pearl bracelet. I painted my nails a nude pink and once they dried, I curled my hair and applied my makeup. It had been a while since I had bothered to dress up, other than the rave we went to, and I stood awestruck, staring at myself in the mirror. For once I didn't see myself as plain and simple, I saw beauty, and grace. I remembered poise and straightened my back, sticking my curves out to what extent I could. I inhaled deeply as I would in meditation, and smiled, "let's do this." Coming down the stairs I was applauded by my family.

"You look gorgeous sweetie."

"Stunning girl!" Luke giggled. I received careful hugs from everyone and just as I hugged the last family member, the doorbell rang. My closest friends joined me for hugs then and I was ecstatic to have them around to support me.

The party went off without a hitch and just before it was time to leave, we put on our caps and gowns and took some photos. We had a neighborhood pond and walked down to it to get some more scenic photos.

"You girls look so cute!" My mom smiled as she took the photos, "I can't wait to put these on Facebook!"

I rolled my eyes and changed poses. The mini photoshoot took us about a half-hour and then mom looked at her watch and gasped, "we gotta get going!"

Each family took off in separate cars and we followed each other to school. The gym was already full of family members awaiting the ceremony. I gave my family another round of hugs and joined my peers in the backup gym. We received our pamphlets and instructions on how to line up, separating me from my group. I knew it was going to be a long ceremony; with 800+ students, it would take a while to get through all the names and speeches.

After what felt like forever, my name was finally called. My family and friends cheered me on, and I waved as I walked across the stage. I shook hands with the principal and raised my certificate in the air; I had finally done it! I finished school! I could move on to such bigger and better things! I was so ready for the next step in becoming a responsible, caring adult, who puts forth positive energy into the world. I blew a kiss to my family as I practically jumped off stage to get back to my seat. They waved me on and took photos the whole time, probably to annoy me with down the road. Even my brother was taking photos, and normally he wasn't one for social media, modern technology, or unessential luxury items. He was leaning towards a more minimalist style, and we were so proud of him for that, but that's why it was usually off to see him taking photos. He loved just living in the moment, and I loved having the photos to look back on.

The rest of the ceremony went by quickly, and once it was time, we ripped up our pamphlets and threw them high into the air. The crowd went crazy, almost as if we were at a concert. Once things finally died down, we evacuated the school and met up for dinner at a Mexican restaurant that had both vegan and non-vegan food.

I got a black bean taco with corn, onions, cilantro, guacamole and salsa. We munched on our food while conversing, just having a good time enjoying each other's company. It was times like these that I really treasured, not for the food, but for the quality time spent with the ones I loved.

"Oh, so I have some exciting news!" I shared with the table. They asked what it was between bites.

"I found a program that I think will be perfect for me. So, with that said, next month I will be temporarily moving to Africa!"

There were a few gasps and some cheers, and my mom nearly shed a tear. "Oh, honey I'm going to miss you so much! But I am so, so proud of you!"

"I'll miss you guys too! But I really think this will be the best thing for me."

"Will you be working with animals or?"

"I'll actually be working on building schools for African children, and maybe I'll even get to teach a bit, well see, but I'm super excited!"

"That's great! They'll be lucky to have you!" My dad exclaimed.

"Education should always be easily accessible to everyone," my mom nodded.

My family's support meant the world to me and even though I would be on the other side of the world, and I would miss them terribly, I knew in my heart it was something I needed and wanted to do.

I fell asleep with a smile on my face that night. No more school, only jobs of helping others from now on. In the morning, I received a text from one of my rave friends of a celebratory party she was throwing that night. We would be going to a bar district downtown. No, we weren't technically old enough to drink, but she was planning on pregaming at her place, then uber-ing downtown. There would be music, and dancing, and it was a good way for us to celebrate graduation, so of course I had to go!

It wasn't a rave though, so instead of glitter and pasties, I wore heels and a sundress. We met up at my friend's house then gathered in the kitchen for shots. The host poured and I served, once we all had our glasses, we clinked them together and downed the hatch. In between shots we played card games and jammed to some music. Two more shots later and we were buzzed and ready to go.

"The uber will be here... in one minute! Shit, we gotta go guys!"

We all jumped up, fuzzy from the alcohol, and ran around, grabbing our things. The uber pulled around the corner and one of the boys yelled at us to hurry up. Out the door, we ran and jumped into the SUV. Even though we were clearly drunk, I'd like to think we were respectful to the driver, we didn't yell, spill anything, or leave any trash behind. Our driver was very kind and even conversed with us on the way there. He dropped us off at the light district and we made our way into the crowd.

An hour into the music we were at our peak

drunkenness and us girls were grinding and swaying to the beat. A few guys approached us, but no one out of the ordinary or creepy.

"Omg girl, hey!" I turned to find my friend Sabrina. She was a couple years older than me, but she was a very non-judgmental type.

"Hey babe!" I exclaimed, shouting so she could hear me over the bass, "Long time no see, what's up?"

"We just rolled hard, man!" She laughed, pointing to her group behind her. They were all laughing and grinding and singing at the top of their lungs.

"You want in?" She asked.

"Oh... I'm not sure if..."

"First one's on the house."

"Well, I guess I don't have to worry about school anymore... sure, what the hell?"

Just this once. I told myself.

She smiled and gave me a big hug, caressing my arms down to my hands where she slid the tab into my fist.

"It's so good to see you!" She exclaimed.

I pretended to sneeze and covered my mouth to insert the pill. Dry swallowing was nasty, so I went over to the bar and asked for water. I knew I needed to drink a lot anyways to not be hungover in the morning.

It took a bit for me to start feeling the effects of the meds, but once I did the party was even more fun. It didn't make me hallucinate or anything weird, it just made me extremely calm and elated, and it made me forget about any troubles I may have had. All responsibility flew out the window and I was free to let loose and enjoy my night.

I met some new friends, one was a girl named

Brenda, she said to call her BB, she was tall and skinny, with short brown hair and lots of freckles. She had on a gorgeous sparkly green dress that accentuated her slender features and heels that were so sharp I had no doubt they could kill a man. She became an instant best friend and we exchanged Instagrams to stay in contact. We bonded over our love of Post Malone and swayed together to the music. Throughout the night I switched back and forth between groups, trying to give my attention to each friend group. At one point all three groups ended up at the center of the dance floor together and someone lit up and passed around. At that point I was already so drunk and high I was to a point I'd say yes to anything, I took a huge hit and struggled to not have a coughing fit in public. The herbs hit me at once and I was further gone than I had ever been. I don't even remember most of what happened in that following hour. All I remember is that it was the greatest night of my life. Being surrounded by close friends and new friends was the highlight I had been yearning for.

The lights, the music, the bass, the dancing, all had me fully hyped up. The district was so full of love and happiness, that I didn't even question when a man approached me and introduced himself. He held his hand out and said he would get me a drink and I took his hand and followed him. He got me a vodka sprite and handed it over to me. We walked back to the back of the building, and I leaned against the wall sloppily.

I tried hard to remember his name, Tony, I think? He was gorgeous. He looked to be around early-twenties, with sandy hair, flawless skin, deep-set blue eyes, and a stunning smile. He was wearing boots and skinny jeans with a clean T-shirt. He was attractive in such a way that I was instantly drawn to him. I felt bad judging him right off the bat by his appearance, but I was so crossfaded I didn't care. My body told me I needed him, and for the first time I listened to that need.

He flirted with me, and I flirted back. Tony, or whatever his name is, leaned over me and tucked my hair behind my ear. I smiled at him and took a sip of my vodka.

"What do you say we get out of here? He asked, a hand on my hip. I nodded and followed him out of the light district. We rounded a corner to the parking garage, and he spun me around once no one was in sight, kissing my neck.

I was engulfed in him, his scent enticing me, his breath on my neck sending shivers down my spine. I turned around and we began making out. He tugged on my hair and pulled me closer to him.

Tony started trailing kisses down my cheek and my neck, caressing my thigh and sliding a finger under my skirt. After a few more kisses I felt a sharp pinch on my neck, as though he was giving me a hickey. It would be my first, but I'd seen it in movies. It was hot. He sucked on my neck as I leaned into him, hanging on to his body in desperation. I wanted more, I needed more.

Tony let go of me and pulled me with him. A few cars down there was a gorgeous neon blue charger. He helped me into the passenger side then climbed into the driver's side. We drove out of town and into the countryside that was nearby; it was only a ten-minute drive before he pulled over... at a cemetery.

I didn't question it at the time, just followed him.

I even giggled a bit as we snuck in. It was fun to be exploring, doing something dangerous and random. I had never really done anything illegal aside from underage partying, and a part of me was excited to be letting loose and being spontaneous.

I practically tripped over my own feet trying to walk through the grass in heels, but quickly we came across a mausoleum. He opened it with a key, and we stepped inside.

Immediately he started kissing me again and I was back in heaven. We made out for a bit, our breathing getting heavier; I lusted for him in a way I had never experienced before, I'd let him do anything to me. He nibbled at my neck again and gave me another hickey. Then he pulled away for a moment to kiss my lips, and looked me in the eye, only to bring his finger to his lips. He gently bit down on the flesh of his fingertip drawing blood. He kissed me again then and put his finger to my lips. His blood covered my bottom lip, and I licked it clean, licking his finger next. The blood was sweet. It wasn't like my blood, which I knew from growing up with bad nosebleeds. From those, the blood would taste salty, almost like a rusty taste, but with a sweet undertone. His was only the sweet, and none of the salty. It made me crave more. I sucked on his finger for a moment before returning to his lips. He kissed me passionately, his hands trailing up and down my body. He wrapped his fingers around my neck, thumbs around my ears; and more instantaneously than I could understand, he snapped my neck, and I was gone.

CHAPTER 2

Realization

I awoke with the worst migraine I had ever experienced. Looking around I struggled to remember where I was. I had forgotten most of the night prior, only remembering bits and pieces of the party and the man I'd met. The room was dark, and I couldn't see much, just small outlines of a casket and the door. I fumbled through the dark, reaching for the handle. A stinging pain hit my stomach and I buckled over. I was hungry, but something felt off. It didn't feel like normal hunger pains, I was craving something. I felt weak, like I hadn't eaten in days. My stomach growled and my throat began to burn. It was so dry and sore I tried to scream but nothing came out.

"Tony!" I coughed.

I wasn't even sure if that was his true name. I saw a flash of him in my mind, remembering how gorgeous he was and then how hands-on he was.

"What did he do to me?" I cried to myself. How long had I been there? I needed to get out and get home, surely my parents would be furious with how late I must be. I cautiously opened the mausoleum door and crept outside. It was still dark, so maybe I wasn't too late. I searched my person for my phone and purse but recalled that I must've left it in the man's car.

"Shit," I growled.

Mom would kill me if she found out, I had to get home before she woke up. I heard a bird start to chirp in the distance and I looked up, the sky to the east was a lighter blue than the west and I knew it wouldn't be long before the sun popped out.

I couldn't believe that Tony would just abandon me in the middle of a cemetery. Did he have no heart? No soul? Of course, he couldn't have. He tricked me into going with him while I was vulnerable.

I walked down the road and tried to figure out where I was. There was a gas station down the way, and I headed there hoping to borrow someone's phone so I could call a friend to give me a ride. The closer I grew to the gas station, the thirstier I became. The burning in my throat was becoming unbearable. My purse was gone though, and I had no money to buy food or drink while waiting for my ride.

Another sting of pain shot through my body, and I put my hand to my chest, breathing through the discomfort. I expected my heart to be beating quickly but instead I felt nothing. I noted it but didn't find it suspicious, assuming I was just momentarily too out of shape to feel it. I reached the gas station; there were no other people around aside from the single employee, and I was grateful for that. Surely I looked like crap after my rough night.

Entering the gas station, I was hit with a stench unlike any other. The smell was musty, reminding me of my grandfather before he passed (may he rest in peace). I held my breath and looked around. The man at the counter was elderly, he looked bored at first, but his gaze grew suspicious upon seeing me.

I gulped, something about him was setting me off. Part of me wanted to jump behind the counter and... what? What feeling is this? Anger? Resentment? Hunger.

I stood my ground at the doorway and raised my voice, "excuse me, can I borrow your phone?" My voice cracked and grumbled, I didn't sound like myself, I sounded sick, like I had a cold.

The man looked behind him at a bulletin board then looked back at me. All the color drained from his face; he looked like he'd seen a ghost.

"Please, sir, I need to get home," I claimed cautiously.

He stared at me, and I looked down at myself, my hair was a tangled mess, my dress was ripped, and there was dried blood streaked from my neck to my legs. I licked my lips and tasted more blood.

An image flashed before my eyes as I recalled licking blood from Tony's finger. I bolted out the door and threw up in the trash bin. What have I done?

I coughed and spit onto the ground. Blood poured from my mouth, and I wiped it on my arm. What was happening to me? I sat there on the ground, unable to move from the pain that was growing throughout my body. My throat only got worse from throwing up; I knew I needed to get home before I passed out, but I could barely move. My head throbbed but I forced myself to gain composure. Then I went back inside the gas station and ran to the bathroom. My face was covered in blood but there were no cuts from what I could tell. However, there was quite a gash surrounded by a huge bruise on my neck. I washed the blood off in the sink and wiped down my arms and legs. Glancing at myself in the mirror was hard, I had never been so appalled by my appearance before. I looked like a train wreck, but I knew I would never get home if I hung out in the bathroom all night. So, ignoring the pain, I swallowed loudly and exited the room.

The man was gone as I approached the desk. Behind it was the bulletin board, and something on it caught my eye. It was... me... on a missing person's poster. There was a picture of me smiling on the flyer and a description beneath. Last seen May 23rd at the light district. How could this be? What day was it that there's a missing person file for me already? Bright blue and red lights outside pulled my attention away and I turned to find the employee pointing at me to a pair of cops.

"Great," I mumbled, I really didn't want to get in trouble for drugs and alcohol, I had to get out of there. I turned on my heel and bolted out the emergency exit. Surprisingly, I could run as easily as I could under normal circumstances. The pain was excruciating, but I powered through.

I cut into a wooded area and ran for as long as I possibly could. Before I knew it, I was just outside my neighborhood. I hadn't recognized the area before, how had I gotten home so quickly? I figured the cops were probably on my tail and I continued to run towards my house. The sun was starting to rise, and I squinted. Something was off about the way the light was coming through. It seemed bolder, brighter. I stopped to breathe once I reached my house, my burning throat urging me to rest a moment.

The door opened and my mom gasped, her hands

swinging up to her mouth. My parents ran over and dropped to the ground with their arms wrapped around me. My mom kissed my forehead, tears streaming down her face.

"Where have you been?" She cried.

"Let's get her inside," my dad whispered, helping me stand. I inhaled and pushed my parents off me. Something was wrong. I felt like sinking my teeth into them... I was so hungry... so thirsty... I...

"Honey, are you okay? What's going on?"

I could only shake my head. They sat me on the couch, my brother joined us then, it looked like he had just woken up. He tried to hug me, but I shoved him off.

"Please... I need some space."

Dad and Jerry took a step back, but my mom sat next to me and held my hand, "where have you been? We were so worried, are you okay? What happened?"

I closed my eyes and focused on breathing. Being next to them was too much. Something about the way they smelled, it was good, enticing even, but a part of me said to stay away from them, the other part wanted to hurt them. I started shaking, was it with fear? Anxiety? Anger? All three? I couldn't tell.

"I think she's in shock" my dad guessed.

"We need to ground her," my mom replied, "honey, your name is Purple Haze Miller. You're 18 years old, you're a beautiful, smart, caring person. You love animals and hanging out with friends. Can you tell me what the last thing you remember is?"

"Take your time babe," Dad soothed, "remember headspace, breathe in... breathe out. Tell us when you're ready."

I meditated as best I could, breathing in and out

without ceasing. It was difficult. With each inhale my throat caught fire. I felt like someone had forced me to swallow acid.

What did I remember? I remembered kissing that man. The man that... did he hurt me?

"Man" I exhaled. Opening my eyes.

"What man?"

"Did someone hurt you?" My brother clenched his fist and my father set his jaw.

I cried again, leaning into my mom. She raised me from the couch and took me to my bedroom. She helped me put pj's on and laid me in bed. The boys stayed downstairs to give me privacy, and I was finally able to start thinking again.

"Mom," I reached out and took her hand.

She nodded and wiped my cheek.

"How long have I been gone?"

She sniffled, "you went out with your friends on Friday."

"And?"

"It's Sunday night, well now Monday morning."

"You mean I've been missing for almost three days?"

Her eyes watered and I could feel my own glaze over as something caught my attention. I focused my vision and suddenly I could see slight movements under her skin, the veins in her cheek trailing down her neck, blood pulsing throughout it.

"I think I died."

The blood drained from her face, and she went pale, "you know you can tell me anything. Please, let me help you. Tell me what happened."

I drank the Kool-Aid and confessed. I knew I could

trust my mom with anything. I had never lied to her before, and I didn't plan on starting now.

"At the party... I got crossfaded. I mean *really* crossfaded. I didn't mean for it to go that far. I'm so sorry mom. I see now that I had poor judgment. But I-I did something I shouldn't have. I followed a man out without thinking, he was cute, and he was so nice, and we started kissing," I paused, not really wanting to tell my mom the gross details.

"Tell me sweetie, I need to know so I can help you get through this."

I pointed to the bruise on my neck, "he uh... he hurt me, and I was too drunk to stop him."

Tears fell down her cheeks, "did he-oh please don't tell me-"

"No! No, well I don't think so; he didn't hurt me like that. I think he broke my neck."

"He broke your neck? Honey, that would kill you."

"That's why I'm so confused. I think he did kill me, and now I'm back to normal? I mean except for my... hunger."

"What do you mean?"

"My stomach, my throat, they hurt. I'm in so much pain. I woke up just a little bit ago. I must've been dead for more than 48 hours... so I must just be dehydrated.

"Oh! Of course, I'll just get you water and something to eat!" She stood up but I grabbed her hand.

"Mom?"

She turned.

"Please don't leave me." She nodded and sat down, then called my dad and had him bring me the food.

I took a swig of water and took a bite of an apple, and the second I swallowed, I felt even worse. I threw it back up, gagging. It didn't taste bad or anything, my stomach just said no. It needed something else.

I shook my head, "I'm so sorry."

"It's okay, shush, it's okay," my mom leaned back, bringing me with her. After crying it out I was able to fall asleep in her arms.

I sat up in bed, the hunger was still there, and it was even more prominent, but I was more focused now. The room was somehow pitch black, but I could still see everything as clear as day, just slightly different colors. My senses seemed heightened. I looked to my sleeping mother, her hair draped across her face. Again, I noticed her pulse and my mouth began to salivate. Why am I drooling?

Hungry.

I stood up carefully and snuck downstairs, I had to eat something. I opened the fridge and grabbed a banana. Then a carrot, then some berries. I stuffed my face, the taste almost seemed heightened, like it was the first time I had ever tried a berry. It was amazing but my stomach wasn't having it. I threw up again, this time making it to the trash bin.

Why can't I keep anything down? I felt so confused, and scared. *What do I do?*

"Purple, did you throw up again?" my mom asked. I nodded.

"You're clearly sick, let's get you back to bed." We went back and by then I was about to pass out. I felt so weak.

The next few days my "condition" only worsened. I couldn't keep anything down, even water. My skin became icy pale, and I was constantly freezing even though I was sweating. My mom thought I had the flu.

She said my cheeks were turning purple and my eyes looked cloudy. I hoped I wasn't losing my sight on top of everything else. I couldn't believe I was so stupid. One bad night out and it's causing all this mess.

I knew that this had to be the end. My family hadn't told anyone that they'd found me yet, I asked them not to, I didn't feel like I was back yet. A part of me died in that cemetery. Also, I'm worried that the other part of me will be gone soon as well. My friends have been worried about me, and it's so hard not to call them and tell them I'm alright, but I'm not alright.

There's something wrong with me, was it the flu? Or was it something else? There is something else weird too. The past couple days I've been sleeping all day, and when I wake up in the middle of the day, my sensitivity to the light has been so bad that I had to have my mom put up black out shades on the windows and rugs under the doors. Sounds were the same, even small things seemed loud to me, as the light strained and pained my eyes, noise gave me headaches and earaches. The smell was awful as well. I could barely stand to be around my family. I only allowed my mother in and only as often as I could handle. My brother went back to his dorm to give me space and said he would keep in contact with Mom to see how I'm doing. Dad went back to work during the day, and Mom stayed to keep an eye on me. I became so weak and thin from not eating for a week I could barely get out of bed. I coughed up blood quite often and it was starting to worry my mother, who decided to look up my symptoms since I refused to let her take me to a doctor. I had a feeling a doctor wouldn't be able to solve my problems.

"Hey Hun, I think I have an idea, but I need you to

tell me something first."

I awaited the question. My voice was so weak I could barely get a word out.

"I need you to tell me exactly what that man did to you."

I swallowed, knowing doing so would make me feel like I was eating glass. "Why?"

"I think I can help you, please, tell me everything you can remember, all the tiny and gross details too."

I nodded and told her everything I could remember, including the biting and blood lust.

"What happened to me?" I asked.

"I think I may know what you need to get better, but it's going to sound really weird."

"What?"

"Well at first I thought maybe he gave you an STD, but since you didn't actually... have sex with him, I started research on what else it could be. Haze, this is going to sound really bizarre, but I think, in order for you to stop being sick, I think you need blood."

"Like a transfusion?"

She sighed, "I think... I sound so stupid saying this, but I think that man may have been a... a vampire."

I wanted to laugh but after everything I had been through, and with how weak I was, a suspicion arose in me.

"But that can't be, right? Vampires aren't real."

"That's the only explanation that makes sense. Is there anything you might have remembered that could confirm or deny this?"

I glanced down at her neck and again noticed the blood rushing underneath her skin. I could even hear it in the same way someone can hear their blood pumping from putting their ear up to a conch shell. I pulled my hand up to my own neck and felt how swollen and sore it was, the bruise had only gotten worse.

"It wasn't a hickey..." I realized.

My mom brushed my hair to the side and inspected my shoulder.

"There is a puncture wound. He bit your neck, not just his finger, didn't he?"

I nodded, "I think so."

"So, it sounds like he bit you, you felt sucking, so it wasn't him making the hickey, he was sucking your blood... and then he made you drink his blood."

"And that's when he killed me."

"If he did... snap your neck," she shivered at the thought, "that means you died with his blood in your system."

"Mom."

"I think you're becoming a vampire!"

A realization shot through me and suddenly everything made sense.

"I can't be a vampire. I'm VEGAN! I don't eat people! And I most certainly will not drink the blood of non-human animals either! What am I going to do?"

"I don't know... but according to every book and movie ever, if you don't drink blood, you're going to die."

"I don't want to die," I cried.

My mom began to cry too, "there's only one thing I can think of."

"What?"

My mom stretched out her arm and I shook my head, "I can't, what if I hurt you?"

"You have to, it's okay."

"No, I won't. I won't do it. What if I can't stop and I do worse than hurt you?"

"I'm willing to take that risk. You're my daughter. I would do anything to protect you."

I shook my head, "Mom, every fiber of my being is crying out for help, but I just can't risk your life. That's not who I am; and even if I've become this monstrous, murderous being, I'm going to fight it."

"You are the strongest young woman I have ever met. We're going to get through this together, okay?"

I nodded, beginning to feel another wave of pain flow through me. It had been almost a week since I had eaten or drank anything, I knew I maybe had days, if not hours left to live.

Mom left me alone with my thoughts then and I contemplated my options. Killing was not one of those options, even though I didn't want to die. I was only 18, I still had so much life to live, so many people I wanted to help. Everything about this was so wrong. Why me? I wasn't built to kill. There wasn't a cell in my body that knew how to track, hunt, or take down prey, nor did I want to. There had to be another way. I couldn't hurt my mother. She meant everything to me. She taught me how to be kind, how to be selfless, she raised me to be myself while also caring for others, it wasn't right. She shouldn't have to suffer from my mistake.

There had to be another way, or I would die trying.

CHAPTER 3

The Change

A knock on my door woke me from my sleep. My mother entered with her hands behind her back.

I blinked through the darkness and asked what she was up to. At this point I was so weak I could barely lift my head and could not sit up to greet her. My father was so worried about me he was constantly suggesting taking me to the hospital, but now knowing what we knew, my mom and I knew that no doctor could help me.

"I got you something, but I need you to keep an open mind."

I closed my eyes, both from barely being able to breathe from the immense pain I was in and from fear of what was in her hand.

She gently grabbed my hand and I felt something squishy inserted into my fist. It was a bag of liquid. I knew that if I opened my eyes, that bag would be bright red.

"How did you get this?" I asked.

"The how's don't matter right now."

"Yes it does mom, did you violate your beliefs to protect me?"

"Well yes and no. Long story short, I stole it from a

doner. So, no animals were harmed... but I did steal. I'm sorry honey, but you won't drink from me. This was the only other thing I could think of. You need blood or you will die. The donors donate blood for transfusions to people who would otherwise die... so they are still doing that."

I had to admit. It was horrendous, but... having the blood so close to me that I could smell it... I was about to go insane thinking about how hungry I was, how weak I felt. My body was signaling that it was what it needed.

I nodded, allowing my mother to open the pouch and bring it to my mouth. The moment the blood touched my lips, my body took over. I was no longer in control of my actions. I sat straight up and squeezed the bag with my nails. It was cold and slimy, and part of me was disgusted, but the monster in me knew this was exactly what I needed. I gulped and gulped without thinking, and within seconds the bag was empty. I gasped, blood dripping over my chin and onto my bed.

I practically growled. "More," I pleaded.

My mom brought her other hand forward, "I kind of thought you might need more than one."

I snatched it out of her hand and tore it open, not caring about a mess. I was hungry, and this was what my body craved. It had been starving for a week and I was dying. No matter how grossed out part of me was, the other part of me was feeling rejuvenated.

I finished the second bag just as quickly as the first and I was still hungry, but I knew I had to stop myself. I had to remain in control. I could not lose myself over this.

My mom grabbed a towel from the bathroom and cautiously approached me. I swallowed, my throat no longer in searing pain, and after a few deep breaths and reminders that I was in control, I was fine. She sat down on the bed next to me and cleaned me up.

"Thank you... I don't know what I would've done if I didn't have you. I could've really hurt someone."

"I'm with you through this, Haze, this doesn't change the way I feel about you. You are still my beautiful daughter, and we will get through this."

I nodded and laid back down. After all that I needed a nap to clear my head. Mom left me to do so, and I fell asleep quickly.

I don't know how long I was asleep for, but it felt like a while. Sitting upright, I stretched. My muscles felt tight, like I was sore from a workout, but I realized then, something felt off about me. I was relaxed, calm, and cheerful, like before the incident. I climbed out of bed, grateful that I had regained my strength, and headed towards the bathroom. As I turned on the light, I swiftly clenched my jaw and shut my eyes tight. The light was so bright and intense that it practically blinded me. I flipped the switch again and stood up; my eyes stung a bit but within a minute they were back to normal. I stood in front of the looking glass, seeing everything with immense clarity but with a dark blue-gray hue. My skin was nearly the color of the room, pale as the moon, as translucent as the moonlight. My eyes were dark, cold almost, but they seemed to twinkle in the dark. My hair was the same in every way except somehow it seemed... shinier? And after a week of no food, I had lost so much weight that I looked anorexic. I opened my mouth and inspected it. My canine teeth were already sharp to begin with but impossibly they seemed even sharper than usual. This was it... my life as I knew it was over.

I'm a vampire.

I can't believe they're even real.

But.

I'm vegan.

Vegan vampires don't exist, they just can't, it is THE definition of an oxymoron. Can I even call myself that anymore? I mean I *drank* human blood.

"Honey? Everything alright in there?" My mom knocked.

"Yeah mom, come on in but don't turn the light on! I stood behind the bathroom door and watched my mom creep into the bedroom.

"Are you okay?" she asked cautiously.

"Shut the door."

She did. "I can't see anything."

"Sorry, I'm just extremely sensitive to the light right now."

"So, it's true then."

"Guess so."

She sighed. I wasn't sure what to say.

"I think... I'm okay now, more or less. I'm not hungry anymore."

"Well, that's good I guess."

I nodded, "but I think it's time to tell dad. Who knows how long it will be before I'm hungry again. I... I can't go back to normal from this."

"What are you saying?"

"I'm saying no one but you two can know about this, I'm dangerous, I don't know if I can control myself. Publicly speaking, we have to pretend I'm still a missing person."

Mom sighed; I could hear the pain in her exhale.

"I love you Mom, I'm so sorry for all the pain I've caused."

"It's not your fault, you were just trying to have a fun night with your friends."

I nodded, momentarily forgetting that I could see her, but she couldn't see me. I reached for her hand and squeezed, "I promise you, I'm going to do everything in my power to not lose myself over this. I don't know how I'm going to do it, but I would rather die than hurt someone."

"I believe you. No matter what happens, you will always be my baby girl."

"Can you bring Dad in?"

She nodded and searched for the door handle. I got it for her, standing behind the frame to avoid any lights.

I could hear them talking from downstairs, although I couldn't quite make out what she was telling him, probably just to be prepared. I sat at the foot of my bed and awaited disaster.

My parents snuck into my room and stood there, unsure what to say or who should start.

"Dad, I know this is going to be hard to believe but I'm just going to rip the Band-Aid off. I'm a vampire."

"That bastard!"

"Dad."

"I'm going to kill him for hurting my daughter!"

"Dad?"

"I'm sorry, I just can't stand the thought of anyone hurting you, much less..."

"Killing me?"

He huffed.

"I'm sorry dad, this is all my fault, I shouldn't have gone to that party."

He sighed, "what are we going to do?

"Well first of all, I'm astounded you didn't even question it, you believe in vampires?"

"Well, not at first, but after everything, it makes sense, kind of explains a lot."

"What time is it?"

"It's a little after 7pm."

"As much as it pains me to say this, I think I have to leave."

"Where will you go?"

"I'm not sure, but I can't stay here. I'm not putting your lives at risk by my being here, and I wouldn't be able to forgive myself if anything happened to you guys."

"We can help though."

"We're not afraid of you," Mom stated.

"It's not that. I know you trust me, but I don't trust me."

My mom exhaled wearily, "do we have a say in the matter?"

I shook my head, "nope."

"Well then... I guess you have to do what you have to do, just promise me one thing?"

"Of course."

"Promise us that you'll keep in contact with us, and you'll keep telling me everything. Vampire or not, you're still my daughter and I'll want to know you're safe. Just... call me every once in a while, eh?"

"I will."

"Okay well, pack light, we don't want it obvious that stuff is missing."

"Oh right... should we fake my death or keep me a missing person?"

"Wow," my mom started tearing up again. I'd never seen her cry as much as I had in the last week.

"I think missing person," Dad huffed, "we don't have a body to fake with."

I nodded, "right."

"Well, we'll give you some privacy."

My parents walked out, closing the door behind them then turning on the hallway light. There was a small amount of light coming through the cracks in the door and that was just enough for me to see everything in the room as well as if it was broad daylight.

I started packing some clothes into my luggage bag, but then realized the police would notice if that was gone. They would probably notice if my toothbrush and paste were gone too. Shit, what was I going to do? A thought came to mind. I was supposed to leave for Africa in a couple weeks anyways, maybe I could say I left early.

However, I also didn't have a car or any money. Where was I supposed to go, how was I supposed to pay for anything? Screw Tony. How dare he ruin my life and then disappear. The angry vampire in me wanted to kick his ass, but the pacifist in me said to forgive and forget. The problem was... the vampire part of me was strong, and it seemed to be trumping the other half. I needed to find him. I needed to know why he did this to me.

It was late at night; I could just search for him overnight and then come home just to sleep. That was another issue. With my stupid light sensitivity, I would have to find a place to sleep that would be pitch-black 24/7. *Good luck, Haze.*

I grabbed my sunglasses off my dresser, ready to

test out a theory.

I stood on the left side of the door, prepared, and cracked it open. Light from the hallway flooded into the room and I was temporarily blinded. I put on the sunglasses, and while I still had to strain my eyes and it was mildly painful to do so, I could function almost normally. Knowing the myths and legends, I was worried about burning in the sunlight, but it wasn't sun, just a lightbulb. Then again, if I was out all night and I didn't make it back in time... I'd better dress for the occasion just in case.

I threw on a hoodie and a hat, hoping it would help. I looked in the mirror and didn't even recognize myself. A realization struck and I took a step back out of shock. Something about wearing the hoodie with the hood up reminded me of the hooded man from the bus, and then again at the protest.

It was the same man. Had to be. It was *him.* He had been following me, that had to be it. The times he was in the hood, it was daytime. The time he was wearing just a T-shirt, it was at night. I mean maybe I'm just overthinking things, but if my memory serves me right, it had to be him.

I braced myself again and threw on my sunglasses.

"Where's your stuff?" Dad asked when I got down to the living room.

I kept my distance so I couldn't smell them as much, and shrugged, "there's something I need to do first. If you don't mind me staying one more day."

"You can stay as long as you feel comfortable."

I nodded, wincing at the light that came through the corner of my glasses.

"Then hopefully I'll be back before sunrise."

I turned around to leave and he called after me.

"Just... be careful."

"Promise. I love you."

"Love you too."

Once I stepped outside, I felt almost refreshed. It was the first time I had been outdoors in over a week. The breeze was cool, but it felt nice. Everything was fully in bloom as summer was just beginning, and I could still smell the rain left over from the previous day's storm. I carefully removed my sunglasses and was astounded by the clarity of my vision. I could see each individual blade of grass blowing in the breeze before me, and glancing down the street I noticed a cat lurking about 5 houses down. I growled under my breath before realizing it. The monster in me wanted to hunt its prey, but I wouldn't let it. I love cats, and never would I hurt one.

My muscles twitched, and I knew I needed to get away before I did something I would regret. So, I decided to test my agility and stamina. I ran as fast as I could, pushing my tired muscles to their peak. Within minutes I was halfway across town, back at the cemetery. I stopped in front of the gates, not even so much as winded from my run. I felt strong. Running was always something I had been good at, but this was unlike any other. If only my track team could see me now.

I sighed in remembrance of my classmates. If only I had not gone to that party, I could be hanging out with my friends right now, but instead I'm hanging out in a graveyard awaiting the man that killed me.

The gates were locked, and I feared not being able to get in, but then I remembered I could just sneak in. It wasn't like me, but *I* wasn't like me anymore. So, I walked around to the backside, away from the street, and climbed the fence.

I took my time walking to the mausoleum, part of me really hoping Tony wasn't there. I wished so badly that he had just been a figment of my imagination, but alas, my bloodlust was proof that he was real, as are vampires.

Carefully, I stepped around gravestones as I walked, apologizing to those I might've disturbed along the way. I wasn't sure if ghosts were real, but now knowing what I know, anything could be real. The loch ness monster could be real for all I know.

A rotten smell crossed my nose and I searched for the cause, finding a dead squirrel underneath a tree about 50 yards away. I wanted so badly to cry for the loss of such an adorable tree creature, but my body would no longer produce tears. My mouth started to water, and I flicked myself in the wrist. I will not eat animals. Even if they are already dead. I won't do it.

"You're going to get hungry if you don't." A deep voice said to me from behind. I spun on my heel.

"Tony."

CHAPTER 4

Tony

"How did you know what I was thinking?" I asked.

"My memory serves me well; I recall being a little virgin vampire. You're hungry, and you don't want to eat that squirrel, but somewhere deep down you know you need to. You need to feed; but considering you're alive after a week I'm assuming you've drunk someone or something's blood. So, tell me, what was your name again, who did you eat?"

"It's Purple Haze; and I did no such thing. By the way, animals are someone's too. They have brains and hearts and thoughts and feelings just like humans do."

"But you're not human."

"Thanks to you."

"Why are you here, Purple Haze?"

"I came to confront you."

He laughed, it was sinister sounding, yet somehow, I was still attracted to this awful excuse of a man.

"You want to do what?... Fight me?"

"No. I know I couldn't beat you in a fight, and not because I'm a female, but because I'm guessing you have quite a bit of experience in the vampire department."

"This is true."

"I just want to ask you... why? Why me?"

He approached me and caressed my cheek. I pointed my chin the other way and stepped back.

"Because," he grinned, "you're different. I've been watching you, Miss Haze, and I'm making you my little science experiment."

"I'm not a science experiment and you're just a creep, watching me? How long has that been going on?"

"Not long, you've noticed me both times." Something told me he was lying but I gave him the benefit of the doubt.

"You were the guy on the bus."

He nodded.

"And the guy at the protest."

Again, he nodded, "you caught my eye, what can I say. You noticed me on the bus, and I found you online. Found out you were going to the protest and watched you there, caught wind you were going to the party, and that's when I decided to make a move."

"Don't say make a move like you wanted my phone number, you took advantage of me while I wasn't sober, and you violated my personal beliefs. I've been vegan my entire life and now I can't survive on anything but animal blood?"

"And human blood."

"I can't tell if that was a joke. Humans are animals. Homo sapiens are classified in the Kingdom Animalia, aka ANIMALS. You would think an old vampire would've learned a thing or two throughout the years."

"You're sassy."

"Angry."

"I like you angry." He winked and I rolled my eyes in response.

"I'm no longer interested."

"You didn't seem uninterested last weekend."

"Don't remind me."

He shoved his hands in his pockets, "so you never did tell me, who did you eat?"

I would not give away my mom's knowledge of my turning, I had to protect my family at all costs, and that included lying and leaving, "I stole a bag from a blood truck."

"Wow, I'm impressed, my protégé is already becoming a thief."

"I'm not your protégé, and I only did it so I wouldn't die. I'm only 18, I still have so much life to live!" I was becoming livid.

"But you have even more time now, you'll be 18 forever!"

I hadn't thought about that yet. Not only would I never get to see any of my friends or family aside from my parents again, but that *never*, would last *forever*. If there is an afterlife, I'll be missing out. I'm going to look and sound like this for the rest of eternity. Who knows what will happen?

"I hate you," I growled.

He wrapped an arm around my waist and kissed me, but I pushed him off, "I mean it."

"Awe come on, you can spend your long life with me!"

"I don't want it! And if I had been given the CHOICE, I would've said NO."

"Well, you *don't* have a choice now, do you?"

"You're a monster!"

"I've been called worse," he shrugged.

"What are you going to do with me?"

"Nothing."

"Nothing?"

"No, this time I am merely an observer."

"And initiator."

"Had to get the party started somewhere."

"What are you observing? You know what? It doesn't matter, you had no right to change me without my permission! You had no right to end my life when I didn't want it to end! It's horribly immoral and wrong!"

"Why? Lions eat antelopes every day."

"Because even though homo sapiens are animals, and therefore are very similar, one crucial way we differ is our intellect, our conscience, and the ability to know right from wrong. Big cats and other non-human animals don't have this, when they kill it is strictly eat or die."

"So that would mean that you are like that now, eat or die."

"Except that I still have a moral conscience that tells me I do not own anyone and therefore have no right to decide if someone's life should end."

"You're a passionate one, aren't you?"

I nodded, crossing my arms, "of course I am."

"And confident."

"What are you, the personality police?"

He laughed like the joke was genuinely funny, even though I knew it was the worst joke I could've come up with.

"And funny," he added. I lowered my eyebrows and grounded my foot.

"You're angry?"

"You mean still? Yes, I am, you took me away from my family, I can never see them again!"

"Don't worry, after a few years they'll forget about you."

"My parents will not forget about me."

"Either that or they die in 50ish years, what does it matter? You can do whatever you want now!"

"There's still a law, I don't have anywhere to live because I don't have money and don't own a car."

"Come stay with me. I'll take you away from all this."

"Don't use some creepy pick-up lines, I'm not coming to live with you."

"Like you said, do you have a choice? No money, no car, no shelter, no food. I can provide all of those things."

I thought about it for a moment, he had a point, I had nowhere to go where anyone would be safe, except for... with him. I shuddered at the thought of having to live with my killer, but maybe I had to.

"Fine. But only until I can get on my own feet, and only if there are separate bedrooms."

"Deal."

"AND let me make this clear, it is in zero way a sexual interest reason for my coming."

"That's what she said?" He smirked. I couldn't help it, I had to smile at that one. It was my favorite reference.

"How do you know about The Office?"

"What? Just because I'm 397 years old means I can't understand modern technology and 'meme culture'?"

"That old, eh? Kinda gross?"

"Not when 400 compares to thousands. I'm actually quite young."

"Are there really vampires that are thousands of

years old?"

"Many. But that's a story for another day."

"If I'm going with you, I need to go home and pack a few things."

"I'll drive," he grinned, flashing his gorgeously lit smile. Damn him for being so attractive.

I followed him to the parking lot where a red convertible mustang sat.

"You have more than one car or you just jacked them?"

"I own, don't worry silly little conformist. What? Are you surprised?"

"I guess not," I sighed.

We arrived back at my house quickly; he drove as fast as he ran.

"Wait a minute, how do you know where I live? I never gave you the address," I realized.

"I do research on all my... clients."

"Client? Is that what we're calling me in your weird little 'experiment'?"

"Sure, why not?"

I slammed the door shut and warned him to stay put. My parents woke up with me coming in and followed me while keeping their distance.
I left my door open and started packing my whole room.

"Why are you packing?" They asked.

"Change of plans. We're going to tell everyone that I was found. That I had met a boy and stayed with him for a week and lost my phone and it was the worst mistake of my life and now I'm leaving for Africa. I had already announced I was going, so it shouldn't be too big a stretch."

"So, after a week you just up and leave?"

"I just graduated; I wasn't going to see 90% of those people ever again anyways."

"I mean I guess, but what about the 10%?"

"I'll text them, tell them myself. I'll stay in contact for a few months then gradually drop off the grid. You'll see, this will work."

"What about your brother?"

"He can't know about this. He's in the loop where everyone else is. I love him, but I've already gotten you two involved, I don't want to add pain anywhere else in the family."

"So, we're just supposed to lie to him?"

I sighed, "well... I mean yeah, I guess... I'm so sorry, but it's for his own safety. I'm putting you both in danger just by my being here. I'm this vicious, blood-drinking monster now, and I'll be damned if I let anything happen to you."

"Well, you swear you'll keep in contact with us at least?"

"Promise. You trust me, right?"

"Of course."

"Then trust that this is what we have to do."

"Okay."

I held my breath and hugged them both for as long as I was able to. After breaking apart, I finished shoving my essentials into a backpack and lugged my bags out to the car.

The vampire popped open the trunk and I threw the bags in, then jumped in the car and we sped off.

"You know what I just realized?" I wondered.

"What's that?" He asked.

"Sober me never asked if Tony is your real name."

"Well, I was born Anthony, but I've gone by many

names over the years."

"I guess you kind of have to huh? I suppose I should go by a different name too. If I'm 'supposedly' in Africa, then my person shouldn't be in the states."

"A new name is always a good idea for a new life."

"I guess, call me Hazel, then."

"Hazel it is," he smiled.

"Where are we going anyways?"

I asked like we were just two friends hanging out, and not the freaks we really are.

"I own 5 houses. Two in the states, one in Germany, one in South America, and one in Japan.

"Oh wow, and you visit them often?"

"I usually stay where it's warm throughout the year. I am cold-blooded."

I nodded, "that makes sense. So, the states, you have one around here I'm guessing?"

"Yeah, just over that hill there, and another in Florida."

"What about the sun?"

"That is why we vampires live our lives in the night. Occasionally I will go out during the day as it rains a lot in my area of Florida. As long as I wear full clothes, hat, day glasses, etc., it's usually not too bad. When it isn't raining though I do stay in."

We pulled into a gated driveway, and he punched in a code to be let through. The driveway was long, winding through a forest-y area. The garage was separate from the house, able to hold six cars. We got out and I stared up at the massive building.

"This is not a house; this is a mansion!"

He shrugged, "it's the second smallest of all my places."

"I thought I had it all," I sighed to myself.

"Well," he gestured, "mi casa es tu casa."

"How many languages do you speak?"

"7 living and 2 dead."

"You must teach me."

"Getting excited, eh? This is the life of an old vampire. You'll get to learn whatever you want with your unlimited amount of time."

I thought about that and could imagine that there might actually be some pros to being immortal, but did those pros outweigh the cons? And that got me thinking, if you could live forever, and you were born millions of years ago, you would've been around to see humans become what we are today, all of recorded history. Maybe stories that were written thousands of years ago were based on real people that others thought of as gods because of their immortality. The Nephilim could be real, the early giants, witches, supernatural beings, all of them, could be real.

Tony snapped me back to reality and gave me a quick tour of the house. There was a ballroom, employee quarters, a huge kitchen, and endless bedrooms and leisure rooms. I was awed by all the beautiful furnishings, most of which were later 19th, early 20th century styled.

The backyard had a hot tub, a pool, and stone path curving into the trees.

"Is there something beyond that tree line?" I asked.

He nodded, "guest house. You can stay there if you want, but I'd prefer you to stay with me."

"Can I see it?"

Without answering, he started walking down the path and I followed closely behind. Once you got closer you could see the outline of a cute little stone cottage house with ivy growing up the sides and wildflowers surrounding.

"It's been a while since anyone's been over here."

"How long is a while?" I asked.

"Maybe 30 years?"

"Is the mansion that old?"

"No, the cottage was built in the 1930s, it was abandoned in the 80s, and I bought the land about 15 years ago, I just left it there. So, I guess there have been one or two encounters in the last 30 years."

He stuck a key in the knob and the stiff door was pried open. The house was incredibly dusty and musty smelling, but it was quaint and adorable. Old furniture was covered in plastic, and oh-my, was it dirty. Definitely not move-in ready. It would need a lot of work if I was going to stay there.

"What do you think?"

"I suppose it would be a good project."

"Just don't invest too much in it, we're moving to Florida once summer is over."

"We?"

"Well, you said you needed to be away from family anyways, what better place than to the south?"

"But what makes you think I want to move anywhere with you?"

"I think in time you will."

"Doubtful."

"We shall see, I guess."

"Shan't."

"Well come on, I have one more thing to show you."

I sighed and followed him back to the mansion.

We went up a long spiral staircase in one corner of the home, to where a set of bedrooms were.

"I think this bedroom will fit you best if you choose to stay in the 'big house'." He gestured to the room and let me open the door. I hated to admit, he was right. The room looked as if it was conjured up just for me.

Inspired by African culture, the room was like a jungle, there were fake plants on every shelf and in every corner, and pictures of different kinds of animals in every free space of eye-level wall. The massive king-sized bed was a canopy, with a light green curtain and a rainbow of colorful sheets and pillows. Hanging from the ceiling above it were dried flowers and herbs, and above that was a string of fairy lights.

"Wow... it's almost like you designed this just for me... how is that?"

"Each room is themed. I hired some of the best architects and interior designers in the area when I built the house."

"So, this isn't a stalker thing?"

"No, you can check the other rooms too, I just thought you might like this one."

"I do, but..." I ran my fingers across the bed sheets, "I'm confused."

"I bet you're wondering where the coffins are?"

"How'd you guess?"

"I do have intellect and also context clues, and yes, there is one, in the gothic-themed room. I sleep in the master, it's more or less old fashioned."

"Not surprising."

"Well, I suppose you'll want to start unpacking, so I'll let you do your thing, and you can hang out for a moment. I'll have whats-his-name bring you your bags."

"You don't even remember the name of who I'm assuming must be your butler? I thought you had a good memory."

"Oh, I have a great memory. What I lack is empathy. He'll be up shortly."

He shut the door behind him and left me to be alone with my thoughts. Those of which were not kind. I laid down on the bed, sighing in sadness, for I could not weep the loss of my own life.

CHAPTER 5

An Escape

I spent the next few days in solitude. I was upset to say the least, but I was also sad and lonely and angry. I felt like an angsty teenager who wouldn't come out of their room. After those few days I started to feel hungry again. I knew it would happen sooner or later; I just wasn't sure when. Where would I get my supply?

I ventured down to the kitchen once it was dark and searched for something. I guess it was more out of habit than anything. I knew there wasn't going to be anything I could eat in there. The kitchen was beautiful and large, but completely empty. There was no human food or otherwise. How did his staff eat? What did his staff eat? Were they vampires too? Doubtful, I hear them vacuuming and talking all day when I'm trying to sleep. Each bedroom in the house had thick blackout curtains, which I was grateful for. Even those sleep masks weren't enough to help through broad daylight. It must be why traditional vampires slept in coffins; it was their only escape from the sunlight. I was just thankful to know I wouldn't explode or burst into flames if I did so encounter said sunlight.

The house was dark and quiet, just the way I liked it, but something was lurking, and my newfound sixth sense... or was it like 7th or 8th... was telling me to investigate. Before I could even turn around, a voice startled me from behind.

"You're not going to find anything in there." My new housemate stated.

"Tony, I am not in the mood for your games right now." I crossed my arms, recalling the pj's I had been living in for the past couple days, "what are you doing down here anyways?"

"It's almost as if you forget you're not the only nocturnal creature here. This is my house you know, I can go wherever I want, whenever I want."

"Why isn't there anything in here? Don't your employees eat?"

"They have their own kitchen in the east wing."

I nodded in understanding. There was a brief pause before I blurted out the truth, "I'm getting hungry."

"Yeah? People tend to do that occasionally."

"No, I mean like-"

"I know what you mean. Why don't you follow me." He turned on his heel and started walking through the corridors. I followed, asking where we were going.

"You'll see."

He led me to a big doorway below an arch and started descending a spiral staircase made of stone.

"This looks like a dungeon." I noted.

"I like to call it a basement, but you can call it whatever."

At the bottom of the stairs was a hallway leading to another door. I felt slightly nervous, the basement had a very creepy aura to it, I almost felt like he was about to murder me but... he had already done that.

Of course, what I saw was even worse than that. The second doorway had a big bolt-lock and two separate key locks, and it opened to what looked like a little basement apartment. At first glance it was nice, quite a bit colder than the rest of the house in both temperature and aesthetics, but there was everything a human would need to get by. There was a set of rooms on the other side of the open layout, each with their own individual locks. I took a quick glance and realized just how big Tony's keychain was. He opened the door cautiously, slowly at first. A man lied on a bed in the corner. It was a minimal room, no decor, just a dresser and a bed. I gasped at the sight and went to check his pulse. The man was still breathing, just sleeping, but that didn't seem to make me feel better.

Tony gestured for me to come back out of the room, and I did so that I could yell at him without disturbing the man.

"Who is that and what's happening!?" I roared.

"I don't know his name, but he's fine."

"That's not one of your employees?"

"No, he's my blood donor."

"So, he's a volunteer?"

"Sure. Would you like to have something to eat?"

Something about the whole situation felt weird and wrong. I shook my head, "on second thought, I'm not that hungry just yet, I'll wait a bit."

"He may not be here for long just FYI, but I can always find you another one."

Without responding I left the conversation and headed back upstairs. Something told me that he wasn't a volunteer, and something told me Tony wasn't going to tell the truth if I asked.

I waited a few more days to make my move. By then I was beginning to get ravenous. I would lash out at minor inconveniences and rage at Tony anytime he passed. I knew he was doing his little observation stuff, so I tried to avoid him as much as possible, but even in such a huge house it was difficult. I finally found some time just before daylight when he had just gone to bed for the day. I snuck into his room, my first time seeing it, and had to momentarily pause at how magnificent it was. It looked like the bedroom from the Marie Antoinette movie, large, with a California King bed and high-arched ceilings and traditional Baroque paintings complete with many nude women and fluffy ethereal clouds. I rolled my eyes and crept around, searching for the keys. I finally discovered them upon entering the bathroom; he had them hanging on a towel hook, in plain sight. I took them as quietly as I could and dashed out. I was lucky to get away without waking him.

There was a little less than an hour before I wouldn't be able to handle the sunlight anymore, so I knew I needed to make my move quickly. I snuck down into the basement, searching for the right key. Once I found the right one, I snuck in, trying to remain as quiet as I could. I passed through the living area to the bedrooms and listened to each door. I was worried there may be more than one "guest" and I was right. None of the doors had windows, so I couldn't see which rooms had occupants, but from one room I could hear a soft cry, and from another I could hear scratching sounds, like someone's nails on the wall. I found the key to the door closest to me, the crier, and the sound was silenced by my jiggling the doorknob.

After finding the right key I slowly opened the

door, nervous about what I would find. A young woman sat on the bed, tear streaks erasing a layer of makeup.

"Oh my god," I gasped. I wanted to run to her and ask if she was okay, but I could smell fresh blood, and I knew if I got too close...

"Are you okay?" I asked, pushing myself against the door. She seemed surprised by my presence, which made sense.

"Did he send you? Are you going to kill me now?" She asked.

I shook my head, trying to hold my breath, then noticed she was handcuffed on one side to the bed. "I'm not going to hurt you. How long have you been like that?"

"Couple days," she sniffled, "a maid comes down a couple times a day to let us go to the bathroom and walk around in the living room for a bit, but then it's back to this bed."

"Us? Do you know how many people are down here?"

"I think there's just one other."

"What has he done to you?"

She moved her hair over to one side, revealing a large neck wound with lots of dried blood.

"Was that recently?"

She nodded, "just a couple hours ago. Are you here to do the same? I thought he was the only vampire." She didn't use his name but we both knew who she was talking about.

"It's a long story, but I'd like to get you out of here."

"Wait, you're here to save me?"

"Let me ask you, are you here voluntarily?"

She shook her head and began to cry again, "I was

hanging out with some friends at Insomnia Cookies, he followed me till I wasn't with them anymore then he chloroformed me and brought me here."

My heart broke for her. No one should ever have to go through that. I was incredibly furious at Tony. He was the monster I feared he was and a liar too.

"I'm going to get you out of here, but in order for me to do that, I need you to stay as still as possible, and cover your neck and as much skin as you can. I tossed my hoodie over to her, hoping it would help cover up the smell and sight of the blood. It masked it a bit, but if I wasn't holding my breath, it was still there underlying.

"I need you to keep your distance from me, do you know which key unlocks your cuffs?"

"I think I can find it," she nodded as I tossed her the ring.

Within a few minutes she had found the right key and unlocked herself. She finished covering up with my hoodie, tightening it around her neck as best she could.

"Use the keys to get the other guy out and I'll keep an eye on the door." She ran to the other room, searching for the right key to unlock his door.

She gasped upon entering the room and I ran to the door.

I gasped along with her, the room was covered in blood, it was the guy that I had seen before. He was torn up pretty good, there was no way he was still alive. I had to step out of the room, my head was spinning, and my throat was closing up. The woman started dry heaving at the sight, she was so disgusted. While a large portion of me was disgusted as well, the other part of me wanted to bolt into the room and start licking the blood off the floor. I was sickened with myself for even having such horrible thoughts. I covered my mouth and nose with my hands trying to not let the smell enter my nostrils. I was fighting my inner demons with everything I could, and I was about to lose my battle.

"Shut the door!" I hollered.

The woman jumped at my sudden outburst, then quickly shut the door in front of her.

"We need to go, now," I boomed, "but I thought I heard banging coming from that door. Check it and then let's get out of here."

Still sobbing, she checked the next bedroom. This time it took her a bit to find the right key and I could feel myself losing my patience. With each intake of breath, I grew hungrier, and it was becoming more and more difficult to hold my composure.

"Hurry!" I growled.

She shook in fear and fumbled with the door for a minute. Finally, she flung the door open, and we entered the room. A man was sitting cross-legged on the bed, cuffed as well. He was hitting his head on the walls in a daze, not even looking up at us when we entered. He had wounds on both sides of his neck and all up his arms. It didn't look like he would last much longer.

"We gotta get him out of here," I stammered.

She searched through the ring again, cursing under her breath, and eventually we set him free. She tried to talk to him, but he was not responding. I heard movement upstairs then and I wasn't sure if it was Tony or his "employees".

"Throw me the keys and pick him up, we need to get out of here."

She did as requested and put the man's arm around her shoulders, helping him walk. He had just enough strength to be helped out of the room, and we exited as quickly as we could. I only knew of the one exit, and I prayed there was no one at the top of the staircase. I kept an ear out for whoever was upstairs and when all was quiet, I turned the knob slowly and cracked the door. The main floor was slowly being flooded with sunrise, it wasn't enough to blind me yet, but I knew I only had minutes before it would start to really bother me.

I whispered for the woman to approach and reached into the pocket of the jacket, where I had stashed my sunglasses. I put them on and told them we had to run but to be as quiet as possible. She nodded and we dashed out the door. We rounded many corners of the house before I heard footsteps. I held my hand up to stop them and we leaned against the wall, holding our breath. One of the caretakers was already up and starting to clean the house for the day, so far oblivious to us. I wondered if it was one of the employees that knew about the basement. We weren't going to take our chances though, so once she left the room we darted across the hallway and out the back door. I led them to the garage, I hadn't been inside the garage just yet, and surprise, surprise, it was locked too. This time with a code. I wasn't sure if it was the same code that opened the gates, but regardless I couldn't remember what he punched in anyway.

"Is there another way?" The woman asked, struggling to carry the man. The sun was just about to pop over the horizon and my forehead beaded with a nervous sweat.

I wiped my brow, "I don't know what to do."

"Are you okay?" She asked.

Such a genuine person, I felt bad she was subjected to all this.

"I will be. Let's just get you guys to a safe place." I looked around for something I could use to break the glass on the garage door, a tool, a rock, anything, but it was all just grass and plants. I guessed it was as good a time as any to test out any vampire skills I might've had, so I steadied my feet and balled up my fist. As quickly and as heavily as I could, I punched the window. It shattered and I grunted in pain. There were shards sticking out of my hand and blood everywhere. Guess vampires do bleed and feel pain.

The woman shrieked and an alarm started blaring.

I rushed her, "find the keys, take whichever car, just drive through the gate and don't stop! Don't look back and don't think about it! Abandon the car when you get to safety or I'm sure he'll find you. Now go!"

The man started groaning as he was coming to.

"What about you?" The woman asked.

I shook my head, "I can't go, I have to stay here. It's complicated, but I'll be okay, you guys just go!"

"I cannot thank you enough!" She shouted as she started speed walking into the garage.

I ran back to the house as quickly as I could and up to my room. All of the staff members were running around trying to figure out where the alarm had been set off and I snuck around them all. I ran to my guest bathroom and ripped out the glass without even thinking. I flinched with each piece, but I was just praying that it wasn't bad enough for stitches. Once all the glass was out, I wrapped my hand in toilet paper and threw on a new black hoodie with extra-long sleeves to cover it up, then I jumped into bed and pretended that I had no idea what was going on. Not even 5 seconds later did a knock strike my door.

Tony entered when I told him to, trying to make my voice sound sleepy. "What's all the commotion?" I yawned.

"The security alarm just went off; you don't know anything about that do you?"

I tried to remember how I would normally act and crossed my arms, lowering my hood, "dude I've been in bed for two hours now, I don't know."

"Here, come with me, I need you in my line of sight." He tossed me sunglasses and I put them on. They seemed to be fancier sunglasses than mine, they were much thicker and darker than my usual pair. I assumed they had been made just for him, maybe like a pair of solar sunglasses for an eclipse or something. I rolled out of bed, trying to keep up my tired persona all without causing more pain to my injuries.

We headed out the door and down to the lobby area, where he stopped someone who was running past.

"Sir," the frightened woman nodded.

"Did you find anything?"

"Yes, the uh... donors... escaped sir."

"They what!" I had never heard him raise his voice like that before. I could tell the maiden was terrified, and frankly so was I.

"They got out somehow, stole one of the cars!"

"That's impossible."

The woman ran away, terrified of Tony. He watched her go, a ferocious growl upon his lips.

"Rick!" He roared.

The man that brought up my luggage on my

first day here approached from around the corner. You could tell he was nervous by the bead of sweat on his forehead.

"You're my most loyal employee, I'm putting you in charge of finding out who helped them escape."

"It will be done," he nodded his head in a tiny bow then turned around and exhaled a sigh of relief before running off.

The alarms were turned off and my ears began to ring in the silence. I looked over at Tony, hoping he couldn't tell how anxious I was.

"Come on, I'm not letting you out of my sight now," he grunted.

He grabbed my wrist (luckily it was my good hand) and pulled me to his bedroom.

"Now, I'm tired and would like to go back to sleep, but I'm keeping my eye on you so you're going to stay right here. Pick the couch or the bed."

He pointed to the luxurious old-fashioned couch in the corner, and normally I would be nice and take the couch, but I really didn't like this man. If you could even call him that.

"Fine, I want the bed."

"As you wish." He plopped down on the couch and seemingly passed out in seconds.

I laid in the bed, waiting till he was in a deep enough sleep for me to return the keys without him noticing. About an hour later and he hadn't stirred at all, so I figured it was as good enough time as any. I snuck out of bed as quietly as possible and entered the bathroom, putting the keys back on the hook. After they settled on the hook, I paused to observe the master bath. It was huge, as large as my bedroom back home, complete with his and hers counters, marquee lighting, a walk-in shower and a huge jacuzzi tub. My parents had a nice bathroom as well, but they never let me use it. I was tempted to jump in and try it out. I looked down at my hand and pushed up the sleeve of my hoodie and unwrapped my makeshift bandage. I was surprised to see that my wounds were nearly healed already, just scars with dried blood at that point.

I sighed and tucked the paper into my hoodie pocket and went back to bed. Sleeping was difficult, my brain just wouldn't shut off. I couldn't stop thinking about what had happened. I decided I needed to find out more about Tony; but first, I needed to find something to eat.

CHAPTER 6

Hunger

The hunger pains were growing more prevalent each hour. I wasn't sure exactly what would happen if I didn't find something to eat, but I was afraid of the answer.

It was the next night, and I was just waking up. I still felt horrible about what happened but at least I got two people out of the basement. The other man, the one that didn't make it, I wasn't sure what became of him. When Tony kills... does he respect the person? Give them their final wish or bury them or contact their relatives? My guess was no. My soul, should I still have one, was telling me I needed to find out more about this man. I cannot stand by while he kidnaps and eats people, if that for sure is what happened. I need the full story. I must investigate. We can't have an immediate reaction. Fear and anger are nasty monsters. We have to control them as we do other emotions. If I were to react without thinking, without getting the truth, it's possible that I could hurt or even kill an innocent person, and I will not let that happen. Problem is: how do I know if he's telling the truth?

"Tony." I looked over at the man who was working on his laptop. He looked up and closed the laptop, "yes

Hazel?"

"I think we need to have a talk, but not here."

"Okay, let's go outside." We headed out to the back patio where we would be away from any employees that were still awake at the time. The moon was full and bright, and it reflected onto the pool like glass, the same way it would to a human seeing the sun's reflection. It wasn't as strong and it wasn't enough to cause my eyes to strain, but it was beautiful and relaxing. I reminded myself not to be relaxed, I needed to stay alert and confident.

"So, what'd you want to talk about?" Tony asked.

"I wanted to be updated on those people that got awa- I mean- escaped, what happened?"

He lowered his eyes, "why does it matter?"

"Because despite being a vampire I still care about people."

He rolled his eyes, "they're fine. They found my car about 20 miles away, abandoned but with no damage."

"I don't care about the damage to your car."

"Ouch," he gasped, a hand to his heart.

"Were they found?"

He shook his head, "no trace."

"Any clues who helped them?"

"All we know is it was someone inside the building. It's a witch hunt now."

"You think one of your employees, did it?" I asked, trying to sound like I had nothing to do with it.

"Had to be. I have a few suspicions about which one."

"Who do you think?"

He rested his chin on his hand and whispered, "I think it could be that older woman who cleans the bathrooms, she has access to my bathroom, where I keep my key."

I acted shocked, like I had no idea he kept his key there, "why do you keep it in your bathroom?"

"I don't know, that's just always where it seems convenient to hook it."

"Well as long as everyone is okay, right?"

"Uh, yeah, right."

Don't think I failed to realize he didn't mention the dead body! But he couldn't know I knew about that. If he knew that I knew there was a body in the basement it was game over, he would know I was the one who helped the victims, and then I'd be kicked out and wouldn't be able to help anyone else that he may try to hurt.

Maybe if I spent some one-on-one time with him, I could appeal to his nicer side. I know he's got one, it might just be very deep down.

"How about a swim? Take your mind off everything?"

Here's my chance, "okay, sure."

Tony took off his clothes leaving just boxers and walked over to the ledge. I joined in, revealing a bralette and thong. He dove in gracefully and I followed. I wasn't a great swimmer, but I wasn't horrible either. We lapped each other a few times until we were worn out. I started feeling like I was dehydrated, like when I was turning, and my throat started getting that burning feeling. I swam over to where my toes could touch the bottom and reached for my throat.

"You okay?" He asked.

"Just really thirsty," I nodded.

"How long has it been since you've had someone to

drink?"

I thought for a moment, "I think about a week? However long it's been since I moved in."

"Why didn't you take the opportunity when I showed you my doner?"

"I just... I can't drink from humans. It's wrong, how could they just let you handcuff them to the bed like that? I'm sorry but it just didn't seem consensual."

He avoided my question and pulled me out of the water, he took my hand and sat me down on the table nearest the pool. It was a low point for me, and I would've cried if I could, "I just... what's going to happen to me? If I can't drink from anyone, am I going to die?"

"You're going to be okay, I promise. Here," he stuck out his arm, palm up. I looked up at him in confusion.

"Drink," he sighed and rolled his eyes.

"Why would I do that?"

"Because you're hungry and you're getting weak because you haven't eaten in a week. I never go a day without sucking."

I shriveled my nose in disgust, "I didn't know I could drink another vampire's blood."

"You can, but it's a taboo in our world because when you do, you become more pure-blooded. The more vampire blood you drink, the stronger you become. Also, you drain the other vampire, so they become weaker and need to feed quickly to regain their strength. So, it's not something you would want to do often, AKA this is a one-time thing. I'll let you drink from me now, but you'll need to find your own source after this. Keep in mind my basement is always open."

"Thanks, but I'll pass."

He held out his fist again. I stared at it

momentarily and realized just how famished I was. His blood pulsed through his veins, and it appealed to me the same way nicecream did before I turned. I gripped his wrist in my hands and brought it closer to me. His natural scent infatuated me, and I couldn't take it. It was almost like the vampire in me awoke and I couldn't control it anymore. I sunk my teeth into his smooth skin and sucked. It was both disgusting and amazing at the same time. The blood poured into my mouth like fruit punch, it was both sweet and salty tasting, and it was everything my deadass needed. I closed my eyes in satisfaction and Tony stroked my hair, pulling me close. Were we having a moment? No, it's just the blood.

He tugged on me gently, "okay Hazel, that's enough, you're gunna knock me out."

I swallowed and released my teeth from his arm.

"Good job," he smiled. He licked his wrist clean then brought his lips to mine. I thought about pushing him away, but I almost felt drunk on the blood, I couldn't stop myself. I kissed him back, sliding my tongue across his lips. My fingers found his chest and caressed down his body to his boxers. This time, I was ready. My body craved him. I hated that I felt that way, but it was almost like an addiction. He trailed kisses down my stomach, tracing my curves with his fingertips. Crickets chirped in the distance and a cool breeze blew through the trees. It was all over after only a few minutes. I was still feeling a bit like I was drunk, but so much for staying alert and confident.

"Wow," I sighed.

He kissed me on the cheek and fixed his boxers; I exhaled deeply and looked up at the stars.

"So, wait, what does this mean?"

"What do you want it to mean?"

"I don't know. I hate you... but like that was kinda nice?"

"I think you'll grow to like me, but we can just have the benefits for now if you want."

I nodded, not sure what else I could say. The hype was dying down and I was beginning to regret what had just happened.

"Do you feel better? Not hungry anymore?"

"No, I feel... better than ever actually," I half lied. Physically I felt amazing. Mentally I was feeling worse than ever. I felt guilty about what had just happened, but I didn't want to admit it.

"Good. I was going to run some errands tonight if you want to join?"

"What are the errands?"

"I have to pick up a package from a friend of mine."

"You have friends?"

He rolled his eyes and tapped my chin with his knuckle, "you think you're so cute."

"Clearly you do too."

"You're not wrong. Now let's go get you dressed; do you have anything nice?"

"No, I only packed essentials."

"Well then go do your makeup or whatever it is you ladies do and I'll see if I can find you something."

"Is this not a casual errand?"

"The place we're meeting him is pretty exclusive, so no."

"Okay then. I'll just... go get ready." I spun on my heel and headed back up to 'my' room. I was both intrigued by the task ahead of me, and frustrated that I let things take the turn that they did. I was just so hungry, and he tasted so good.

I groaned out loud, just thinking those words were disgusting to me. He said the place was exclusive, so I wore dark, smokey eyeshadow and blood-red lipstick. I hadn't brought much jewelry with me, just a couple items that meant something to me, like a necklace and bracelet set that my mom bought for my birthday, and a little set of rings that I've been wearing almost every day since I was 14.

There was a knock on my door, and I opened it cautiously. Tony stood there with a garment bag and some strappy black heels.

"Oh, wow. Where did you get those?"

He shrugged, "guest rooms. Few bought for guests, few things left behind. I think it should fit you though."

"Well, I'll give it a try... thanks I guess."

He handed me the items and walked away without another word. I laid the garment bag down on the bed and unzipped it, pulling out a dark blue dress with a deep V-neck and shimmers throughout. I rolled my eyes at the extravagant dress and changed into it. It fit nearly perfectly, and I stood in front of the mirror, gawking at my own reflection. The deep blue went well with my pale skin, highlighting my cheeks and collarbone. The chest part could've used more boobs, as mine are pretty small, but even so, it made them appear bigger, which normally I wouldn't care for, but it was a surprisingly nice change from the hoodies. There was also a slit in the side, revealing my upper thigh, making my legs appear thicker and my ass rounder. It was a good look for me. I strapped on the heels and completed the look. I wasn't used to wearing stilettos, but I would just have to remember to keep my shoulders back and head strong.

Tony barged in without knocking and I chastised him for it.

"Really? What if I was naked!"

"Nothing I haven't seen before," he replied.

"You're the worst," I grumbled.

"So I've been told."

"Well, what do you think?" I asked, gesturing to the dress.

He bobbed his head, "I think... I think I could just rip that dress off you right now. It's hot."

I sized him up, taking in his own appearance. He was wearing a clean tuxedo and had his hair slid back.

"You clean up well too," I half-laughed.

"Let's get going."

I followed him out and to the garage. The window had already been fixed and the car already replaced. He pointed to a black car, and we got into the brand-new Mercedes, speeding off just as quickly as usual. We drove for what felt like forever, but was maybe a half hour, a very awkward silence throughout. I just sat and watched the trees zoom by, wondering where we were headed.

Once I saw a mansion that was lit up like the fourth of July, I knew we were going to a fancy mansion party. A man approached us at a gate leading up to the house. Tony and a plus one were on the list so we rounded the driveway and pulled up to the house. We stepped out in front of the beige mansion and observed the huge, rounded fountain and driveway, then gawked at the building. It was like Tony's yet vastly different.

There were women and men dressed in the finest modern gowns and tuxedos walking around, laughing, each with a drink in hand. It was a real-life Gatsby party.

I would know, it was one of my favorite books, at least, of the ones we were required to read in school that is.

"Wow," I gaped, "I'm surprised we're not all wearing masquerade masks."

"They have those kinds of parties too, but not this one."

I nodded and a server approached us with a tray of wine glasses. He offered us some and I took it without even thinking. I assumed it was just red wine, forgetting that I would have an aversion to wine, but when I took a sip, I was surprised to realize it was something completely different. I wanted to spit it out, but I also didn't want to cause a scene, so I swallowed with a frown and turned to Tony.

"Is this-"

I didn't need to finish my question to receive my answer, as Tony chugged the red liquid. It was a glass filled with blood. The question was, who's? He could tell I was beginning to panic and rested a hand on my bare shoulder. "Volunteers! It's fine!"

So, this was a vampire party, "is everyone here... like us?"

"Not everyone, the servers are human, and then there's the go-go girls, oh and the volunteers of course." Again, with the volunteers. I handed him my glass as we walked into the ballroom. I didn't want unknown blood, and something told me Tony might not have been telling the truth.

The party was roaring in this room. Music was blaring from a professional DJ set, complete with lights and bass and grinding bodies. It was almost like a classier version of a rave.

"So, this is your errand you had to run? A house

rave?"

He pointed a finger to a curtain in the corner, "not the party, but what lies beyond it."

"And what exactly lies beyond it?"

"You'll see."

We made our way through the crowd and over to the corner with the curtain. Tony pulled it to the side, revealing a long hallway overdosed with red curtains. I followed him cautiously, prepared for anything.

He knocked on a door at the end of the hallway in what sounded like a secret knock. One tap, 4 taps, 2 taps. The door opened on its own and Tony strolled in with me tagging behind. The door shut behind me with no one guiding it and I wondered how it was done but I knew other things were more important at the time. The room appeared to be a study. Bookcases lined the wall, filled with old encyclopedias and what I assumed were old novels. A man sat at a desk in the middle of the room. Sprawled on the table was a map and some candles. You could hear the bass booming from the other room, and it created a very eerie environment.

"Anthony," The man smiled.

"Bobby!" Tony laughed.

"Anthony, I told you not to call me that, it's Richard."

"I never did understand how they got Bob from Richard anyways."

I leaned in, "I think you're thinking of Robert."

"Ah, well anyways, I'm here to pick up."

"What's your rush, have a drink!" He pushed a button, and a server came in with some more glasses. I shook my head when offered but the boys clanked their drinks."

"Don't you want one?" Richard asked.

"I don't drink," I replied firmly.

"Oh Hun, they're nonalcoholic."

"Yes, I'm very aware."

His eyes darted between me and Tony.

"Oh yeah, Richard this is Hazel, the one I've been telling you about."

He started laughing hysterically, "oh you're the vegan vampire."

"Why's that so funny?"

He nearly choked with how hard he was laughing, "wow. Okay sorry, I needed that, it's just, the oxymoron is hilarious."

"Yeah, yeah, refusing to cause harm to another is sooo extreme."

"Feisty. You may have something here, Anthony."

"I sure do." He looked at me with those eyes that just made me what to take his clothes off, but I frowned. Now was certainly not the time to flirt.

"Come on, I'll show you guys the playroom," Richard smiled.

"Excuse me?" I asked.

"Not like that, this isn't a brothel," he laughed.

I cleared my throat. The whole situation was intensely awkward, and I certainly didn't want to see his 'playroom', but I had to keep my cool. I had to pretend I was one of these guys.

He led us back into the hallway and through a different door, one with yet another curtain behind it. Behind the curtain was a small circular space with a couch and pole in the middle. Off to the side was an altar of sorts, with cabinet doors locked with a bolt. Richard opened the lock and pulled out a bag filled with white tablets.

They exchanged the bag for a wad of cash and shook hands. All while laughing and joking around. I was familiar with what the bag held but was concerned with why he was buying it.

"Um, is that?" I asked.

"Hell yeah, this was the errand."

"Why did you need that?"

"To have some fun, what else?"

"I'm just surprised I guess."

He stuffed the bag in his pocket and pressed his fingers into my elbow, "come on."

"Please don't man-handle me." I frowned.

A woman wearing only pasties and a g-string came in then and Richard clapped, "Awe yes. Okay well our time is up, I'm sure you can find your way out?"

"Pleasure as usual, have a good night." Tony waved to Richard, winked to the woman, and led me out. He stopped around the corner and removed 2 tabs from the bag, not even bothering to hide it. He handed one to me, but I pushed his fist back.

"I don't want that!"

"Why not?"

"This is not what I came for."

"What did you come for? You could've stayed home."

"Okay let's get a couple things straight. Firstly, that place is not my home, it's a temporary place for me to sleep. Secondly, I don't take drugs from strangers, especially that kind of drug, which I believe is acid, am I right? And thirdly I came with you because I thought maybe we were becoming... friends... or something."

"I'd be your friend more if you take this with me.

Watch, I'll show you it's not poisoned or anything." He placed the tablet under his tongue and let it dissolve then showed me that it was gone.

"Good for you, now can we go?"

He laughed, "we can't leave now, I just took acid, I can't drive anywhere for a while."

"Are you kidding me? A little warning would've been nice! Never mind, I'll drive, come on!"

"Absolutely not. I came here to have fun, you're really disappointing me, you know."

"What about your little experiment? I told you I don't want any part of that."

"Fine, don't drink the Kool-Aid, but you still gotta stay and hang for a bit, dance with me? Come on, you were doing molly just a few weeks ago!"

I shook my head, "that was Adderall! You go ahead, I'm gunna just go find the bathroom."

"Suit yourself. Oh, hey Marco!" He laughed and ran off to chat with someone. For being centuries old, he sure was a child. Although maybe it was the acid kicking in, I wasn't sure.

If I had been with my friends and I wasn't a vampire, things could've been different. Maybe I would've said yes, but not here, not with him.
I found the bathroom and locked myself in, beginning to shake with anxiety. Why did I just blindly jump to follow him? It's not like I cared about him.

Tony is a dick, especially for what he did to me. I don't regret having sex with him, because that's all it was, there was no infatuation, no love, just physical attraction and nothing else. What he did to those people, and what I'm sure he's done to so many others, is unforgivable.

I had to leave; I couldn't be there anymore. I looked at myself in the mirror and didn't recognize myself. This isn't me. I need to find my roots again. What happened to the woman who went to protests and ate tofu and had chill, stoner friends? This person in front of me looked like me, but she was someone else, someone who craved murder; but I would not give in to her obsession with death.

I exited the bathroom and went back to the party. I found Tony swaying to the music with a group of women, two of them grinding on him. I tapped him on the shoulder, and he turned with a goofy grin.

"Hey you're back! Did you change your mind?"

"Uh, yeah! I did, can I have one?"

"Absolutely." He fished a tab from his pocket and folded it into my hand. I gave him a handsy hug, searching for his keys, but he didn't seem to mind.

"You know what?" I smiled; keys clutched behind my back.

"I think I need something to wash this down, I'm gunna go find some of those fancy blood drinks."

He laughed, "okay, but hurry back."

I smiled back and practically ran out the door, stealing his car and driving it back to the mansion. On one hand it was nice to be around a group of people that didn't make me want to slit their throats and suck them dry, but on the other hand, I wasn't like them. Sure, I partied on occasion, but I didn't murder people for fun, I didn't strip down to my underwear and dance for free drinks, and I didn't do hard-core LSD.

I was not in the mood to be peer pressured by a bunch of vampires.

When I got back to the mansion, I threw the dress

on the floor and leaned against the wall. I so badly just wanted to call my mom or one of my close friends and cry to them and tell them how much I missed them, but they would all be asleep. Even though I did know and feel like I could tell my mom anything, I didn't want to burden her with my problems. She has enough to deal with just worrying about my safety, let alone worrying about my hanging out with a bunch of murderers, because that's who I am now, isn't it?

I dropped my head into my hands and cried, "what do I do?"

I plopped face-first onto my bed and sighed.

I'll figure things out tomorrow. I've got the rest of eternity to figure it out. I thought to myself. Even though it was only 3 am, I passed out, not even worrying about my skin routine or nightly meditation.

CHAPTER 7

Infatuation

Someone shook me awake.

"How dare you!" Tony shouted.

"What?" I sat up, rubbing my eyes, completely forgetting about what happened.

"You left me at the party! You STOLE MY CAR! WHO GAVE YOU THE RIGHT?"

"Excuse me?" I blinked back my frustration and stood up.

"You've got some nerve stealing from me! Did you forget who I am? What I can *do* to you?"

"Oh, you mean like kill me and turn me into a vampire?"

"Now is not the time for the attitude. What did you think you were doing? You knew I wasn't in the right mindset to be left there!"

I hadn't ever seen this side of him before, he had never been this angry with me. It really showed me his true colors. When I remembered the basement, I realized it was completely possible that the worst-case scenario was indeed the case.

"Exactly," I replied trying to keep my cool while being brave and confident at the same time, "you drag me to that party without telling me where we were going or what we were doing, then you take highly psychological drugs without a plan and just leave me there to fend for myself? You need to check your privilege; I am not here to be your housekeeper or your chauffeur. I am a human being who deserves to be treated with respect."

"Respect? I opened my home to you, I gave you clothes, shoes, fuck, I even gave you my blood! And you have the audacity to demand respect from me?"

"You murdered me!"

"You're not going to get over that are you?"

"No!"

"Well, Hazel, I suggest you do, because unless you want to end up with a stake to the heart, you're stuck like this whether you like it or not."

"You're a monster!"

"I've been called worse."

"Get out of my room."

"This is my house, and I will go wherever I damn well please. You. Do. Not. Own. Me. I. Own. You."

"You can't own a person."

"Don't worry, I've been around the block. There's nothing you can do or say to save yourself."

"I thought I was here on my own free will."

"You thought that, sure. Have a good night, Hazel."

He left the room abruptly. I wasn't done yelling at him, but what else could I do. He was seemingly imprisoning me in this house; and I would not stand for that. This situation really showed me his true side. It was time to call my mom. The Fourth of July was in just a couple days, and it had been almost a month since I'd spoken to her. I pulled my phone off the charger, hoping it wasn't too late. The sky was already dark, and my phone read 11 pm. *She probably just went to sleep.* I debated whether to wake her or not, and decided that if the situation was reversed, I would want my kid to call me, so I did.

I video called my mom, and it took many rings for her to pick up. She was in bed, and when she saw it was me, she sat right up and left the bedroom to talk to me.

"Hey sweetie, what's going on?" She asked.

"Hey Mom, sorry to be calling you so late."

"It's alright! I suppose it is morning for you huh? Are you okay?"

"Not really, I was hoping I could get your advice."

"Of course, you can always talk to me, I'm here for you night or day."

I thanked her and told her everything that was going on, asking what she thought I should do.

"Well, honey, that's a tough one, he's clearly very unstable. I'm no psychologist, but that man sounds kind of crazy, are you sure you should be staying there?"

"Yeah, I mean, I have nowhere else to go."

"Well maybe we could make it work here! We could get you a coffin I guess?"

I laughed genuinely for the first time in what felt like a very long time, "no coffins, Mom, but thank you, I appreciate that. No but really, I don't think it would be safe. My cravings... are just too strong."

"Oh... right. How are you doing with that? "

"Well... since I tell you everything... Tony let me drink from him. But he said it was a one-time thing because it's not good for him. I don't know what I'll do in a few days when I get hungry again."

"It's times like these I wish I'd gone to medical school; I could get you all the blood you needed. Wow, I feel so weird saying that."

"I know, but I just want you to know that I've still never hurt anyone or any animals. I'm going to stay true to myself and my morals."

"I know this must be so difficult for you, but I am so, so proud of you."

"Thanks Mom, that makes me feel a bit better."

"I wish there was more I could do to help."

"I just wish I knew what to do about Tony. He's such a different person when he's angry. I'm so mad at myself for ever thinking that he could be a good person."

"We always have hope but sometimes we can't change who a person is. If a person wants to be better, they have to change on their own, we can't force people to be better."

"I know, I wish we could."

She sighed with a short chuckle, "oh what a conundrum huh?"

"Yes, I wish things could just go back to the way they were but-"

"The past is in the past," we synchronized.

We talked for a bit longer then said our goodbyes so she could get back to sleep. I decided to roam the house again, to see if I could discover any secrets or clues, or maybe just to calm down, I wasn't really sure. I just couldn't sit in that room anymore. I missed my friends, my family, and my lifestyle. I had been happy before this all began, what did I do to deserve this?

I found myself wandering outside, past the pool and into the forest beyond the yard. The one nice thing about being a vampire seemed to be a lack of anxiety. Before I turned, I would've been terrified to wander through the forest alone, for fear of predators (and by that, I mostly mean human predators). However, with the newfound strength and speed I had, I had no fear at all. The sounds of the forest even calmed me down further. An owl hooted from what I sensed to be about a half-mile away, the trees swayed in the wind, and there was a scent that I picked up from who knows where, but it wasn't a pleasant one. I followed the scent the best I could. It was a scent that was like blood mixed with something terrible. My instincts craved the blood, but my brain told me this had bad news written all over it. I told myself I needed to get away so as not to be tempted, but another part of me wondered if it was someone, human or not, that needed help.

I followed the ghastly smell to a location roughly a mile away from the lining of the trees. Deep into the forest was a collection of recently unearthed dirt and my heart sank. A toe stuck out from under the mound, and I rushed over to it. I unburied the human then jumped back, shocked by the mess and the stench. My teeth gnashed together as I wrapped my arms around my face, trying to block the scent. The sight was horrifying. Any human bit of me left was screaming in fear. Should I call the cops? Should I tell Tony? *Tony... no... he probably did this.*

I sighed then took a sharp inhale and held my breath, releasing my arms and going back to the corpse. I was no CSI, but I had seen enough of the show to know that the body was fresh, maybe only a day or two old. I was surprised that Tony (if this was his fault) would've been so careless with the victim.

There was no way to help them at that point. I took a closer look to observe the injuries. Maybe it was a human murderer, not that that would make it any better, but for my own sake I just hoped the culprit wasn't Anthony. Of course, the first thing I noticed was that most of the blood was sourced from wounds in the neck and arms. I dropped to my knees and leaned over for a better look, and in doing so, accidentally let go of my breath. As I inhaled again the smell of blood hit me so hard my fangs barred, and I growled under my breath. It was so instantaneous that I felt I had no control over it, I sunk my teeth into the flesh and sucked. I only got a few drops as most of the blood had already been taken or had probably pooled to the lower half of the body, and what little I did tasted terrible. It was exactly as you'd expect, rusty, thick, and dry around the edges. It was enough to satisfy the craving but then the sane part of my brain kicked back in, and I was disgusted. I sat back and put my head in my hands in shame.

How could I have let myself be so careless and stupid? Not even just that but how could I let my instincts take over when I've worked so hard to build up my mental strength and keep my morality even as a vampire? I shuddered to think about what I had done, and wondered what I should do then. I couldn't tell my mom, even though I told her everything, this would have to be an exclusion, we had literally just talked about how I had been doing well about keeping my wits. I couldn't go to Tony either; I didn't know if there were other vampires in the area but even if there were, this victim was just too close to the house. With that being said, I couldn't go to the police either, both he and I would be arrested; and Tony being arrested... didn't sound like a smart idea. We would probably end up with more victims. This time, they would be cops. I had to protect myself and my family and play it cool until I could figure out what to do. Who knows what an angry Tony was truly capable of. I needed to re-bury the body so no one would suspect anything if they came back or if someone else stumbled upon it.

I opened my eyes and looked around. It only took a second before I noticed something else in the distance. I stood up to get a better look and was shocked to find another mound of dirt, this one much bigger, big enough to have at least ten bodies underneath. You could tell that one had been properly dug up because it was mostly flat, but there was no grass, just leaves, and the rest of the forest was grassy. I was too scared to investigate further so I quickly covered the recently deceased person back up, ensuring this time there was no foot left sticking out. Part of me gagged at doing this, I wanted so badly to throw up at the horrific sight, but the other part of me was unbothered by the mess I unveiled as that's what it craved. I was sickened not just by the human loss, but also by the monster I was becoming.

A firework exploded in the distance and alarmed me as I wasn't expecting it; it was the middle of the night and the 4th of July was a few days away, so I rushed back to the house and locked myself in my room.

After three days of being holed up in my room, there was a knock at the door.

"Go away," I growled, knowing it was Tony. I still hadn't figured out what I was going to do. Although I would have to leave the room sooner or later, the hunger was starting to come back, and I would have to find a food source quickly.

Tony turned the doorknob with such strength

that he broke the lock and barged in. I assumed he was going to yell at me some more but instead he just stood there and stared at me.

"What?"

"Look, I just wanted to say that I'm sorry about the other day. I shouldn't have yelled at you like that."

"Wow, I'm shocked, you're apologizing?"

"Yes, I think you should come out of your room and let's go do something together, the sun will be down soon, and we could go watch the fireworks."

Just as he said that we heard a bang outside. Growing up I always loved going to firework shows, but knowing now how devastating they can be to animals, it just didn't feel right. Dogs and cats and other non-human companions are terrified by the sounds, and some of them run away and get lost because of this. Squirrels and bunnies and birds will become disoriented from the sounds and lights, and many don't make it home to their babies. Not to mention the PTSD symptoms that veterans get from the fireworks. But again, I had to keep my cool or Tony would know something was up. I had to regain his trust before I could do anything. An idea came to mind, but it could be difficult and time-consuming to execute. However, it would give me the stability and insurance I needed for my safety so that I could do what needed to be done to save others from Tony's wrath.

"Okay, fine, I'll go with you, but you gotta make it nice."

"What do you mean?"

"I mean no drugs; you have to treat it like a date."

"You want to go on a date?"

"I mean if we're gunna do this then we gotta do it

right, right?"

"I mean yeah, okay, let's go on a date. Wouldn't be the first time I've gone on one."

"Really? Why do I not find that entirely convincing?"

"Cause you think I'm all about the sex, don't you? Well, little did you know, I'm actually pretty good at dates."

"We shall see, won't we?"

"Go get ready and you will."

Locked and loaded. I had him right where I needed him. I went and got ready for our fake date, sliding on a strappy black dress with an exposed back and thigh-high boots, then I rolled my hair into a ballet bun and added some dangling earrings (all courtesy of Tony's guest closet). I then emerged from my room, it finally being dark enough for me to do so, and waited for Tony in the den. It wasn't long before he walked in, this time not in a tux, but a nice white button-down and black slacks. He rolled up his sleeves and I admired his muscular forearms.

Tony grinned at me and kissed my cheek, "you look stunning."

"Thanks, you too," I fumbled. I found it difficult to concentrate on my plan when he was so dashing. Even just the way he smiled at me made me want to swoon. I had to keep it together though. Despite the man's gorgeous appearance, on the inside he was truly ugly.

"Ready?" I asked. He took the jacket that I was holding onto and swung it over his shoulder then held my hand. He really was taking the date seriously. We drove in his new car down to the nearby lake and walked down to the beach, where other viewers were setting up. Tony laid a big blanket and bottle of what looked like champagne onto the sand and patted the spot next to him. He handed me the black bottle and gestured for me to sit with him. I sat but did not drink, for I knew what was really in that bottle. We looked up at the night sky and noticed lights in the distance followed by the sounds of the fireworks.

"Isn't this nice?" Tony asked as I sat next to him.

"Fantastic," I lied. A cloud of smoke settled into the area like a fog, and if it weren't for all the humans around, it would have looked very creepy. In the passing minutes more people crowded onto the little beach and the smell of being around so many humans was beginning to bother me. Tony somehow noticed this and offered me the bottle again. I shook my head.

"Come on, it'll help take the edge off. It's the only way I can be around this many people without wanting to tear them all apart."

I shushed him, "don't say that so casually, someone may hear you."

"People vent and say they want to kill people all the time, everyone knows they don't actually mean it."

"Not with strangers."

"Hey, don't be such a sourpuss, we're on a date remember? Let's enjoy our evening together."

I nodded to keep up the charade and let him put his arm around me. The show started then, and fireworks lit up the night sky. The people around us cheered and oo-ed and awe-ed and I just sat there trying not to frown. I felt bad that the animals from the neighboring forest were probably scared out of their minds but there wasn't much I could do about it. I suppose my animal rescuing days were over now too, since I couldn't be near any animals anymore without wanting to... hurt them. I couldn't take that risk, I had to stay as far away from anyone human or nonhuman as possible. Even just being in the somewhat close proximity that I was in then was difficult for me, especially since I haven't had anything to drink in days. Unfortunately, it only got worse when the show was over and the people around us became restless. A young man passed by us then and noticed me.

"Purple Haze, is that you?" He smiled and attempted to give me a hug, but I took a step back next to Tony.

"I'm sorry I think you have me confused for someone else."

"Come on you can't be serious. Weren't you supposed to be in Africa, why are you still here?"

The man was right, he did know me, and I knew him. We went to high school together. We weren't close, but close enough that he knew I was lying. I had to think quickly, was it better to lie again and risk confronting him about it, or was it better to acknowledge him and move on with the empty promise of a coffee-catch-up? In this case, with Tony by my side, I knew things could get ugly fast, so I knew I needed to get rid of him.

"I'm sorry, but you don't know me," I said, lowering my voice.

He leaned in and whispered, "are you okay? Is this guy bothering you?" He was too close for comfort. I could smell his freshly washed hair, sharp body spray, and his sweet blood underneath those layers. I blinked a few times as my body stiffened before Tony pulled me back and glared at my old friend.

"She said she doesn't know you, so I think it's time

you go," he growled.

"Uh... yeah, just... DM me... if you change your mind on that," he said to me before slowly slinking back to his group of people.

"We need to go," I stammered.

Tony nodded and we hopped in the car and sped off.

"That was too close," I sighed.

"Who was that?" he asked.

"A classmate. I'm not supposed to exist in this world anymore, I shouldn't be going to events like that. If I can't control myself... if I can't control my hunger... someone I care about could get hurt."

"Then vampire events only from now on. Got it."

"That's the problem though, I don't want to go to vampire events either."

"Then what do you want?"

"I want my old life back," I grumbled. I was losing my grip; I could feel my sanity falling off the wagon.

Tony sighed, "it's a bit late for that."

It took everything I had in me not to just climb over the car seats and rip his throat open. I was just so pissed at him for doing this to me, and so pissed at myself for allowing things to go the way they had. The vampire in me wanted to kill, and the other part of me wanted it to be him that I killed. However, if every life is precious, does that include the undead?

We were quiet for the rest of the ride until we pulled up to the last place I would ever want to go. The cemetery that he murdered me in.

"What the hell are we doing here?" I boomed.

"Chill, I thought maybe coming back here may be good for you."

"In what world would coming back to the place I died be good for me?"

"To fight your demons. I thought bringing you here could help you come to the decision of whether you want to be a vampire or not."

"What do you mean?"

He gestured to me to get out of the car and for whatever reason, I did. I followed him into the graveyard, stopping just in front of the mausoleum that led to my death. It may still have my blood on the floor.

The vengeance lingered on my tongue.

"Again, why did you bring me here?" I asked.

Tony stepped forward and rested his thumb on my cheek, kissing me gently on the lips. "I want you to have what you want."

"What do you think that is?"

"You didn't choose this life. I chose it for you. This time I'm giving you the choice." He was right in a way. He never gave me the choice. It was never about consent; it was about power.

"Can you please stop speaking in riddles and just tell me what you mean?"

"Hazel. Do you want to be a vampire or not?"

I paused, "no... but."

"But?"

"But what would my other choice be? I mean you can't just make me human again, can you?"

"No, I'm afraid not."

I looked around, starting to feel something weird in the pit of my gut. The surrounding area was clouded with firework smoke and the sky was littered with flashing lights. What sounded like bombs would go off every few seconds, and they made me flinch every time.

The wind had blown my hair loose and it fell from its bun, cascading down into messy curls.

"Tony... what's my other option?" I needed him to say it. I knew what the answer was; there was only one way this could go. I don't think he knew I was faking the date or even my 'feelings' for him, but he knew I never wanted this life.

"The other choice is to kill you. For good this time."

"Why?"

"Because you can never go back to being human once you're a vampire."

"No, I mean, why would you want to kill me for good? I thought you wanted me to be a vampire for your little experiment thing?"

He shrugged his shoulders.

"Wait." I took a step closer to him and stared into his eyes. He looked back at me with an odd sense of sadness, and I was both confused and enlightened at the same time.

"Do you... do you have actual feelings for me?"

He rolled his eyes, "no I would never have actual feelings for a test subject."

"So, then that's all I am to you, a test subject? A lab rat?"

"No, I mean-"

"Just admit it, you like me."

"You can either die here tonight or you can come home and be with me," he growled.

"That's not fair."

"You can't have it both ways. You can't live in the human world anymore; this is how it must be."

I was silent for a moment, he was giving me an

out, but not really. I could choose to either die and let him live to eat people the next day or be his girlfriend and probably be forced to do the same. Some sort of rage snapped inside my body and before I even knew it, a third possibility appeared. I could just kill him.

My right arm lunged forward and punched Tony right in the cheek. He could feel it, for he did flinch and take a step back, but I surely felt it more in my hand. I felt like I had broken every knuckle. Tony reached out to grab me but the karate lessons I had taken when I was younger began to kick in and I was able to swiftly avoid his grasp. Even though I had never made it to black-belt status, somehow the muscle memory was still there, and it gave me a fighting chance.

"I don't want to hurt you," Tony said as he reached for me again. I took his arm in mine and swung it down, twisted it over, and kneed him in the chest.

"Then you will lose," I stated.

Tony stood from his crouched position and smiled, "you know, you're cute when you're angry."

"Where have I heard that before?" I rolled my eyes before lunging at him. He held his arms out and as I jumped to kick him, he grabbed my foot and flipped me back over. I landed on my ass and cringed. He gave me time to stand up and I realized my high heels would be the death of me, so I took them off and threw them at him one by one, screaming at the top of my lungs.

"Why are you so angry at me?" he asked, dodging the boots.

"Why am I angry? Because you murdered me! Right over there! And not only that but then you bring me back to this place, and ask me if I want you to murder me a second time?"

"I thought it was the right thing to do. I thought maybe if I gave you this you might forgive me."

"How can I forgive you if I'm dead?"

"Well, I believe in an afterlife, so that's how I guess."

"Doesn't matter, it still doesn't make this okay. You will never be able to make this okay!" I yelled again, it honestly felt so good to get out all that aggression, even if I knew I had no chance of defeating the man. I came at him again and this time he just picked me up and held me over his shoulder.

"Put me down!"

"Not until you've calmed down."

"Calmed down? I'm trying to fight you and you just keep pushing me away!"

"Babe, you do not want me to fight you, I will destroy you."

"Better that than this."

He set me back down, "you would rather die fighting than be a vampire?"

I shrugged my shoulders; I was honestly going back and forth so much I had no clue at that point.

"Please, just give me a chance, let me show you how fun being a vampire can be. If it really means that much to you, I won't offer you drinks anymore, but I will teach you how to get your own."

"What, do you mean how to hunt and eat people?"

He looked around and spotted a deer in the distance, "no, you could drink animal blood instead of humans."

A nearby deer's ears perked up as if she could tell what we were talking about, and when she noticed us, she darted back into the trees.

"You still don't get it, do you?"

"No animals either?"

I shook my head, "in my eyes, humans and nonhuman animals are the same. I mean I know obviously there are differences, but like humans, they have a beating heart that pumps blood through their bodies, a brain that functions alongside their muscles, and like us, they too feel emotions like pain and loss and pride and joy. They love and care for their families just like we do, and if we're going off straight intellect, pigs and dolphins are some of the world's most intelligent creatures, they can learn how to count and do puzzles and express their feelings. Apes can learn sign language and have been known to sign the words for sorrow and love. I could never, ever harm a loving, innocent creature like that, they are not alive for our amusement or taste pleasure. Murder is murder."

Tony was at a loss for words. His hair was tousled from our one-sided fight and his eyes were low, but I couldn't tell if it was from remorse or something else.

My breathing had calmed by then, so I took a step closer to Tony and ran a hand through my hair. He stared down at me and waited for me to speak again.

"I don't want to die, Tony... but I don't want others to die because of me either. If I can't find a way to be alive without harming someone else, then I would rather be dead."

"So, if I tell you I can find a way for you to get what you want, you'll stay with me?"

I thought about this, could I really change this man's way of thinking? Maybe getting close to me was a good thing, maybe I could get him to stop harming people without me killing or harming him. This was it; this was how I could save people. If I let him kill me right then, then I wouldn't be around to stop him from hurting other people; and unfortunately, I was not strong enough to beat him in battle, I knew that now. So, I vowed to myself then and there that I would either get him to stop drinking from people all together, or I would end his life so that he never could. To do that though, I would need to get stronger first. I will keep up the charade for as long as I can until I am either strong enough to defeat him, or until he changes.

"Ask me, Tony."

"Ask you what?"

"You know what, ask me."

Tony closed the space between us and tilted my chin up to him, "Do you want me to kill you right here, right now, or do you want to be a vampire?"

I lowered my eyebrows and stared into his eyes, "I want to be a vampire."

CHAPTER 8

Courage

When we got home from the firework show, and after our little one-sided fight, Tony started kissing and touching me. I had to remind myself that this was part of the plan. I pretend to be Tony's girlfriend, his faithful, loyal vampire servant girl, and in turn he teaches me, unknowingly, how to kill him. If it so happens that he actually does change along the way, then maybe things will work out. For now, though, I play the role and sleep with one eye open.

Tony kissed my neck and led me towards the bedroom. I knew where this was leading and I knew that for it to not be an excruciating experience I had to get turned on for real, so I kissed him back and wrapped my arms around his neck. His cologne had an intoxicating smell and if it weren't for my bloodlust, I would've fallen for that alone. Already barefoot, I let Tony pull off my dress and caress my skin as I removed his suit. Once it was gone, I sat him on the edge of the bed and saddled onto his lap, kissing his neck with what he probably assumed was passion. Then, in the heat of the moment, I bared my fangs and bit into the flesh of his neck. I sucked as much as I could before Tony stopped me.

"What are you doing? I told you we couldn't do that anymore." He kept me on his lap and spoke gently, which came as a surprise, maybe it was the bloodletting that calmed him down. Guess I would need to keep that in mind. I licked my lips and kissed him.

"I'm sorry," I said innocently, "it's just that you smell so yummy and I'm just so hungry."

He kissed my chest a few times and glided his hands down my back to rest on my ass.

"Okay, fine, but this is the last time, I swear," he sighed and extended his neck for me. I couldn't believe I was about to get away with this. Maybe it was just as much of an addiction for him as it was for me. The vampire in me seemingly took over and went in for the bite again. I knew doing this would make him weaker and me stronger, not to mention the nearly drunk feeling you got from drinking a vampire's blood was heavenly. No, it wasn't quite like being drunk, it was more like being high. It made you serene and jubilant and ready to take on anything.

Once he wouldn't let me take anymore, he tapped my arm and pulled me back onto the bed. He licked the blood from my lips and stuck his tongue in my mouth. Human me would've been disgusted, but it wasn't that bad and the next thirty minutes went by quickly without issue. I ended up asleep in his arms and I awoke the next evening feeling sore but elated and full. I wondered if I should feel bad about what I did because while technically he did give me consent, I did try to sway him to let me drink, but I wasn't sure when or where my next meal would come. Besides, it wasn't like he asked for my consent when he turned me. If I had to feed from someone, at least it was a stone-cold murderer like him. Was it really that bad to get rid of someone that was costing innocent lives? Maybe. As a human I never believed in capital punishment. Murderers and rapists should spend their lives in prison, and people in prison for drugs should be either decriminalized or rehabilitated. However, now that I have a vampire's brain, that part of me wants to kill just about anyone and everyone, especially people like him. Of course, as I've been doing, I will keep my sanity and my humanity, and if I do have to harm someone, it will only be someone that truly deserves it.

Tony hadn't stirred yet, so I went into the master bathroom and showered, then put on a robe and went back to my room for some clothes. At some point he woke up and came into my room without knocking and waited for me to finish getting dressed.

"So, what're we doing today?" he asked.

"Don't you have a job?" I unauthentically teased.

"Well yes and no. I own a few companies, but my people do all the work."

"Yeah, that sounds about right. At least you're honest about it"

"I do sometimes have to get on my laptop or my phone for business purposes but only when my right hand is desperate."

"Well, I hope you pay them well."

"I should think so. Do you want to try another date today?"

"Ah, well actually I was thinking you could show me that thing we were talking about?"

"Yes! Wait, what thing?"

"You said you would show me just how fun being a vampire can be."

"Ah yes, that, well mostly we just party, drink blood, hunt for sport, and partake in hobbies. I know some vampires well beyond my years that all they do is paint. Did you know that De Vinci is a vampire?"

"Wait, really? How come you never hear about him anymore?"

He rolled his eyes, "it's not exactly inauspicious if he used the same name for hundreds of years. In today's world he's known as Leo Vincent, a black-market seller."

My mouth gaped open thinking about how one of my favorite historic artists was not only alive but now works in the black-market trade.

"Okay I feel like you have a lot of other stories like that and in time I would love for you to tell me ALL of them."

"It's a date," he grinned.

"So, what other celebrities are vampires? Wait, I've thought about this before. If vampires are real, what other kinds of supernatural creatures exist? Do you know what happens when we die, or when humans die? How long can a vampire live for, are we completely immortal or just mostly?" I rambled on, taking a seat on the bed next to Tony. Suddenly the subject came alive for me, and I was genuinely curious about vampirism, but I was also asking because the more I know, hopefully the easier my task will become. I had to know everything.

"My, quite the curious cat now, huh? Well, there's Nicolas Cage for example, oh and Abraham Lincoln was a vampire hunter. A large portion, not all, but most, serial killers are vampires. For example, Jack the Ripper, Elizabeth Bathory, John Brennan Crutchley; and then Dracula was based on a real vampire. Uh... oh bigfoot is real, I've encountered a few, mermaids live in the unexplored ocean, and of course witches and aliens. I have met a couple of witches, all of them were disgustingly nice."

"What? Oh, do you mean like Wiccans?"

"Some, yes. All of them, at least of the ones I met, were spiritual witches, not like the Wicked Witch of the West, but more like the Good Witch of the North."

I nodded, "okay what about us? What can we do? How long do we live, that sort of thing?"

"You're really starting to get into this aren't you? Good okay, well as vampires we are quite a bit stronger and faster than humans, and as you already know, we do have major light sensitivity, but the sun won't really kill us. It has to do with us being nocturnal, we have eyes that can see in the dark, so light isn't usually necessary. Our skin does burn easily, so although the sun doesn't kill us, that is why we rarely go out in the daylight. The day glasses help though, I'll get you a pair like mine if you want."

"That would be great! What else is there?"

"Well, we don't have any special powers per say, it's mostly just heightened senses. We can see, hear, and smell better, and like I said we're stronger and faster. Although there are rumors that some vampires can influence humans."

"You mean like mind control?"

"More like seduction, but I've never actually seen it in person."

"How long can we live?"

"Well, we don't die of natural causes because we don't age, so in theory we can live forever, but we can be killed. A stake through the heart can do it, but really it can be done using anything if the heart is completely destroyed or if the brain and heart are separated indefinitely."

"Like a lynching?"

"Exactly. It is best to burn the bodies, as there is a legend that if body pieces remain together that the vampire could come back, but I don't think that part of the legend is true, it's never been seen in my lifetime."

"What happens when a vampire doesn't feed for a really long time?"

"They go in sort of like a coma, they die, but not completely. After a week we start to weaken and after about a month we go into a coma-more or less-and appear to be dead, but let's say if someone were to come up and pour a bucket of blood in your mouth then you would come back good as new after a couple of hours. Wait, why am I telling you all of this? You don't need to know how to kill a vampire," he lowered his eyebrows in suspicion.

I rolled my eyes like he had nothing to worry about, "sorry for trying to stay alive, what if I meet a vampire and they don't like me and try to hurt me?"

"I won't let that happen, okay? You're with me now and nothing will harm you, I promise."

I nodded, coast clear. "So how many vampires do you know?"

"So many," he laughed, "wouldn't be able to count. Most of us are very social creatures if you can believe that. We don't like to be outed, but we do also like to grow in numbers."

"So how many people have you turned?"

"Ah, well I've sort of lost count."

"Were they all your 'experiments'?"

"No, most of them started out as companions, especially in the beginning."

"Where's the beginning?"

"You want my origin story?"

I shrugged.

"Uh okay well, long story short, I was born in Europe in the 17th century, 1624 to be exact, and I came from a very poor family, my mother died in childbirth, and I was raised by my aunt after my father offed himself a few years later. I became a vampire at 20 years old when I met one at a brothel. We got into a brawl over some maiden, and he took me around back, beat the shit out of me and sucked my blood, then told me I would spend the rest of eternity regretting that decision but at this point I rarely think about it."

"What happened to the woman that he got so angry over?"

"I apparently slept with a woman that he had been making one of his slaves at the time. The worst part wasn't even that, it was just that by that point, I was on my own. I had no family, and no genuine companions, and no vampire guidance of any kind. I ended up going on a killing spree for about 30 years until I learned how to control my rage."

"What do you mean?"

"I mean instead of just taking what I needed and letting the human be, I would suck them completely dry with no remorse."

My eyes widened and I hoped he couldn't tell how stunned I was.

"How many?"

He sighed and shook his head. "In those 30 years? Probably hundreds. I moved around a lot, no one ever caught me. For most I tried to cover my tracks, but it was after those 30 years I came across another vampire who helped me get my rage under control and taught me how to... well... be a vampire. It was after that that I turned someone for the first time."

I lowered my head into my hands. He had killed HUNDREDS of people? And that was just in 30 years? How many has he killed since then? I knew not all of his victims have returned home, so just how many lives has he taken over his 400 years?

He laid a hand on my back gently and I tried my best not to flinch at his touch. This news was utterly shocking, and I had no idea how to go about things. I had to remember to pretend to be on his side.

"I'm sorry if that's disturbing news, I didn't mean to upset you, but I figured I should tell the truth since you asked. I promise I'm not like that anymore, I only take what I need and nothing more."

I wanted so badly to tell him how I knew he was lying, but I had to hold my tongue, so I just nodded and leaned into him. He wrapped an arm around me and patted my hair with his other hand. After a few minutes I sat up, "so... if you're from Europe how come you don't have a European accent?"

He laughed and sat up with me. "Oh, don't you worry Darlin, I got lots'a accents for ya," he said with a country twang. I smiled at him, and he continued, "no I just prefer this one, seems to be the easiest, I don't have to enunciate as often. Okay, so you've now asked me a million questions, it's my turn to ask you a few," Tony stated.

"Shoot," I nodded.

"When did you first go vegan?"

"Is this an experimental question or genuine curiosity?" I pondered.

Tony rested a hand on my shoulder with his thumb on my cheek, "genuine question. I was honest with you that I had, as they say, 'caught the feels' so you know that you're more to me than that stupid experiment idea." He looked into my eyes lovingly as he said that and I did my best to give him the same look back, but I saw right through the lies. Even if he did have actual feelings for me, I would never reciprocate them. I could never love a man that is so two-faced.

"Well, I've been vegan all my life actually, my parents went vegetarian in their teenage years, and by the time I was born they were fully vegan."

"And you have a brother, correct? Is he vegan also?"

"Yes, born and raised like me."

"So how do you know that you don't, or rather didn't, want to eat meat if you've never tried it?"

"I don't feel I need to know what meat tastes like to know I don't want it. When I ate food, it was to fuel my body, not for taste pleasure, although as veganism grows so does how yummy the food is. My parents make the BEST tasting healthy food. Also, because again, it's not for taste pleasure, and most meat-eaters won't stop eating meat because they like the taste of it, but this shouldn't matter because A, meat is almost always seasoned or breaded using plants anyways, and B, because it's about who you're eating, not what. Once you see that what's on your plate is either life or death, it becomes an easy decision."

"So basically, you don't eat meat because you view it as kind of like... cannibalism?"

"In a way, yeah, that's a good comparison. I know

it's not *exactly* the same, but like I've said before, they have beating hearts and functioning brains. Like I guess I could just never eat anything that had eyes for example, but it goes farther than that. Deeper down the rabbit hole. Also, I do have many friends that were not born vegan and remember what meat tastes like, and they all say the only regret they have is not going vegan sooner."

"Interesting." Tony rested his hand on his knee and thought about my rant, "okay so how does a vegan make sure they get all the nutrients they need? I mean as a vampire all I need is blood, but humans need so much more."

"You know, I get the nutrient question a lot and the answer is that it's surprisingly easy, a lot of plant-based foods have a lot of nutrients so really as long as you're eating a variety of foods that are healthy like fruits, vegetables, whole grains, nuts and lentils, and some people will need the occasional vitamin, then you're pretty set. It's the vegans that just eat nothing but Oreos that give the rest of us a bad name. Not that Oreos aren't delicious because trust me they are, but you can't live off them."

"I see. Okay so switching topics a bit here but what were you, and are you, wanting to get out of life?"

I thought about that for a moment. My ultimate goal was always to help people and animals. I wasn't sure how to do that now that I was... this thing. "I guess I'm not sure about now, but before this," I gestured to myself, "happened, I really just wanted to travel, meet people, and be as earth friendly as I could. And now..."

"Now you don't know where to go?"

"I mean yeah, you kinda changed my life." Not for

the better of course, but he didn't have to know that.

"We can still do that, I have money, we can travel as much as you want!"

"Yeah, I mean I guess, but my mom would be so worried about me, and I don't know, things are just different now."

"Well, you have made sacrifices for me, maybe I could make a sacrifice for you. What would you say if I told you no more blood from civilians, only from volunteer donations from now on."

If I could roll my eyes without giving myself away then I would have, "weren't you already doing that?"

"Uh, yeah, well like 99% of the time, now it'll be 100%." I couldn't tell if his lies were getting worse or if my ability to see his bullshit was getting better. Or maybe I was starting to get through to him, maybe this really would be his turnaround.

"Well, I think that it's time you started teaching me how to be a vampire right? And I'll teach you how to be human."

"I'd like that." He kissed me on the cheek then got up and started the shower. He pulled me in with him and part of me just wished he'd leave me alone. I hated that he was being so kind and generous to me, knowing that that wasn't the case for any other people he crossed paths with. What was it about me that he loved so well? What was it about me that made him not be such an asshole?

After we got ready for the day, or rather night, he took me to the city. I guess he figured the city would be the only place where there would be people out so late. First, we went to the crossroads, where they were celebrating First Fridays with food trucks, art vendors, and bars. We walked around a bit, and the night was still young so there were a lot of people out, but I found that my bloodlust wasn't as bad as it usually was. I could smell those that were nearest to me, but I didn't really feel hungry like I normally would. Sure, the vampire in me was like 'hey what if you just grabbed this person and pulled them into the alley and-' but that part was such a small fraction compared to the last time I was near a human that it was almost easy to be near them. It was almost like I was back to normal for a bit. Not quite, but close.

"I can tell you're having thoughts," Tony wrapped my arm around his, "what are they?"

I looked up at him, "I'm... surprisingly fine. Ish."

"You know why?"

I shook my head.

He leaned in and whispered in my ear, giving me goosebumps, "it's because you fed on me last night," then in a louder tone and further away he added, "when you do that you're not as hungry so it's easier, and it also depends on who and how much. Since it was me, it helped more than any of these people would."

"So, I'm hearing that there's a lot of positives to drinking... well that, as opposed to drinking..." I gestured with my eyes to the humans nearby. I had to be careful with my words so as not to raise any suspicions.

"Yes and no, it's positive for you, but negative for me. For example, I'm feeling quite sluggish today and unlike you, I am very thirsty."

I stopped in my tracks when I realized something. Yeah, feeding from him made me not hungry, which meant that I wouldn't feed from any innocent humans, but it made him hungry, and when Tony gets hungry...

who knows what will happen. I could've just screwed somebody over because I drank from Tony rather than finding a blood truck. The problem was I wasn't sure how hard those were to come by. I needed an excuse to get us back to the mansion before his hunger took over.

"Tony... I'm suddenly starting to not feel very well, can we go back home?"

"I find it odd that you say you're not feeling well because vampires don't get sick, but since you called it home and not the mansion or the house, I shall take you there. Come on, let's go," he held my hand and led me back to the car.

Once we got back to the mansion, I said I needed some time alone and for whatever reason, he not only believed me but didn't ask questions. He just said that he would be in his office if I needed anything. So, I headed up to my room and laid on my bed, debating what to do. It was about midnight, but since it was the weekend, I figured my mom would either still be up or she would be in bed but still awake, so I called her, and she answered on the second ring. We turned on the cameras so we could see each other as we spoke, and it was so good to see her. It was the first time I had in more than a month.

"Hey sweetie!" she grinned. It was always so good to see her smile. I hoped she could still do so often even though she now had an empty nest.

"Hey Mom, how are you doing?"

"I'm okay, don't you worry about me, how are you holding up? Have you eaten recently?"

"Yeah, actually that's kind of what I was hoping to talk to you about."

"Of course, what's going on? You've got that tone

in your voice, did something bad happen?"

I could tell she was worried about me, and I didn't blame her. I don't know how she could stay so calm knowing what I am now and what I could do to people.

"Not exactly," I told her everything that had happened since I last talked to her, all of which took maybe half an hour to explain, but she stayed on the phone listening quietly till I finished the story. Never once did she question my integrity or tell me I was in the wrong. Honestly though, she probably should have.

"What do you think I should do?" I asked.

"Well, it sounds to me like you're doing the best you can. You haven't given into your cravings in a devastating way, and you might have even gotten him to change his thoughts on veganism and well... eating people." She shuddered at the thought, and I wished I could just give her a hug.

"Maybe, but my gut tells me something's not right. I'm worried that he's still hurting people, or at least will when he gets hungry, which is apparently now. I think... I think I might have made a mistake."

"Honey, I'm so sorry, I'm sure everything will be okay. Do you know what his food source is right now?"

I shook my head, "no idea. He hasn't shown me or talked about it at all. And the basement... I'm scared to go down there."

"I don't blame you at all baby, I would be too. The only thing I could think of would be to continue what you've been doing, keeping an eye on him. Keep your friends close-"

"And your enemies closer," I synched.

"Exactly. If he can never get alone time, then he will never have the opportunity to do the thing he told you he wouldn't do anymore. Although... if you're wanting to learn how to fight, how could you do that around him without raising any suspicion?"

"I don't know. That was another dilemma I was trying to figure out. I'm not sure if he'll even let me leave the house without him. I feel like I'm a prisoner here, but I can't really compare this amazing mansion to a prison cell."

"I suppose it may not look the same but if you're being held there against your will then that's not good. As your mother I would really like to get you out of that house."

"No, it's okay Mom, you don't need to worry, he won't hurt me, that much I know."

"You sure?"

"Yeah. I mean, I think I'm the first person he's actually had feelings for in... well... who knows how long. I would feel bad about leading him on if he were anything other than a monster."

"So how do we go about solving your problem then?"

"I need two things. I need blood, and I need strength. I need to keep him sated on a humane supply until I've gotten strong enough to take him down."

"And how do we do that?"

I hesitated, "I need to rob a blood bank and I need to find a way out of this house."

She sighed, "I get why you need to, it's just... stealing one bag to feed yourself for a week is one thing, but to take a whole bunch to keep him sated... I mean what about the people that need that blood for surgeries?"

"I know, I feel so bad about this, but I don't know

what else to do."

"I'll find one, okay? Next week I will find the closest blood drive, and your dad and I will donate, and I know it won't be enough, but if I can help you in any way, I'm going to do it."

"No Mom, you really don't have to do that."

"I'm going to, don't even try to talk me out of it, I've already made up my mind. I want to help you. I will let you know next week which one I go to and then once it's dark out you go and do what you need to do, okay?"

My mom was filled with sorrow and I so badly wanted to take everything back. I shouldn't have burdened her with my problems. She shouldn't have to be dealing with all of this. I created this problem and I needed to fix it, but for now, I needed to just change the subject and see my mom smile again.

"Hey, never mind that, things will be okay, just like you said. I will figure this out, okay? Guess what, I might be able to come to see you soon! I've been practicing being around humans and I think I know what I need to do to be able to come visit!"

She smiled at that, and I smiled back. "Really?" she asked.

"Yep, if I feed beforehand, I shouldn't really get those urges. I can hang out with you and not feel like I'm going mad."

"That's great! I would love to see you in person! But what about Tony, do you think he'll let you leave?"

"I think... I think if I can continue to earn his trust, maybe a few more days or a week or so, I think he'll let me. He's never really told me I can't leave the house; I'm just sort of scared about what may happen if I do. So, I think if I talk to him maybe... for me, he will let me."

"That would be wonderful, just let me know, okay? Don't be a stranger."

"I won't, I promise. I'm going to go do like you said and keep an eye on him, so I'll talk to you later, okay?"

"Okay yeah, I'll text you tomorrow about the blood bank, okay?"

"Okay thanks Mom, I love you!"

"I love you too!"

We hung up and I sighed in relief. I felt much better after talking to my mom. With her and my dad's support, even from far away, I knew I could do this.

CHAPTER 9

First Kill

Nearly a week later I still hadn't found any people that would consent to letting me drink from them, and I knew it wouldn't be much longer before my body started to break down. I suspected that Tony may feel even worse because it had been a bit longer for him, plus I had drained him of his own blood. This was going to be harder than I thought. I didn't even know where to begin to look anyways. I couldn't talk to anyone I knew, such as old classmates, because then they would know I wasn't in Africa; and I couldn't just go up to a random person and ask them because just blatantly telling someone you're a vampire would send them running.

My mother plans on going to the blood bank tomorrow but at this point I'm so hungry and weak that I'm not sure how I'm going to do it. Not to mention Tony hasn't been doing anything but laying around the past few days because of how hungry he is. I was proud of him for sticking to his word and not feeding until I found a willing volunteer, but it was getting more and more difficult.

We had to do something... find someone. Someone that we could trust.

It was around two in the morning when I finally

gained the courage and strength to abandon my bed and find my way down to the den. Tony was there resting on the couch, watching TV of all things. I folded myself into the chair with him and asked why he was watching TV.

"What, vampires aren't allowed to just relax and watch some Rick and Morty?"

"I mean yeah, I just didn't know you were into that kind of thing?"

"When you've been around the block like I have you learn that you gotta keep up with the times or fall behind."

"Meaning?"

"I don't know, there are just some modern-day amenities that I enjoy, okay?"

"Okay cranky," I smirked and turned the volume down a bit.

"I'm sorry. I'm just... so hungry."

I sighed, "I know, me too."

"We should really go find something to eat, I don't know how much longer I can take this."

"How though?"

"Okay well, I do know one place we could try."

"What place?" I frowned. It had been decided over the last few days that he would let me do all the work to ensure the authenticity of wherever or whoever we found our food from. Was that because I didn't trust Tony with the task? Absolutely, but he didn't have to know that.

"There's this place, this park, near the city, where a bunch of homeless people live-"

I frowned, wondering where this was going as he paused.

"Look, I know how that sounds but hear me out. These particular people are super nice, and they love to help other people. I could offer them some money in exchange for their help with our problem."

"I don't know... that doesn't really sit right with me."

"Well at least just come see for yourself and talk with them and then decide."

"But if they're homeless, we should really be helping them, not the other way around."

"No see, that's the thing, I've met these guys, they like being homeless. It's like a stick-it-to-the-man kind of sitch for them, like they aren't going to let anyone control or dictate how they live their lives."

"You have a lot of money."

"Irrelevant but yes."

"So, you can use your money to help them."

"Well, I'm not going to give them all of it, but I'll certainly offer a bit if they help us."

"You're treating this like it's some mundane exchange, we're talking about people who are dealing with a really bad point in their life, and you want to just take more from them?"

"I'll be giving them some back in return! Think of it this way. They could go into a plasma donation center and make like 600 dollars; this would be just like that. We're not going to take enough blood to harm them."

I sighed; I was so hungry I could barely keep my head clear. The demons inside me were crying out for food no matter the source, and they kept trying to justify it. I gave in and said we would go just to check it out, but if there was any uncertainty on their part that we would leave and not come back or bother them ever again. Tony agreed and turned off the tv.

"Right now?" I asked, standing up.

"Right now, I can't take a minute longer of this."

I nodded, "I feel so drained and hungry... I'll do almost anything."

My body was sore all over, and the pain in my stomach from being empty for so long was nearing unbearable, even my teeth seemed to be in pain, almost like the bloodlust was causing my fangs to tug or shift or something, causing irritation in my mouth. It wasn't a good feeling, and I just couldn't do it anymore. I would check this place out but trust my human gut, and if my training on how to be around humans has improved at all we should be fine.

I could tell Tony was feeling sore and worn out like me and he didn't walk quickly like he normally would, and he didn't stand as erect as normal either. His posture had gone out the window and he kept rubbing his chin like his gums were bothering him too. With that being said, I felt secure in knowing that he was indeed hungry; and *if* he was indeed hungry, then that meant he truly had gone a week without harming anyone or worse. In a way it did make me feel better to see him suffer. I knew that if he was suffering, then no one else was suffering because of him. Okay, maybe I thought he deserved it a bit too. Especially if what I think happened at those unmarked graves really did happen.

I shuddered at the thought as we hopped into the Lamborghini. The drive felt long even though Tony was going well beyond the speed limit. I wondered how he had never gotten caught before, and to pass the time and to get my mind off the pain, I asked him about it.

"You mean how have I never gotten a speeding ticket?"

"Yeah."

He laughed, "I'm just that good."

I rolled my eyes, "no for real."

"One of the things you learn in four hundred years is how to sense things around you, like cops for example."

"You can just... sense... them?"

"In a sense," he laughed again, and I frowned at his verbiage. I dropped the question as we pulled into a parking lot across the street from a large-looking park just outside of the city.

"Ready?" he asked.

I nodded, knowing that was quite a lie. I wasn't ready at all, but something had to be done. If we didn't feed soon, I knew it would be too late. If these guys could help us in a way that would do no harm to them, then maybe we could make this work, but I didn't get my hopes up just in case. I would remain true to myself and be careful.

We walked down a trail into the woods and eventually came across a bridge. There was one person sitting on the bridge smoking a cigarette. He didn't give the stereotypical appearance of a homeless person: his clothes were dirty, but he didn't have a backpack with him or any kind of gear, just the cigarette and his lighter that he kept flicking on and off. He looked at me and grinned. His teeth were straight but yellow, and something about his smile seemed off to me. I tried to read his aura like my mother taught me, but I really struggled with it. I told myself to just relax and focus and trust my gut. My human gut told me to run. My vampire gut told me to kill. Something was not right. Tony tugged on my arm and led me away from the man. Without my asking, he knew I wanted to know why he pulled me away but all he said was that the camp was "this way".

The trail was gone and I felt like we were just wandering through the forest aimlessly, but Tony assured me that he knew where he was going. Why he knew where this group of people holed up was confusing to me, and I reminded myself to ask him about it later. The wind blew through the trees then and it reminded me just how different everything felt as a vampire in the night versus a human in the day. It was pitch black outside as there was no moon and clouds covered the stars, yet we could see everything that was in our path just as well anyways. The breeze was cool and felt much more comforting than the 105-degree heatwave that had been going through the town this week.

As we got closer to the campsite, I began to see the light of a fire I assumed was meant to keep them warm, and once we approached, the group became frightened.

There was a family, plus four men and a woman in the group, and a part of my soul broke to see them like that. The family huddled while the others approached us.

"How'd you find us?" A man asked. Tony started to speak but something came over me and I pushed him back. I knew I needed to feel the situation out before I asked them the question I needed to ask.

"Hi, I'm sorry, my boyfriend and I were just taking a stroll and came across your site. I apologize for disturbing you, we really mean no harm."

"Well tell your friend to stop looking at me like that, it's creeping me out."

I looked back at Tony, and he was all but drooling. He was so hungry he could barely contain himself. I needed him to control his emotions.

"Tony," I whispered, "check yourself right now or we're leaving."

I don't know why he listened to me, but he did. He closed his mouth and kept his eyes on me to stay focused and I turned back to the group.

"Um, do you mind if we sit with you for a bit? To warm up by the fire before we head back to our car?"

The mom of the group looked at me and nodded to the others, I hoped she could tell that I was no threat to them. Well, not in certain ways at least. They allowed us to sit with them, so we did, exchanging names before they began telling us their stories. The more I heard from them the less I wanted to ask them the question. Even though my throat was burning, and it was taking everything I had in me not to just go all crazy vampire on them, I held my tongue. Tony reached for my hand and squeezed. Although, I wasn't sure if that was to keep up the charade of just a young couple taking a walk through the park who got lost off the trail, or if he was doing so to keep his composure. I knew it had to be difficult for him since he was so used to just eating whoever whenever. These people had just fallen into hard times and couldn't get back on their feet and I felt so bad for them. I wanted to do what I could to help but what could I do? I personally didn't have any money or resources for them, all I could do was take, and that didn't feel right. Even if Tony gave them money, how much was worth of the blood that we took from them, plus how much would it take to get all nine people back on their feet again?

I began to question everything. These people were so kind and thoughtful and even though they worried about us being a danger to them they still opened up their space for us to join and I knew I couldn't drink from these people.

"Babe, I think I'm ready to go home," I nudged Tony hoping he would take the hint, but his eyes were practically glazed over. His body was going into hunt mode.

"You know, I think he's not feeling that well. I'll get him back to the car, but thank you so much for letting us sit with you and I hope things get better. If I ever see you again, I'll have a care package prepared, I promise!"

"You just take care of yourself, okay?" They waved goodbye as I stood Tony up and dragged him away. Doing so was harder than I thought it would be. His muscles were fighting me, and he was fighting himself. Once we were too far away for them to hear he started growling at me.

"Why did you pull me away? Why did you not want to drink from them? They were perfect candidates!"

"Because this isn't right, Tony! I can't just walk up to someone and be like 'hey can I chop off your arm and eat it because I'm a cannibal, but I don't want to kill you? Huh? Because that's how crazy that would sound to them. I can't... I just can't do it."

"I was about to lose it back there."

"I know, I was too. It literally took all the restraint I had not to go after their throats, but I had to pull myself out of that mentality and remember that they are people too and they deserve to be treated with love and respect and appreciation like everyone else!"

"But-"

"You lied. You said they were nice people, and that part was true, but you also said that they enjoyed being homeless and their goal was to help other people and that was not the case!"

"Can I please just take the old one? He's lived a long enough life anyways!"

"No! I can't believe you would even sug-"

I paused mid-sentence as a scream filled my ears. Tony looked around and sniffed the air. His eyes went wide as we smelled what could only be identified as blood and I knew we were in trouble. As I swallowed, the burning in my throat became a thousand times more prevalent and I couldn't control it any longer. My mind and body went into hunt mode and there was nothing I could do to stop it.

Tony and I ran through the forest in search of the source of the smell. It was only a few seconds before we came across a horrific sight. The man from before-the person on the bridge smoking a cigarette-he was standing over someone. Seeing and smelling it was too much for Tony and he began drinking from the victim. Blood covered the man from head to toe in splatters and pooled into the ground below his victim.

"What have you done?" I shrieked. He tried to run then but I gathered all the energy I had left and threw him to the ground. Without a second thought my instincts took over and my fangs bared. I bit a hole in his neck and began to feed. I didn't have time to think of the consequences. All that was going through my mind was that he was a murderer and he deserved punishment, and the vampire took over and did the rest. After a minute or so Tony pulled me off him.

"Why did you do that?" I asked, "he's a murderer! He killed that woman!" I was livid, insane even, but Tony was calm and collected.

"I know," he sighed, wiping the blood from his cheeks, "but I figured you of all people wouldn't want to kill even someone like him. However, I think it may be too late."

Realization struck and I turned around to check for a pulse. The man was gone. I sat on the grass and put my head in my hands, contemplating what I did.

"This can't be happening. Nonono, I promised! I promised I would never hurt a single living being!"

Tony kneeled beside me and laid a hand on my back, but I pushed him off and crawled over to the woman. My thirst had been sated so I could now look at her without feeling the need to drain her, but she was in awful condition. Her head had been bashed multiple times and she has at least three stab wounds. I couldn't tell how old she was, but she looked young. I wondered where she had come from, but she was wearing yoga shorts and a sports tank, so I assumed she was the kind of woman that just wanted to go for a late-night jog. It was so heartbreaking that this poor woman just wanted to live her best life and was murdered for it.

I wanted so badly to just curl up in my bed and cry, but something had to be done. There were two dead people right in front of me, and one of them was dead because of me. Nothing would ever be the same.

"What do I do?"

"You mean what do we do?" Tony gestured for me to give him a hug and I don't know why, but I did. I wrapped my arms around him and buried my head in his chest. I was just so upset by what happened, by what I did, that I didn't know if I could live with myself. Yes, he murdered that woman, but he deserved to rot in prison for the rest of his life, not be killed by a vampire. It's not my job to play God, it's not my job to decide who lives and who dies. There was nothing I could do for the woman; it was already too late for her unfortunately... but I didn't have to kill him. I could have just broken his leg, or something, then taken him to the police station, or I could have used my vampire strength to hold him down and...

"I know what you're thinking," Tony brushed my hair back and looked into my eyes. I shook my head and tried to take a step back, but he pulled me back in.

"It okay, it is,"

"No, it's not! Look what I did! How could I let this happen!"

"You're still a young vampire, you don't have control over your thirst like I do."

"Like you do?" I started yelling, I so badly wanted to just break down and cry but all I could do was get angry, and I did. "Like you do? You should've seen your face back there at the camp! They feared you because you just looked like you wanted to eat them. You can't control your thirst any better than I can! You were practically drooling! And you didn't even wait to see who this woman was before you started drinking her blood! This is all your fault! If we had done things the way I wanted to do them this wouldn't have happened! We would have never been out here in the woods in the first place!"

Tony shushed me and that only made me angrier. I

pushed him off me and turned back to the woman. The scene was bloody and human-me probably would've puked at the sight, but something in me couldn't look away.

"Look, I'm sorry to tell you to be quiet, but there are other people out here and if you're too loud they will come and find us and think that *we* are responsible for this mess! We must do something with these bodies, quickly."

"This can't be happening." I felt like I was going insane. "This shouldn't have happened. We shouldn't have been here."

"Hazel this isn't your fault. That woman would have died whether we were out here or not."

I thought about that. If only I had known. I had sensed something was off the first time I saw the man, if I had just listened to my instincts, I could've prevented this. Something in my bones had told me he was a bad guy and I just walked away because I feared harming an innocent man.

"You're right, we have to do something. Can we just call an anonymous tip to the police?"

"No way, they'll trace the call or recognize a voice or something, we have to bury the bodies where no one will ever find them."

"No, we can't do that! Her family needs to grieve! She needs a funeral, a time of remembrance."

"She's already been given vengeance, what else is there?'

"It's not just about revenge, it's about the people she left behind. She could have siblings, parents, a significant other, they will be missing her. They'll need closure. They need to know what happened to her."

"Okay but you killed him, your DNA is all over his neck. He has to go."

"Is your DNA not all over her?"

"I don't think so, I didn't bite her."

"Just licked her clean."

He licked his lips in answer.

"You're disgusting."

"Tomato-tomahto"

"Why are you so apathetic about all of this? Two people are dead!"

"I'm a vampire sweetie, I see death all the time."

"Yea, because you're a murderer too!"

"I meant because the people around me grow old and die and I forever remain this age, but you know I'm a changed man now, you've seen it, no more killing for me, remember? I drank from her because she was already dead. It was already too late for her. She didn't have the ability to give consent because her soul was no longer with her body."

"Are you saying she's in a better place?"

He shrugged, "I just know she's not here anymore."

"So, then what do you suggest we do?"

"I say we take the man and bury his body and leave the girl here, someone will find her, and then the police will take care of the rest."

"Do we have to?"

"Yes, this is the only way."

I sighed, "I cannot believe this is happening."

Before anything else I checked the man's pockets and found his wallet. I shoved the wallet into my pocket so I could ID him later, then I grabbed his feet and Tony grabbed his shoulders and together we got him back to the car. Much to my dismay, we stuffed him in the trunk then quickly got into the car and drove off. When we got back to the house, instead of pulling into the garage, Tony drove the car through the grass all the way down to the line of trees where he reversed the car as far into the forest as he could. He then got out of the car, and I followed. We opened the trunk and pulled him out. I was utterly sickened by what we were doing but I was so dazed from all the fresh blood in my system that things Tony said kinda made sense. Maybe he was right. We'll hide the man's body and it'll seem like the woman's attacker ran off. If anything, they would search for an alive person.

The body wasn't as heavy as I expected it to be, but I don't know if that was because I was no longer human, or if it was because I had fresh blood in my system, or because the man was seemingly malnourished. Maybe it was all the above.

We carried him a ways through the forest until we got to a small clearing that seemed very familiar. After setting the man down and looking around I realized where we were and gulped some air, nearly choking on my own breath from the shock. Tony patted my back and asked if I was okay. I knew this was going to change everything, but I couldn't let him get away with this.

"You did this?" I accused.

"Did what?"

I stretched my arm out, "I've seen this before. I didn't want to believe it was you."

"What?" He tried to play the fool, but I knew better.

"Look at the ground, Tony. This isn't a game. I know there are bodies here. I don't know how many, but

I know it's more than one, and even one is too many. You've been burying people here. People that you're killing."

"What? I wouldn't do that, you know that."

"Actually, I don't."

"Prove it."

"You have the shovel."

He did conveniently have a shovel in the trunk, and he brought it with him as we carried the man. I pointed to the spot where I found a body the last time I was here and told him to dig. He did, and of course it only took two shovels of dirt before he hit something. We unearthed the same body that I had found before, however this time it was further decayed and smelled even worse.

"Proof."

"So, there's a body here, that doesn't prove it was me. The real question is how did YOU know exactly where to dig to find a body?"

"Oh, don't you try to turn this around on me! This isn't a courtroom; you and I both know that you did this. I came across it while exploring one day."

"I guess I'm gunna have to start being smart about where I hide the bodies huh?" He laughed but I frowned.

"This isn't a joke! How many bodies do you have here?"

"I've... lost count," he stammered.

I wanted to puke. I had my proof. I knew what I needed to do.

Tony has to die.

CHAPTER 10

A New Friend

My foot almost automatically swung out and smacked Tony right between the legs. He bent over in pain for a moment before grabbing my leg and yanking me, so I fell onto my back.

"Screw you, Tony," I stammered as I pulled myself up off the ground.

"Really? I thought we were over this. You know what I've done in my past, none of these kills were recent."

"This one was!" I took another swing, but he was ready this time and dodged my blow. I went in for another punch and it was dodged again. I growled and just started throwing hands and kicking as hard as I could, and I got a few in but most were avoided. Tony eventually just grabbed my arms and held me up like a child. He wasn't more than 6 inches taller than me, but he was much stronger.

"Stop trying to fight me!"

"Why! You're a maniac! A murderer!"

He dropped me and I fell to the ground. My heavy breathing was apparent, and my hair was surely full of knots. I took a few deep breaths to regain my composure then stood up.

"I'm getting really tired of you accusing me of being a bad person all the time."

"It's not an accusation, it's just a statement of fact."

"It's not though, I kill to survive, not for fun."

"THAT'S not true though, you killed me! And that was just for fun."

"I didn't kill you, I made you better!"

"If you think killing innocent people, not being able to go out during the day, and living so long you get tired of existing is truly living, you're sadly mistaken. I would've rather you just murdered me for good than turned me into this... monster."

"I'm sorry you're upset with me, and I guess I'm sorry that I turned you, but I really think that I can show you the beauty of this kind of life."

I sighed. I either had to kill him now or go back to pretending I believed his lies until I could kill him. I was tired of going back and forth between pretending to love him and hating him, and with that thought, I jumped up and wrapped my arms around him. I tried to behead him, but I was neither strong enough nor was I fast enough. He saw it coming and this time he was done with the battle too.

"Do you want to get your ass beat? Because that's how this is going to end. I can block your throws all day." He was using his angry voice, a voice I had only heard twice, and I could feel my body going numb with fear.
I couldn't let that stop me though, so I tried a third time, and this time he punched me back. I could feel my nose begin to bleed but I refused to care.

"You know, I don't usually like to hit women." He claimed.

"I really don't care."

We fought then; it was mostly one-sided though, as he kept blocking me then tossing me to the ground. Unfortunately, it wasn't a cute wrestle-fight, it was more of him just beating me up. I was more than sure I had a black eye and possibly a broken nose, but I wasn't ready to give up just yet.

"Mark my words, I will kill you." I threatened.

"You can try," he laughed, not a scratch on him. Which gave me an idea.

I got as close as I could then jumped up and instead of going for a punch, I used my naturally long nails to claw at his face. I got him and blood drew from the scratch.

"Ouch." He said nonchalantly.

I used the opportunity to swing my leg under his and knock him down, then I jumped onto his stomach to hold him down while I threw more punches. I got him on the first one but before the second he grabbed my wrists and flipped me over, so I was on my back, and he was then straddled on top of me.

"You're done." He snapped at me and yanked me upright then dragged me back to the car.

"What're you gunna do?" I asked.

"I am going to take you back to the house so you have some time to calm down and then I'll come back and deal with this mess." His voice was low, and I could tell he was furious.

"Why didn't you kill me?"

"I should have."

"But you didn't."

"I don't know why. Maybe cause part of me thinks you'll get over this anger issue just like last time and in a couple of days you'll stop hating me again."

"That's not true. I will never not hate you after this." I tried to get out of his grip, but he wasn't letting go. "I will never love you," I huffed.

"Is that so? Then I guess I have no choice."

He picked me up and threw me over his shoulder. I kicked and slapped and clawed and yanked out some of his hair, but he wouldn't relent. He then shoved me into the car from the driver's side and held on the whole way back to the house, traveling through the grass as he did so. He left the car on the back porch, didn't even turn the engine off, and pulled me out from the driver's side. He charged into the house while towing my screaming and kicking ass. I prayed that one of the employees would wake up, hear me, and come to help, but unfortunately, this might've been something they were used to. I wondered just how many people had been taken down here against their will. How many women's' screams have haunted these halls?

Tony pulled me down the staircase and I knew exactly what he would do with me. He took me into one of the 'bedrooms' and handcuffed me to the bed, the same way he had for who knows how many of his victims. I wailed and kicked and attempted to bite but he overpowered me in every way. Apparently weakening him by drinking from him and keeping him hungry had not helped at all, but then again, he had just fed off that poor girl at the park.

Without another word, I was left alone in this cell of a room. I yelled after him, asking what he was going to do with me, but he ignored my cries and went back upstairs. I had no idea how long I would be in there, or if he was going to let me starve to death, or if he would bring another victim down here and force me to drink from them, or if he would eventually get off his high horse and realize that I was right. The odds of that last one were slim. The possibilities: endless. He had the rest of eternity to decide what to do with me, but I didn't have that kind of time.

I have to get out of here.

I thought about all the people that had occupied this room. There was little evidence of the number of occupants, the only recent one being the scratches on the wall behind the bed. Tony wasn't just a murderer; he was a serial killer. I guess I should've assumed as much. Most vampires probably were serial killers. They believe it is in their nature to kill, and maybe in some ways it is, but that still doesn't excuse the horrible things they do. In this day and age, there is no excuse for abuse. There is no excuse for brutality, inequality, racism, sexism, or speciesism.

I looked around the room for anything that could help me escape but there was nothing in the room except for the bed. I leaned over the side of the bed and looked underneath it. The only thing underneath was an old, dirty tennis shoe, but I had seen a video before that taught me exactly how the shoe would be helpful, so I picked it up and started tearing out the laces. Once I got the lace out, I strung it through a chain link on the handcuff then peddled it with my feet. It took a while, but the friction eventually caused the link to snap, and I was relatively free.

I listened at the door with a hand on the handle to make sure no one was on the other side but instead I heard small cries coming from the room next to me. I realized there was another victim down here and I became FURIOUS. Had Tony had victims down here this whole time? He had lied to me in more ways than one. I could feel my rage growing by the second and the handle on the door snapped off. I shrugged to myself and yanked the door open. I still had enough rage in me to do the same to the door handle of the room next to me.

The woman lying on the bed was soaked with what I assumed was her own blood and tears streamed down her face. She jumped when I smashed into the room, curling up into the corner and crying harder. I calmly shushed her and sat on the bed. She was a young woman appearing to be about my age; she had green hair and a fair complexion with a nose ring, and a tattoo on her clavicle.

"Hey," I whispered, "it's going to be okay; I'm going to get you out of here. I'm not going to hurt you, I promise. Did Tony do this?" I began threading the shoelace through her cuff link again. She didn't respond at first, so I asked again.

"I'm sorry, I know you're probably traumatized but it's really important that I know who did this to you. I can only assume it must be the man that owns the building, but I have to be sure."

She didn't know her kidnapper's name, but she gave the description of a person I knew was Tony. This confirmed my fueled hatred for the man and my vampiric urge to slaughter him.

"Did he do that to you?" She asked in response to seeing my bloody face.

"Yes actually." I paused and looked her in the eyes. I was taken aback for a brief moment as her eyes were a stunning golden hue but quickly regained my composure and explained what happened. As I did so I finally let a breath in and realized something.

"Wait, did he hurt you? Well, obviously he hurt you. What happened exactly?"

"I was at a friend's house the other night, we're neighbors so I was walking home. He just grabbed me and brought me here. He came out of nowhere so fast I had no idea he was anywhere near me. He cuffed me to the bed and fed from me and then..." she trailed off.

"Then?"

She leaned up and revealed a deep gash in her throat. It had already closed but was still fresh. He had killed her.

"You're turning."

She cried, "I'm turning into a vampire? Wait no I can't be! Vampires aren't real! And I'm vegetarian so I don't know how that's going to work."

"You are? Wait..." I thought for a moment. This was planned. Tony knew she didn't eat meat, and if he knew that, that meant he'd been watching her. He had planned to kidnap and kill her the same way he did with me. He was replacing me. Which probably meant he was planning to get rid of me. It also meant that he never had any intention of doing his feeding the way we agreed on. Once again, I realized the only way to end this suffering, this mass number of victims, is to end Tony's life. I would try to get him sent to prison but I know that he'd either kill the cops taking him in or kill his cell mates once he got hungry. I knew he would find a way out.

There was only one way.

The link finally snapped, and she was released from the bed.

"Thank you," she sniffled. "I'm Amity."

"Call me Hazel." I half smiled and helped her off the bed. She was weak and growing weaker every minute she didn't get her first meal as a vampire. If we didn't find her something to eat soon, she would perish. Together Amity and I headed up the stairs but were stopped by the locked door. This time I didn't have keys, or any adrenaline left. I shook the door as a failed attempt to break through, then sighed in defeat.

Amity looked like she was about to pass out, so we went back down and sat on the main-room couch. She began to cry again and I hugged her, "we'll figure this out. There's a way out of here. Tony makes mistakes."

I suddenly realized that my pockets had never been emptied. I still had the man from the park's wallet and... my cell phone.

"Example number one, he forgot to take my phone." Amity gave a weak smile and I thought about who to call. The police weren't an option. If they found out about this, they'd find out about that man. I had no friends that I could trust with this secret, and that's if they even believed me. They all thought I was in another country. The only person that I trusted enough to help me was... my mom. I sighed, not wanting to get her involved in this. Her involvement would mean if we didn't come up with the perfect plan, she would die. She would die by Tony's hand and there would be nothing I could do to stop it. He's already proven that he would win against a vampire in a fight. A human had no chance.

I could tell that Amity was nervous, but she stayed strong and asked how she could help.

"Don't you worry about a thing. I'll figure this out." Who knows how much time we had till either Tony came back for us or before sunrise. In the chaos I had lost track of time, and I wondered where Tony had gone to after he left the basement. He could've gone to bed, but he also could've gone back out to get the car and finish burying... what's his name. I looked around the room and wondered what I could use to get us out. There was a small kitchenette in the corner; it didn't have much but there was a gas stove, sink, microwave, and a few human-friendly food items. There was a fridge, but nothing in it, it wasn't even plugged in, and there were utensils but only spoons.

"Ug, there has to be something we can use," I grumbled.

I searched high and low and finally found a paper clip stuck in between the cabinet and the fridge.

"Yes!"

Sitting down next to Amity I gently grabbed her hand and started picking at the lock. Lucky for me the handcuffs were the cheap adult-store kind and not the actual police kind. It didn't take me long to get both of our handcuffs off. Amity shook out her hands and thanked me. I nodded and whipped out my phone, ready to call my mother.

My mom answered on the 5th ring with a sleepy tone.

"911!"

She gasped and asked me what was wrong, much more alert this time. I told her a short version of what happened, "so what do you think? I need a plan. My thought process is I need to get out of this house and as far away as possible as quickly as possible, and I need to make it so that Tony can't bring people down here anymore."

"What about barricading the door?"

"Nah he'll just tear it down faster than we can put it up. I think I need to destroy the place, what's the fastest way to do that? Fire. I start a fire right as we escape and hope he doesn't notice it quick enough to get it stopped. However, I happened to notice that there's a gas stove and no smoke detectors down here, nor is there a fire extinguisher. He won't notice till it's too late."

"Okay, good plan. Next thing, you need a getaway car. That's where I come in. I'm leaving right now, tell me where you are, and we can discuss further."

I told her the location as I stood up and started getting things ready; I turned on the stove and lit it with the matches from the junk drawer. I was both surprised and unsurprised that Tony allowed matches down here, but maybe it was something one of his employees left behind. Either way, it made my life easier.

Together my mother and I came up with a plan: carefully unlock the basement door, start the fire, and run. My mom stayed on the phone the whole time and let me know when she was just outside the gates. The bars on the gate were thin enough to let people through but not cars so all we had to do was get to the gate. I put my mom in my pocket and helped Amity to her feet. We were both a mess but together we made a good team. I stood at the top of the stairs and worked on getting the door unlocked while she started the fire.

Once I got the door unlocked, I called it and Amity started to run towards me. She was weak but she was brave. I rushed back down the stairs and helped her up and we dashed out. The house was quiet until we got to the south wing. One of the employees was awake and walking in between rooms. They saw us and the color drained from their face, and they ran in the opposite direction. I led Amity down the hallway, and we darted out the door as fast as we could. We took a shortcut through the front yard which had a line of trees that gave the house more privacy so at that point we wouldn't be able to be seen from the house. It was dark and I could see perfectly well, but Amity, who was still more human than vampire, didn't have the same great eyesight, and to her it was probably pitch-black outside. She stumbled upon something as we ran and took a tumble.

"Amity, are you okay?" I cried.

She held onto her ankle for a moment and sharply inhaled, "my foot!" I looked down and she was bleeding badly around the ankle and a bit on her knee. I wasn't sure if it was broken, or just a scratch, or something that would need stitches, but we didn't have time to find out.

"Amity, hold onto me."

Her eyes went wide, and I slipped my arms underneath her and scooped her up. I couldn't lift Tony, but I could lift Amity, so I did and carried her all the way to the car. She had tried to complain at first but knew it was pointless. We had to get out ASAP; I could see my mother's car from a distance, even though she had kept the lights off to be a bit less obvious. It wasn't far. We made it to the car in seconds. My mother had already opened the door for a smoother escape. I popped Amity into the backside and climbed in beside her, slamming the door behind me. My mom spun her tires trying to accelerate so quickly. As we sped off there was a loud boom and a bright light emitting from the mansion, but we paid no attention and kept going.

"What happened, do we need to go to the hospital?" she asked as she sped off, keeping an eye on both the road in front of her and behind her. I did the same, too paranoid not to look for someone following us. So far, we were in the clear. I gently laid Amity's foot in my lap and examined it. I was no doctor but I had passed multiple certifications on first aid so I could at least tell if she needed stitches. The wound looked more like a bad rug burn than a couple of cuts so she must have scraped it on a big rock or something. I was able to look out for those, but she wasn't.

"I should've just carried you from the start, I'm so sorry," I told her. She looked me in the eyes and smiled, "are you kidding? You just saved my life! I would have died back there if you hadn't helped me."

"But you did die back there. You're in the process of turning into a vampire."

"I know but... with you I know I'll be okay."

Amity blushed and my eyes grew wide.

She laughed in a nervous giggle and changed the subject, "so where are we going?

"Home, right?" Mom responded.

"No!" I exclaimed, "I mean, if there's someone following us, we'll lead them straight to the house."

"Yes, but we have nowhere else to go, and we need to treat Amity's wound... and get her something to drink... right?"

"Yeah... I guess Tony already knows of the house so if he is going to, he'll go there first, and if we weren't there but Dad was..." I shuddered at the thought. I could not let Tony hurt anyone else.

"Okay we'll go to our house, wait it out till Amity feels better, but then we have to leave. I can't let you guys get hurt, and my being here puts you guys in danger."

The sky was getting lighter, and I knew that if we had not gotten out sooner, it would've been too late.

CHAPTER 11

Moving On

Amity, my mother, and I hid in my old bedroom with the blackout curtains tightly pinned to the wall. My dad had awoken from all the commotion and joined us. He hugged me and asked about my bruises.

"I'm fine, it'll heal in a few more hours probably." It was still sore but no longer painful.

My dad looked at Amity and asked who she was. She then extended her arm and shook his hand, "I'm Amity."

"What happened to you girls?"

"It's nothing dear, why don't you go back to sleep so they can get some rest?" My mother suggested.

"But you're covered in blood, shouldn't we go to the hospital?"

"It was just an accident, but the bleeding has stopped, and no one needs stitches, so it'll be okay, I promise," she added.

"Well, are you sure?"

"I'm sure Dad, I promise everything is okay."

"Okay... but I can't go back to bed now that the sun's up. So, I'll go get some coffee and give you all some alone time. Anybody want anything?"

Amity and I shook our heads and my mom asked

for a Chai Latte. Once my dad was out of the room I checked on Amity.

"I feel very hungry and tired but I'm okay," she responded.

"Why don't we get you cleaned up and into bed so you can rest and then we'll worry about food, okay?"

She nodded and I led her into my old bathroom. I helped her get the water turned on then dug through my closet for some comfy clothes for her.

"Any requests?" I asked.

"Anything in black?"

"You got it."

I found a black t-shirt and some sweatpants for her and laid them out on the countertop.

"Okay, I'll be in the other room if you need me."

I started to walk away but she grabbed my hand, and I turned back. The look she gave me was pleading, and I felt so bad that she was having to go through what I had gone through not more than a few months ago.

"Thank you, Hazel. I appreciate everything you've done for me."

"It's the least I could do, really. I'm so sorry Amity."

"For what?"

"For what you've gone through. Tony had no right to lay a hand on you and I promise... I will make him regret it."

Amity and I locked eyes for a moment, and I could feel my face getting hot, but I wasn't sure if that was from anger... or something else. Her porcelain skin, golden brown eyes, and tiny pointed chin caught my eye, and I took in how pretty she was. I could hear Amity's heart skip a beat and she let go of my hand.

"Well thanks again," she turned back to the

shower and started undressing so I headed back into the bedroom and closed the door behind me. My mom came back into the room with a thermometer, blankets, washcloths, and heating pads and prepared the bed for our patient. While we waited for her to get out of the shower my mother examined my wounds.

"Wow that's amazing," she exclaimed.

"What?" I asked.

"I think even just since you got home it's already improved a bit; the bruising is starting to turn green."

She gently wiped some blood off my face, and I could tell she was fighting the urge to lick her thumb and rub it on my cheek to get it off. As my mother, that was something she had done a lot of over the years. The shower turned off then as my dad walked in with the coffee. He handed my mom hers then kissed her on the cheek, "I'm just gunna go ahead and get ready for work and go in early today so you ladies can do what you need to do, I love you."

"I love you too," my mom told him.

I smiled at their conversation. At times I wished I had a real relationship like that. I had never had anything serious before, I was always just too busy for that kind of commitment. I guess now I could take things slow, I had the rest of eternity. Granted that's only if Tony doesn't come to finish what he started and if I could even find another vampire like me. Dating a human would be completely irresponsible.

My dad left the room again just as Amity opened the door. She looked cute in my clothes, but she appeared completely exhausted.

"Um... I don't feel so good," Amity leaned back and tried to catch herself on the door and I just knew she was about to go down, so I ran over and caught her. She passed out and I picked her up and carried her to the bed. She woke back up and immediately apologized.

"Girl do not be sorry, seriously it's fine. I'm here for you, okay?"

My mom handed me a wet washcloth and I dampened her forehead with it, then sat at the end of the bed and put her feet in my lap. Together my mother and I examined and wrapped the wound on her ankle. It wasn't bad, and like my own wounds, was healing quickly, but while her wounds were healing quickly, her body was not, and she looked more ill by the minute. My mom could tell she was about to puke and ran to grab a bin.

"How could you tell?" I asked after she had laid back down.

"A mom knows," she laughed. I shrugged and continued pampering her foot. Once it was all wrapped in bandages, I checked her throat. The shower had rinsed off all the blood and all that remained was a line of scar tissue, and eventually that would be gone too.

My mom took Amity's temperature, and it was way off the charts. She sighed and grabbed a blanket then wrapped it snuggly around Amity, who then shivered and nuzzled into the blanket. After a few minutes she had fallen asleep, and we let her. Her body needed to heal from the trauma... but she also needed food.

"What are we going to do?" I whispered, "she needs blood. If we don't get her some, she's going to die. I can't let that happen."

"Well, we never did go to that blood truck, I could go as soon as I find out where it'll be and when, it may take a few days though."

"I don't know if she has a few days... she seems so weak, and I'd hate to chance it. She needs to heal; she needs to feed."

"Then... I'll do it. She can drink from me."

"No, Mom, I can't let you-"

"Why not? My body, my choice, right? I want to help."

"What if she can't stop? The other night... I couldn't stop myself... and it was too late for them. I hurt someone, no, I killed someone. I can't let that happen to you and I can't let that happen to her."

"Yes, but she has one thing that you didn't have."

"What's that?"

"She has you. I trust you and I trust that if she can't stop on her own then you will help her. You will make sure that I will be fine, I believe in that, and if you need some too, I'm sure I have enough for the both of you."

"Doubtful. Remember how much I needed when I had my first taste? Nothing was enough. She's going to wake up very hungry."

"Then I will help her not be hungry anymore and then you can teach her the ways of a good vampire."

I smiled, "thanks Mom, but I'm not up for a pep talk. Let's just wait till she wakes up and then if she's okay with it... we can try your idea."

She nodded and we changed the subject, talking until I grew so tired, I laid back on the bed with Amity's feet still in my lap. My mom put another blanket on top of me and I passed out.

I awoke sometime later to Amity coughing, it sounded bad, so I was concerned. I sat her up and pulled her hair back so she could puke as my mom came running into the room. I sat behind Amity and as she calmed down, she laid back against me. At least if she was sitting up, she couldn't choke.

"Are you okay?" I asked.

She nodded, "why do I feel like this?"

"It's because you're turning, it gives you a bad fever for a couple days. Once you feed, you should start to feel better."

"You mean... I have to drink blood?"

My mother nodded, "Purple... I mean Hazel... had to too. Unfortunately, I don't have blood bags this time, but she and I were talking about it and... I'd like to volunteer for you to drink my blood."

"You would do that for me?"

"A friend of my daughters is a friend of mine, and we do anything for those we care about, don't we?" They both looked at me and I looked at Amity. Her eyes were more on the brown side of golden brown this time, and she looked sad but confused.

I nodded, "are you okay with that? We want both parties to be consenting."

"I... don't know if I can, I mean, how do I even do it, do I even have fangs?"

"I mean your teeth don't really sharpen overnight per se but maybe I can sort of... get it started?" My mom looked at me with confidence and held out her wrist.

"Are you both ready?" I asked.

They both nodded and I took my mom's hand. Hesitantly I bared my teeth and as gently as I could, bit into the flesh. The blood instantly touched my taste buds and before I took it too far, I quickly transferred her wrist to Amity. Once she got her first taste it was just like how it happened for me. The vampire sort of knew what to do and took over. She fed for a bit and once my mom started to look faint, I pried her off and laid her back. Amity gasped for air but was relatively okay.

"Mom?" I asked.

She was dazed momentarily but came around, "I'm okay, I think I just need to go lie down."

She left the room, and I got out from behind Amity and let her lay back down, "how are you feeling now?" I asked.

"Not perfect, but so much better. I didn't imagine it would taste good."

I got another washcloth from earlier and handed it to her. She wiped the blood off her chin and sighed.

"So, this is what I've become huh."

"I'm sorry," I sighed and kneeled beside the bed.

"Why are you always sorry?" She turned to her side to face me better and propped herself up on an elbow.

"I don't know, I just feel like you're in this situation because of me. If I had ended it with Tony sooner, he never would've hurt you, and I never would've hurt that man."

"What man?"

"Right, I guess I hadn't told you, well let me just start from the beginning."

I told her the story of my meeting with Tony and everything after that up till we met in the basement. She listened closely and never interrupted. As I finished telling the story I realized I still had the wallet (and also that I was still wearing the same clothes as yesterday).

"Hey uh I think I'm gunna go take a shower, do you think you'll be okay for a few minutes?"

"Of course, thank you."

I nodded, "just holler if you need anything."

I took my shower with the heat turned up all the way and basked in the steam. I took some deep breaths and tried to relax, but I couldn't stop thinking about everything that had happened. What would I do now? My parents would be in danger if I stayed, but I had nowhere else to go.

Continuing my thought process as I got out of the shower, I threw on a blue and white hoodie and some jean shorts then wiped the fog off my looking glass. I detangled my long blonde hair and put on some moisturizer I had left behind. I looked like an absolute wreck, but the bruises were yellow now. Not much longer before they would be completely healed. I sighed and exited the bathroom. Amity was waiting up for me and patted the spot on the bed next to her. I sat down crisscrossed, and she tossed me the wallet.

I gave her a questioning look and she told me to open it. I did so and pulled out the photo ID. It was the same man I had encountered, but he was younger and cleaner. The card was about five years expired and rough around the edges. Apparently, his name was Kyle Jones, age 45, 5 foot 9 and 190 pounds.

"Let's look him up," she suggested, "I don't have my phone."

I pulled mine out of my pocket and googled Kyle. What came up horrified us both. Apparently, Kyle had been living off the grid for the last 6 years because he was A WANTED CRIMINAL. Not only was he found guilty of three counts of murder, which was his wife and 2 children, but he's suspected to be a pedophile who has destroyed the lives of many children.

"OH my-" Amity gasped.

"What the hell?"

"So, this means-"

"Amity, I don't like that I'm having this feeling, but I think I'm glad he didn't make it."

"No, you're so right. He might be worse than Tony. At least Tony never hurt any children... right?"

"None that I'm aware of. What a freak. Those poor kids."

Amity put a hand on my shoulder, "Hazel, you did the right thing. He got what was coming to him. His not surviving being fed on was destiny... or something."

"Is it bad that I'm actually feeling a major sense of relief? I mean, I still feel bad that he didn't get to spend the rest of his life in prison but..."

"No of course not, that's a big plate to carry. You deserve some relief wherever you can get it."

I smiled, "thanks. You know, you are so easy to talk to."

"I think we make a good team; and now that I'm a vampire... well I'll need some new friends. Whatdya say, besties?"

Amity held out her pinky and I took it in mine, "besties."

We laughed and let our hands go. Even though the reasoning behind it was horrific, it still made my soul feel fulfilled to know I had made a new friend in the world.

"Seriously though, what am I supposed to do? I don't think my parents will be as cool as yours."

"Yeah, it's kinda just my mom. My dad knows I'm a vampire and that something funky is up but he's respectful enough not to push, and my mom is... just my rock, I've always told her everything."

"That sounds nice. My dad is more like that for me. My mom is the 'You have to play this sport because I used to be popular in high school when I played this sport' kind of character."

"If you don't want to tell them, that's up to you, but I do think it's best that you don't live there anymore. Who knows what could happen when you get hungry again."

"I don't want to hurt them."

"I know you don't; and I don't want to hurt mine either. Maybe we could be roomies for a bit and help each other."

"I would love that. I'd prefer to be as far away from here as possible. I do not want to be in the same town as Tony," she shuddered.

"I agree. Where could we go though? Where would we go that would have a large portion of willing donors?"

"Beats me. Maybe we can think about that while we pack."

"Good idea." I stood up and grabbed my old backpack and started dropping things into it.

"We'll go get some stuff from your place then we'll get the next bus ticket out of here."

"But if we don't know where to go... I mean how will we get food wherever we're going? Here we have your mom to help us with that blood truck, right? We won't have that option if we leave."

"Good point." I paused for thought, "Tony was talking about going to another party on Friday night."

"And?"

"Well, it's a vampire party. I mean, surely we aren't

the only vampires around that don't *kill* to eat, right?"

"Hopefully. So, you want to just go to this party and start asking everyone if they are or know a vampire like that? What if Tony is there?"

"Yeah, I guess. I mean, I don't think that'll be a problem, right? Maybe we could come up with an excuse as to why, and if Tony is there, he'll probably be too messed up on drugs to notice us, but maybe we could switch up our looks just in case."

"Honestly, since we're escape victims and neither of us want people recognizing us or searching for us... it may be a good idea to just permanently change our looks."

I grabbed a lock of my blonde hair and thought about it, "yeah I think you're right, I could totally go for a different color."

"Mandatory montage!" She laughed and I smiled. Seeing her radiant smile made me feel better about everything.

"So how do we want to do this? I guess we should make a run to the mall?"

Amity grabbed my hand and nodded, "I'm feeling much better now!"

"You sure? If you need to wait another day, we can. If Tony hasn't come to this house by now, I doubt he's going to."

"No, I'm okay, if we only have till tomorrow night that doesn't leave us with much time to bleach our hair. It's such a process, but we can do it at my house and then head out from there. I also have blackout curtains... and a bigger bed. So, we will go to the mall tonight, sleep at my place during the day and do our montage and then we will head to the party."

I looked at my twin sized bed and laughed, "Yeah, sorry my bed isn't the most comfortable."

"Sorry, that's not what I meant, I just meant like, so you don't have to sleep on the floor or couch or under my feet... or anything."

"I made it work last night," I waved it off and finished packing my things. I mostly packed clothes that I didn't wear very often for part of my "new look" and some books that were important to me. I looked at my phone and saw it was finally time for it to be dark out, so we left my room and went to check on my mom. My dad was in the living room with my mom asleep on the couch.

"Hey, do you guys know what's up with her? She's been sleeping since I got home from work."

"Uh yeah, she was just up all night helping us so she's pretty tired."

I leaned over the couch and noticed my mom was smart enough to put a big Band-Aid on her wrist before passing out.

"Hey mom," I gently shook her for a moment and her eyes fluttered open.

"You okay?" I asked.

She stretched and sat up, "yeah I'm sorry, I'm just a bit groggy."

"As long as you're okay, that's what matters."

"Yeah, I'm okay."

"Dad, can you get her something to eat? Mom, I think you need to replenish, you need food with lots of nutrition and maybe some sugar."

"Yeah, I think you're right," she rubbed her eyes and yawned as my father went to go get her something to eat.

"So, we've decided it would be best if we sort of... changed our looks and moved in together somewhere. That way Tony doesn't know where we are, and our family stays safe."

"You're going away?"

"I think I have to, but you know I've always wanted to travel. I can finally do that now. Money would be the only issue."

"Well, we could give you some, to get you going until you find a place. I will miss you, but I think I agree that you should probably leave town."

I hugged my mom, and she started crying. "I'm gunna miss you so much."

"I'll miss you too sweetie," she replied.

"Where are we going?" Dad asked as he walked in with a plate of food for my mom. He handed it to her and sat a glass of water down on the coffee table.

"Oh uh, Amity and I have decided to be roommates so we're gunna go find a place to stay, but we're thinking of going pretty far out."

"Are you sure you're ready for that?"

"Honey, she's been living without us for a few months now, and you know our daughter, she's very smart and resourceful." My mom looked from my dad to me and smirked.

"Yeah. Just hard to believe our nest is truly empty."

"I love you Dad, I'll be right here, okay?" I put a hand to my heart.

We chatted for a bit till my mom was done with her meal and the color had returned to her face.

"I feel so much better now," she grinned.

"I'm sorry," Amity sighed.

"It's okay hun, you needed it more than me."

Amity smiled with her perfectly straight teeth, and I couldn't help but smile too.

"We should probably get going before the mall closes for the night."

"You're right, we only have a couple hours."

We gathered my stuff and headed for the door. I was fully prepared to either walk or take the bus, but my mom came over to me and handed me her car keys.

"No mom, I can't do that."

"You need it to get where you're going."

"But you need it."

"Your dad and I can carpool, it's okay."

"You guys are too nice, I don't deserve you."

"That's not true, *we* don't deserve such an amazing daughter. We're so proud of you and if this will help you to continue to be the bigger person and help people rather than what those other vampires do, then I'm glad to contribute. Here, also take this."

She handed me a credit card, "it's one of many so don't worry, you're not taking my only one. It has a couple hundred dollars on it so that should be enough to get you to your destination and then I can just cancel it once you're settled in and ready to get your own."

I hugged my mom tightly and thanked her for everything she was doing for us. She hugged me back and then hugged Amity too.

"And you, Miss Amity, you are welcome here anytime, so don't be a stranger, okay?"

"I won't." Amity released from the embrace and waved goodbye.

My mom turned to me and winked, and I felt my cheeks get hot. Why did she just wink at me? I shook my head as we headed out, loading up my bag into the car before driving off. Once we were alone in the car, I asked how she was doing.

"Better every minute," she smiled.

"And your foot?"

"Honestly, I don't even feel it now."

"We'll take off the bandages when we get to your place and see how it's doing. Oh man, it's been a while since I've been to the mall," I stated as we arrived.

We walked in through the Nordstrom entrance and without even noticing we headed straight to Hot Topic. We got a few things from there, then went to the next hot spot, Spencer's. Amity found some awesome things there including a new nose stud. She told me she usually wore rings, but since she was changing her look a bit she opted for a stud.

"I think that will look so cute on you," I smiled, "oo look!" I grabbed her hand and led her to the back of the store where they had a few Wiccan books.

"I've always wanted to read about witches, and now that I know they're totally real. I think I'm going to."

"Heck yeah, I've always loved witches and all types of mystical beings."

After Spencer's we ran to Sally's. The mall was about to close so we had to be quick. We bought a couple of boxes of bleach and then wondered what color to do.

"Well, as the expert of hair dying, I think since your hair is naturally blonde, you should go dark. Maybe red or black?"

"I'm not sure I'd look good in black, what about a dark brown?"

Amity held up a swatch to my face and grinned, "yes I see it! You would look amazing in this color."

"I trust your judgment, let's do it. What color are you going for?"

She thought for a moment, "we'll I've never done pink before, what about this one?" She held up a bubblegum pink swatch and awaited my response.

"I like it! That's a super cool color!"

"It's probably going to take two bleaches to get it this color, but it'll be worth it."

We paid for our stuff and went back to the car. Amity navigated us back to her house and surprisingly enough she was only about 15 minutes away from where I lived, but I guess that wasn't super surprising. We entered her house quietly in case her parents were already asleep, and they were.

"They sleep a lot," she frowned and led me to her room. She shut the door and made sure to check her curtains for any holes that would lead to the sunlight coming through, then held her hands out.

"Well, this is it. Luckily my bathroom is also connected to my bedroom, but it's not quite as nice as yours."

Her room was smaller than mine, but she still had a bigger bed, and she had plenty of knick-knacks and posters and things that made the room special. My room was boring compared to hers and I told her that.

"I like to switch up hobbies, I love art and music most."

"I love music too, what genres do you listen to?"

"Honestly a pretty wide variety. Some days I wanna rock out and other days I want to rave, and some days, like when I really need to focus, I'll listen to lo-fi."

"Girl yaasss, you rave?"

"I've been to a couple, but what I really like is

underground clubbing, you know like that scene in the matrix? Except I've never been because they're always 21+."

"That's amazing! Actually, the place we're going is kind of like that. I mean, it's a vampire den essentially, and they play like dark synthwave club music."

"Really? Okay, now I'm super excited!"

"Let's get this montage going!"

She turned on the radio then got our purchases out of the bags and laid them on the bed.

"Okay, your hair is gunna be the easy one so let's do it first." She sat me down in her computer chair and went into the bathroom. She came out with towels, brushes, and bowls and set them on her computer desk. Then she wrapped one of the towels around me like a cape and pulled my hair out.

"So how short are we going?" she asked as she began brushing my hair.

I pulled a strand down and observed it for a moment. While sitting it almost reached my hips. "You know, let's go big or go home. Let's do like right at shoulder length. Also... how do you think I would look with bangs?"

She came around and put some hair over my eyes to visualize, "I think you'd look super pretty with some light, wispy, witchy looking bangs."

"Let's do it!"

"Awesome! Okay, so normally you wanna cut after you dye, but since your hair is currently so long I think we'd run out of dye so I'm just going to cut it to about here-and then I'll trim it up and do the bangs once we're done with the color."

"You seem to know what you're doing, and I don't,

so I'm just gunna let you do your thing." I smiled and she got back to brushing my hair. It had been a long time since someone had pampered me, and it felt nice. It was also gratifying to just be hanging out with a friend, giving each other makeovers like when I was a kid. I felt like I was finally able to breathe and relax for the first time in months.

I looked around Amity's room as she did my hair and was in awe of all her cute trinkets. She had a lot of skulls and dragons and "spooky" stuff, but she also had some stuffies and sports trophies. Alongside one of her trophies was a picture of her in a softball uniform wielding a bat.

"You play?" I asked.

"Captain of the team actually."

"You must be good then!"

"Most of those trophies are from little leagues, my parents kinda made me do it but I grew to like it, I get my aggression out when I hit the ball."

"I'm not great at sports, but I did do a little bit of karate when I was a kid and track up until recently."

"Oh, nice! You'll have to teach me some moves," she karate chopped the air and I laughed.

"No moves left to teach you I'm afraid. I couldn't even defend myself against Tony."

"Yeah, but he has hundreds of years of experience so don't be so hard on yourself. Speaking of which... how are we going to take him down?"

"I'm not sure, we definitely have to start with a training montage though."

"Oo yes, we'll go to the gym, lift some books, do some jogging. Man, that sounds like a lot of work."

"Yeah... but maybe with the two of us, we won't

need as much physical strength. Maybe we can trick him somehow and defeat him then."

"We'll figure it out, we have all the time in the world."

"You seem so... calm, about all of this. I was freaking the hell out when I realized what I was."

"Well... I've always been into the macabre, I've read tons of books about vampires, and I think the concept is really interesting. Besides, it's like your mom said. I have something you didn't. I have YOU."

I blushed, "you heard that?"

"I was half asleep, but yeah I heard that part. I'm grateful that I have you to help me through this, and I'm sorry you didn't have the same support."

"It's no big."

She had finished applying the dye then and wrapped my hair in a cap, "okay now we do mine while that sets for about 30 minutes and then we'll rinse it out."

I stood up and she took my place in the chair.

"Wait, I need a mirror. Hang on." She got up and grabbed a makeup pallet that had a mirror in it and leaned it up against her computer, then she parted her hair. She then showed me how to help her do her hair and together we had it all bleached in 30 minutes.

After rinsing out each other's hair I blow-dried mine for a few minutes till it was just barely damp, then I sat back down for Amity to cut it. She trimmed the ends up to my shoulders then took her time with the bangs.

"Now don't peek until I'm totally done! Ugh, it looks so good! You're going to love it!"

Amity's hair had lightened up but still had some

light blue left behind, so we went to bed for the day and when we woke up in the evening, she bleached it again. While we waited for that to process, she did my makeup using dark colors for both the eyes and the lips.

"Okay now put this on," she handed me the black dress I had found at the mall. It was slimming at the waist, with a poofy skirt and heart shaped neckline. I was never really one to care if another girl saw me changing, so I started taking off my clothes there and Amity quickly turned around.

"Oh, you're okay don't worry," I told her, "I wouldn't want to go to the bathroom and accidentally look in the mirror now, would I?"

She turned back as I was getting into the dress and her face was beet red.

"Can you zip me?" I asked. I turned around and pulled my hair back as she zipped me in.

"Well, what do you think?"

The red in her face deepened, "you look stunning."

"Thanks! So do you!"

She rolled her eyes, are you kidding? I'm a hot mess." At that point, it was time to get the bleach out and after that, we were finally ready to put the pink in. After rinsing that out, changing clothes, and putting on makeup, Amity was ready to party. The pink looked gorgeous on her, she was like some sort of cotton candy-haired goddess, and I was in love. She did her makeup like mine and put in her new nose stud, and wore a black, long-sleeved dress with boots and a crescent moon pendant necklace.

"You look amazing!" I was astounded by how gorgeous she looked, in fact maybe even a bit jealous.

"Okay and now the reveal! She led me to the

bathroom with a hand over my eyes and then lifted her hand up once we were settled in.

I looked like a completely different person. I had never had dark hair or bangs before and it was a huge difference, but it was a good difference. I looked a bit older and more mature, and the bangs did complement my face shape well which was also surprising.

"Woah," was all I could say.

"Woah is right," Amity chuckled.

"Thank you so much it looks amazing! And I love how you did my makeup, it's all so perfect!"

"Of course!" I hugged her carefully to not get makeup on either of our clothes, "alright, I guess we're ready to party!"

After all that the sun was gone, and it was time to go.

"Wow, we just barely finished in time; I never knew how hard it was to do your hair."

"Yeah, it's a process, I usually open my schedule for a whole day anytime I have to bleach. Even if it's just my roots."

"Good call."

With our new "disguises" we set off to find the party. Luckily it was in the same house as the last one I had gone to with Tony. I think most of them were at that location. Someone sure knew how to party. We rolled up and slithered in, trying to scope out the crowd. If either of us saw Tony, the plan was to ditch. Neither of us saw him with the first round of guests but the night was still young.

The music blared and it was just the music I expected, French underground synthwave. It sounded so different from the poppy rave music I usually listened to, but I really liked it and was tapping my foot next to Amity.

"Do you wanna dance?" she asked me, holding out a hand.

I smiled and put my hand in hers, "with you? But of course!"

The last time I was there I had zero intention or will to dance, but with Amity I felt so carefree and serene. We danced for a good half hour, totally forgetting about our quest for a bit, and when we finally remembered that we were supposed to be mingling, we started talking to the dancers around us.

After a few attempts, we still hadn't gotten any useful information, mostly just stoners that were too high to understand their own thoughts. Not that that's a bad thing because I've been there, done that, but it wasn't helpful to us.

We stepped out of the dance zone, the whole time keeping an eye out for Tony, but he was nowhere to be found.

"Hey, is that what I think it is?" Amity asked while pointing to a punch bowl and "chocolate" fountain, both of which had blood in them.

"Uh yeah... but I wouldn't drink it, who knows how it was sourced." She nodded, but I could tell she was uncomfortable to be near it, so we walked over to the other side of the ballroom. We talked to a few more people who were at least not *as* high, and finally got something.

"Word is, there's some hippy ring in the mountains," someone told us.

"Really? Tell me more, I'm so curious... how anyone could live like that." I made it seem like I was shocked that anyone would NOT kill their meal and hoped that no one would notice my lies.

The woman rolled her eyes, "I don't know, some sort of progressive, cliché human-wannabes are out in the wilderness just having drum circles and getting their blood from... get this... donors. Can you believe that?"

Amity's mouth dropped open in shock.

"Wow really? What a crazy world we live in huh? I would love to see such backward ideas! Where do they live exactly?" I added.

She shrugged, "somewhere in Colorado Springs I think."

"Crazy hippies," I shook my head in fake disgust and thanked them for their time.

"Oh, have you seen Tony? He was supposed to be here."

My body went cold, but I kept my cool, "who?"

"Never mind."

Amity and I walked away from the group and huddled up.

"Well, do you think we have what we came for?"

"Yes. Colorado, here we come!"

CHAPTER 12

Colorado

After the party, we changed into pj's and sat crisscrossed on the bed. We stayed up for a bit talking and getting to know each other and laughing and playing stupid games like Fuck Marry Kill. It was like the perfect sleepover, and I hadn't had a sleepover since I was 10.

We passed out just as the sun started to rise and woke up again as it was setting.

"Morning," I yawned and stretched next to my new best friend, and she replied with the same.

"Well today's the day, you ready?"

"I'm ready."

"Fresh start for both of us."

"Yes, I am so excited. I've never been to Colorado before."

"I've been once, the mountains are super cool, and there are some caves that are amazing too."

"Oo exploring a cave sounds so fun!"

"I'll take you some time!"

"It's a date!" I realized what I said and blushed then quickly changed the subject. "Ah, so we have a long drive."

"Yeahh," she replied with a hand on her neck,

"guess I should get started on a rad playlist huh?"

"Rezz?"

"Yes!"

"Deadmau5?"

"YES!"

"Liquid Stranger?"

"Yeessss one of my favs. How about Trisekt?"

"Okay, I don't know if I've heard of that one."

"Omg, you're going to love them!"

"Bet!"

"This is going to be a GREAT road trip."

"Hell yeah."

We heard her parents come upstairs then and they knocked on her door. We looked at each other and I told her it would be okay and to just hold her breath if she felt uncomfortable.

"Yeah?" Her mom opened the door with her dad beside her.

"Where were you the past couple days?"

"Uh, I've been hanging out with my new friend."

"And this is?" Amity's father asked.

"I'm Hazel," I waved.

"Nice to meet you, were heading to bed so-"

"Oh okay, we were actually just about to head out."

"Where are you going?"

"Actually, we're road tripping to Colorado."

"Right now? Why?"

"Hazel had a... death in the family, so I'm coming with her in support. We may be there for a while."

"I suppose you are an adult that can make your own choices now so... okay, but please be safe."

"I will." Her dad gave her a hug and nodded at me and then her mom shut the door behind them.

"Well then," I cringed.

"Yeah, my parents are weird. I'm sure after a few days they'll totally forget about me."

We waited a few minutes for her parents to settle in bed and then lugged our bags to the car.

"So, it's about an 8-hour drive to Denver. I say we stop there for the day and then continue on to Colorado Springs. We need to be fast though because that doesn't give us much time before sunrise."

"Okay let's get going then, do you want me to take the first shift with driving?"

"That's okay, I can, plus you have to compose our playlist remember?"

She clasped her hands together, "of course! I think first up will be some Kaskade!"

"Excellent choice."

We hopped in the car and set up the GPS. The way there was spent laughing and singing and sharing stories. Once we were deep into the middle of nowhere, we pulled over and laid on the backend of the car to stare up at the stars for a bit. It was a clear, cool night and you could see a bit of the Milky Way, something I had never seen before.

"It's so beautiful," Amity smiled and pointed up at a few stars, "there's Orion's Belt."

"And there's Little Dipper!" I only knew the ones I had learned in school, and that was so long ago I only remembered a few, but it was so magnificent to be able to just forget about the world for a bit and stare into the dome.

"Do you remember that Area 51 release everyone was talking about?" Amity asked.

"The one where they said UFOs are real?"

"Yeah."

"They also said that they believe we're living in a simulation too."

"Really? That would be so crazy... like if we were just characters in a movie or a game or a book or something."

"Yeah, I mean there could be someone out there just writing our story right now."

"What if what we see in the sky right now is just a snow globe of reality. We think it's real because we live inside the snow globe, but maybe there's a whole other life form out there."

She turned to me with her mouth open, "woah, those are some high thoughts."

"And we're not even in Colorado yet," I giggled.

"Speaking of which, we should probably get going. We don't want to get too far behind and not have anywhere to go when the sun comes up."

"True, but I guess even if we do, it won't kill us," I stated as we got back in the car and drove off.

"It won't?"

"No, that's one of the many myths about being a vampire."

"Then why are we concerned about it? And what are the others?"

"Well, the light does affect us, it just doesn't kill us. We're nocturnal creatures by nature with very sensitive eyes. Have you noticed since you've turned that you can see much better in the dark?"

"Actually yeah, I just thought I was crazy, so I didn't say anything. I also just feel so much more... powerful? I think? Maybe that's not the right word but I just feel... better. Is that bad?"

"No, that's just the perk I guess of not being human anymore. Vampires are predators. Humans aren't exactly made to kill food with their bare hands, that's why we're better gatherers; or they, I guess I should say. That's why I'm vegan... or was, unfortunately, because with where we live and with it being the 21st century, there's really no need to eat meat. I can get all the nutrition I need from a variety of fruits, vegetables, lentils, grains, etcetera."

"I've been vegetarian for a while. I've always wanted to go vegan, but my parents were so pro-meat they wouldn't let me. They always said, 'not while living under our roof'. I was already trying to look for a roommate when we met so I could get the hell out of there."

"Well, I'm sorry that you can't be that anymore." I frowned and gripped the steering wheel, thinking again about my hatred for the man that turned us.

"Well, at least I can still be the best that I'm able to now. If I can continue to find ethical sources of nourishment, then I think I can live with myself. I'm just so lucky to have you."

I turned my head for a moment and half-smiled, "I'm lucky to have you too. If it weren't for you, I'd probably have been stuck in that basement or pretending to be into Tony again until I could finally get rid of him."

A few hours later we had made it into the city and stopped at the cheapest hotel we could find. We then got all of our stuff out of the car and headed into the building.

"I'm sorry, but we're pretty full tonight, all we have left is a one-bed, is that okay?" The clerk asked as we were checking in. We turned to each other and shrugged.

"Sure. Why are you so full, is there an event going on?" I asked.

"I think there's a couple of events actually, there's some kind of convention and there's also a concert."

"Nice, who's the artist?"

"Some Alison Wonderland or something like that."

Amity and I both gasped.

"Yes!"

"We are so going!" I grinned.

The clerk gave us our room keys and we excitedly went to find it. Once in our room, we closed the curtains and pinned them to the wall with furniture and blankets. We then turned on the tv and sat on the bed.

"Alright well, it's been a super long night and I'm ready to get to sleep."

"Yeah, me too," Amity agreed.

"When we wake up, we'll figure out what the next move is."

We climbed under the covers and passed out quickly. In the evening, I woke up early and Amity was still asleep, so I took a shower. Once out I realized I had forgotten to grab clothes beforehand, so I went back into the room in just my towel. Amity had woken up but was still lying in bed.

"Morning," she yawned.

"Morning sleepy head, you ready to party?"

"Always."

I sat down and started getting concert info. "Okay, so the doors open at 7, so if we leave soon, we'll be able to make it in time to see Alison. They have resale tickets available online."

"Sweet, I'll get mine now. What should we wear?"

"Uh... I don't know. I didn't really bring any rave clothes. I guess we could just go in bras and fishnets. I do have glitter."

"You always carry body glitter on you?" She laughed.

"Always." I joked.

"I know we're supposed to be looking for our vampire siblings but I'm glad we're taking some time to just go to a show and have fun."

"Yeah, I am too, but we will need to find food soon; it's been three days, I'm starting to get hungry again."

"Yeah, me too," she sighed with a hand on her stomach."

"The concert will probably be over at about midnight, so we'll have plenty of time after to start our search. We could even kinda ask around while we're there too."

"Okay good plan."

"Hope you brought hiking boots and bear repellant," I half-joked.

"No... I guess I should have. We also might need to find a more permanent residence."

"True. Do you want to take a shower? I can look on Zillow while you do that if you want."

"I would love a shower." She got out of bed and started digging through her bags.

"What about this?" she asked, holding up a see-through top and short pink skirt that matched her hair.

"Perfect! What about mine?" I held up a fishnet crop top and booty shorts.

"Cute," she agreed.

"Sweet." I started changing into the outfit and she went into the bathroom. For some reason I felt anxious; I normally wasn't the kind of person to get anxious easily, and although Amity made me feel safe and happy, I always got nervous when I really thought about it. I wondered for a moment why that was but did some deep breathing, shook it off, and put my outfit on.

Once Amity was out of the shower, we shared the bathroom to do our makeup. Instead of her typical all-black look Amity went for more color, she did pinks, and I did purples, and we both added lots of body glitter. Together we made a cute pairing.

"Hey, so not sure how you feel about this-" Amity started.

"Yeah?" I wondered.

"But we are in Colorado... so we could-"

I laughed, knowing where she was going with that, "I'll check dispensaries nearby, we can get a pre-roll and some gummies?"

"I've never had gummies before. Wait, if we can't eat food, can we eat edibles?"

"Oh, I didn't even think of that. I've only ever seen vampires snort cocaine, smoke weed, and take pills. I've never seen one eat an edible... maybe we can't."

"Guess we could try one and see, but I'm not really wanting to spend money on something that I'm just gunna... wait what happens?"

"Right, um... your body just can't really process it, so you end up spitting it out or throwing it up."

"Bummer, guess that means I'll never have ice cream again huh?"

"Yeah... but that's okay, maybe after a while we will get used to it. After these couple months, I've started to. Sometimes I really miss my mom's homemade vegan Mac 'n Cheese though."

"That sounds delicious, what does she make it out of?"

"It's a cashew base with soy and nutritional yeast."

"Is nutritional yeast good? My parents were always afraid of that stuff, same with tofu."

"Yes, it is so good! I'm sorry you won't get to try it now... but surely there are pros to not eating Americanized junk food. We won't get unhealthily overweight."

She looked down at herself. "True. I didn't even think about that, but I have slimmed down a bit."

"Don't get me wrong, you'd be beautiful no matter what your weight is, my point in saying that is that certain types of human food are so bad for you."

She blushed, "I get it. Oh, hang on, you have a sparkle in your lashes." Amity got closer and tried to pick the sparkle. She couldn't get it at first, so she put her other hand on my shoulder to steady us. As soon as she touched me, I got shivers and stood back.

"Sorry! Your hand was just cold," I said, my face turning as red as hers.

"All good," she shrugged, "I got it."

"Thank you. Oh, so I found this place outside of Colorado Springs that's available for rent, it's kind of expensive... but it's a perfect hiding place."

"Awesome, can you message the owner and see if they'll let us come take a look?"

"Yeah. I just hope they won't mind it being a meeting during non-business hours."

"If not, we'll keep looking. Maybe we should try to get jobs too if we're gunna be here for a while."

"That's not a bad idea. What job will hire us overnight though?"

"Um, maybe we could be stockmen at Walmart or something?"

"Yeah, or maybe we could be strippers."

She laughed, "not a bad idea, they do make great tips."

"I'm not even joking, I'll do it." I smiled while saying this even though I said I wasn't joking, but I couldn't help myself.

After we finished getting ready, we left the hotel room and went through the lobby to leave. We weren't the only ones doing so, there were three other groups that we passed by, one of which was dressed for the rave like we were and two of which were dressed in cosplay. One person from a cosplay group was dressed as a vampire, I recognized it as a specific character from an anime, but I wondered if he knew anything.

I pointed, "you should talk to him, see if he knows anything."

"Why me?" She frowned.

"Because you're prettier than me, I don't know."

"Let's just go together, and by the way, that is absolutely not true."

I rolled my eyes, and we walked up to the group.

"Hey guys," I smiled, "I love your cosplays."

"Thanks!" They replied.

Amity looked at the vampire, "especially yours! Are you Dracula from Castlevania?"

"Yeah," he replied.

"You wouldn't happen to know of any real vampires around here, would you? Or are you?" I could tell she was trying to sound flirty, but it just wasn't really working, and the guy wasn't going to take the bait even if he did know anything.

"You're joking, right? Or is this part of your cosplay? What are you guys anyways?"

"Oh, we're not going to the convention, we're going to Red Rocks."

He nodded, "Well gotta go, see you."

His group walked one way and we walked another.

"Dang it," Amity frowned.

"I didn't realize you were such a bad actor," I teased.

"Sorry, I just... got nervous, I guess. But I'm excited for this concert so let's get going."

We got to the Red Rocks Amphitheater just in time for Alison to come on stage. Everyone was dressed in such a wide variety of clothes, yet everyone was just vibing, jovial, and carefree. Some people were wearing sweats and t-shirts, some people were wearing coats and pants, some were wearing hardly anything at all, just pasties and panties, and everything in-between. It was chilly up in the mountain, so I wished we had chosen to wear more clothes. I shivered and Amity noticed and wrapped her arms around me.

"Maybe we should go further down where there are more people, it'll be warmer there."

"Yeah, you're right, and we can make some small talk."

"Right."

We went into the pit and took a few minutes to dance with the crowd. Once we were loose and comfortable, we pulled out the pre-roll and lit up. We offered to share it with the people around us to open room for conversation.

Amity and I talked to a few people, none of which thought we were being serious. At some point, I was looking around and saw a guy drinking from a hydration pack, but the substance coming out of it was dark red. It could've been wine, but I had to find out.

I grabbed Amity's hand so we wouldn't get separated and moved a few rows back to get closer.

"Here's a good spot," I fibbed.

Being high while doing this was quite a bit different, but I wasn't quite high enough to be a lost cause. I turned back and asked the guy if he had some water.

"Oh, uh... it's not water."

"That's okay, anything will do, I'm just super thirsty."

"I'm sorry, I'm... germophobic," he lied.

I leaned in, pretending I was being flirty and got close enough to smell that it was for sure blood in the pack.

"Don't worry," I winked, "I've uh... already lost my V card if you catch my drift."

"How is that related to my beverage? Oh are you a-"

I nodded, "but would it be okay if I asked um... if your drink was ethically sourced?"

"Absolutely, I run with those guys," he pointed to a group of people that were walking in our direction. They were mostly dressed in hippy-like clothing, with flowers and tassels and drapey outfits.

"We don't exactly like to announce our dietary decisions for obvious reasons, but something tells me I can trust you two."

"You can actually. We are sort of here in Colorado specifically to find... you." Amity admitted.

The rest of the group arrived then, and we introduced ourselves.

"Do you think we could all chat after the show?"

"Of course!" One of the women in the group smiled and hugged us, "I love you guys; it's so cool we found more people like us!" I could tell she was on something, but I wasn't sure what.

"I will share my hydration pack though, now that I know you guys are chill. That is, if you need it, I mean."

I put a hand on my stomach, thinking about how long it had been since my last real meal.

"It's been days," I told him.

"Jesus, I'm sorry, you must be starving, here, this batch is locally sourced," he leaned in to whisper, "blood donor at the hospital."

I looked at Amity and she nodded for me to go ahead. She trusted him, and so did I. I took a sip from the pack and fought a gasp of pleasure.

"Here," I handed the nozzle to Amity, and she took a sip. Her eyes grew wide, and I could tell she was struggling to pull away, so I tapped her shoulder as a reminder.

"Sorry," she apologized.

"No, it's okay, I would've done the same if it had been that long."

We felt so much better and more refreshed after our little snack that we decided we could let loose and just enjoy the music for the rest of the night. So, we spent the next hour bouncing to the music and looking up at the stars, awestruck by the beauty of the landscape. The venue was high up on a mountain overlooking Denver and a few other cities below, right in-between two huge rocks.

Seeing the city sparkle below and the mountains next to you with the stage in the middle and the lights flashing all around you was such an incredible experience. At the height of that experience, Alison played a remix of the song Midnight City by M83, and after that, she played Innerbloom by Rüfüs Du Sol, two songs that I never thought I'd get to hear in person, and I looked up and just took a deep breath and it was almost like my third eye had momentarily opened. I listened closely to the lyrics and closed my eyes.

"Feels like I'm dreaming
Like I'm walking
Walking by your side
Keeps on repeating
Repeating
So free my mind
All the talking
Wasting all your time
I'm giving all
That I've got
If you want me
If you need me
I'm yours"

As the bridge repeated, I opened my eyes and saw the world for its beauty, and as the twinkling lights around us had focused, I looked to my best friend and reached for her hand as the words "I'm yours" melodically repeated. We looked up at the sky together and saw a shooting star. I made a wish that the happiness I was feeling would never go away, and I hoped that it would come true.

Once the show was over, we walked out to the

parking lot with our new group of friends.

"So, there's this awesome late-night bookstore that we like to hit up when we're in the city, you guys want to go? It's super chill, I promise," our new friend Matt shared.

Amity grinned, "are you kidding? I love books!"

"Yeah, I've never heard of one that's open this late," I agreed.

"It's newer, it's built around the idea that bibliophiles need a space 24/7. So, you can go in and just read like at a library, but you can also buy books, and there's a lounge area out back, and for others, you can buy coffee and smoothies too."

"That sounds amazing, yes let's go."

We followed the group to this late-night bookstore, and it was beautiful. It was a cute little brick shop at the end of a strip complete with a chalkboard sign out front and patio outback. The inside had a small coffee/smoothie bar and surrounding that were all the glorious books. Amity and I were both in awe of the cute little shop and we spent a few minutes looking around before the group led us to the back patio where we all sat around a lit, gas fire pit.

"So, introductions?" I began, "I'm Hazel, and this is Amity."

"Well as I said earlier, my name is Matt," our man with the hydration pack stated, "and I enjoy hiking." He was a tall but scrawny man, with dark brown hair and eyes to match. His shoes and backpack indicated that yes, he did enjoy hiking.

"Call me Sasha," the next person shook our hands. She was a queen of a woman, with skin as dark as obsidian, and eyes that twinkled like the same. Her hair was natural and short, and she wore stunning body jewelry, "I enjoy art, I own a small handmade jewelry business."

"Wow, I was just about to say how much I loved your jewelry," Amity was as amazed as I was. I wasn't super fluent in gemstones, but it looked like she had mostly turquoise on.

"Oh, thank you! I'll show you my shop sometime!" She had a thin accent that sounded Nigerian, but I couldn't be sure.

"That would be awesome-" I started as the next person cleared their throat.

"I'm William, you can call me Will. I was a teenager in the 70s and have been stuck there ever since. I love swimming and kayaking." Will was the palest of all the vampires that sat before me, with blue eyes and blonde hair, he was dressed in just a t-shirt and bootcut jeans, with a big hole in each knee.

"Wow, sounds fun! I haven't been kayaking in ages," Amity added.

He nodded and the second to last person went.

"James, pronouns he/him," the man waved, "I'm a fan of rock climbing and animal advocacy."

"I mean we're all fans of advocacy," the last person announced, "that's why we're here. We're a group." The woman stood and shook our hands next, "my name's Margaret but you can just call me M."

M gave the appearance of being the youngest in the group, she looked maybe 15 at the most, but something told me she was probably actually the oldest in the group.

"So how did you guys come to be a group, what do you guys do exactly?" I asked.

"Well, that's quite the question, we all have very different backgrounds. But as for a group, we all just sort of found each other over time, understood that we have similar goals in life, and made a pact. We have a place in Pike-San and we mostly spend our days enjoying nature and everything that mother earth has given us." M was a passionate person, that much I could tell. She had a flowery maxi dress on and a flower crown around her head. Her long, dirty-blond hair was in loose curls and bounced when she talked.

"That sounds amazing."

"Um yeah, where do we sign up?" Amity agreed.

"You should join us at our next support group meeting, the Peaceful Vampires," James said.

"There are more people like you?" I asked.

"Of course, there are tons of people who are like-minded. You just gotta know where to find them."

"And now you have," Matt added.

"We kind of thought there weren't that many."

"Well, there probably aren't in comparison to the number of humans in the world... or the number of 'regular' vampires. When did you guys turn?" M asked.

"I was turned in May, and the man that turned me did some really horrible things, it's a long story, but he also turned Amity here too."

"Less than a week ago," she added.

"Ah so young," Sasha smiled with a hand on her heart.

"Neither of us agrees in killing people or even hurting them just so we can eat, so we've been in search of people that are also like that so we can learn how to find ethical sources of food and just, in general, be happier, better people," Amity told them.

"Well, you're in luck, we are just the people to help you do that."

After a while of talking the sky was starting to get lighter and we decided to call it a night.

"So, we have a thing tomorrow night, but you guys should come to see us the following night, we'll show you the group."

We agreed and shook everyone's hands before separating.

"They were all so nice," I said once we were back in our hotel room.

"Yes, I think they're perfect for our quest."

"Now we just need to find a place to rent and jobs."

"The hard part," she frowned.

"We'll figure it out!"

"Yeah," she sighed so I put my hand on her shoulder to show my support.

"Hey, when are we gunna go see that cave you were talking about?"

She shrugged, "well I think they only have tours during the day."

"Do they?"

She got out her phone and checked Google, "oh sweet, they do ghost tours! I could sign us up for one tomorrow night! The latest one they have is from 9 pm-10!"

"It's perfect!" I sang.

She laughed, "I'll get our tickets right now then. Hey, maybe after the caves we could go for a walk in the park?"

"I would love that."

CHAPTER 13

Peace

"So, are you ready for our date, I mean, friend date?" Amity asked.

I brushed out my fluffy hair and grinned, "ready! I can't wait to see the caves with you."

"Just remember to bring a jacket, it gets pretty cold in there."

I nodded and searched for a jacket, "um, I think that may be the one thing I forgot to bring, I guess I'm going to have to find some good winter clothes since the winters get pretty harsh in the mountains."

"Yeah, that would be a good idea," she said, taking off her jacket and handing it to me, "here, take mine, I've got another."

"Thanks," I replied, strapping the jacket to my waist.

We drove out of the city and into the mountains, in awe of how beautiful they were.

"No matter how many times I see them up close like this, I will never get used to it."

"I know right? They're so beautiful," Amity agreed. As she said this my brain automatically thought the words 'just like you' and I turned my head as I could feel the blush coming on. Why was I thinking things like that?

We drove the car up a sharp, winding road, and at the top was a large parking lot that dropped off, overlooking the mountains. We stood for a bit at the edge and watched birds float around for a bit.

"So cool," was all I could say.

"Come on, we should probably get going, we have to check-in," Amity said, pulling my arm. Her hand slid down to mine, and I gripped it. Something told me not to let go. We walked hand in hand up until we got to the check-in table. I wasn't sure if Amity wanted to keep holding my hand or if she just hadn't really noticed that it was happening, but something about it just felt so comfortable and... right... so I was a bit sad when she let go.

We were told to go wait for the rest of the tour group at a bear statue, so we found it and waited a few minutes. The tour guide was a couple minutes late, but once she arrived, she sent us underground quickly.

"You doing alright?" I whispered. I knew it couldn't have been easy for a new vampire to be around this many living beings in such close proximity. I had (more or less) gotten used to it.

She nodded, "I'm good, aren't these caves so cool?"

"Absolutely."

While walking through, the guide also showed us things that were growing inside the caves and how they had changed over the thousands of years they had been there. We were then led into a deeper part of the cave and the tour guide shut off the lights and explained how complete cave darkness can affect people. After that, she dove into the ghost stories which fascinated Amity more than anything. She was almost giddy with excitement.

Once the tour was over, we stood and overlooked the mountains again, breathing in the fresh air, neither of us wanting to leave. We googled where there was a good place to go on a walk and it led us to a nearby park. We followed the instructions and got back in the car. As we were getting out, Amity pulled out a blanket.

"What's that for, are you cold?" I asked.

"No, I brought it because I figured we may want to lay down and stargaze. I kinda thought maybe we could treat this like a picnic, but without the food obviously, is that okay?"

"Yeah, that sounds awesome! That'll give us some time to start researching and applying for jobs too."

"Yeah... exactly."

I frowned at her wording and wondered if maybe I missed something. We started our walk, following a path that wound around the trees and hills. It was such a beautiful landscape with the mountains in the background and the moon shining brightly above our heads. It was a cool night but in a relaxing, early autumn sort of way.

"Oh look, there's a perfect spot," Amity pointed towards a clearing off to our right, so we stepped off the pathway and into the grass. We headed far enough out that if anyone else was walking the path late at night they wouldn't be able to see us, then laid the blanket out and sat down.We began by doing some job searches on our phones and we had both ended up applying for a job at the late-night bookstore alongside many others. I hoped we would get the jobs but tried not to get my hopes up too much.

"Okay, we've done enough adulting for the day,"

Amity frowned and laid down on the blanket, pulling me with her. We looked up at the stars and started talking about other things, like school and hobbies and Amity's softball team. At some point, Amity sat up quickly and screeched. I sat up too, wondering what was wrong.

She swiped her hands on her legs, "ew!"

"What?" I asked.

"Sorry, there was a spider, it's gone now."

I laughed, "babe, you're a vampire now? There's no need to be afraid of spiders."

She looked at me with a twinkle in her eyes, "psh, yeah I know that."

I grinned and patted her shoulder, she shivered a bit, and I figured it was because she was cold, so I sat closer and gave her a side hug, rubbing my hands on her arms to warm her.

"I'm okay actually, but thank you," she smirked.

"You're not cold? Then why did you shiver?"

"I don't know," she waved, "anyways."

"How about you tell me more about yourself?" I suggested.

"Like what?"

"Like what your past friends have been like, what your favorite foods were, most important memories you have, previous boyfriends?"

Her cheeks turned red, "I've never had a boyfriend."

"Girl, that's nothing to be embarrassed about! I get it, boys kind of... suck."

She giggled, "no that's not why. I mean they do suck but... uh... actually, I'm sort of... lesbian?"

"Oh! You are?"

"Yeah... I'm sorry. I should've told you sooner... I just didn't want you to think I was hitting on you or something, I'm a very touchy person and I know that can get annoying to people who aren't that way."

"You say that like it's a bad thing."

"It isn't? The few people I've told haven't responded well to it, so I just don't really tell people. Besides... I thought you were straight? You've only ever talked about men in your life, like Tony."

I shrugged, "I've never dated a woman before... but only because I've never really dated anyone before. I've never really had a serious relationship at all. I've had a few f-buddies and that's all. That's all Tony ever was to me too. And of course it's not a bad thing, my brother is gay, and I've never once loved him any less even for a second; and same with my trans-cousin. Truth is, I don't know what I am... but I know I'm not straight. Maybe I'm bi," I shrugged and looked up from eyeballing my feet. Amity was looking right into my eyes, and I felt all the blood drain from my face. Her pink hair blew in the gentle breeze and as she gazed at me, I knew she was the person I had been looking for. I had found a best friend, and it was beautiful and amazing, but I had also found love, and I was not about to let that go.

"But I know I'm not straight... when I... look at you," I admitted.

She blushed, "So what does that mean... for us?"

"Amity, there's something I've been wanting to ask you," I paused from the shock, was I really about to do this? It would change everything, but it would be a good change. I saw the care and passion in her eyes, and I knew I wanted to be more than just friends.

Before I knew it Amity blurted out: "do you wanna

go out with me?"

I facepalmed, "no! I was so ready!"

We laughed and Amity waved her hand, "I'm sorry, you say it!"

"Amity, will you go out with me?"

"Yes!" She grinned and I reached out for her, wrapping my arms around her neck. She wrapped her arms around my waist and hugged me back. Butterflies fluttered around in my stomach and my heart could've jumped from my chest. It was the happiest I'd been in a long time.

I pulled away from the hug slowly and cupped her face in my hands, "you are the most beautiful person I've ever met, and I've been dying to tell you that." I grinned and she leaned closer. I took that as my cue, and I leaned in to kiss her. We kissed for a moment, it was slow and soft, and my body tingled as the butterflies intensified. I knew at that moment that my wish had been granted.

Amity knocked me down to the ground and snuggled up to me. I laughed and wrapped my arm around her lovingly. Together we looked up at the stars for a while longer.

"So, this was a date then?" Amity asked.

I laughed, "it was from the second I said it was."

"Okay good, I thought I had misread that. This is perfect."

"I agree, best date I've ever been on."

She looked up at me with adoration and I pulled her closer. After a few minutes of silence, we heard a noise and sat upright. A deer spun their head around to look at us and I sighed in relief.

"Just a deer," I said to myself.

Amity stood up and started walking towards it. I jumped up and grabbed the blanket so we wouldn't lose it, "Amity what're you doing?"

"Trying to see if I have any cool vampire powers like in the movies."

I rolled my eyes and thought to myself how adorable she was. She carefully approached the deer and let him sniff her hand. You could tell the deer was nervous, but it wasn't until she tried to pet him that he ran away into the woods. Amity sighed and turned back to me.

"Hey, you got close enough to touch, a deer wouldn't have done that with a human," I consoled, taking her hand in mine.

She blushed, "you're right, maybe since we're not human anymore, they're not as afraid of us."

"Anyways, we should probably be getting back, it's getting late."

She agreed and we started making our way back to the car. It was about a half-hour walk back and we held hands the entire time. It was so weird to think that a week ago I was being mentally abused by the man that killed me and now I'm in Colorado with my more-than-best friend.

When we got back to the hotel, I checked my phone and realized I had an unread message. It was from the owner of one of the houses for rent saying it would be fine to show us the house in the early nighttime in a couple of days. I replied that we would be there and penciled it into my schedule, then notified Amity.

She grinned. "Yey! It would be so awesome to get out of this crappy hotel."

"I mean, yeah it's a crappy hotel, but at least it's a crappy hotel with the best person ever."

"That's true, I am with the best person ever!"

I smiled and opened my suitcase to find some PJs. I didn't have much left that was clean, just shorts and a Cami, so I started to put that on.

"Oh okay," Amity flushed.

"Sorry, I thought this was allowed since you're my girlfriend now. Do you want me to take it to the bathroom?"

She gulped and focused on my forehead, "nope you're good."

I laughed and put my shirt on then gave her a peck on the nose, "you're cute."

"No," she said bashfully, "you are."

Amity turned around and got her PJs out of her suitcase, "I think we'll need to find a laundromat soon."

"Actually, I think the hotel has one. It's probably awful though."

"Probably, but that's okay, better than nothing."

Her PJs were black sweatpants and a tank top, and after throwing those on she jumped onto the bed and turned on the tv. I climbed in next to her and laid down. She followed and got on her phone, researching more jobs for a bit before going to sleep. I texted my mom, telling her about how we were dating now, with lots of heart emojis. I knew she wouldn't see it for another couple of hours, but I sent it anyway because I was too excited. We passed out curled up next to each other and it was the one night I didn't have a single bad dream since becoming a vampire.

The next night when I woke up, Amity was already up and ready for the night.

"Woah, how long have I been asleep?" I asked.

"Not too long, I just woke up kind of early. What time are we going to meet up with the gang?"

"12."

"Midnight. Okay, we'll we have plenty of time then. We can check our applications and keep looking for more apartments."

"Yeah, good plan."

"Hey, you know what's one thing I miss about being human?"

"What's that?"

"I miss going out for late-night snacks."

"Did you do that often?" I teased.

"I would. I snuck out of the house a lot. There's a gas station right next to my house that I would go get chips from at like 3 am during the summer."

"Yeah, that makes sense. We could always go to the dispensary before they close, that's kind of similar."

She shrugged, "yeah close enough, let's do it!"

I checked my phone then and my mom had texted back 'congratulations' and a winky face. I replied asking how she knew but assumed it was just a mom thing.

We walked down to a nearby dispensary and smoked it on our way back. Our conversations while high got even more chaotic than usual.

"Okay no but listen," she started, "you've heard of the Mandela effect, right?"

"Yes, that shit is so creepy. Like no its definitely 'Berenstein bears' not 'Berenstain'."

"Right? Exactly! And the mysterious case of Elisa Lam?"

"Definitely supernatural... maybe it was a vampire thing!"

Her eyers went wide, "woah, that would make so much sense!"

We stopped on a bench just outside of the hotel and talked for a bit, Amity laying her legs in my lap and leaning her head on my shoulder. Once our time was up, we started our journey to the Peaceful Vampires group get-together near Colorado Springs. I was surprised to see that the meeting was in an old, abandoned church but honestly, not that surprised. The church in a little graveyard at the bottom of the mountain hill. It was made of stone and beginning to crumble, and the inside was covered in dust and debris.

"I would have expected this from a more... violent... group of vampires," Amity whispered.

"Yeah, me too," I smiled and waved to the group as they noticed us. There were six other people that I did not recognize, and they were all sitting in a circle of chairs around the altar.

"Welcome," a man I presumed to be the group leader waved us up to the altar and pointed to some free chairs. He looked like a man that had come straight from the office. He was bald, with glasses, and was wearing khakis, a button-up, and a sweater vest. He even had a briefcase leaned upright behind his chair.

"You must be the newcomers I've heard so much about," he smiled, "please, introduce yourself in AA fashion."

"AA fashion? Uh okay. Hi everyone, I'm Hazel and I'm a vampire."

"Hi Hazel," the group synchronized.

"And I'm Amity, also a vampire," she waved.

"Hi Amity," they replied.

"So, we were just talking about the blood drive

that we'll be having next week, would you ladies like to join?"

We nodded.

"Great! You guys can help with check-ins and making sure each participant fills out the proper paperwork which I can give you on the day of. Now it depends on how much blood we are given, but we usually split the final amount as evenly as possible but 10 percent plus the odd one or two if any will be given to a hospital so it can be used by humans that need it. Do you both agree to these terms?"

"You give a percentage to charity? That's so awesome of you guys, I'm in, how about you Amity?"

"Absolutely."

Going counterclockwise, each member of the group announced themselves, even those we already knew, and I waved, telling them how glad I was to be there.

"It is so refreshing to meet people who want to change the world for the better," Amity added.

"Likewise," the leader, Collin, responded.

We settled in with the group and by the end of it, we were all best friends. At some point Amity and I exchanged a look and held hands for a moment and Sasha excitedly asked if we were together. We looked at each other then turned back and enthusiastically said yes, to which the group replied with 'awe's and 'nice job's. Not one of them was judgmental or unsupportive.

"You guys are amazing," I thanked them, "it's nice to see people who have been around a while be so open and supportive."

"Yeah, I'm not even out to my parents yet because I know exactly how they'd, or at least my mom, would react." Amity sighed, crossing her arms.

"For me personally," M responded, "I believe that as immortals it is our duty to care for the planet that we will forever live on. If we do not teach the mortals how to be kind, and generous people, then this planet will not survive long. Too many people these days create chaos and ruin with every step, not once thinking about the consequences of their actions. I chose to live in peace and love for all and only surround myself with those who feel the same."

"How... many years have you been around if you don't mind me asking?"

"I was born in 1813, and if there is ever anything I learned from being alive in the great depression and many other horrible times, it's that family doesn't come from blood, it comes from love. You have an infinite amount of time and an infinite amount of love. You can always make more room and you can always, always expand. Time is relative."

I was still too high for that even though for the most part I had come down. I nodded and put thought into it. She was right, it was what I had been saying all my life. We choose kindness, we choose love, we choose happiness. We have the ability to make choices for better or for worse, so why would we choose the latter? As vampires, we could torture, kill, and eat the people that we used to be just like, or we could ask them to donate the extra blood that they can spare.

Amity and I discussed this on the way back to the hotel and unsurprisingly, we agreed. We had finally made it where we wanted to be, we were living our best lives in Colorado, while also getting to help others.

"Hey," I turned to Amity as we were walking up to

the hotel and took her hand in mine, "we still have time, do you want to go on a date? We could get all dressed up, go to the only place that's open at 4 am, order some coffee and pancakes and pretend to eat it?"

Amity giggled, her free hand smacking her leg.

"What's so funny?" I asked.

She took some deep breaths and squeezed my hand. "That sounds like the most perfect date ever, I love it."

"Great!" We went inside and changed into fancy dresses; I was in a short, light pink dress that was strapless and had an A-line frame, and Amity was in a very Aphrodite-looking gown, light gold with a belt just below the bust and a slit in the fabric in front of each leg. It was very flowy and beautiful and made me self-conscious in my dumb pink dress.

"Okay not fair, you're over here looking like some cotton candy-haired goddess, and I just got pink... fluff."

Her face turned bright red, and she patted her hair down, "what? No way, you look gorgeous."

"Aw thanks," I blushed.

We went for our date and by the time we got back, we were relaxed and tired from all the laughing we did. The server at the restaurant was so confused that we paid in full plus a good tip for a plate of pancakes we never touched. I felt bad for being a bit wasteful, but I told the server they could have it and I hoped that they were allowed to do so. I would have if I worked there.

Once back in the hotel room Amity went to get her pajamas from her suitcase and I wrapped my arms around her waist from behind. She paused and wrapped her arms around mine, then turned around to kiss me. My grip on her got tighter and I kissed her back, then she leaned into me and wrapped her arms around my neck. We kissed for a few minutes before I let go.

With a heavy breath, I pointed to her PJs, "suppose we should probably get you into those huh?"

She playfully slapped my arm and smiled, "I can do that by myself thank you."

I shrugged, "suit yourself, I'll just be over here... taking my dress off... by myself."

She rolled her eyes and unzipped the back of my dress, "there, I helped."

I laughed and slid the dress down then put on some boxer shorts and a spaghetti strap shirt, then went into the bathroom to take my makeup off and brush my teeth. Amity undressed and joined me. The bed called our name and we hopped into it, cuddling for warmth.

"I'm so glad I have an awesome girlfriend," I ran my fingers through Amity's hair and kissed her forehead.

"I am an awesome girlfriend," she laughed and snuggled closer. We said our goodnights and fell asleep just as the sun was rising.

CHAPTER 14

The Hunter

A few days later we went to meet the landlord of the house we were looking to rent, and we arrived not long after the sun had set.

"You must be Hunter, I'm Amity, and this is Hazel," Amity greeted upon our arrival.

"Yes, that's me, it's nice to meet you guys."

"Sorry it's so late," I apologized, "we have a... very busy work schedule."

He waved his hand and squinted, "it's no biggie, it is Saturday night anyways. Besides, it's so peaceful at night, wouldn't you agree?"

We agreed and he led us into the house. It was a cute little stone cabin that was not far away from the church where the Peaceful Vampires meet.

"It's a beautiful home," Amity was in awe, looking around the place with the wonder of a child.

The furniture was all wooden minus the couch, and it was decorated with old-fashioned lanterns on the wall that reminded me of "old witch living in the woods" vibes and I absolutely loved it.

"Hazel, look!" Amity pointed to the fireplace which had a crescent moon carved into it.

"That's so cool!"

"So, you guys like it here?" Hunter asked.

"Love it!" Amity replied, "it kind of reminds me of a vampire's den or something."

"Vampires you say? That would be so cool if they were real, right?"

"Uh..." she looked at me and I shrugged, "sure I guess."

"Have you guys heard of the vampire serial killer?"

It was a weird thing to bring up during our first meeting, but I gave him the benefit of the doubt.

"No," we replied.

"Well, apparently it's this guy who is still alive and out there somewhere, who is suspected to be the murderer of more than 40 people. All of the victims were completely drained of blood."

"That's crazy."

"Right? People like that should really be put down, don't you think?"

"Yeah, I suppose," I said. He took a step towards us, and my intuition told me to take a stance. Amity did the same and stepped in front of me.

"Are YOU a vampire?" She asked.

"Are you saying you do believe in vampires?"

"You first."

"I do. But I am not."

She frowned, "then why do you want to know?"

"So I know who to kill!"

Hunter lunged at us, pulling a stake from behind his back. We jumped to the side, and he fell between us. We scrambled to stand and took a few seconds to check on each other.

"Who do you think you are?" I asked.

"Who do you think I am?" He growled.

He was a scary man, very military type, and as he stood a foot taller than me, I was a bit nervous, but I remembered who I was, and who I wanted to protect, and I set my body into a fighting position.

"My name is Hunter? And I'm asking you about vampires? It's quite obvious I'm a vampire hunter."

"Way to be self-aware," Amity rolled her eyes.

He lunged at us again and this time I blocked the blow while Amity gave him a swift kick to the crotch. "You're messing with the wrong girls," she spat.

He snapped back and the three of us fought. We held our own for a bit, he picked on me first, kicking me to the ground and raising the stake above my head. I scrambled backward as Amity pounced on him from behind. He struggled to get her off and I took the opportunity to grab the stake and toss it across the room. I refused to kill this human, but I was also unsure of how I would stop him without hurting him. Hunter gripped Amity and yanked her off, tossing her to the ground. I ran over to her and fell to my knees to make sure she was okay. Hunter took out another hidden weapon and used that moment to tackle us onto our stomachs, a knee to each neck. He was strong and had the two of us pinned down tightly.

"Why us? We've never hurt anybody?" I gasped, honestly confused.

"It's true! We're vegan vampires!" Amity admitted.

Hunter relaxed a bit and chuckled. I wanted to tell him it wasn't funny, but I didn't want a stake through my back.

"So, you don't kill people and drink their blood?"

"NO! Never have never will. We are peaceful vampires!"

"Really!" I agreed.

"And you expect me to believe that?"

"Dude, you believe in vampires! Something that should totally be fictional, is it really that hard to believe that there are vampires out there that are kind and would never hurt a fly?"

"But how do you survive?" he asked genuinely as he released the pressure from our necks. We sat up slowly and I rested a hand on Amity's shoulder to make sure she was okay, then continued.

"We only take blood from the bag; we get them from willing donors, and no one is ever hurt in the process. It's like giving someone a kidney or donating plasma. We need it to survive, and they can spare a bit if they're up to it."

"That can't be," he lowered his weapon in a very confused state.

"Actually, we kind of agree to killing certain vampires. For a bit, and still mostly now, we wanted to kill the man that turned us because he was a total prick," I added.

"What did he do?"

"He killed a bunch of humans, like too many to count, practically enslaved them in his home, and kidnapped and turned girls like us into vampires for personal gain. No, not even for gain, it was just because he could. He's an evil man and deserves to rot in hell."

"He sounds like a total dickhead."

"You're telling me," Amity sighed.

He put the stake away and helped us to our feet. We took a step back, still cautious. "Look, we'll tell you whatever you want to know, we have nothing to hide. That man, his name is Tony. He had us imprisoned in his basement and we escaped. We came to Colorado to get away from him but also to find someone to teach us how to fight so we can go back and kill him when we're strong enough."

"Hazel put up quite the fight before he locked her away, but he's just too experienced."

"Wait, so you guys are vampires, but the only person you would ever hurt is another vampire who has murdered a bunch of people?"

I nodded, "Tony has to die. If he doesn't, then more humans will."

"That's why I'm a vampire hunter, to save the people they would otherwise kill for food or even pleasure," he shuddered.

"Exactly. We would never harm an innocent fly."

"You know, kinda like Dexter," Amity added.

He gave us a questioning look and Amity smiled, "it's a show, it's awesome and you would probably love it! But yes, we're like that in a way, but we haven't killed anyone at all yet, not even a bad guy."

"And that's what you want to learn how to do?"

"Yes. We don't want to let that man get away with harming anyone else. We're just not strong enough to defeat him yet."

"Then it sounds like we have similar goals... maybe we could be of help to one another."

"Maybe we could."

"We really do need a place to stay," Amity admitted.

"Heard. I'll give you a one-month trial. Try anything though, and you're out faster than lightning. And if I find out that you've been lying and you bring humans in here, deal's off, and I kill you."

"Deal."

"I'll get the contract and we'll meet up again tomorrow and discuss details."

"When can we move in? We're kind of tired of being in a hotel."

"The house is move-in ready, including furniture, so as soon as you sign the contract you can move in. That's the nice thing about renting from someone like me instead of an apartment."

"Well let's just meet here, same time tomorrow, and we'll bring our stuff with us then."

"Sounds good."

We went outside the house and as soon as Hunter was gone, I squealed, "we got a house!"

Amity jumped up to hug me and I swung her around. "I mean look at this place! It's amazing!"

We looked around and I took a deep breath.

"Yeah! I feel like I can actually breathe here, it's so... tranquil."

"Perfect place for us to stargaze?"

"I think that's our thing now, isn't it?" She grinned.

"I believe so, now we just need a song!"

"The one from Alison Wonderland's set where uh... where you held my hand and there was a shooting star, and it was just very..."

"Otherworldly?"

"Yes, it was really nice. I actually made a wish on that star."

"I did too, what did you wish for?"

"Well, I suppose I can tell you because it already came true. I sort of wished that I would gain the courage to ask you out."

We blushed as we made eye contact, "and I wished

that I could stay as euphoric as I was in that moment forever, and that came true too. Well, at least so far, it's staying true. You make me happier than anyone else ever has."

Amity smiled and leaned up to kiss me. I was only two-ish inches taller, but I thought it was cute that she leaned up. I kissed her back with my arms wrapped around her waist as I pulled her closer.

"Is Hunter even going to know if we do or don't stay here tonight?"

I smiled, "he might find out if his lock is broken in the morning, best not break our contract before we've even signed it."

She sighed, "good point."

"But we have all night now, how about a short hike?"

"Sounds perfect."

We drove down to the nearest hiking trail and started our journey. This one was going up one of the mountains and it was very curvy and rocky. I was leading the way for most of it, but I was quickly becoming out of breath. While struggling to breathe through the pain, I wasn't watching my feet and tripped on a rock. I started falling forward and would've landed flat on my face if Amity hadn't reached out and caught me. She was fast as lightning with her reaction and, as I was going down, she spun me so that I landed on my butt, pulling her down with me. We fell onto the ground with Amity landing in my lap. I couldn't help but laugh at my own stupidity and Amity followed the lead.

"Sorry about that," I said.

"No worries, are you okay?" She asked.

"I'm good now," I smiled and put my hands on her

cheeks, "you know, we're totally alone for probably at least a few miles."

"You're right, we are completely alone," she flushed. I pulled her in for another kiss and we sat there in the cool dirt, making out till we ran out of breath.

Time rolled forward a day and we were all packed up and ready to move into our new place. We met Hunter at the house and went over the contract. For the most part, it seemed fairly standard: keep the house clean, rent due on the 15th of every month, no pets allowed, and no outrageous parties. However, then it got into the handwritten part of the contract.

"Now I want to trust you guys," he started, "but you are the one thing in the entire world that I completely despise and do not trust. So, you're going to have to earn that."

"Well Hunter, as we said, we aren't like the vampires you know. We would never hurt anyone," Amity shrugged.

"You did try to hurt me."

"That was in self-defense! You attacked us first!"

"I suppose I'll let that one slide, but don't think I won't keep an eye on you."

"Look," I frowned, "we thought that we had mutual grounds, that we would help each other. Can we do that or not?"

"Perhaps. The question is, are you willing to learn? Are you willing to do what it takes?"

"As long as the only person we hurt is someone that truly deserves it, then yes, I am."

"Me too," Amity agreed.

"Then we start our training in a week. I know you guys aren't big fans of the sunlight, so I will do my best to switch to a sleep schedule that fits both of our needs."

"What kind of training will we be doing exactly?" She asked.

"We'll start right at morning time for you and evening for me, and we'll start with some basic self-defense tactics. Well throw in some mountain hiking to build up strength and endurance and once I feel you're ready, I'll teach you how to fight, then how to kill."

"We can't just skip to the killing part?"

I nudged her and she rolled her eyes, "What?"

"No, we can't skip. If we skipped, then you'd be the one who'd end up dead," Hunter warned.

"Fine, fine, I see your point. It's just that, well, it's already been a week since Tony... who knows how many people he's hurt since then. How long have you been a hunter, Hunter?"

"Long enough."

"How many vampires have you killed?"

"On average, about one a month for the last ten years, so maybe around 100 to 150ish."

"I'm sure that adds up but that number kind of surprises me, I figured it would be more than one a month." I replied.

"Some vampires are pretty hard to find actually."

"You found us pretty easily."

"You guys are newbs; you were pretty easy."

Amity started to protest but I pushed her back, "he's right. We should be more careful."

"Plus, I technically wasn't 100% sure, the thing that tipped me off was you wanting to meet at night."

"Yeah, that figures," I shrugged. "We need to find some more of those special sunglasses that Tony had."

"What glasses?" Amity asked.

"Tony had these special sunglasses that made it so we could go out in the sunlight with barely a bother. They were cool. I didn't have any on me when we escaped."

"I wonder if any of the Peaceful Vampires would have some or know where to get them."

"I bet they would, we'll ask next time we see them."

"Peaceful Vampires?" Hunter asked.

"Uh yeah. There are some other vampires like us."

"Oh cool, where are they?"

I shook my head, "you want us to earn our trust with you, but you have to earn yours with us too."

"That's fair. Anyways it's getting late, are we in agreement?"

Amity and I exchanged glances and nodded.

"Then both of you sign here and here," he demanded, pointing to lines on the page.

We signed the contract and stood up.

"We'll meet at dusk a week from today at Pikes Peak to begin your training. Your homework is to get used to the altitude if you haven't already, that would make it harder."

"Why are we going all the way up to Pikes Peak?" I asked.

"Because I said so, and because it's cool, okay?"

"Okay," we agreed.

"I shall see myself out, enjoy your new home." Hunter handed us the keys, put two fingers to his forehead and waved them, then turned around and slammed the door behind him.

I followed him to the door and locked it behind him, then turned back to Amity and smiled.

"Welcome home!" She laughed.

"Home sweet home!" I hugged her and led her into the living room. The first thing we wanted to do was explore the place more in depth.

On each side of the stone fireplace was a bookshelf. There weren't many books on it, but I knew we could fill it in no time. The kitchen was in the back of the house; it was nearly useless to us, but we kept the refrigerator plugged in so we could keep a fresh supply when ready. The house had an amazing view, especially from the upper level. It was a small, loft-style house, so the only bedroom was just a space above the living room, but it was quaint and quiet. The one place we had yet to explore was a trap door we found hidden underneath the living room rug.

"Woah," Amity gasped, "what is that?"

"I don't know, it's definitely not a basement, maybe a panic room?"

We opened the door and looked down into the hole. At first all you could see was cement and a wooden ladder, so we decided to crawl in and investigate. Amity was enthusiastic about our find and went first. She helped me down next, and we turned to find a small room encased in cement. The room was empty aside from a shelf, a toilet, a sink, and a metal bed with a thin mattress.

"Well, that's not creepy at all," I shivered.

"Yeah... this is either a prison cell or a bomb shelter. Hoping it's the latter."

"I don't think the contract said anything about a prison cell, but considering who the owner is... I wouldn't be surprised."

"What, you think he's kept vampires down here?"

"I'm just saying it's possible, and it's kind of creeping me out, let's go back upstairs."

"Okay."

We went back up to the main level and began unpacking our things. We didn't have much, and we had quite the load of laundry, but it was nice to have a place to put our things and a place to call home. It was also nice knowing we were far away from civilization. There were a few neighbors, but no one closer than a mile and a half.

Once done with laundry we sat on the couch and this time I put my legs up on Amity, who then rested her arms on my thighs and checked her phone.

"Ah guess what!" she exclaimed.

"What?" I grinned.

"I got a job interview! It's at that bookstore!"

"That's awesome, congratulations!" I squeezed her shoulders and gave her a kiss on the cheek, "I just know you're going to get the job, you're perfect for it!"

"Thanks! Check yours, maybe you have one too!"

"Okay," I pulled out my phone and noticed I had a couple messages and a couple emails. That was my fault for not checking it in a couple days. I opened the emails first and I had gotten two interviews, one at a grocery store in Colorado Springs and one at the bookstore. I told Amity about both, and she practically squealed with excitement.

"Let's set up our interviews for the bookstore about the same time, I hope we get it!"

"I hope so too! We kind of have to anyway, we only have one car and it's not exactly a quick drive."

"Yeah, you have a point, but I think it will work out just fine!"

I checked my other messages, and one was from my mother, replying that she knew about Amity and me because of 'motherly intuition', whatever that meant. My brother also texted me saying he missed me. I thought about replying but I figured that it was for the best that I didn't.

"Guess we should start our homework then?" I thought.

"What, getting used to the altitude?"

"No, our bookstore homework, we should probably get to reading!"

"Good point!" We each picked out books to read and returned to our place on the couch, reading until we couldn't keep our eyes open any longer.

CHAPTER 15

Something Unexpected

We awoke when the sunlight beamed through the windows and struck our spot on the couch.

"Ah!" I screeched. Amity and I were immediately blinded by the light.

"How did we manage to fall asleep before putting up curtains?" Amity cried. She reached for me as I did for her, and we held each other close. I grabbed the blanket that was behind us on the couch and threw it over our heads. It didn't filter the light completely, but it was enough that we could open our eyes and slowly adjust.

"Are you okay?" she asked me.

"Yeah, you?"

"Yeah, I just feel really stupid right about now."

"Hey," she soothed, a finger under my chin, "it could've happened to anyone, I guess we may just be stuck under this blanket for a bit yeah?"

I looked at my wonderful girlfriend and saw the love in her eyes. My heart swooned and I laughed away the butterflies.

"Well, if we're going to be stuck here for a bit, we should get comfortable," I pulled the blanket down, so it was just barely covering our heads, but also covered the rest of us, and we curled up on the couch together. In that moment I was wide awake, and I figured Amity was too. The sun was something I hadn't seen in a long time, and it was quite a shock to my system. Although, all was forgotten when I looked at Amity. I leaned over her to give her a kiss and she kissed me back, pulling my hair away from my face. Straddling her hips, I deepened the kiss until we ran out of breath and then I trailed the kisses down her neck.

It was a while before we fell back to sleep but eventually, we did, cuddled cozy into the couch. When we woke it was thankfully dark out, and the first thing we did was make a run to town to get some blackout curtains. We also got a few other things for the house to make it cozier and more our own, then we went to meet the Peaceful Vampires at the blood drive. The drive was being held in a blood truck outside of a care center, we met up there and received name badges and paperwork.

"Okay, so with every donating patient you'll have them fill out this form, and then when they leave you can give them one of these cookies." Collin gave us a basket of cookies and my mouth dropped open.

"Those look delicious, did you make them?"

"No, Sasha did, she's an excellent baker. Although, not like I would actually know."

"I have some human friends that I like to cook for, and they always say they're amazing," Sasha shared, coming out from behind the truck.

"Hey, how are you?" I waved.

"Great thanks!" How are you two, did you get that house you were hoping to get?"

"Yes!" Amity cheered, "it's amazing and we'd love to have you over sometime!"

"That sounds great, I would love that!"

"Oh, and just so I know, I understand that you guys are still kinda new to this lifestyle, are you guys okay with being around blood and not drinking it?" Collin asked.

"I am, you?" I pointed to Amity with my eyes.

"I think so... you've taught me well."

"Excellent, you guys are strong, most vampires really struggle with that in the beginning."

M came around the truck then and said hello to us. This time she was wearing scrubs and a white coat with her hair pulled back tightly.

"Hey M. Wow, you look so professional!" I cheered.

She laughed, "I would hope! I am a doctor!"

"Really? That's awesome... but how, don't the humans think you're like 15 or something?"

"They think I'm one of those child prodigy types, they get over it pretty quickly."

"Sweet," Amity fawned.

"We're about ready to open up, how about out here?" She asked Collin.

"I think we're good, hey did you know-" his voice trailed off as they went back into the truck and left us out of it. It was still early on, the nights were getting longer as the season steered towards autumn, but I wondered what kind of crazy human would go to a parking lot blood drive at night. I certainly wouldn't have six months ago.

My wonder turned into surprise as we checked in more than a hundred volunteers over the course of 2 hours. We even ran out of cookies and Amity had to run to the store to buy more.

At the end of the event, we gathered to celebrate

with a bottle filled with the stuff.

"I can't believe so many people were willing to donate. How often do you guys run these? "

"Our drives are every other week, James is an excellent salesman," Will grinned, a grip on James' shoulder.

"You guys are amazing," Amity toasted and we all cheered in unison. M then counted and portioned out everyone's dividends, and with 8 of us participating we each took home 14 bags, enough for every day for two weeks, or a lot longer if needed, and then we still got to donate 21 more bags to the care center.

"Great job guys!" M smiled and locked up the truck, "let's meet up at the church next week and we can discuss the next drive!"

Amity and I agreed to meet them and before they left, we were invited to a private party that the clan was having.

"Sure, why not?"

We followed the group's car into the mountains and more than an hour later we had finally arrived at our destination. It was quite literally in the middle of nowhere, on a stretch of land at the top of a hill. It wasn't quite the height of the mountains it was surrounded by, but with those in view in every direction it was a breathtaking sight. Seeing it at night was like seeing a 360-degree galaxy. The small number of houses scattered below looked like the stars in the eastern sky and the lake at the bottom reflected the clouds to the west.

The clans' house was a series of very elaborate yet simple tree houses in a triangle formation with a fire pit in the center. They had clotheslines and hammocks and lots of outdoor furniture and you could genuinely tell these people absolutely loved nature.

"Would you like a tour?" Matt asked as we got out of the car.

I was speechless and had to nod.

"We wash all of our clothes by hand, and we bathe in the waterfall just behind that tree line there," he pointed down a hill and I could see a line of rocks that led to what I could hear was rushing water.

"We also grow our own food, behind the house over there. Well, we can't eat it of course, but we've got some green thumbs in the group so we grow and then donate, it can be very therapeutic. The treehouses are mainly to shield from the sun, storms, and snow as we spend most of our time outside, in our hammocks over there, or our fireplace here." As he said this the fireplace was being lit by James and M, while Will and Sasha brought out a tray and a mason jar.

"Is that?" Amity asked, eyebrows both lowered and raised.

"You bet," Sasha smiled and set the tray down on a wooden table next to the floor pillows that surrounded the pit. "We grow some of this in the garden too, but not enough to get in trouble."

"As if *that* would be the thing that would get us in trouble," she added with a laugh.

Matt nudged us away for a tour then and showed us the inside of one of the three treehouses, "this one is mine, the girls stay in one of the others and James and Will in the last."

The entire thing was one singular room with just a bed, lots of books and magazines, and hiking gear. There was no kitchen, but there was something so alluring about the place I couldn't help but wish I lived there. Then I remembered the amazing new house I just got with my even more amazing girlfriend, and I couldn't help but be grateful for the way my life had changed recently. Amity took my hand in hers and squeezed almost as if she had read my mind.

"We're completely off the grid, doesn't cost us a cent to live here."

My eyes grew wide at his words, "isn't that technically illegal?"

He grimaced, "yeah, we technically live inside a national park illegally, our location isn't something you can find on Zillow, but we live off the land and we give back where we can. Instead of jobs, we do all volunteer work and a bit of travelogging, oh and Sasha's artwork."

"You guys are literally living the dream," Amity beamed.

Matt shrugged, "I just try to leave as little footprint as I can and appreciate this big world for all of its many years of caring for me."

"That's beautiful." I could've been moved to tears. He was a way better person than I could ever dream of being; and my new dream was quickly becoming that dream.

The group called to us from outside and we joined them at the firepit. Will rolled a blunt as we started chatting and James turned on a battery-operated music box and danced over to his spot.

"Ah, you know I have a sort of mild hatred for these newer songs," M joked.

"Oh, come on, you know you love them," James laughed.

"Amity, Hazel, what do you girls listen to?"

"Ah, I don't think you could handle Amity's music," I teased.

M tossed her head back and Will handed me the blunt.

"Guest's first," he grinned.

I took a hit and passed it to Amity, who then passed it to Matt, who then passed it to M, who passed it to Sasha, who passed it to James, who passed it back to Will. We did two rounds of that before the blunt was out. Amity put her arm around my waist, and I inched closer. I kissed her on her cheek, and she looked at me and blushed. James caught our attention then as he stood from his place in the circle. We watched as he pulled Will and Sasha up from their spots as well and began dancing. The fire crackled over the music as we all got up to join them in their dance. I wasn't too familiar with the song, but I could dance to anything with a beat, especially after a couple hits.

Amity raised my arm and twirled me in circles, and I did the same to her. We lowered our arms around each other and pulled apart, then spun back in and laughed at the dizzy feeling we got. James, Will, and Sasha were dancing in a circle hand in hand, M was doing some beautiful interpretive dance, and Matt was bobbing his head and tapping his foot, a grin on his face. Together we danced the night away around the fire. It felt like some sort of bonfire ritual, but everything was all love and happiness. There wasn't a shred of negativity in the space at all.

After a while, we were so worn out from all the dancing we had to stop and sit back down. We each took a few sips of a glass of not-wine and went back to relaxing. I noticed Will gave James a kiss on the lips and

I grinned, "aw! You guys are so cute, I didn't know you were together!"

"Yeah, actually, we're all together, we're a throuple," Sasha announced, putting her arms around both boys.

"It's complicated," Will expanded, "it's more of a poly relationship, I'm gay, and with James, James is Bi and is with both me and Sasha, and Sasha is pansexual, and she also sometimes has a side piece."

"We have a more go with the flow relationship," Sasha continued.

"No explanation necessary, if you're good, then I'm good."

"Same," Amity smiled.

"How about you, are you in a relationship?" I asked Matt.

"No. I'm straight, but there's no one right now, and I'm okay with that, I'm glad to just be here, in the moment."

"You're always so positive, I wish I was more like you," Amity told him.

"It's all in your head really, it takes some rewiring and some de-brainwashing, but anyone can do it."

"And you, M?"

"Oh, I'm Ace. I'm not looking for sex at all- which is rare for a vampire- but I'm also not really interested in any formal relationships either. I'm good just knowing I have friends who care."

"And we care a lot," Sasha said, resting her hand on M's shoulder.

"I'm so glad you guys have each other," I shared.

"I'm so glad I have you," Amity assured me.

"I'm glad I have you too. I'm really glad I'm not

going through this alone."

"You are never alone, Hazel," M frowned, "no matter how alone you feel in this world there will always be someone or something that cares for you, even if you don't know it."

"Thanks," I sighed and laid my head on Amity's shoulder.

Suddenly a yelp could be heard in the distance. The sound shook me to my core.

"Uh..."

"What was that?"

The scream was followed by a loud growl, and I was even more terrified. What on earth could've made a noise like that?

"That sounded like a bear," Matt stated.

We all stood up and ran towards the sound, heading into the woods beyond the houses. Matt took lead and we followed him about a mile into the forest until we noticed a woman hiding behind a tree and a man running towards her. We got in front of the woman and Matt continued towards the man, who had a bear close behind him.

"Are you okay?" I asked her.

She was completely out of breath and hunkered over trying to catch it. She nodded in response and looked up to see if her companion was okay. He ran over to the group and hugged her while Matt stood in front of the bear.

The bear stood on his back legs and roared, attempting to scare Matt, but he felt no such fear. Instead, he bared his fangs and hissed loudly with his arms outstretched. Amity ran over to him and did the same, then Sasha and James followed too. The rest of us stayed back to keep an eye on the couple and make sure they were okay.

With the four of them standing up to the bear, he finally got back down to all fours and started sniffing around, then huffed and turned around. Amity sighed in relief and they all walked back to us, Matt walking backward to keep an eye on the bear. The bear never returned, and we stood around the couple, asking what happened.

"Nothing really, we were just camping nearby and..."

"Our tent!" The woman cried. M put a hand on her shoulder and tried to calm her down.

"Where's your campsite? We'll escort you back and make sure the bear is gone."

"That way," the man pointed. He took the woman's hand, and they led the way.

"What're your names?

"I'm John, and this is Betty," he sighed.

We introduced ourselves and told them they were in good hands.

"What're you guys doing out here?" Betty asked.

"We were camping too," James lied, "we heard you scream."

"How did you get the bear to go away?"

"Ah, you know, pretending to be big and scary," Matt laughed.

"Wait, I could've sworn it was right here," John pondered, "where is it?"

"OH no, we probably got lost, we didn't bring anything with us when we ran out of our tent," Betty replied.

"Don't worry, we'll find it, it can't be too far," I

assured her.

After a few moments of hunting, we found the abandoned campsite. The bear was gone but the campsite was destroyed; the tent was ripped open and there was food and supplies scattered everywhere.

"Jesus, it looks like a tornado went through here!" Betty cried.

"I think there were two of them," John added.

"Looks like it," Matt noted, squatting down and looking at tracks in the dirt.

I wondered how he could tell but Betty started crying over her broken supplies.

"How'd this happen?" She asked.

"Bears are strong," John replied.

"I mean, we should've been more careful."

"Were you guys sleeping?" I asked. I didn't know much about camping, and this was a good learning experience for me since I was now going to be living in the area.

"Yeah. We should've had noise traps or something; and we left our food out, we shouldn't have done that," John sighed.

"Normally bears don't get too close to campsites, but you guys are pretty far out here, how come you didn't stay with the campgrounds?" Matt asked.

"We wanted to just get as far away from civilization as we could. Technically we're here illegally because we don't have a wilderness permit... but we thought we'd be okay; we've been camping before."

"I don't blame you, sometimes it's nice to just get away for a while and forget that the rest of the world exists."

"I'm just glad you guys were around to help us,

thank you for that."

Some of us nodded and others said variations of you're welcome, and Sasha offered for them to pack up and come back with us where they'd be safe. They agreed and we helped them salvage what we could from the wreckage, then took them back to the tree houses. They were in awe just like we had been.

"One thing I gotta tell you though," Matt said to them, "technically we're not supposed to be here, so you gotta keep our secret, just like we'll keep yours about you camping illegally."

"Fair enough, we just appreciate your help," they replied.

We took our spots back at the fireplace and M left to go grab more pillows. The 9 of us hung out and chatted for a bit then the couple got tired so Sasha let them sleep in her cabin and said she would sleep in Will and James' cabin if she needed to.

We knew the sun would be up in just two short hours, and we had a bit of a hike to get back to the car, so we packed up and said our goodbyes. We made plans for the next meeting and then we were on our way. When we got back to the house Amity stopped and grabbed my hand. I turned around with a confused look on my face.

"You okay?" I asked her.

She nodded and looked up at the sky. Clouds had rolled in in the last hour or so and there was lightning in the distance.

"Isn't it beautiful?" She asked. "I love a good thunderstorm."

"Me too, they always help me sleep."

She nodded, "so soothing."

"Hey, you were really brave today. I love that you're

always headfirst into the fray."

She blushed, "I'm really not that brave, honestly. Actually, I was quite terrified, a bear is pretty serious."

"Well, to a human yeah, but it shouldn't be a problem for us, right?"

"Yeah, I don't know, whenever I feel like you're being threatened I feel a bit defensive is all. Like when we met Hunter."

"That's sweet of you. I can handle myself though, just so you're aware."

She laughed, "Yeah I know. You did bust down my cell door when we met."

I rolled my eyes in thought, "yeah that's right I did."

"And that was after getting a black eye and a nearly broken nose."

"What can I say? I'm tough when life depends on it."

"Well, I would bet my life on that."

"I would do anything for you, Amity."

"I would do anything for you too."

Thunder roared above our heads and the clouds opened the floodgates. It poured down onto us just as we leaned in for a kiss. The rain was cold and momentarily shocked us, as we both took a step back and rapidly blinked, looking up at the sky and laughing. It was one of those moments where for just a split second you get angry. Your clothes are wet, it's cold, and it was unexpected, but then you realize, who cares? You can change clothes, you can go inside, you can wrap up in a blanket. Just shut up and enjoy the little things.

I looked back at Amity and smiled. She grinned as well and pulled me back in to kiss her again. The rain poured onto our cheeks as we kissed, our hair and clothes clinging to our skin. The serenity and love that I felt at that moment was surreal and I never wanted it to end.

CHAPTER 16

An Odd Encounter

"What do you want to do tonight?" Amity asked.

"Hmm," I thought, a finger to my chin, "we should explore the mountains!"

"Yes, that sounds great!" Amity plopped onto the couch and researched trails deep into the mountains to hike through.

"How about a haunted trail?" She asked.

"I'm intrigued, tell me more," I grinned as I sat down beside her. She showed me the pictures that Google had listed, then showed me an article beneath the listing about how the trail was known to be haunted. It claimed that it carried the spirits of all the hundreds of people who have either gone missing from the trail or found dead. It was well known as the deadliest trail in the state.

"I wonder why so many people have died on this particular trail."

"It must be a tough hike. May be a good challenge for us."

Amity nodded and put the address into the GPS. It would take a while to get there, but we had all night. Hunter went out of town for the week to visit some family so we could either train without him, go to the gym, or take a hike to keep up with our exercise routine. Part of us wanted to just take the whole night off from responsibilities and go do something fun, but what was more fun than going for a scenic walk with your date?

We packed some go bags and tossed them into the car, then rolled out of the driveway. The 2 hours it took to get there were well worth it. The views were amazing. We passed by rivers and waterfalls and forests and even rocky areas that reminded me of the Grand Canyon. I could understand why it took so long to get there. Most of the road was single-lane, and people drove slowly not only because of the twists and turns but also, I assume, because they wanted to take their time and admire the beauty of the mountains. At one point we even pulled over just before a bridge overlooking a huge waterfall. We walked to the middle of the overpass and gazed at the sight. Amity held my hand as we both took deep breaths. We meditated the best we could while standing against the railing, although it wasn't hard. Aside from a few passing cars behind us, it was an incredibly serene location.

Mist rained down on us and soaked our hair and clothes, but we had spares and towels in the car, so we didn't care. The water was cool, almost cold, but that didn't bother us either. We just focused on peace and serenity. The only thing missing was a good playlist to have in the background, like theme music in a melancholy series.

After about half an hour, we decided to continue on, lest we lose too much time and get stuck out in the sun. We took turns hiding each other behind towels to change into our spare clothes, then we hopped back in the car and sped off. It wasn't long before we reached our next destination, where we parked in an empty parking lot at the beginning of a few hiking trails. The park was technically closed, but like, who was going to stop us from walking on a path? It was not like we could go during open hours.

Amity and I looked at the park map and decided which route to take, then double checked to make sure we had everything in our drawstring bags. In hindsight maybe we should have had more supplies, but we figured, we're vampires, what all could we need? We kept some toiletries, first aid, pocketknives, and a couple stakes that Hunter had given us for emergencies. 'You never know,' he told us.

The beginning of our hike was easy, the path went uphill, but it wasn't steep, and it was also very smooth, with lots of leaves covering the rocks beneath. We passed by many fallen trees and random boulders and even some formations that went over our heads. Occasionally there was a fairy circle or gnome garden, and we stopped to admire those for a few minutes before we carried on.

The rest of the hike was more difficult. The pathway grew rocky and much steeper. We had to stop often to catch our breath. At one point, we had stopped to sit on a log, and a critter crawled past us then hid in a bush nearby. It popped out again a minute later but out of nowhere was scooped up by a large brown owl. Sadness overcame me as I watched the poor little chipmunk get snatched up, but unfortunately there was nothing I could do at that point. It was just nature being nature. At least his death was quick. It reminded me of how most vampires would kill their victims slowly, or even torture them for long periods before eventually killing them. At least owls didn't do that.

Off to the side a bit further up there was a small opening between the foliage, where you could tell there was a path not well traveled. Amity encouraged us to explore the unknown, so we crouched down and nearly crawled through the space. This path took us to a stream that was flowing smoothly with crystal clear water. We followed the side of the river on the rocks, sometimes having to hop from rock to rock, and in the distance was the sound of a speedy rapid. The water seemed to increase in speed as the land started sloping. It wasn't steep, but it was enough to create a lot of movement.

Just before the rapids was an excellent spot to hop to the other side of the stream. As we continued following the river, the trees grew thin and eventually opened up to a valley. To our right the water dropped down over a sharp edge, and to the left was a flattened space that seemed to circle the valley. It was about 10 to 15 feet wide with a steep incline on one side, and a drop off on the other. Amity tiptoed over to the edge, and I followed. Looking down I noticed there were lots of bluffs sticking out of the wall of the cliff, then about halfway down it started to round off back into a hill, where the waterfall turned into a river.

"This is incredible!" I exclaimed.

"True, but maybe this is why there's been so many deaths and missing persons. They've probably all fallen off this cliff."

I lowered my chin, "yeah, you're probably right."

While following the flattened rock we noticed a hole in the formation. It was large enough for a human to walk into, but nothing much bigger.

"Do you think a bear could fit through there?" Amity wondered.

I took a step back and observed. "I hope not."

It was then that we heard an ominous sound. A low growl emitted from somewhere above us, and we looked around trying to find the source.

"That didn't sound like a bear," Amity observed.

I nodded, "but what else could that have been? It almost sounded... human."

We stepped away from the cave entrance cautiously. I wasn't sure what I expected, but I know I didn't expect to be tackled to the ground. Amity and I were both knocked down. Amity caught herself hands up, but I wasn't quick enough and hit my head on the stone ground.

Amity jumped up and stood over me to protect me as I took a minute to collect myself. I looked up from the ground with scrapped knees and a bleeding forehead, and was shocked to see not some wild animal, but something way more human looking. Something was off though, it was more like something in between human and gorilla. Something feral. A very harry-looking naked man. He looked like bigfoot, but smaller. He looked like... a caveman.

I stood up with a hand to my head and took a closer look. The creature was a tall, bulky man covered in thick hair from head to toe. His beard and head hair were exceptionally long, and he carried a sharpened stick. Almost like a stake. He was completely naked, and his bare feet seemed rough and flat, like they had formed with the stone ground.

The man-thing was in a slightly crouched position, stick ready to use. He barred his teeth and made the same growling sound again.

Amity gaped, "is that-"

Before she could finish her question, the man was coming at us again. We dodged his stick and Amity got in a swift kick. He stumbled back, seemingly surprised, but then lowered himself even more. He put his fists to the ground like Tarzan, then pounced up. He leaped higher than I had ever seen someone jump. It was almost... supernatural. As he landed, he made some noises that resembled a monkey, and sped around us intimidatingly. He was supernaturally fast too. Little did he know that so were we.

The feral man jumped again and almost caught me. He reached his neck out and attempted to bite me. That was when I noticed the fangs. A vampire.

I pushed the man off and waved the white flag. "Hey, look, we're vampires too, you don't need to be afraid of us. You don't need to attack us, we're the same!"

Showing him my teeth did nothing. It seemed as though he didn't understand a word I said. Maybe it just went right over his head. He lunged at us again and the three of us fought. I remembered my tools in my bag and told Amity to hold him off while I got them out. Quickly I spun the bag around to my front and reached in. Just as I got ahold of the stake the bag was kicked out of my hands. It rolled over to the edge of the cliff and settled. The stake was still in hand, so I did my best to use it to my advantage.

Amity used her quick thinking to fake-out the man then grab his sharp stick, but he held on to it tightly. They fought over the stick, Amity stabilized herself then jumped up and flipped over the man, turning to pull the stick back to his throat. As they did so I jumped in and stabbed him with the stake. A last second movement forced me to miss my target, and I stabbed his stomach instead. The man bellowed but it only made him angrier. He then let go of Amity and shoved me as hard as he could. I fell back and rolled over to the edge of the cliff. It was then I truly felt the adrenaline kick in. They both ran over to me, Amity trying to save me, and the caveman trying to finish me off. The man got to me first.

As fast as lightning, he crouched down onto his fists and kicked me in the stomach. My arms reached up to catch myself, but the man grabbed them first. He bit into my left wrist then sat back, probably confused by the difference in taste. Amity grabbed my right hand just at the last second and saved me from falling. My wrist hurt a lot, but I didn't allow myself to genuinely feel the pain.

Together Amity and I tried to get me up from the cliff's edge, but at the same time she was trying to fight off the caveman by kicking him away from herself. I made the mistake of glancing down and seeing just how far of a fall it would be to go all the way to the bottom. My heart fell into my stomach. There was a bluff below, but it was small, and concerningly thin. I heard the grumbling of the caveman and Amity talking to him, trying to get him to understand, but he just didn't, and she lost the battle.

I heard Amity scream, and our hands broke apart. I grabbed the edge just in time and held on for dear life. Amity was picked up and thrown over the ledge. I reached out to her with one hand, but I underestimated how hard it would be to hold on to the edge of a cliff and also grab someone else who was falling over. Our fingers touched as she fell, but it was no use. It was then my turn to scream as I watched my best friend fall. Luckily, she didn't fall too far out, and the bluff caught her. Unluckily, it seemed she had hit her head pretty good and was knocked unconscious.

"Amity!" I shrieked.

I looked up and the caveman looked back at me, grunting. He then tried to pry my fingers off and pull my hair. I realized I had two options. I could try to pull myself back up while he was simultaneously trying to push me back down, or I could let go in the hopes that I would land down on the bluff with Amity. There wasn't much time to decide, my arms were growing tired, and my fingers were getting sweaty. I looked down again. The bluff was around 8 to 10 feet down and the edges looked very unstable.

Remembering that as a vampire, the odds were good that I would survive the fall even if I missed the bluff; so, I decided to take my chances with it. If I fell, it could still be painful, but if I landed correctly, maybe it wouldn't be too bad. So, as carefully as I could, I let go of the cliff's edge and let myself fall down to the bluff. I kept as straight as I could, then bent my knees. It was a rough landing, and I fell back onto my butt, but I had made it with barely a scratch.

I crawled a few feet over to Amity; she was near the edge where the formation was thin. I was worried that with both of us, it would crack and crumble.

"Amity, Amity!" I shook her gently, but she didn't wake up. It took a minute to get her wiggled over to the other side, but slowly, I got her to safety. She was bleeding from a large gash on the back of her head, and it almost looked like she had broken her leg, but without an X-ray I couldn't be sure. I held her in my lap and cradled her head into my arm so the wound wouldn't have anything touching it. After a few minutes she still hadn't woken up, but I could hear the caveman pacing and huffing and puffing. It made me wonder where he came from, who he was, and why he acted so strangely. It seemed to me that this was no ordinary vampire.

He waited for us at the top, angry that he couldn't get to us. The wall that I was leaning on was cold and jaggy, but I wondered if I could climb it. I didn't think I could jump that high, and if Amity did have a broken leg, she surely wouldn't be able to either. A few more minutes later she started to stir. I brushed her hair away from her face and spoke slowly.

"Hey, how you doin'?" I asked her, "you really scared me."

She looked up at me and gave a weak smile, "been better."

"We have to figure out a way to get back up to the top, without that guy pushing us back down."

"Could we wait until my wounds are healed?"

I shook my head, "I don't think so, your head wound is bad and, is your leg broken?"

She looked down and wiggled her foot. "It's painful, but I don't think its broken."

"It still may take a day or two for your head to heal. We don't have that kind of time; we can't be out here in the sun all day."

"You're right, I'll figure this out, we'll get out of this," she promised.

Amity began to stand up, so I jumped to help her. She put some weight on her foot and winced in pain.

"Are you okay?"

"Well, it may not be broken but it's definitely sprained. I don't think I can climb up with this."

I looked around for anything that could help us. Amity's bag had fallen off before she went over the edge, and mine was still up top too. Not that we had anything in them that would have helped us anyways. There was a tree near the ledge on the right side which had a ton of roots poking out, but they didn't seem sturdy enough to help us either. Maybe they could if Amity was able to climb.

"I think we're on our own," I sighed. Both of us had left our cell phones in our bags, and I regretted not leaving it in my back pocket. We could have called someone to come rescue us, but alas, we were unable to.

Using my heightened sense of hearing, I listened to the caveman stop pacing and walk away, and then there was silence. I wondered if he had given up or heard some other prey moving about. It gave me a sketchy idea.

"Okay, given our wounds, I think the best way we can do this is if I hoist you up and then try to climb up myself."

"That sounds dangerous," she stuttered.

"The only other way is for one of us to pull the other up, but you would need both feet to do it."

"Well, maybe not, my knee isn't too bad, and I'll have to be on my knees to be able to reach you anyways. We could try it."

"Not much else we can try." I shrugged.

"We should probably hurry then, I bet he'll come back."

I nodded and looked for the best spot to climb the

wall. It reminded me of freshman year of high school. For a few weeks that year I was all about rock climbing, and then my hyper fixation wore off and I never did it again. Not until now.

"Okay give me your good foot."

Amity limped over to me and braced herself against the wall. I kneeled down and locked my hands over my thigh. She looked up to gage her space then put her foot in my hands. Using my back and legs more than my arms I lifted her up as high as I could. She stretched her arms out but still couldn't reach. The training with Hunter was beginning to make me stronger, but I still hadn't reached my bench goal yet. However, I was determined to get Amity to safety, so with everything I had, I jumped and pushed her up like a cheerleader would. It was high enough up then that she could catch her elbow on the ledge and swing her good leg up. She crawled the rest of the way up then rolled onto her stomach to look down at me.

"You did it!" I cheered.

"Um no. You did all the hard work," she grinned.

I shook my head and reached out to find a spot to begin my climb. The spots were thin, but I managed to secure my footing enough to pull myself up a few feet, enough for Amity to reach my outstretched arm. Once our hands were clasped together, I pushed my foot against the wall as hard as I could, and she yanked as hard as she could, and we did the impossible.

With heavy breaths, we rolled away from the ledge and hugged. Together we celebrated the victory of not falling off a cliff, but the celebration quickly turned into more adrenaline when the caveman made his reappearance. He must've heard us talking and came back. This time we would not let him overtake us.

We stood our ground, Amity behind me for protection. With her injured leg, she wouldn't be able to do much in a fight. The caveman roared at us again. I had never seen such a... lack of emotion or compassion... in someone's eyes before. It was like he was barely human at all. Technically, he wasn't- he's a vampire- but even vampires seemed to have a spark in their eyes. This one didn't.

"Hi, uh, greetings? Look, I know you probably don't understand what I'm saying, but we can help you. We can show you what the world is like today. Uh... we have new ways to light fires, and cook food, and softer things to sleep on than the ground and... we are friends, okay?"

Despite all my belief, I could tell the words, fire, food, and friend somehow rang a bell to him, so I rolled with it.

Keep It Simple, Stupid. I told myself.

I pointed to him, and then myself, and then back to him, "friends."

The man sniffed the air like a dog then stood from his gorilla stance and stepped gingerly towards us. He made a sound like he was trying to speak, which excited me. Maybe I got through to him.

When he was close enough to touch, he stopped and looked at us up and down. He opened his mouth again like he was going to speak, and his facial expression switched from curious to furious.

"BLOOD!" He howled.

I screeched out of pure shock as he went in for another bite, pushing Amity to the side and leaning back like I was doing the limbo. Before he could even grab me, I put my arms out and did a backbend, then kicked my foot up and flipped over, smacking him right in the chin as I did so. It was hard enough to break his jaw, and Amity was sure to give him another punch right after. He jumped back into his crouched position and circled us like a wolf. Amity limped over to pick up the dropped stake and tossed it to me. I promptly utilized the weapon and staked him right through the chest. I was pretty sure I missed his heart, but it was enough to momentarily immobilize him. Amity was right behind, ready to push. Together we shoved him over the cliff's edge and sighed in relief. We watched as he fell, his head colliding with the thin part of the bluff. It cracked and fell apart and they tumbled down together. He landed somewhere in the foliage below and we could no longer see him.

"Are you okay?" Amity asked me.

"I think so, you?"

She nodded, "I will be."

We were both out of breath, but relieved that the threat was eliminated. However, I still felt bad that we couldn't get through to him. Maybe if we could have just found a way to communicate, we could have taken him back with us and integrated him into the real world.

"What choice did we have?" Amity read my thoughts and patted my back.

We picked our bags up and dug through them. I pulled out my cell phone and shoved it into my back pocket, then led Amity towards the hole in the wall. My curiosity overcame my urgency, and we turned on the flash on our phones and trekked into the cave. It was small at first, then it opened up to a fairly large cavern. Inside the room was a collection of found goods that had been hoarded: bags, food, shoes, trash, and a pile of bones next to it. There was a fire pit in the middle, and a lump of fur a few feet away. I was disgusted by all the animal fur, but I understood. There was also a stack of very sharp spears, sticks, and rocks on the other side of the room.

What fascinated me the most was what we found on the wall. Amity and I held up our flashlights to the wall and observed cave drawings covering nearly every inch. We scoured to find significant pieces, and Amity managed to find the most remarkable one of all: where it must have all began. It depicted an encounter with another caveman, only to be bitten and grow sick. The man ate raw meat and (seemingly) discovered that the blood was what he needed. After that he started biting during his hunts. Most of the rest of the depictions implied that there were a huge number of deaths by his hand, both animals, and more recently, humans. The pictures also indicated the changes in mankind. They started as other cavemen, eventually there were native tribes, and then people with bonnets and horses and some supplies. After that it phased into people we know today, hikers with backpacks.

Amity and I gaped at all the information that was being downloaded into our brains.

"He's occupied this cave for a long time." Amity observed.

"Do you know what this means?" I asked her.

"That this guy is probably the oldest vampire ever?"

"Unless the one that turned him is still alive, yea, I'd say so."

"I mean he has to be *thousands* of years old."

"Considering when the paleolithic era was, he could be anywhere from 11,000 years old to millions of years old."

"I remember learning in school that they came down through Canada, I wonder where vampires first began."

I shrugged, "that's a heavy question."

We heard some rustling outside the cave then. It might have just been the wind and trees, but it reminded us that the man could very possibly still be alive, since we didn't carve out the heart or burn the body.

"Come on, we should probably go."

Amity nodded in agreement and took some pictures on her phone before we left. Once we got back to the car, we sighed in relief.

What a crazy night.

CHAPTER 17

Strength

A few weeks later the leaves were finally changing colors and the sky was growing darker. We could wake up earlier, stay out longer, and go to bed later. The blood drives were going well. We brought in tons of volunteers, and the Peaceful Vampires were as amazing as always. We were fortunate enough to both get jobs at the bookstore and due to driving arrangements we were able to get shifts at the same time. So, whenever we weren't training with Hunter, we were working at one of the coolest shops in town. I was grateful to not only have a job but to have one that didn't discriminate against night owls.

Amity and I had been training with Hunter four nights a week and between that and the adequate amounts of food, I was feeling stronger than I ever had. I was truly starting to feel more like how I felt a vampire should. Willed, powerful, brave, I felt like I could take on the world. There was still a long way to go until I would be ready to take on Tony, but at least it wasn't a fight I would have to do solo.

Training up to that point had mainly been straight-up exercise, going to the gym, hiking, rock climbing, some yoga, and lots of stretching. Finally,

Hunter thought we were at a point where we were ready to start learning combat and soon he would start teaching us about weapons too.

Feeling confident wasn't something I was new to, but never had I felt this level of confidence before. My body had started taking more of the shape of someone who worked out, and something excited me about getting abs, it was like a show of accomplishment or something. Amity... well she was more beautiful than ever, and by that, I meant she looked healthier. She had gained some weight, but it was all muscle. It was almost like she hadn't been fed at all when she was human, and now with all this training and daily meals she was getting everything she needed to be in a more nourished state. Even her hair seemed to be shinier and her eyes much more golden than brown.

Amity and I had also grown in our relationship too. We had our first disagreement; it was over something super petty, and we got over it quickly, but it was almost refreshing, like our minds had just gotten kind of tired from being so nice all the time. Being good is difficult at times. You are constantly, 24/7, having to fight the good and evil battle. Someone who didn't care wouldn't have to fight that battle. Although doing the right thing is always best, it's not always the easiest. Amity and I realized our mistake and were able to get back on track quickly. We mostly just thought to ourselves, 'what would the Peaceful Vampires do?' and went with that. Always the answer was peace, of course.

After the weeks had passed, I'd like to think that I would've forgotten about Tony long ago, but it had seemed that I only thought about him more every day. I wanted to know where he was, and what he was doing. I also wanted to know why he hadn't come for us that day and every day since. Knowing him I would've expected him to have shown up at my parents' house while Amity and I were there. Don't get me wrong, I'm glad he never did, but it still begs the question, why? If he was as interested in me as he said, if he cared as much as he claimed, whether that being good form or bad, why didn't he come to kill me? I betrayed him, I lied to him, I tried multiple times to kill him, I set his basement on fire, and I helped not one but three of his prisoner's escape. If I were him, I'd probably want to kill me too.

A part of me hopes that maybe he realized he was in the wrong and decided to let us go, but something tells me he more than likely ended up taking two steps back and may now be hurting more people than when I was around. Also, what became of his basement? Were they able to stop the fire quickly enough that it didn't cause much damage or did the fire grow exponentially until it became uncontrollable and took the whole house down? I hope it's the latter. Maybe the explosion was bigger than it sounded. Maybe Tony died in that fire. Probably not though. It would take a *lot* for a fire to kill a vampire, if they even can die from that. I mean, I guess I don't know specifically, but from what I've read and heard, yes vampires can be killed by fire, but they would have to be thoroughly turned to ashes for it to work.

Hunter hasn't really gotten into the how-tos of killing vampires yet, but one thing he has told us is that the easiest way to kill a vampire and know for sure they're gone for good is to rip out the heart and destroy it. His theory is that we still have our souls until that moment and then we can no longer heal ourselves to recover. You can't fix what's not there. That's also made me think about how I thought Tony was a lost cause. He was living in his own world, not reality. He would or will never be a better person because he is not in this world. Well, in a manner of speaking. I just hoped that I could gain the strength, knowledge, and courage I needed to end him quickly. The faster I prepare, the more lives I could save. That being said, my awesome girlfriend and I were heading out for a night of training, and we readied ourselves with leggings, sports bras, water, towels, and high ponytails.

"Ready?" I asked as we headed for the door.

"Ready," she replied as she shoved her foot into her shoe and swung her backpack over her shoulder.

I gave Amity a quick kiss on the lips and opened the door.

We met Hunter in our usual spot just like always; he had never allowed us over to his home, and part of me wondered if that was because he didn't trust us. While I suppose I don't fully trust the vampire hunter not to harm me, a vampire, I still have faith that he's generally a good man. So far so good, it's been weeks and he's held up his end of the bargain.

"Good night," he greeted.

"Good night, how are you?" I asked.

"Ready to start our training, are you guys stretched out yet?"

Amity shook her head, "we just got here."

"That's fine, me neither."

We spent about 20 to 30 minutes stretching out, Amity and I helping each other with the ones that we could. After that, Hunter got a bag out and laid it down in front of us.

"What's this?" I asked.

He opened the bag and revealed a full case of a variety of weapons. Off the top I noticed a bow and arrow, a bunch of stakes, and some guns. Hunter took them all out and separated them, and under those revealed a couple grenades and an assortment of knives.

"Wow, do you really need all of that?" Amity asked.

"It never hurts to be prepared," he shrugged.

He went through and explained each one, how to use it and when.

"Do you really think it's that hard to kill a vampire?" I asked, "you know, if they can be killed by just taking out the heart, shouldn't you really only need a knife?"

Hunter frowned, "you've never really seen a vampire at full power, have you?"

"I mean I've seen Tony pretty dang angry... but no, I guess not really."

"A newbie like yourself may be pretty easy to kill, yes, but the older vampires, and especially the ancient ones, are extremely difficult to kill. They've got heightened senses of smell, sight, and hearing, and not to mention hundreds of years to build up their strength and endurance. Then you also have years of experience which makes them more cunning and alert. Vampires are immortal, therefore unlike humans, they only get stronger with age."

"Like how we're getting stronger now," Amity nodded.

"Which is why I'm putting all my trust into you guys now. You were weak before. I could've easily killed you if I needed to, but now I'm teaching you how to be unkillable, so you can defy the odds."

"Ah yes, we were so easy to kill that that's why you struggled so much for a few minutes before you pinned us down when we met."

"I wasn't struggling," he scoffed, "I was going easy on you."

"Wanna bet?"

"You're fucking ON."

Hunter spread his feet apart and held up his fists. I cracked my knuckles in anticipation. It was my first fight since before starting my training, and I could feel how much stronger and more prepared I was this time. He ran at me, and I braced myself, then ducked at the last second. His arms swooped over me as I slid around, coming up behind him and swinging my legs underneath. He caught himself on me and brought my neck down in a headlock. For a split second I thought I was done for, but I could hear Amity encouraging me from a few feet away, so I took a deep breath and remembered my training. Whipping up all the strength I could muster, I kicked up my feet and threw Hunter off me. He lost his grip and stumbled, and but didn't completely fall over. Swinging his leg up to kick me, I ducked again, this time reaching up and grabbing his leg, then thrusting it as hard as I could. I couldn't throw the man, I wasn't that strong, but I did make him lose his balance and this time he fell, ass onto grass. He grunted in response and jumped right back up. Amity cheered in the background.

"Not bad, rookie," Hunter smirked.

"You haven't seen the best of me yet," I replied.

"You're nothing compared to what you could be."

I took that as a personal attack and responded with an actual attack, punching him right in the jaw.

"Okay, ouch," he rubbed his jaw for a moment before revving up for another attack. He came at me in a crouched position, picked me up and threw me down to the ground. A pain shot up my back and through my neck and for a split second I thought I had really damaged something. Hunter generously gave me a minute to catch my breath and I was back in. Catching his leg in mine before he got the chance to run, I tightened my grip and twisted my legs around, knocking Hunter to the ground. Before he could even react, I was on top of him with the blunt end of a knife to his chest. He tapped the ground and nodded his head in approval. I stood up with an arm outstretched and he took the offer.

Amity ran over to me and gave me a big hug, "you did amazing!"

"Thanks!" I grinned, hugging her back.

"You just may be ready," Hunter approved.

"Sweeettt."

"Your turn," he pointed to Amity.

"Oof, okay here goes nothing."

Amity and I switched places so that I could be her cheerleader and she could knock Hunter off his feet again. They each took a moment to gain composure then braced themselves.

"Come on babe, you've got this!" I encouraged.

She grinned and waved then got serious again and lowered her stance. She then lunged forward and tried to knock Hunter over, but he stood his ground and barely felt her blow. He grabbed her by the waist and flipped her up over his shoulder. Thinking quickly, Amity used the gravitational pull of him flipping her to pull herself down, bringing Hunter down with her. He landed on his back in the grass but then flipped over and got up to a crouched position. He jumped at Amity who then rolled over to avoid him. They both stood up and circled each other like wolves. Amity lowered her eyes and stretched her arms out in front of her. She reached for Hunter and pulled him back. He momentarily lost his balance but regained it just as easily. With her hands in his he swung her around, tossing her back to the ground like a rag doll.

"Are you okay?" I asked.

Amity nodded and reached for one of the weapons from the bag nearby. She grabbed the first thing she could, which ended up being a handgun, then aimed for the open space next to Hunter and pulled the trigger. No bullets came out of the gun, but we were all aware of who technically won this round.

Hunter relaxed his muscles and spoke, "okay, okay, I think we're getting ahead of ourselves. Besides, you know it's not just as easy as pointing and shooting a gun at a vampire. If you don't hit the bullseye on the *first* try: *you're* dead."

"For real? I don't get a good job like she did?"

He shook his head, "it wasn't bad, but you both have a long way to go until you can do this on your own. You were clumsy and impulsive. You need more control; and Hazel you were too confident, you need to slow down and anticipate your opponents' next move."

"Well, I think you did amazing babe," I told Amity with a pat on the back.

"Thanks cutie, so did you."

"Ugh you guys are disgusting, go be adorable and sweet somewhere else," Hunter groaned.

"You're just jealous that you don't have an amazing

woman in your life like I do," I reassured him.

"Who says I don't?"

"Do you?"

"Well... no. But you didn't just have to make that assumption."

We laughed and got back to our originally scheduled training program. Finally, Hunter began showing us fighting stances and blocking positions. It reminded me of the karate classes I had taken in grade school. Back then, I never had the self-control or discipline it takes to enjoy the sport, but now I have a much better appreciation for it.

At the end of the day's training, Hunter pulled the two of us into a huddle and told us we did a good job and that we had homework, then stood back and clapped his hands together.

I gave him a questioning look and he raised his hand, "now before we go, I have one more thing."

Amity and I looked at each other inquisitively and awaited his reply.

"Well?" I pushed.

"I have a job for us."

"What do you mean?"

"There's a vampire in the area that I've found that needs to be taken care of. I think you girls are ready for your first mission. Supervised of course."

"What do you mean? Is it Tony, is he here?" Amity asked, a scowl on her face.

"No, it's not Tony, it's a woman by the name of Lucida. The police have a warrant out for her arrest under suspicion of killing her boyfriend, who was found completely drained of blood."

"I mean that's awful, but we're not here to turn a

woman into the police, we aren't FBI, we're here so that you can teach us how to kill one very specific person," I reminded.

"Who said anything about turning her into the police? She's obviously a vampire, prison wouldn't work for her even if we could bring her into the police alive. No, I'm talking about ending her existence so that she can't hurt anyone else. I'm talking about the contract that you two signed and agreed to."

"Was killing more people than Tony in the contract?" Amity inquired.

"Yes, it was, did you even read it? We went over it together, were you not paying attention?"

We looked at each other and shrugged, "who reads contracts anyways? It's like terms and conditions on any website."

"Yeah, and then they steal your data, that's why I never agree to those things."

I cringed, "you must not get on the internet often then... or at all."

"Rarely. Anyways yes, this is your assignment, and depending on how it goes, we may need to have a few more before I can send you out on your own. We start with this woman tomorrow night, using tonight to do all the research we can on her to get the story straight, and then after all is said and done, we go back to training. But let me just say this: after tomorrow the training will get much more intense."

"Well don't worry, we can handle anything you throw at us, right babe?" Amity looked at me and smiled.

"Is that so?" Hunter reached down and pulled a thick pocketknife out of the weapons bag and threw it in our direction. Amity reached out faster than I could blink and caught it gracefully.

"Told you," she laughed.

"Wow," I gaped, "beautiful and a great catch." She smiled and took my hand in her free one, using the other to put the knife in her back pocket.

"Amusing," Hunter rolled his eyes, "keep that, you never know when you'll need it."

We nodded and picked up our gym bags.

"Meet back here tomorrow, same time, and I'll text you the details as soon as I get home."

"And we will definitely read them," I replied sarcastically.

"You'd better. Don't forget your homework." Hunter picked up the bag full of guns and knives and walked away, leaving Amity and I all alone.

When we got back to the house, we figured we would start our 'homework' sooner rather than later to get it over with, so we sat our gym bags down and pushed the couch back for more space. Sparring with Amity was always a good time. We were great at positive reinforcement and supporting each other. Together we practiced blocks and stances and at one point we had blocked each other at the same time. Our breath was heavy from all the exercise and as I gazed at my partner, I couldn't help but laugh. Amity giggled in response and gave me a peck on the nose. Before she could pull away, I grabbed her cheeks and pulled her in for a real kiss. When we finally broke apart Amity snickered.

"I can only imagine what Hunter thinks goes on in this house of his."

"Oh, I'm sure he knows, and he probably cringes anytime he thinks about it."

"Good. It's my goal in life to be so in love with someone that other people cringe at the thought."

My smile turned serious, "did you say?"

She blushed, "uh yeah. I mean I do. I love you. These past 2 months we've spent together has honestly been the best couple months of my life."

"It's a shame we had to meet in such unfortunate circumstances. But... I love you too," I replied.

"Hey," she brushed a strand of hair back from my face and held her hand up to my cheek, "I wouldn't change a thing. If I had to suffer for a bit to meet you, I am totally okay with that, I would do it again and again."

I smiled and hugged my best friend, the woman that I loved.

"Now, I feel gross so I'm gunna go take a shower. Care to join?" Amity winked at me, and I laughed.

"Is that even a question?" I responded.

Amity took my hand in hers and led me through the house.

CHAPTER 18

First Hunt

By the time we got out of the shower, Hunter had texted us his research information. There were several documents and pictures that we had to look through and piece together. As if Hunter couldn't just tell us what he had already pieced together. I suppose he wanted us to learn how to do it ourselves, but neither Amity nor I want to continue to be hunters after the Tony fiasco is over. Once our portion of the contract was finished, we wanted out. Of course, we wanted to help people, but we weren't really wanting to help people by killing others. That part of the plan was lost on me. Of course, part of me knew it was a necessary step to ensure the safety of humans, but there will always be another bad guy. That was one of the problems of humanity and consciousness; and the one major difference between humans and non-human animals. When we know there is a choice, you can be good, or you can be bad, sometimes people choose bad.

"Look here," Amity pointed out. We were cuddled up in bed, the room only lit by a string of fairy lights above our heads. She opened one of the photos and zoomed in. In one of the gruesome crime photos, next to the body, lay a very interesting object.

"Can you zoom in any further?" I asked.

Amity shook her head, "what is that?" she asked.

"Looks like a gem of some kind. Correct me if I'm wrong, but I think that's a blood diamond."

"Wouldn't that be fitting. You know, I bet there's a very fancy ring that's missing its gemstone. We find this woman's jewelry collection, I bet we'll find that empty ring, and boom we have proof that she's the killer."

"Check the documents, what was the cause of death again?"

Amity closed out of the picture and pulled up the police report for the victim, "it says that the autopsy revealed an initial blunt force trauma to the head, bite wounds to the neck and arms, and defensive wounds on the hands. The official cause of death was blood loss."

"So, the victim died while trying to fight his attacker. How do we know it was a woman?"

"We'll they're not sure for the other victims, but this one was found in the women's restroom at a club in downtown Denver."

"Why was he in the women's restroom?"

She shrugged, "it's even more confusing when most bathrooms in Denver are gender neutral."

"Oh right, well I feel like we need to do some more sleuthing before we decide to... terminate the assailant or not. Hunter acts like he's got it all figured out, but how does he know? If the police aren't doing anything to find her, why should we assume that she's the culprit?"

"I mean he has been doing this for a while."

"But what if he's just going around killing people that he thinks are vampires but without any actual evidence?" I wondered.

"I guess that's possible, but do we really think he's the kind of person that would do that?"

"Who knows. We know nothing about this guy honestly. He could just be using that as his excuse to kill people."

"Like the Dexter scenario. Well maybe if we crack this code we'll determine if he's legit or not."

"How exactly are we supposed to crack this case? Neither of us have experience in criminal investigation. How are we supposed to determine something that not even the police could figure out with certainty?"

"You know what this calls for?"

"What's that?"

I turned to Amity, a smile growing on her lips.

"An adventure!"

"Right now? But we were just about to go to bed. The sun will be up in less than an hour and I'm exhausted."

Amity tapped her finger on her chin.

"Maybe you're right. However, if this woman really is a vampire, she wouldn't be expecting us to show up during the daytime."

"How exactly are we going to do that?'"

She thought for a moment, "don't we just need those cool sunglasses?"

"We don't have any. Where are we supposed to get some? Only the most elite vampires have them."

"Then we need to be elite vampires. We need to join the *it* crowd."

"Remember all the parties Tony would attend? Surely there's another group here in Colorado that does the same thing. All the older, richer, fancier vampires love to show off."

"We get into that group, and we'll have all the answers we could ever need. The who's-who would lead us straight to the worst of the worst."

"All we need to do is convince Hunter to give us some more time to go undercover."

Amity nodded and nestled into me, "let's get our beauty rest and tomorrow we will begin our sleuthing."

"Hunter will just have to start playing by our rules if he wants us to continue helping him," I agreed.

It wasn't long before we were both out like a light and when we woke up the next night it was to the sound of Hunter calling my phone. I answered with a groggy tone, asking him what he wanted.

"You're late!" he scolded.

Amity and I sat upright, yawning and stretching.

"Bro, you need to chill," I sighed.

"Why are you not here?" He asked.

"Sorry we were up late looking at those files, we must've forgotten to set the alarm. Give us 15 minutes to get ready then we'll be there."

"Hurry, we have much to discuss."

I rolled my eyes and hung up the phone.

"Someone woke up on the wrong side of the bed," Amity yawned.

"Well, it wasn't the beautiful woman next to me," I grinned and kissed my girlfriend before crawling out of bed.

"It's times like this I wish I could drink coffee," Amity stretched, twisting her arms back and forth.

"You're telling me," I agreed, doing the same.

We got ready quickly and met up with Hunter at our designated spot. We could tell he was furious, so I tried to diffuse the situation.

"Hey, come on, we aren't *that* late."

"I'm the kind of person that believes if you're on time, you're already late, so to me you are very late. Don't let it happen again."

"Yes sir," I groaned.

His face had been a bright red, but finally his organic color was coming back, and he exhaled, "anyways. How did your homework go? What did ya'll discover?"

"We discovered a hidden gem in one of the photos," Amity announced.

"Great, what kind of hidden gem?"

"A literal gem," I revealed, pulling up the picture on my phone. We zoomed in and showed Hunter the diamond and what our suspicions were.

"Wow, I hadn't even noticed that before, great jobs guys."

"Woah, was that a compliment?" I was shocked.

"Don't get too big a head, did you actually solve the mystery?"

"Well, no, but didn't you?"

"Yes, like I told you yesterday, Lucida is the vampire to find."

"How do you know that, and why couldn't you just tell us this yesterday?"

"I wanted you guys to discover the answer on your own so that when your training is over, you'll be able to find more vampires like this on your own."

"I think we found a solution to that that's much easier."

"What do you mean?"

"Well... *we're* vampires. We don't exactly need a

crime scene to meet other vampires. Which means we can maybe get into exclusive parties and groups that would reveal which vampires are the ones that need to be killed."

"Spoiler alert," Hunter announced, "they all need to be killed."

"You gotta stop thinking like that," Amity told him, "you've already admitted that not all vampires are like that, AKA me and Hazel. If we don't deserve to die than neither do most other vampires."

"I understand that there are some vampires out there that maybe could be useful to the cause... but if all vampires were extinct then we wouldn't have any of them running around killing people."

"I guess you're not technically wrong, but humans kill other humans too; and you know that may just be worse because at least some vampires probably only do it out of instinct and the fact that they have to drink blood in order to stay alive. It's not always someone living to kill, some kill to live."

"That's a good way to put it," I nodded to Amity, "maybe some vampires don't even realize what they're doing is wrong. If they live forever, then really, some of them are just like toddlers, learning how to survive in the world they've been forced into."

"Look, let us just try it this way first, I promise you it will work." I pleaded.

He thought for a moment, "how will you get in?"

"If the parties here are anything like the few I've gone too, it won't be hard. Even if it is, we can get in because we're vampires. We'll prove it whatever way we have to."

"What if the way they make you prove it is by

killing someone?"

"I mean... it's not a cult, it's a party. Although, that does make me wonder if there are vampire cults to worry about."

Amity shuddered, "I'm sure there's at least one. That would for sure be something we'll want to investigate."

"Agreed," Hunter nodded.

The three of us made our arrangements and piled into Hunter's car. He drove us into the mountains to the suspect's home address. Unfortunately, there was a gate at the drive, and we had to abandon the car and walk the rest of the way. Before leaving the car, we hid as many weapons on us as we could. Amity and I were both wearing knee-high combat boots where we stuffed several knives, biker shorts with pocketknives tucked into the waist, and faux leather jackets with small handguns stashed in the inside pockets. Hunter was even more dressed to impress. As a human he wore much more protective clothing, including a bullet proof vest and thick combat boots. He was concealing more knives, guns, and even ninja stars in his own jacket as well. Even at night he was sweating heavily.

"Jeeze, what else you packing?" I teased.

"Wouldn't you like to know," he joked in response. He then shushed me and waved his hand, gesturing for us to get moving. We followed the road most of the way up to the house, but when we got close enough to see it, we moved into the trees and went around to the back. All the windows on the second floor were open, the purple curtains swaying in the breeze. None of the lights were on but we didn't assume that no one was around.

"Okay here's the plan. You guys boost me up into the window, I'll check to make sure the coast is clear, then pull you guys up with me."

We nodded and moved closer to the house. Amity and I put our knees and hands together to allow Hunter to step into our grip, then we lifted him up. He was heavier than he looked, but together we were able to raise him up to the window and he climbed in. I told Amity to go next, and Hunter reached out to catch her as I pushed her up. Once she was in, I realized I was too far out of Hunter's reach and I had to think quickly.

"Hazel," Amity encouraged, "you're a vampire, you can do this."

She was right. I looked around and took a few steps back, then lowered my gaze and focused on my goal. Taking a deep breath, I steadied myself then ran as fast as I could to the wall. I pushed myself up the wall and jumped as high as I could. It was more than enough to reach Hunter's extended hand, and we fell back into the house.

"Okay that was awesome!" I whispered.

"That was the coolest thing I've ever seen! For a split second I thought you were going to fly!" Amity squealed, "I wonder what else we can do!"

Hunter shushed her and stood up, "split up, find the vampire, and take her down. If we hear anything, we come running to help the other person, got it?"

We nodded and left the room, all going in separate directions. I went down the staircase, listening carefully for any household inhabitants. I never came across any, but I did find a clue in the very fancy cottage-core kitchen.

Amity's voice could be heard shouting from

upstairs and in my startled state I grabbed the paper and shoved it in my pocket as I ran up the stairs.

"Are you okay?" I asked as I was entering a massive master bedroom. Amity called me into the closet, and I rounded the corner into the bathroom then into the closet beyond. Both were nearly as big as the rooms in Tony's mansion.

Hunter had already made it in and upon seeing me, he pointed to Amity, who was holding something up in her hand.

"Is that what I think it is?" I asked.

She nodded, "the ring with the missing gemstone!"

"So, it's true. Lucida did kill that man in the photo. Shouldn't we take this to the police?"

"And say what?" Hunter was flabbergasted, "oh hey, we broke into this woman's house because we think she's a vampire who's killed a lot more than this guy?"

I shrugged, "maybe."

"Regardless, we have the evidence we need now. We know who, for sure, needs to be terminated."

"You're right, but where is she?" Amity asked, looking around the room.

"Good question babe, where is Lucida? Her windows were open, but she isn't home?"

"Maybe she went out?"

"Oh, wait I almost forgot," I pulled the flyer out of my pocket and uncrumpled it. The sheet was mostly black with bright red splatters throughout, with the title 'BLOOD RAVE'. I wasn't surprised in the least, but it did remind me of that scene in the Blade movie and I hoped this one wouldn't be nearly the same. According to the flyer, the rave was happening right then, so if we wanted to participate, we would need to get our butts into gear.

I showed the others the flyer and they agreed that we should all try to get in. Luckily the address was right on the flyer, so we didn't even have to think about where to go.

"Lucida is clearly not here, and if she's anywhere, she's at this party," I announced.

"We can't just murder her right in the middle of a party though," Amity reminded.

"True. Hunter, what do you think, maybe we could befriend her, get her to leave the party? She'll probably be high as hell and out of her mind anyways, we could lead her into the woods and take care of her there."

"It might work. Although I must admit I'm a little scared to find out what a blood rave is," Hunter recoiled at the thought.

"Me too honestly," I agreed.

"We're not exactly dressed for a party," Amity said, looking down at all her faux leather.

"Yeah, I don't think my bulletproof vest is going to look in place there, is it?" Hunter asked.

"Deff not. I mean... Lucida won't exactly be needing these clothes anymore, right? Maybe we could just sort of... borrow them?"

"I don't know... isn't that a bit much?" I wondered.

"She's dead, who cares?" Hunter shrugged.

"I guess the plan may not work if we don't... and we don't exactly have time to be driving all the way back to our place, decide what to wear, then drive all the way to this rave. Its location is another hour further into the mountains," I sighed and looked around the closet.

"I think that's my cue to book it, I'll be keeping

watch downstairs," Hunter swooped out of the room faster than we could acknowledge him and headed downstairs.

Unsurprisingly, Lucida had a lovely shoe collection and wardrobe. It wasn't hard to find something to wear, but we were both quite a bit smaller than Lucida, so the attire didn't exactly fit, especially in the chest region. We made do with what we had, and I picked out a cute bright red halter top and a sleek black pencil skirt. Amity picked out a deep purple plunging V-neck dress with a short asymmetrical skirt and looked gorgeous in it. The shoes were way too big for us so we were stuck wearing the big combat boots, but it honestly didn't look too bad, and we figured considering it was a rave, there would probably be tons of people wearing big boots. After fluffing up our hair in the mirror we went back downstairs to find Hunter waiting impatiently in the living room.

"Why do girls always take so long to get ready?" he asked, arms crossed.

I rolled my eyes, "omg. We weren't even in there for more than 15 minutes. Calm down with that toxic masculinity."

"Yeah, you know it wouldn't kill you to zhuzh a little." Amity said.

"Huh?" his mouth dropped open like he had just heard something incredibly stupid.

This time it was Amity's turn to roll her eyes, "you know, zhuzh. Spike what little hair you have, pop a collar, untuck your shirt, stop being such a bore."

"I'll have you know, I'm a very exciting person. You guys just don't see it because when we're together its strictly business."

"Well then, let's get you off to clock and into that party huh?"

"You know I can't be off the clock in a room full of vampires."

"Maybe, but just so we're clear, you cannot just start killing them all willy nilly. We have our mission and that is the only vampire that is going down tonight, got it?"

"Understood. It would jeopardize the mission to just blow down the whole party."

"Plus, there's a good chance that there will be humans in there too," I reminded.

"Why would there be humans there?"

"I'll give you one guess."

He shook his head, "no I get it."

CHAPTER 19

Blood Rave

The blood rave was in a very sketchy roadhouse in the middle of nowhere. The building looked like it had been abandoned for more than a century, with stone bricks, wood, and railroad spikes littering the lands surrounding it. The roundhouse was a curved-shaped building with six severely faded red garage doors and the remains of a circle track out front. What seemed like a hundred cars were parked in the field next to the building and I assumed those were the cars of the partygoers as there were a few groups of people spread out, smoking cigarettes and drinking out of wine bottles. Heaven only knew what was actually in those wine bottles; I'd be willing to bet that it was not really wine.

A booming bass track could be heard from inside the roundhouse, but you couldn't see into it as there were no windows, so the only way we knew we were in the right place was the music and the bouncer standing guard at the side door. I turned to look at our group to make sure we were ready; Hunter had unwillingly taken off his bulletproof vest but refused to remove the weapons in his pockets. Amity looked as beautiful as ever and I gave her hand a squeeze to make sure she was okay. She squeezed back and gave me a quick smile in response.

"Alright, does everyone remember the plan?" I asked.

"Yes, we are vampires who received the invitational flyer, and this is our human that we keep on hand. If we need a name, Lucida should be on the list," Amity nodded.

"And if anyone asks my name is not Hunter, and I refer to you both as master," Hunter added.

"Good job," I reached up and patted his head like a dog and led my group towards the door, striding with as much confidence as I could muster.

"Flyer?" the bouncer asked. I handed him the flyer and shifted my weight as if impatient. He looked at the three of us and stopped on Hunter, then back to Amity and me.

"No humans allowed," He frowned.

"Apologies, he's my emergency support human. I keep him around in case I get hungry."

"Don't worry, there will be plenty to drink in there. The human stays outside."

I turned to Hunter and glared, "Brandon, go back to the car."

"Uh, yes... Ma'am," Hunter lowered his head then walked away and I turned back to the bouncer. He let us in then and we took the opportunity without hesitation.

Once we were out of earshot Amity whispered, "how do you think he could tell that we were both vampires, but Hunter wasn't?"

"Good question, maybe the eyes? We have much better night vision, maybe he could tell by the pupils or something."

"Or maybe the smell?"

"Could be."

Whatever DJ was running the show was playing Tarik Bouisfi and it was a welcome change to the dubstep that was played at the other parties. It was much darker and ominous sounding, much more fitting for this scenario. The lights danced around us from the curved stage just behind the garage doors. There was a lot of smoke floating around and the crowd was going crazy. Thankfully there weren't any sprinklers spraying blood onto the crowd of people. At least, not yet.

The next song that was played I recognized instantly to be In Your Lungs by Street Fever. It was a little bit more upbeat than the last song, but still very underground-club sounding. The crowd started cheering and I took Amity's hand in mine.

"Want to dance?" I asked.

"Shouldn't we be focusing on our mission?"

"Ah, don't start sounding like Hunter now, babe. He's outside; let's have a few minutes of fun before we find you-know-who. Besides, it might look kind of weird to go to an underground rave and not dance, right?"

She nodded and followed me to the dance floor. The beat dropped then, and we cheered, pushing our way into the middle of the pit. The lights flashed and the crowd jumped to the beat and for a moment I forgot that we were at a vampire party and that every single person around us drinks blood to survive. As the song came to an end and the next one began, I remembered this, and I shuddered to think there were so many monsters nearby. What was unfortunate was that in this setting it didn't seem like there were any monsters around, just a bunch of normal people, dancing their night away and enjoying the freedom of their youth. However, so many of these party people held glasses with deep red liquids and I had to hold back and swallow my disgust.

How many people had to be drained of their blood to fill the requirements for tonight's rave? Just one? Ten maybe? Potentially a hundred? The bar in the back was serving a steady flow of said red liquid and I approached the bartender to see if I could find out.

"You want organic, tainted, or bland?" the bartender asked.

"Uh, remind me the difference?"

The woman lowered an eyebrow, "bland is your average human. Organic is vegan blood, and tainted is blood on drugs. Tainted is the choice drink of the night, and we're having a two for one special."

"Huh, let me just go see what my girlfriend wants," I tried to sound nonchalant, but I hoped it hadn't come off as confused or disgusted. They not only had different kinds of human blood, but the blood of vegans specifically? And it was seen as a delicacy? I was utterly repulsed. There was no way they had obtained all that blood legally or morally.

I was honest with Amity when I got back over to her, and she was equally horrified. If I hadn't needed to keep up the charade I probably would've broken down. It was one thing to have human blood, but for them to go out of their way to hunt down vegans and murder them for taste pleasure was cruel and uncalled for, not to mention morbidly ironic. Now it seemed more personal than ever, and I wasn't even human anymore.

"Maybe Hunter has a point," I sighed.

"I mean, yeah maybe most vampires... well, suck... but not all of them. Don't forget about the Peaceful Vampires. Maybe we should go spend some more time with them to get in a better headspace."

"Yeah, you're right, vampires do suck."

She laughed, "well you're not wrong, but come on, we should get going on our mission. Who knows what time Lucida will dip."

I nodded and we split up to find her. We knew what she looked like based on the photos from Hunter's files, but it was so dark that it was hard to look at each person, much less be able to tell which one was her. I ended up just asking each person that even slightly resembled her if they were her or knew where she was and every time, I was told no. After circling the floor, I decided to check bathrooms and backrooms, and the backrooms were where things got interesting. Along a hallway in the back were three doors all labeled 'red room'. I opened one up to see what exactly a red room was, fearing the worst, and was shocked to find out my fears were true.

A woman straddled over a man on a bright red couch, blood pouring from his neck. I slammed the door shut and grabbed the woman by her hair, yanking her back. The woman hissed like a cat and swatted her claws at me. I bashed her head into the wall and kept a tight grip so I could pull out my phone and call Amity. As I'm about to hang up the phone the woman pulled her strength together and ripped herself from my grip, losing a few hairs in the process. She growled at me and jumped to attack, but I dodged in time and she ran headfirst into the wall.

The man on the couch was passed out, I assumed this was from blood loss, but I just hoped he was still alive. Unfortunately, I had to deal with the woman before checking to see if the man still had a heartbeat. As such, the woman came at me again and we fought aggressively. I tried to sway her by sharing my thoughts on the matter, but she was not having any of it and refused to listen to a word I said. She was out for blood, and she wasn't going to stop until she got what she was after.

While kicking and avoiding punches, I took a moment to look at her appearance and realized she fit the description of the woman we were after, and I was pretty sure this was Lucida. I just needed confirmation before I proceeded any further.

"Look, my friend and I were just trying to find someone. Someone by the name of Lucida. Does that name ring a bell?"

As soon as the name escaped my lips, she straightened her back and closed her mouth.

"Who's looking for me, and why?" She asked, a scowl on her face. Amity came in then, locking the door behind her.

"It's her," I whispered, knowing that Lucida would still be able to hear even at the low volume.

"Again, I ask of you," Lucida growled.

"You know, originally, I had planned on telling you that I was a big fan of your work and maybe offer you something you couldn't refuse, lead you out into the woods then take care of you there, but you have officially crossed the line. Did this man consent to you biting him and sucking his blood to a point where he's out cold, if not, dead?"

"That's what the red room is, I *paid* for this pleasure."

"As in- the club provided the human and you paid to drink from him?"

She nodded and shrugged simultaneously, "they said he was special. Some kind of fancy neurosurgeon or something. I just thought that sounded delicious."

I sighed in defeat, "is he dead?"

"He is now," she smirked, wiping a sliver of blood from the corner of her mouth.

It took all I had in me not to scream at the top of my lungs, but I knew that would cause a stir and we would be busted. So instead, I drew a knife from my clutch and threw it at Lucida like a magician throwing a dart. It landed just shy of her heart and knocked her down. Amity ran over and pinned her arms up behind her and kneeled on them so she couldn't get up.

"Now, babe, finish this!" She howled.

I leaned over Lucida, a knee to her stomach, and gripped the handle of the knife. Her eyes grew wide as fear overcame her. I hesitated as I saw this, my humanity tugging at my soul. She was once a person too.

"Please," Lucida begged.

"How many humans have you killed?" I asked, putting pressure on the wound.

She cried out in pain, "a few okay!"

"How many!"

"Too many to count! I'm sorry, please don't kill me!"

I looked up at Amity, sweat beading down my forehead.

"It's okay if you can't, I can do it," She suggested.

I didn't want her to do that though. She was too kind, too loving, too innocent for this cruel world. I hated the thought that if she killed this woman tonight, that would change her life forever. I on the other hand, had already killed someone. It was on accident of course, and the person was a child rapist, but... I still played God and ended their life. What gave me the right? Who gave me the authority?

"Someone has to," Amity pleaded.

Lucida tried to push me off her, but I twisted the knife. She pleaded as I shushed her. Blood poured from Lucida's wound, and I knew all it would take was a bit of carving and her life would be over. Time was running out. Someone would find us sooner or later or Lucida would win. It was kill or be killed. As much as I hated it, I had made my decision.

"It's going to be okay," Amity reassured, applying pressure to Lucida's arms and head.

I glared down at the murderer before me and blinked back the fear, replacing it with rage. The knife burned into my hand as I pushed it further into Lucida's chest. She roared in pain and Amity covered her mouth with her hand. I carved into Lucida and plucked out her heart and as soon as the cord was cut, she was gone.

As a vampire, the smell of her blood was strong and sweet, but as much as I craved it, there was a stronger force at will. My pent-up rage had overflowed, and I was off the deep end. Holding Lucida's heart in my hand, I dropped the knife and collapsed to the ground. The puddle of blood soaked into my clothes as it did Amity's when she joined me on the floor. My hands and legs shook like I was hypothermic, but it was all just anxiety.

Amity patted my hair and soothed me until I was calm enough to sit back up, then reminded me that I did the right thing; that all of this was for the better because now there was one less person in the world killing innocent people. All I could think about was how this time it wasn't an accident. If I wasn't already doomed to hell, I am now.

"We need to go, before someone figures out what happened," Amity sighed, looking down at our blood-stained clothes.

"What do we do about her?" I asked.

"Honestly, I don't know. I really didn't think we would end up doing it here, but she started this, she had already killed him. Now there's two bodies. I'm calling Hunter."

"He'll just want to try to get inside, that will jeopardize us more."

"I'll make sure he stays put and just gives advice."

Amity pulled up Hunter on her phone and turned on the speaker. We explained what had happened and he lectured us for being so stupid and naive. We really weren't in the mood to take his bullshit so we told him to shut up and give us some advice rather than yelling about something that couldn't be undone. He felt that there was no way we could get those bodies out without someone realizing what we had done, and we couldn't just wait until the rave was over because, more than likely, the employees would come check the rooms for stragglers. I also noted that Lucida had claimed to pay for her victim to be brought in, which meant someone was getting paid to take the victim back out of the room too most likely. Hunter took this to mean maybe they would just deal with Lucida too and not ask questions.

He genuinely believed that the best way to proceed furthermore was to just sneak out with the heart and leave Lucida behind. As much as I hated to agree with him, on this one I had to. I just couldn't see a scenario in which the other vampires wouldn't come for us after seeing what we had done. No one in the building could know what had transpired here.

Amity had much less blood on her, so I recommended that she take the lead, and make sure the coast is clear, then lead us the heck out of the building. She nodded and stood at the door, listening for anyone nearby. Once she believed the hallway to be clear, she unlocked the door and cracked it open. Confirming that the coast was clear, Amity took my hand and led us out of the red room, shutting the door behind us. Unfortunately, we had to go back through the dance floor to exit the building, and we bumped into a couple people while wading through the crowd. One of the people we bumped into stopped to apologize, and upon doing so, noticed my appearance.

"Oh no! It looks like you spilled your drink!" They gaped.

"Ah, yeah! Yes, that's exactly what happened! I'm very clumsy, as you can see!"

I started to pull away from them, but they pulled me back, "I have a bleach stick in my purse, here let me find it!"

I shook my head, "that's okay, I have a change of clothes in my car so we're just gunna go get it now. Thank you!"

They waved and smiled and was quite honestly the kindest interaction I had had all night, but now was not the time to make friends. We ran the rest of the way back to the car and jumped in. Hunter had had the engine running and ready to go and we bolted out of there faster than the Flash.

"I cannot believe that just happened," I exhaled deeply and leaned my head on Amity's shoulder. She patted my hair and agreed.

"Did you guys make it out okay?" Hunter asked.

"One person asked me about the blood, but they just thought I had spilled my drink, so it was okay. No one suspected anything... but I'm still worried about what's going to happen once they find the body."

"Fair point, but honestly, what if nothing happens?" Amity wondered, "vampires see bodies all the time. Well, at least those kinds of vampires do. There are dead bodies everywhere. Heck, their drinks were made from dead bodies."

"Don't remind me," I frowned.

"Sorry. I just mean that maybe they won't think anything of it, and they'll just see it as an inconvenience that they have to clean up someone's dinner."

"But-" I pulled the heart out of my clutch and gazed at it. Amity understood what I was thinking and wrapped her arms around me.

"For what it's worth," Hunter sighed, looking at us in his rear-view mirror, "I think you guys did pretty good for your first mission. You found the clues, followed your lead, and did the hard job that no one else wanted to do. And you know why? It's because you are good people. I'm sorry for being hard on you back there. We're definitely going to work on your anger management skills and better ways that that could've been handled, but overall, I'm proud of you. That person will no longer harm any living being ever again."

"I know you're right, but why do I still feel so... dirty?"

"That would be because of the blood on your hands." Amity half-teased.

I moaned, "seriously."

"No really, let's get you home and you can take a shower and I promise you'll feel better. I always do."

"I hope you're right."

When we got back to the house, I went straight up to take a shower. As the blood washed down my body, I thought about what it meant to be a vampire hunter and what my future would hold. I knew this wasn't the life I had originally planned, but it was the life I was thrust into, and it was the life that I would be forced to live for the rest of eternity. I didn't want this. No part of me was excited to be a vampire. I was happy to have Amity in my life, but she was the only good outcome in this lonely new world I was in. Eventually my family and friends would die, and I would be left behind, cursed to perpetually walk through blood and war to find my just path.

I had killed a person tonight.

Plain and simple. I had ended someone's existence, and that was something I could never take back; but I chose my life, and my girlfriend's life, over the life of someone I knew would abuse their power. There was no point in feeling guilty. Yet... I did. Was it because I was engrained to believe that over everything else in life, morality was the most important aspect? Or was it because I truly believe I did something wrong, something... bad. Am I a bad person? Am I the villain?

These thoughts continued to swirl through my mind as Amity and I went out back to dispose of the remains of Lucida. Starting a fire in the tiny pit we had, Amity took the reins and held the heart, along with the clothes we had 'borrowed', above the flame. Just as she was about to drop it in, I stopped her, taking the heart in my own hands.

"Can I just say... after everything... I'm sorry things had to go the way they did. I wish we could've just persuaded you to be a better person, but psychotic people can't be persuaded. I hope that you are able to be a better... thing... for wherever the universe takes you next."

It wasn't my best speech, but it was the best I could come up with for someone who did such unspeakable things. I then closed my eyes and tossed the heart in, feeling the warmth of the fire as it expanded around the object. As Amity threw the clothes in, the flames grew brighter, and I tightened my eyes shut and held onto her. She embraced me back and I knew that through everything, she was the one person that would always be there for me. The one person in the entire world that would help me bury the body.

CHAPTER 20

Guilt

Winter had arrived too soon. Two months had passed since Lucida's death, and I was still dealing with all the emotional pain in the ways that I could. We had to move our training sessions indoors as it became too cold for the human to be comfortable, which meant we finally got to see Hunter's house for the first time. Understandably so, it was chaotically messy. He lived by himself, so that part I understood, but with his military-like personality I really figured he would've had a spotless house.

Regardless, Amity and I had discovered that the longer we were vampires and the stronger we got, the more we became like the vampires on tv. Our fangs never really got sharper as others did, and I assumed that was from a lack of biting into people to eat; but we got stronger, faster, more intelligent, and less susceptible to temperatures. The only downside was that our night vision had gotten better too. This meant that the sunlight bothered us even more, but at the same time we were getting more used to night-time lights such as streetlights, fires, table lamps, etcetera.

Amity was always there for me when I started getting worked up over Lucida, but my heart was torn in two. On one hand I was glad that Lucida could no longer harm innocent people, but on the other hand I still wished we could've found another way. We had only had one other mission since Lucida, and with that one, Hunter did the deed. I still felt bad, but I was glad it was him and not me. I needed time to heal from the trauma of committing my first premeditated murder.

"You okay?" Amity asked, resting a hand on my thigh. I turned to her and gave a weak smile, "yeah I'm fine."

She frowned, "no you're not, you've got that look, what are you thinking about?"

"Lucida... I just still can't get the image out of my brain. I know you think what I did was the right way to go but... I'm just not so sure."

"I understand how difficult this must be for you. I'm here for you though, okay? Your feelings are valid, and I must say, I trust you more than anyone else on this planet. If in that moment you felt what you were doing was right, then it was. I love you for standing up for what you believe in and staying strong."

"Thanks, you always know what to say."

She hugged me tightly and kissed me on the cheek, "it will be okay, I promise. Lucida got what she deserved."

"You're right, it's just hard for me to think that way."

I stood up from the couch and put my book away on the shelf. Amity went to the kitchen and grabbed two tumblers for us.

"You hungry?" she asked.

I nodded, "famished."

It had taken a while, but eventually we had both

gotten used to drinking from the donation blood. We did try to keep it to a minimum, only drinking what we really needed to survive so as not to waste any blood that the donators generously gave us, but sometimes we just really needed breakfast. I still wished there was another way, but there really wasn't. It's not like there was a blood substitute the way there are meat substitutes for vegans.

"Did you hear Kat is pregnant?" Amity's eyes grew wide as she remembered to tell me. Kat was one of our coworkers who was notoriously known for all her hookups not just with some of the male team members but also some of the customers, not to mention whoever else she hooks up with from her social media apps and weekly clubbing activities. It wasn't exactly a surprise to me that she would end up pregnant.

I rolled my eyes, "of course she is, does she know who the father is?"

She shook her head, "I don't think so, I think she has it narrowed down to two guys though, one of them being Stewart."

Stewart was another of our coworkers, which again, was not a surprise.

"She does realize that not every time she has sex has to be unprotected, right?"

Amity laughed, "apparently not."

I sat back down on the couch and Amity joined me, sitting in my lap. I put my arms around her waist, and she put hers around my neck.

"I'm really glad we don't have to worry about that."

"For more than one reason," she added.

I smiled as she brushed my hair back and kissed my neck. Amity trailed kisses up my neck and to my lips where I kissed her back, and as we were making out, I received a phone call. We groaned and ignored the call, but whoever was on the other end called again as soon as it went to voicemail. Moaning, I turned away from Amity and grabbed my phone from the other side of the couch.

"Hunter," I stated as I answered the phone, putting it on speaker.

"Guys, I uh... I need your help."

"What's going on?" I asked.

"I hate to admit it, but I took a job... and I've seemed to have gotten myself into a bit of a pickle. They're stronger than I anticipated."

"Are you okay? Where are you?" Amity inquired.

"I thought I could sneak up on them while they were still asleep, now he has me hanging from the ceiling, please, you have to come help me!"
Hunter was sounding increasingly scared, and Amity and I jumped into action. Hunter explained where to go as we got dressed.

"Who is this vampire?" I asked while throwing on a shirt.

"Elijah Westley. I pinned the location a while back and finally got my proof. I'll tell you the rest later, please, the blood is rushing to my head, you need to come quick! Who knows when he'll come back to finish me off."

"Hunter, we're on our way, there's just one problem."

"I know, its daylight, I thought I would have the advantage on this one."

"Why did you take the job without us anyways?"

"No time to explain, I think I hear him coming,

please, just hurry!"

The phone was hung up then and I feared the worst.

"We have to go help him," I urged.

Amity ran to our secret hiding spot, the saferoom underneath the house, and retrieved the only two pairs of day glasses we had. We had more-or-less stolen them off a vampire at the last party we went to, one where we were looking for a particular vampire, but had no luck. We had yet had a true reason to use them, but now we did.

"I hope they work," I frowned.

"They're gunna have to," Amity sighed, and we rushed outside in our hooded cloaks, winter gear, hidden weapons, and day glasses. It had snowed the previous day, and there was a good foot and a half of ground coverage. Our car wasn't the best for this kind of weather, but luckily where we lived wasn't too far into the mountains and most of the roads had been cleared. We had also continuously shoveled every couple of hours throughout the previous night as it snowed so that we wouldn't have to shovel all 18 inches in one go. Carefully, we climbed into the car and sped off into the setting sun. It was difficult to drive with the glasses on, because it had to block out so much sunlight that it was barely transparent, but I did my best and eventually we made it to the location Hunter had described.

Our car spun into the driveway of an old log house, one that was big enough to be a small mansion. I'm beginning to see a pattern in these vampires. The house even had a -not one- but *four* car garage behind it. A man dressed like an FBI agent, ear wire included, stood guard at the front door and there were cameras in each corner.

I wondered how Hunter had even made it into the house in the first place.

We got out of the car and the man at the front door charged towards us, yelling that we needed to leave.

"You have a friend of ours in there and we're not leaving till he is safely returned to us," I told him, glaring through my glasses.

"Oh sure, let me just go get him," he half-smiled and turned around as if to head back to the house, then immediately turned back around, thrusting a fist directly to my cheekbone. It was painful and I was startled, but Amity jumped into action. Her cloak floated up as she jumped into the air and brought down her wrath upon the man. He grunted and staggered back, then brought a leg up to kick her. She thought quickly and grabbed his leg, swinging it up further and making him fall backwards. I pushed on his chest to knock him down harder and he grunted as he landed.

"Like I said, we're not leaving until we get our friend back."

The man jumped back up and started throwing more punches and kicks, he got a few in, and we got a few in, but once I kicked him in the groin and he was down for the count, Amity pulled out a knife and raised it above her head.

"Wait!" I hollered.

She looked at me with confusion, and he looked at us with fear.

"Don't kill him, I think he's human," I realized this when I noticed he was out in the remains of sunlight with no problem.

"Do you have a vampire in the house?" I asked the man. He nodded in response, still grimacing over the painful kick to the nuts.

Amity sighed and hit him over the head with the blunt end of her knife, knocking him unconscious. We dragged his sleeping body up to the front of the house and checked to see if the door was unlocked: it wasn't but a quick body search and we were able to find the keys. We opened the huge wooden doors and laid the man in the foyer. Shutting the doors behind us, we took off our glasses and tossed them on the floor. The house was pitch black apart from the light from the fireplace and minimal lamps. Quickly we ran in a circle around the house trying to find Hunter, assuming that if this scenario were anything like Tony, we would find Hunter below ground. Eventually we found the door to the basement, but it too, was locked. I shook the door handle as hard as I could to try to break it, but it was not going to budge.

Deep, long screams could be heard then, emitting from beyond this particular door, and I knew that it had to be Hunter. Amity and I gasped and charged at the door, and together we were able to knock it down. I had no idea if it was vampire strength or pure adrenaline, but I knew we were going to do everything in our power to save our friend.

We rushed down the staircase and followed a trail of blood down a corridor. This basement was unlike anything I had ever seen. It was straight out of a jigsaw movie. There were cages and tools and blood everywhere. We found Hunter in the back, hanging upside down by his ankles, his face as red as his blood underneath, and his arms swinging beside his head. A bucket was on the ground below him, and beside him was a table, with a man standing before it. He was tall, with a long leather coat and thick boots, and hair that was waist length and pinned back like someone from the revolution.

He knew we were there, yet he didn't turn around. We had stopped running upon seeing him, he was way out of our league in terms of an even fight, but maybe since there was two of us...

I looked back to Hunter, who had tears streaming down his forehead and blood dripping from a cut on his side. He was bruised from head to toe and his face had been beaten to a pulp. It was the worst I had ever seen him (or anyone), and my heart hurt to see him in so much pain. This Elijah person was the worst vampire I had seen yet, an absolute psychopath that not only drank blood from humans but got enjoyment out of their slow torture. I took Amity's hand and just as I was about to lunge forward, the man spoke.

"I wouldn't do that if I was you," he said without turning around.

"Look, hey man, we're vampires too, okay? We get it, we don't want any trouble here."

Elijah turned towards us, a blade in hand. He twirled and admired the weapon as he spoke, "you're vampires you say?"

"Yes, we are. This human, he's a friend of ours, and he meant you no harm, but we'd really like him back now, please."

Something about this man really terrified me. The look in his eyes was ice-cold and hollow, as if he had no soul left at all, like the caveman. At least we could communicate with this man. His hair was white, but his skin was tan and youthful, and when I looked at him all I could think of was fear. I had no idea how we were gunna get Hunter out of there alive. He had passed out at some point from all the blood loss, and I just hoped he would be okay.

"This *human* here broke into my house and tried to kill me!"

I took a few steps forwards and held up my palms, "I think this is all just a big misunderstanding, he didn't mean to scare you."

Elijah lowered the knife and got closer to us, "I eat humans like him for *fun*. Do you really think I'm going to let this man go?"

I mustered up all the confidence I could and lowered my eyebrows, "if you don't, you will die here tonight."

Elijah laughed and turned the knife around in his hand, so it faced backwards. He ran at us at speeds I could barely fathom, but somehow, we managed to jump to the side and pull our own weapons out.

My weapon of choice was a small dagger I hid in my waistband, and Amity's was a Glock that she had stashed in her pocket. She shot him and I threw my knife at his heart. He dodged the knife but was grazed by the bullet. He never staggered though, barely even blinked! Amity shot again just before he knocked it out of her hand. The bullet went into his stomach, and that time I could tell he felt it, but he all but flinched.

"Amity!" I cried. Elijah tossed her to the side and turned back towards his table. I stared in disbelief for a moment, then darted forward to attack. I had my backup knife out in a second and I jumped onto his back.

Something in me snapped and I went straight for his neck. However, he was so fast that before I could even think about cutting his throat, he had already pushed me off. The blade had barely broken skin, but at least it did some damage.

They say, 'if looks could kill', this would've been that moment. Elijah roared like an animal, barring his fangs. It was still just the two canine teeth but those two were sharper than I had ever seen on a vampire. He bent down and sunk his teeth into my arm, and I howled in agony. He didn't suck on me, but instead spat out the blood that graced his lips. Amity rushed over, probably fearing the worst.

"I'm okay," I nodded, standing back up and bracing myself for whatever was next.

"Your blood tastes disgusting. It's far too sweet," Elijah spat.

"You're so kind," I grumbled.

He yanked my arm forward and held me in place in front of Hunter and did the same with Amity. His grip on my wrist was so tight that I couldn't feel my fingers after just a few seconds. I gritted my teeth as he pushed me closer to Hunter.

"Since you're here, you might as well help me drain my next victim.

This one here is just breakfast. Maybe you guys could come back for dinner?"

"What's dinner?"

"Let's just say.... more than one."

"Not a chance in HELL," Amity growled.

"Been there, done that." He let go of us and picked a knife off the table, handing it to me.

"Slit his throat," he ordered.

I shook my head, "I won't do that."

"You're a vampire, dear, it's only in your nature to

do so. Besides, weren't you just about to do the same to me? It's only fair."

"You're wrong. I would never hurt someone I care about."

"Why should you care for this man anyways? He's a vampire slasher. He could turn on you at any moment. Does he even know what you really are?"

"She's a good person, that's what she is!" Amity stood her ground, and I appreciated it, but I was more scared for her than anything else. I feel like I've said it before, but more-so now than any other time, truly was my nightmares come to life. My biggest fear at that moment was that one or both people I cared about wouldn't make it through the night.

"Fine," Elijah took the knife back and slit one of Hunter's wrists, holding the bucket up to his hand. It startled Hunter awake, and he screamed.

"No!" I shouted. Elijah looked back at Amity and me with eyes that dared us to move any closer. Once the blood slowed to just a drip Elijah took the bucket and shoved it into my hands.

"Drink," he demanded.

"No!" I cried, "I can't do that."

"I know you want to. I can tell you haven't got any real meat on your bones. You're weak. You're no true vampire."

"I don't care! He's my friend and I won't do that to him."

"Leave her alone!" Hunter slurred.

"Hunter, you're gunna be okay, we'll get you out of here!"

"Shut up! Now drink this or I'll kill all three of you right here, right now."

"Why? Why do you want me to drink it?"

"Because I can smell how weak you are, and unlike you, I care about other vampires."

"I care about other vampires, I just don't care about murderers like you!"

Elijah picked a stake off the table and held it against my chest, "drink now or I'll shove this through your heart."

"It's okay," Hunter cried, his breath staggered, "drink it, I give you permission."

I looked at my friend with fear in my eyes and looked down at the small bucket in my hands. Just as I brought it to my lips, it was kicked out from under me. The blood splattered all over us and the ground as Amity pushed me behind her and held her gun up. She shot as many rounds as she had and as close to his heart as she could. At such a close range she was able to hit the target twice, which knocked Elijah down. His eyes were closed but I didn't dare believe he was dead.

"Quick! Cut him down!" I yelped.

I held up Hunter's top half while Amity cut the rope that he was hanging from. He fell into my lap, groaning.

"We need to apply pressure to the wounds!"

"Here!" Amity used my dagger to cut her top layer of clothing into a tourniquet, wrapping the cloth around Hunter's wrist. His breathing was labored but he was alive and that's what mattered.

"We need to get him to a hospital."

"Yes, but what do we do about *him*?" Amity asked.

I looked behind at Elijah and he was still lying there, motionless, "I honestly don't know."

I got back to tending Hunter's wounds and Amity

assessed the situation, looking around the room for anything that might help. Hunter had passed out cold and I was worried about all the blood he had lost. Even though it had been months on a steady diet and being around human coworkers, having all that fresh blood near me (and on me) was not easy to handle. I really had to fight the half of myself that wanted to sink my teeth in, but I wouldn't give in. Fear drove me farther than my bloodlust, so I held my tongue and thought about how I would get my friend the help he needed. I guessed this was a scenario that the cops could handle, it was self-defense after all. If the cops got here and Elijah was still alive but too weak to do anything, he would be taken to prison where he would hopefully get solitary confinement for being a serial killer and eventually starve to death. I pulled my phone out of my back pocket but just as I did so, I was grabbed by the neck and pulled back, dropping the phone in the process. I shrieked and Amity spun on her heal. Elijah had a blade to my throat and hollered at Amity to stay put.

"Please. Please don't hurt her!" She cried.

"I could end her right now," he was weak from the bullets, that much I could tell. If I could just find a way to end it for good. He stood up, pulling me with him, but struggled to stay standing.

Amity inched closer, holding out her hand.

"What do you want from us?" She asked.

His grip on me tightened and I struggled to breathe. I wrapped my hands around his arm and pushed against him as hard as I could, then tucked and rolled. As I rolled away Amity lunged towards him and grabbed the blade. They fought over the knife but in his weakened state, Elijah was unable to hold on. Amity then pushed him down and kicked him. He jumped back into a crab position to avoid her, but this time he wasn't quite quick enough, and she slashed his arm open. Feeling the pain, he held his bad arm with his good one and inched backwards. Amity followed him and kneeled over his chest.

"This is the last time you will ever hurt anyone," her voice was cold. I had never heard her speak like that before. It was both terrifying and adorable at the same time, but I didn't have time to think about that. Hunter didn't have time for me to think about that.

CHAPTER 21

Saving Hunter

I didn't even try to stop her this time. Amity slit Elijah's throat, just like he had asked her to do to Hunter, and he choked on his own blood. Then she pulled a wooden stake from her back pocket and drove it through his heart. After a moment he stopped breathing, and I walked over to them.

"We have to destroy the heart, just to be sure," I told her.

She nodded and pulled out the stake, seeing the holes and cringing at the gore. "There's fragments everywhere, if I carve out the heart, it wouldn't be in one piece."

"Then we'll have to burn all of him just to be safe. Let's just get Hunter in the car, you take him to the hospital, and I'll stay here and take care of this."

"No way. I'm not leaving you alone in this house!"

"It's okay, he's gone now, I'll find some gas and I'll burn this whole place to shit if I have to."

"You're quite the pyromaniac, aren't you?" she smirked.

"And you're quite the vampire slayer, aren't you?" I wanted to wink but now was not the time for flirting. We had just been through so much. It was really going to take time to heal from this. Especially for Hunter.

"You sure you'll be okay?" she asked.

I nodded, "just don't say anything about vampires, okay? I don't know what you'll have to tell them, just something about being kidnapped and beaten or whatever, you got this okay? I trust you."

"I love you," she sighed and pushed her messy hair away from her face.

"I love you too, come on, I'll help you get Hunter to the car."

Together we picked up Hunter and carried him up the staircase. Once we got to the front door, we realized something very important was missing. The man in black was gone. Which meant he was awake and most likely hiding in the house somewhere.

"Ugh," I growled.

Amity opened the door and searched for him, "well he's not in sight, he's either gone or he's hiding in the house somewhere."

"Let's just focus on Hunter, then we'll worry about the other human."

I took off my cloak and wrapped it around Hunter, then we carried him out into the cold to get back to the car. The sun had set while we were in the house and the dark didn't help the freezing temperatures. We got him situated in the back seat and then I gave Amity a hug.

"You really won't come with me? We can always come back later, I'm sure he won't wake up from that, I mean he wasn't breathing, he had no pulse!"

I shook my head, "Hunter always said you have to completely destroy their heart, that's the only way to know they're gone for good."

"But how will you get out of here? Maybe I could

come back to get you or-"

I looked at the garage, "I can just about 100% guarantee there's more than one car in there, I'll take one when I'm done here and I'll meet you at the hospital, okay?"

"Okay... but call me every five minutes until you're away from this house. I swear if anything bad were to happen to you..."

"I promise you I won't let anything bad happen, I'll be careful."

We said our goodbyes and then Amity sped off as quickly as she was able to on the icy roads. I was slowly starting to feel the cold then, so I ran back inside and attempted to find the human. It felt so weird thinking that less than 9 months ago, I wouldn't have described someone as being human or not, I would've just thought 'person'; but to describe Elijah was not to describe a human: he was far too gone for that. Elijah was something else entirely. A vampire, yes, but more authentically, a demon spawn straight from hell.

After searching the main floor, I still hadn't come across the human, so I went back downstairs to check there and get started on figuring out what to do with Elijah's body. When I got down to the spot though, the body was gone. A trail of dark-red blood led me to a back room, where I found the man in black leaning over Elijah's body which he had laid on a table of sorts. The room was just like the rest of the basement, covered in old-dried blood and guts with torture devices hanging all over the wall. It looked like a sadistic BDSM nightmare... only worse for obvious reasons.

"What's your name?" I asked the man, approaching cautiously.

He looked at me with a whimper, half of his bottom lip swollen from one of the punches Amity hit him with earlier.

"Jaden," he sniffled, "what am I going to do? When he wakes up, he's going to kill me... just like the others."

I steadied my hands and took a few steps towards him, "Jaden... look, I understand you're scared, you may even fear me too, but I promise you, I will not kill you, and I will not let him kill you either. See those wounds he has? That means that he's dying, and if we finish this, he will be dead for good, and he cannot come back to hurt you."

He looked back at me, and I could tell he was contemplating his next move. He was wondering whether he should believe me or stay loyal to his 'master'.

"How did you get here Jaden? What did he do to you?"

More tears fell as he recalled. "He killed her... my wife... we were out hiking, he ambushed us, brought us back here. He hooked her up to some spikey chair and whipped her till her whole body was covered in lashes. He had me in one of those nasty cages, forced me to watch the whole thing. Just before she died, he sliced her open and gathered her... blood. All of it. He drank some of it and then cut her body into pieces. I didn't see what he did with her remains after that."

I gulped, "Jaden... I'm *so* sorry. You never should have had to go through that."

"After the whole thing he told me I was to be his slave, or he would do the same thing to me. I was too scared to fight back, so I let him dress me up and play butler, but I've been trying to figure out how to escape ever since."

"This is it then, Jaden, you're free now. He can't hurt you anymore, just let me take care of the rest, and you go home. Go to your parents, your friends, whoever, and hold them tight."

"But how can I come home without her? They'll think I did it. A couple doesn't just go hiking and only one come back. They'll never believe my story."

"Yeah, no, they wouldn't understand, but I think I know some people that can help."

I told Jaden about the Peaceful Vampires group and to seek help from them and then said that maybe his best bet was to just move somewhere else and start over.

"You're right, this has all been so traumatizing. I honestly don't know how to go on without her, but being here, there's too many painful memories. Maybe starting somewhere fresh, somewhere where vampires are less likely to be, might help."

"It can't hurt. Just, let me take over here. You take one of his cars and I'll make sure he stays dead."

"I want to do it."

I nodded in understanding, "then help me get his body to a burnable location.

"Easy, he has an incinerator out back."

I shuddered to wonder why he would have an incinerator out back, but I didn't have to guess. My phone rang then, the vibrations coming from the other room, and I remembered that I had dropped it when Elijah grabbed me earlier. I followed the sound and found my phone on the ground near where Hunter had been hung. It was covered in his blood, so I wiped it off on my pants before putting it up to my ear.

"Amity," I sighed with relief.

"Thank goodness you're okay! It's been ten minutes, you didn't call!"

"I'm sorry, I honestly forgot all about my phone. I had to fish it out of the basement here."

"Well, you're okay right? What's going on?"

"So, Jaden, my new friend here, is helping me out. We're gunna make sure this is finished for good and then I'm coming straight to the hospital. How are you guys holding up?"

"Well, I'm driving as fast as I can but it's gunna be a bit before I get there. Hunter's woken up again, but he's not doing good."

I exhaled and put my hand on my forehead, "oh no. It's okay, you'll get him there, I know it, he'll be okay."

"He's lost so much blood."

"I know, he'll probably need a transfusion but if he's awake that probably a good sign. Just keep doing what you're doing, you got this babe."

"So do you, call me again in 5, okay?"

I agreed and hung up, then went back to Jaden, who was strapping Elijah down to the table.

"What's that for? I asked.

"It's like a gurney, like the ones they use in morgues."

"Understood, now how do we get him out of here?"

"There's a back door, follow me."

I let Jaden lead me back through the basement to an emergency exit on the other side. We had to go up a flight of stairs, carrying Elijah with us as we did. At the top we were greeted by the freezing wind and a snowdrift 3 feet high.

"How are we supposed to get him through this?" I

shouted through the wind.

"Honestly I don't know, other than shoveling."

"That'll take forever!"

"It's just a few feet, it won't take that long. "

"Rather just throw him over and hope for the best."

"I mean... we could."

"It's pretty disrespectful, but in my opinion, he doesn't deserve our respect."

"You're not wrong. Let's give it a try."

We took Elijah off the table and threw him onto the snow mound. His body rolled down, blood soaking the snow beneath him.

"Maybe this was a bad idea," I wondered.

Jaden jumped over the tall part of the drift and shuffled through the snow, then offered a hand to help me do the same. Together we carried the body out to the incinerator, a huge stone building in the backyard.

"Now what?"

"I've seen him use this a thousand times; he uses it so often that the machine is never turned off. All we have to do is throw him in and push a few buttons."

"Ironic that his life would end the same way as his victims. You say you've seen him use it a lot? Those times were for his victims?"

He nodded, "he preferred this method because it destroys the evidence."

Without another word we gathered up Elijah and tossed him into the giant oven. Jaden pushed some buttons and in seconds the small room was completely ingulfed in flames.

"It looks fast, but it will take a while to fully cremate him. We should head back inside in the meantime."

I agreed but gave the incinerator one last look before walking away. There were so many thoughts floating around my head that it was difficult to organize them. So much had happened in the last couple hours. Hunter had been attacked, the sun had gone down, I was nearly forced to drink Hunters blood and then nearly killed, Amity committed her first murder, and I committed my first cover-up. It was hard information to swallow. After calling and checking up with Amity, Jaden and I agreed to stay at the house until the process was done, to make sure there was absolutely no way Elijah could come back. We retired to the living room, and each took a couch. The silence was quite awkward, so I tried to make small talk.

"So how long have you been here? Uh... in this house I mean."

"You mean how long have I been a slave? Few months. In that time, I learned a lot about Elijah, and yet nothing at the same time. He never shared anything with me or told me anything about his background. Not that that's surprising by any means. However, I did learn a lot about him through observation and sneaking around during the day. He's at least 300 years old, probably older, he drinks blood a few times a day, killing at least three people a week if not more. In the time I've been here he's killed somewhere around 4 dozen people. He's a cruel, soulless man that only cares about his next meal and the pleasure he gets from torturing that meal before he eats them."

"Why did he choose you to be his slave? Why not others?"

"There were others. There was one at the time of my kidnapping. Elijah killed him because he was too weak to carry a victim's body out of the room. Then there were four more over the course of those three months. All murdered for different reasons, one of them for trying to escape."

"All that time though, you didn't try to run away during daylight hours?"

"After what had happened with one of the other slaves I couldn't risk it. I knew he would come for me. That he would find me. As hard as it is to live without my wife, I'm just not ready to die yet."

"Hey, you do not have to justify saving your own life. You did what you had to do, just like Amity and I did what we had to do."

"Amity, that was the girl that was with you? Do you guys do that often?"

I shook my head, "no, that was the first time Amity had ever killed a vampire. I've only done it twice in total. The man we were trying to save is Hunter, he's been teaching us how to kill vampires because we want to find the man that turned us and make sure he can never do the same to anyone else."

"Was he like Elijah?"

"Tony... wasn't really like him per-say. Now that I've witnessed this evil masochist known as Elijah, I'd say Tony could've been much worse. He stalked me, seduced me, killed me, and then convinced me that I'd be better off with him. So, I abandoned my parents and went with him. Come to find out that that was all just a manipulation tactic. He did have a basement, but it was finished and mostly clean and comfortable. His victims were just handcuffed to a bed rather than... all this, but he still killed so many people and then Amity and I were just his guinea pigs. When I found her locked up in the basement, we found a way to escape and ran away to Colorado, and here we are."

"I'm so sorry," he sighed.

"It's okay, I guess. I got to meet my girlfriend because of it. Now she and I get to spend forever together."

"Amity?"

I nodded.

"Thats sweet, I'm glad you have each other."

"Thank you; and again, I'm so sorry about your wife. I really wish I would've found this guy sooner so I could've helped. Who knows how many people he's killed in the 300 years he's been around."

"Way too many to count unfortunately, but thank you, I appreciate it. Now I just have to figure out where I'm going to go... or what I'm going to do."

"You've lived through a very traumatic event. Maybe there's some way you could benefit from that. A TED Talk, or a book maybe? You could be an inspirational speaker or go back to school to be a psychologist, or maybe you could just start fresh somewhere you've never been before, find a hobby and excel in that."

"Yeah maybe, what place is most likely to not have any vampires?"

"I'm sorry, I wish I knew. If I've learned anything from running away to Colorado it's that vampires are everywhere. Also, that they all seem to be rich for some reason, oh and apparently, they all love raves."

Jaden smirked, it was the first time I had seen even half a smile on his face, and I was glad that I was able to give him even just a fraction of a second of happiness. I felt so bad for the man before me, he had been through so much, and seen so many people perish over the last few months. I don't know how anyone could come back from something like that.

"Well, it's been an hour, do you think it's done?"

"More than likely, let's go take a look."

Jaden and I headed back out into the cold to check on the incinerator and sure enough, there was nothing left of Elijah but bones and ashes. Not one bit of me felt sorry for him either. I wanted to feel bad about ending his life... but I just couldn't. He had hurt so many people. The four of us were lucky to get out of there alive.

"I guess it's done then," I stated.

"Good riddance."

We headed to the garage to scope out the car situation, and just like I assumed, there was more than one car. Jaden and I searched for the keys, and each took one. He took a rather expensive looking black Lambo, saying if he was gunna get something out of this terrible event that it had 'better been good' and left it at that. I took the keys to the slightly less luxurious but way more efficient yellow Hummer. It was more fun to drive but also drove way better in all the snow. I was honestly worried for Jaden in that poor little sports car.

With the new wheels it didn't take long to get to the hospital, and when I found Amity, we embraced tightly and spun in circles.

"I'm so glad you're okay!" She cheered.

"I am thanks to you and Jaden."

"Jaden was that human, right? What happened?"

Taking a seat in the waiting area of the hospital, I told Amity everything that had happened in the last hour and a half, even the little details. She felt horrible over Jaden's loss, and I wasn't sure how to respond.

"What happened in the past can't be changed, but at least the people that were around are okay now and Elijah will never hurt or kill or kidnap anyone ever again."

"True."

"How is he doing by the way?"

"I've been waiting this whole time for someone to tell me. Oh, there's his doctor now."

A woman in a blood-stained lab coat approached us and asked if we were Hunter's emergency contacts. We told her who we were and why we were here with Amity taking the lead on the story of what happened.

"Can you tell us if he's going to be okay?" Amity asked.

"Well, his injuries were severe, and he lost a lot of blood, but he took the transfusion well and there's a good chance he'll pull through. As soon as he's stable and in recovery I'll let you know, and you can go see him."

We nodded and thanked the doctor, then sat back down in the waiting room chairs.

"He's going to be okay," I grinned, "all thanks to you!"

CHAPTER 22

Recovery

Hunter woke up a few hours later and we ran into his hospital room to see him. We approached his bedside and Amity took his hand in hers.

"I'm so glad you're going to be okay," she smiled.

"Thank you, both, for saving me."

"No big," I shushed, waving my hand.

"How do you feel?"

"Been better," he joked.

"I'm so sorry about what happened."

"It's my own fault, I shouldn't have gone alone, and I shouldn't have underestimated him."

"He was tough for sure," I agreed.

"Is it over?" he asked, choosing his words carefully.

"It is. Amity was very brave," I told him. I looked at my girlfriend and rested my hand on her back. She smiled at me with a sad look in her eyes and I understood better than anyone the feelings that she must have been going through.

"He's gone now," she added.

"Good. I'm proud of you guys. I also underestimated you two too, and for that, I'm so sorry."

"No need to apologize, you just get well rested and heal up quickly, okay?"

"Yes, we still have plenty to do, and lots more training."

"More training? Are we not done with that yet? I think we're both fully fledged... hunters... now."

"Yeah, I suppose you're right. No more training then, but we still need to practice and keep up with our skills. There's always room for improvement."

"Of course you would say that, but you're right. This fight was a close one, I think we all have room to grow stronger."

"I agree," I added, "who knows what the next one will be like. And I don't know about you but I'm ready. I want to make sure that the vampire world realizes that if they're anything like Elijah... I'm coming for them."

Amity looked up to me and rested her hand on mine, "we're coming for them."

I smiled at her and rubbed her back with my other hand. We spoke with Hunter for a while longer then left to let him get some rest. He was in the hospital for a few days, but it took a few weeks for him to finally feel good enough to get back to normal. It was interesting to compare how quickly a human healed compared to how quickly I healed. Of course, I only had one deep bite mark and a few bruises while hunter had wounds all over his body, but my bite mark was gone in a day, and even the scar was healed the day after that.

By the beginning of February, we were back to a normal schedule and for the most part back to normal emotionally speaking as well. Amity was a tough cookie. She appeared sad for a bit, but unless she was hiding it well, she was coping with the whole situation just fine. She got back to her bubbly self in no time, and I couldn't have been prouder of her or admired her more. She was stronger than I gave her credit for. The moment that I was in danger she had stepped up to the plate while I had just frozen in my panic. Truthfully, my biggest fear from that whole situation was that Elijah was going to hurt my Amity. I felt bad for that, because that meant that Hunter, even in his injured state, was still not my number one priority. Honestly though, I couldn't help it. I cared more about Amity than I cared about anyone else, and I was prepared to die for her if needed.

My phone buzzed then, and I pulled it out of my pocket. Sasha was calling me and when I answered, she was excited to speak with me.

"Hey girl! I know it's been a bit, but Peaceful Vampires is having a fundraiser next month and we were wondering if you and Amity would like to help."

Amity could hear the other end of the conversation and nodded with excitement.

"We'd love to!"

"Great, can you meet us at the church tonight for some collaborations?"

"We'd normally have a thing with our friend, but I'm sure we can cancel!"

"Well, if you can we'd love to have you, we're meeting at midnight like usual."

"Great, see you then!"

I hung up and texted Hunter, letting him know that we wouldn't be able to make it to practice because something came up, and he was fine with it and just said that he would take an easy day at the gym instead. Since the Elijah incident, Hunter had been a lot more trusting, kind, and understanding. It was strange and unusual to see him not so uptight all the time, but I guess that must come with the near-death experience. Said experience was quite traumatizing for all of us, but for him most of all.

While he was healing, he was quite reserved about going back to hunting. I think he felt like there wasn't a point to killing the unkillable, but he quickly realized that that wasn't the case. The three of us made a good team, and if we stayed a team, there was no vampire that we couldn't defeat.

Of course, I had my own reservations as I had changed from a human who only wanted the best for the world and always thought there had to be another way when it came to a violent character. Growing up, I had never believed in capital punishment. Things change though, and in less than a year I had now become someone who kills... well, not *people*... but something. That was the only way I could justify the whole situation.

The Peaceful Vampires didn't agree with killing other vampires because they believed it was up to the others to make the choice of being good. However, from what I've learned and witnessed, some vampires just weren't worth trying to save. Some of them would never learn, would never grow, and would never choose to be good. They would starve to death before they let go of their pride. Of course, I say some because we have proof that there are good vampires out there. I try my best to be one of them, but at this point if I must kill one vampire to save hundreds of human lives, I'm going to do it.

I love all of earth's inhabitants, and I want to cause the least amount of harm possible. Some may say, well it's just in their nature to eat people, or that they need to kill some humans to survive, so it's okay; but the truth is, that's just not the case. Every vampire has the capacity for compassion, and every vampire has the ability to get food from willing volunteers or donors, or at least to just take what they need and not let the human die. There was no excuse.

Sure, I was conflicted about it at first, but after doing the math, I could be saving so many more lives by not letting people like Tony or Elijah continue to do what they do-or did.

That said though, I still wanted to do what I could to help the Peaceful Vampires spread the word of love and kindness. Of course, they were also my food resource, so if I wanted to continue eating the way I did, I would need to continue helping them. So off we went to meet with the gang. Amity and I arrived fashionably on time at the creepy abandoned church where the Peaceful Vampires met up. They welcomed us in with open arms and we all sat together in fold-up chairs where an altar used to lie.

"Let's begin," announced the leader of the group, Collin. "First order of business is to welcome our newcomer, if you don't mind introducing yourself and telling us a little bit about you?" Collin pointed to the one member that I hadn't recognized, and they spoke up.

"Hi everyone, my name is Oliver, nickname Oli, either is fine. I was born in 1857 and turned when I was 32. When I first turned, I was concerned for the people that I was hurting, but after a while and with some truly bad advice from the person who turned me, I became a cold, bloodsucking creature that killed people. In the last decade or so I started to kind of wake up and realize that what I was doing was wrong. I moved into my own place and started making better decisions, and just recently I met Sasha, and here I am."

This was interesting to me especially since I had just been talking with Amity about how so many vampires were a lost cause. Then here right in front of us was one that was about 160 years old that recently decided to choose good. Maybe I had just been proven wrong.

"Well, let me just say that we are all happy to have you here and proud that you have made the effort to better yourself." Collin stated.

Oliver nodded with a smile and the meeting continued.

"So, with our expansion of the group, Oli, and the girls a few months ago, we feel we also need to expand our doner numbers too. Hince the fundraiser. So, what we'd like to do is get some venders together, and a couple guest speakers, and get people excited about giving blood!"

"We'd like to find one more doctor or nurse and open a second blood truck so we can do one event in two locations so we can get more volunteers. Colorado is huge and the cities are densely populated, so we'll do one in Denver and one in Colorado Springs," M added. As the only Doctor in the group, M was the busiest member, and did most of the work. I admired her for being so amazing and helpful to everyone.

"How will you find another doctor that's like us though?" Amity asked.

"It may not be easy, but I think I stand the best chance as the person to figure that out. I may spend some time at other hospitals and see what information

I can gather and just maybe I can find one." M nodded and stood from her chair. The remainder of the group did the same, knowing we were nearing the end of our meeting.

"Ah, actually, it may be easier than you think," Sasha announced with a point of her finger.

M gave her a questioning look and Oli raised his hand, "one of the reasons Sasha asked me to join the group was because I briefly told her about my background. Before I had turned, I was actually a couple years out of medical school and was in residency in my local hospital. After turning I had to quit because the blood was too much to handle, but now that it's been so long, I think I may have the skills to get back into it. If all you need is someone to help with the donations, I'm your person."

"That would be amazing, thank you so much Oli, and welcome to the team!"

"We'll be able to make twice as many blood bags now!" Will Exclaimed.

The meeting ended and we gathered our things to leave. Oli approached Amity and I and shook our hands.

"It's great to meet the two of you," he smiled, "Sasha has told me a lot."

"All good things I hope," I responded.

"Of course! I just wanted to say that you two are a bit of an inspiration for me, she told me about how you escaped your abuser and are striving for a better life now."

"Goal achieved so far!" Amity grinned.

"That's great, I'm so glad! Maybe we could get together sometime and kind of help each other through this transition."

"Sounds like a plan, would tomorrow night work for you?"

"Sure, we could meet at the bar downtown If you're up for that?"

Amity and I glanced at each other and nodded, "sure why not?"

So, the next night Amity and I ended up at a neat bar in the city. The theme of the bar was retro, so it had a lot of arcade games and 80's music playing. It didn't seem like the kind of place that people danced at, more solely for drinks and games. Surprisingly, we weren't carded at the door, which I worried about since neither of us were legally 21 yet. We noticed Oli at the end of the bar and went over to join him.

"Hey guys! Thanks for joining me!" He grinned.

"Of course!"

"Yeah! This place looks awesome I can't wait to play some pinball!" Amity cheered.

"Let me get you guys some drinks, so we look human," Oli offered.

"Oh, that's okay, you don't have to do that. I'm sure there's plenty of people here not drinking." We looked around and everyone either had a drink in hand or had it sitting next to them while they gamed.

"I'll get us some drinks," he repeated.

"Okay, well thank you!"

The bartender glided over to us as if on cue and asked for our orders.

"I'll get a Berry Noir if you have it."

"And I'll take a Bud Light please," Amity smiled.

The bartender nodded and pulled out two cans from the fridge behind him.

"So, Oli, tell us about yourself," I suggested.

"Hmm, well, I've traveled a lot. Between being alive and the last 2 years, I've gone to 7 different countries, each more amazing than the last; but that was with the man that killed me, so parts of it wasn't great."

"Maybe this is a loaded question," Amity started, "but what motivated you to be better?"

"Honestly, after decades and decades of being his slave, I just realized I had had enough, and I left. I came back to the states and found my own place, and started making my own decisions and I realized I liked being my own person, and I liked being nice. It just feels good to help people and give back, you know?"

"Absolutely."

"What about you guys?"

I shared my story about life before being a vampire, and then Amity did the same, and Oliver seemed intrigued by all of it. He listened closely without interrupting, and asked his questions only when we were done.

"So even when you were alive, you never ate meat?"

I shook my head, "nope."

"And you did these… protests? Tell me about those."

"Well, there's a couple different kinds, there's silent protests, which are the ones I like to participate in the most, then there's rallies and a lot of signage, and there's ones where we go to the slaughterhouses or factories and try to give care to the animals in their final moments or document their mistreatment to spread awareness. I suppose I wasn't as involved in the lifestyle as I could have been, but I was a bit more focused on my education. Some people dedicate their entire lives to exposing the truth behind the industry."

"I've never been to a protest in my life, of any kind."

"I went to the Black Lives Matter protest a couple years back, it got intense and a bit scary. There's a lot of risk involved; but I feel like when you are adamant about doing the right thing, don't you want people to be aware? Change won't happen unless we make it happen," Amity added.

"Exactly. I haven't gone to one since before becoming a vampire because I feel like what's the point? I'm not technically vegan anymore so isn't it a bit hypocritical of me to partake in activities like that?" I sighed.

"I mean, maybe a bit," Oli noted, "but it's not like you're doing it on purpose. If you really want to do the least harm in the world, I think you're doing that already every day. You drink blood or you die. That's the reality you're living in now... but you're making sure that no one else must die for you or even suffer for you to do that. So, I think that's awesome, and I aspire to be like you. We should all three do one of these protests."

"You think?"

"I mean, there's nothing stopping us," Amity assured.

"It would pull away from our training."

"Not too much, we can make time."

"Most protests are during the day."

"Then we'll convince the community to do it at night."

I pulled up the local vegan group page on social media and requested to follow. Amity did the same and we waited for the approval. It could be minutes, or it could be days, so we resumed our conversation.

"You know, if the locals don't have anything planned right away, I think I know a place we could protest." Oliver stated.

"What's that?" I asked.

"I like going for nightly strolls, and there's this local 24-hour coffee shop downtown that I'm a regular at, so I'll go get a coffee and then walk around for a bit, people watching and site seeing. I don't drink the coffee of course, but I love the smell and the warmth from the cup. Anyways, there's this massive butcher shop that I pass by every day, and every day that I pass it I get more and more curious about it. Something has always just seemed off about it. The most curious thing that I noticed was that it has some odd hours. Well, at least, odd to a human, because it's open late at night."

"That's strange."

"Yeah, that is strange. It sounds like it could be a good place to protest," Amity figured.

It was at that point that we both got notifications on our phones that our request to join the local vegan group had been approved, so I typed out a post seeing if anyone would want to start a protest and sent it.

We hung out with Oliver for a bit longer at the bar then went around playing the arcade games. My favorites were most of the classics, Pac-Man, Dig Dug, Galaga, and Pinball. We also played against each other in rounds of Skee ball and Mario Kart. I won a couple rounds of Skee ball, and Amity and Oli both won a round of Mario Kart. It was a super fun night and by the end of it we were all exhausted both physically and socially.

Over the next week the three of us plus some vegans from the group organized a protest to be held outside of the butcher shop with signs and flyers. I was both excited and nervous to be getting back into activism, but mostly nervous. It was a bit scary to be telling people not to eat meat when I drank blood for nourishment. Not like any of them would find out, but I still just felt like a hypocrite.

Hunter didn't understand. Amity and I tried to explain to him why we wanted to do this, but it didn't make sense to him. He wasn't vegan or even vegetarian, he cared about the lives of humans, but in his eyes, non-humans were different. However, that didn't mean he didn't support us in our own endeavors. He told us to go have fun and that we would see him the next day for practice.

We took our signs and met up a block away from the location in a parking lot. I greeted the people I had only ever spoken to online and introduced myself. They all seemed like very nice people, and I was excited to work with them.

A few of us sat on the curb while a few others stood behind us and we held our signs up without speaking. It was cold and dark out but that didn't seem to stop anyone from wanting to be there. A few people passed us without a word, others went inside the shop with menacing glares, and a couple people stopped to say hello and ask what we were all about, but after a while, an employee came out of the shop and told us to leave.

"You can't tell us to leave, we're on public property," one member of the group shouted.

The man nearly growled, "if you don't leave right

now, I'm calling the cops!"

The group tried to reason with him, legally we were doing nothing wrong, but from a business standpoint we understood why he didn't want us there. Oliver was right, something about the man, and his shop, just seemed off. I scrutinized the man, taking in all his features. He was short with all-black clothing and a baseball cap. He had buzzed hair and dark, malicious looking eyes. The veins in his muscular arms and hands were bright blue and highly visible, as if he was straining them with tension. I squinted at him, something in my guts told me he was a vampire. Why would a vampire sell meat to humans? Was it solely about the money?

"Ah guys," I whispered to Amity and Oli, "I think we have a code V."

The two of them looked up at him from the curb and gaped.

"I think you're right," Oli whispered back.

"What does that mean?" Amity asked.

"It means either he's a broke, newbie vampire or something fishy is going on here."

"I mean, I'm sure it's nothing weird. Well, nothing weirder than a human selling the dead flesh of poor little pigs and cows."

The man huffed and went back inside the shop and our group decided it was probably best to move on. We had at least talked a few people out of going in there, so it was at least mildly successful, so we decided to call it a night.

The group said our goodbyes in the parking lot and made promises to keep in touch for future opportunities then went our separate ways. Oli left too, walking in the other direction to go get his nightly coffee.

"I think we need to go back," I told Amity.

"Why?" She asked.

"Because I need to know why my Spidey-senses are tingling."

"Oh, your Spidey-senses are tingling huh? Well okay let's do some sleuthing!"

I laughed and gave her a kiss on the cheek, "I love how unquestioningly supportive you are."

"I believe in you and your vampire superpowers," she laughed back.

We walked back to the shop then and entered the building like any customer would. The sight of all the slabs of meat sickened me and I had to hold back a gag. The man that was outside yelling at us earlier was walking back to the back, carefully closing a door behind him, and a woman and another man stood at the counter.

"Hi there! What can we get for ya?" the woman asked politely.

"Hi, um... we're new around here and were walking around the city, doing some sight-seeing, and we noticed your shop open," Amity lied.

"That's right, we are the only late-night butcher shop in all of Colorado! You guys just moved to town?"

"Uh, yeah," I nodded.

"Congratulations, are you liking it so far?"

As Amity answered her mundane questions, I took the opportunity to look around the shop and take in anything that seemed suspicious. One thing I instantly noticed was that it wasn't just steak and ribs, it was intestines, brains, and all kinds of other body parts. I had never wanted to vomit more in my life. The woman behind the counter seemed innocent and friendly, just a woman selling a product; but the man next to her seemed cold and rude. Unlike the other man, this man was tall with grey eyes and blonde hair, but like the other man, he had a buzz cut and muscular features. They were all wearing the same all-black uniform and baseball cap, but this man's apron was covered in what I assumed was dried "food".

They both gave me the same vibe as the man from the sidewalk. Were they all vampires?

"You guys have a lot of variety," I mentioned.

"We try to be very eco-friendly and not waste any part of the animal," the woman smiled.

I forced a smile in return and continued to look around. The walls were painted red, and the furniture and counters were black, almost like they were trying to hide something. Stains perhaps. To the far right of the glass display there was a sign that read 'ask us about our rare meats'. I wasn't sure I wanted to know, but I figured it needed to.

"What is your 'rare meats'?"

"Oh, you'll love it! It's a very rare, delicious type of meat that you can only get from overseas. It might not technically be legal, but I promise it is the best food investment you'll ever make."

The man jabbed the woman in her side with his elbow, she winced briefly but smiled through.

"Don't tell them it's illegal, remember?" he grunted.

"Oh right, sorry."

"It tastes just like beef, but way better. Our more… lavish… clientele really enjoy it," he told us.

We nodded and asked a few more questions to make sure we were in the clear of them being suspicious of us, and then we booked it out of there.

The moment we exited the shop I had to find a trashcan because I couldn't hold back the gag anymore. Amity pulled my hair away from my face, massaged my back, and soothed me with her calming voice.

"How are you not throwing up too?" I asked her.

"My parents exposed me to a lot of disgusting meats, I guess I'm used to it."

"Ug, that was awful." I corrected my posture and took a deep breath, "they admitted to doing illegal things, so even if they aren't vampires, they're still criminals."

"I know... I think we need to tell Hunter about this one though, he can use his skills to figure out if they really are vampires and if so, what we should do about it."

I nodded. She was right, Hunter would know what to do.

CHAPTER 23

The Butcher Shop

Once we awoke the next night, the first thing we did was call Hunter for an emergency meeting, which just meant that we were meeting up at his place an hour earlier than we would have anyways. Instead of immediately heading for the home-gym like we normally would at Hunter's house, this time he led us to the kitchen and got himself an energy drink out of the fridge. He tried to offer a drink to us, remembered why he shouldn't, then told us to have a seat at the dining table.

"So, what's wrong?" he asked, sipping his drink.

"We have a possible new mission," Amity told him.

"Do tell."

We told him everything about our previous night at the butcher shop and he listened intently. He agreed that something seemed strange; and mentioned that if our gut was telling us they were vampires, they probably were.

"We should get more information before we just bust in on them, so let's do our research."

We followed Hunter to a front room where he had an office space. He hopped on the computer and did some digging on the shop and the people who own it.

Amity and I did the same on our phones. As it turns out, the couple that spoke to us were the owners of the shop. It was a small local business and they only had about 3 other employees that we knew of.

"If it is such a small business, why is the building so big?" I wondered.

"Maybe there's a different business on the other side?" Amity suggested.

"I never saw any signs or doors or anything on the other side."

"Maybe they like live back there or something."

"Or maybe that's where the meat comes from," Hunter added.

"Don't they get it shipped in from a farm or... slaughterhouse? I mean I feel like it would be difficult to get some cows into that building when it's in the city."

"True, maybe they do, or maybe they don't, I think we need to find out."

"You mean like go there?"

"Yeah, we need to sneak in."

"Why are we always sneaking into places? I feel like such a criminal," Amity half-joked.

"We're only criminals if they're innocent and it really is just a butcher shop."

"That's not how the law works," I scoffed.

"I mean what else would it be?" Amity asked.

"A front for something. The question is, what?"

"Could be a drug den?"

"Yeah, could be. Or it could be something a lot worse."

I wasn't sure I wanted to know, but I think I needed to. Hunter threw his energy drink in a nearby trashcan and left the room, assuming we would just follow behind. We did and he led us to his car, where we got in and drove off, heading downtown.

It took a while to get there, but once we did, I was more nervous than ever. We parked in the same lot as the night before and walked the rest of the way. This time though, we walked down the next street over and back around so we could approach the building from the back. It was a large, stone-brick building with graffiti art on the side of a cow cooking on a grill (how ironic) and a few parking spots reserved for employees in the back. A large dumpster was hidden behind a fence close to the back door, where I'm assuming the employees entered. The closer we got, the more rancid the smell of it became. It was horrifying. I didn't dare look. I could imagine what was in there.

Amity covered her nose with her shirt and Hunter rolled his eyes at her. "I've smelled worse," he claimed.

"You mean your BO?" Amity teased. We all knew what a stickler Hunter was about making sure he always smelled good. He nudged her and tugged her closer to him as someone exited the building. It was the same short employee from the day before. He hopped into one of the vehicles and drove off, leaving only 2 cars left in the lot.

"Two cars. That means, there's probably three people in there," Hunter examined, "if the owners are married, they most likely drove here together, and then one other employee."

We were hidden on the side of the building with graffiti, peeking our heads around the corner. Once the coast was clear, we stalked back to the door. Lucky for us the door had one of those pull handles that don't shut well, and it did not shut all the way when the employee left. Hunter gently inched the door open and peered inside. The coast must've been clear because he ushered us inside and shut the door quietly behind him.

Suddenly we found ourselves in a dark broom closet. There was a shelving filled with aprons, shirts, and boxes of random tools to our right, and mops and brooms to our left. In front of us was yet another door; this one was wide open, revealing a kitchen on the other side.

I was the first to step through the doorway, and at first it seemed like a normal, restaurant kitchen, except there was something off. Most of it was very clean, except for two areas: the dish-washing station, and the meat slicing area.

We could hear the owners talking with customers in the front room, so we figured we were momentarily safe, but Hunter chose to stand near the door to the front to keep watch. Part of me wished I would've been the one to just keep watch, as what I saw in the next moment absolutely disgusted me. I looked back at the dish-washing station, and it was loaded with dishes and trays stacked tall. They were coated in a dark, slimy liquid that oozed down into a full sink. The water in the sink was black with what I assumed was the blood and guts from the meats.

"Ew," Amity gagged upon seeing the mess.

"Agreed," I whispered, my throat feeling tight.

We kept wandering around and found our way over to the grinders and slicers, of which there were many. A couple of them were clean, but the rest of them were covered in slabs of raw meat, the "juice" spilling all over the table and floor below.

"Does this smell weird to you?" Amity asked.

As much as I hated the thought of not only seeing the meat, but also smelling it (I had been holding my breath as much as I could), I inhaled deeply to smell what she smelled. She was right, it didn't quite smell the way I thought it should. I wasn't too familiar with the scent of raw meat, since I had never eaten it before, but I had been around non-vegan friends and their dinners before, and this didn't smell like that. I couldn't quite put my finger on what the difference was.

"Let's move on," I pleaded.

On a random wall in the middle was mostly shelving, including many chef knives. Hanging on the wall above that were butcher knives and huge, long knives that could only be described as swords.

"Why would they have a katanas, machetes, and a… garden scythe?"

"Uhh…" Amity had no answer.

There was a door in one corner with a window, the manager's office, and another door in the other corner. The room to that door seemed much larger, and I could tell by the type of door that this was their freezer. I approached the door cautiously, terrified of what I was about to find, when Hunter gave the signal.

He ran over to us as quickly as he could, but we needed to hide, or we were about to be found. I did the first thing I could think of and pushed us all into the freezer, keeping the door cracked and hoping they wouldn't be coming our way. The freezer was completely pitch black other than one little red light. A human would have a hard time seeing much of anything, but as we turned around to look at our surroundings, we were surprised by something much worse than what I could've ever imagined.

The freezer was the largest freezer I had ever stepped into. Not that I had been in many, but regardless, it was huge. There was shelving all the way around, but I glossed over what was on the shelving because what really caught my attention was what was in the middle of the room. Hanging from the ceiling on one side was what many people probably would expect from a butcher shop, the remains of multiple cows. On the other side... the same remains, but they were not cows, they were humans.

Hunter took one look and couldn't hold back the puke. His bile spewed all over the floor, mixing in with blood and puss and fat, and escaping down a drain in the middle. A human torso hung from its back muscle towards the center of the room, followed by an even more gruesome, full-bodied corpse, only thing missing was the skin.

I had to shut my eyes then. Amity did everything she could to hold in her shriek so the owners wouldn't hear us, turning into my shoulder to hide herself.

"Oh my god," I cried.

Hunter was gasping for air for several minutes before he finally tapped us. We looked up at him and he was staring beyond the bodies.

"It gets worse," he shuddered. Tears silently fell from his lashes, something I had never seen of him before, he wasn't the type to cry for anything. His 'masculinity' would never allow that. Amity clung onto me as we followed his gaze. The back wall had another door, and a long window overlooking what appeared to be none other than a slaughterhouse. The worst part, we noticed as we walked closer to it, was that it wasn't just any slaughterhouse. It was *all* human.

"Oh my god," I repeated.

My throat was searing with pain, and I couldn't even tell if it was just from the horrifying sight mixed with anxiety, or from the bloodlust that I was fighting off.

I hardly noticed the cold as we moved through the room, as much as I wanted to just burn the place down without even looking anymore, a part of me said I had to finish what I started. I had to go into that slaughterhouse. So, I shuffled forward, pulling Amity beside me and Hunter slowly tracing behind. The door was locked with a keypad, but I could tell by the fingerprints what the four numbers were. I told Hunter to keep watch as I tried to figure out the right combination and in three tries, I got it right. Amity and I stepped inside and were immediately hit with the smell of rotting flesh and fresh blood. It was cold in there too, but not quite as cold as the last room.

Human corpses were strung up in a long que, awaiting their next destination, and behind that were huge machines and a large conveyor belt. I wasn't sure what they did, but I could imagine it was nothing good. To the right of the machines was a trough, coated in a dried, dark red substance I could only assume was blood. In front of that was another wall covered in knives and swords and weapons of various kinds.

The corpses were all naked, and all beaten and bruised. The body of a young woman lay on the conveyor belt, her long hair draped over her body and hanging off the edge. She looked so alive that I ran over to her, hoping there was a chance to save her, but her throat had been slit and her body had been drained of its blood, and it was too late.

"What do we do?" I whispered to Amity.

Before she could respond we heard a shout and Hunter rushed in, yanking us by the arms and hiding us behind some machinery.

A young boy was wailing and begging for his life, and I could hear his feet stomping the floor as if he was being dragged by someone. The owners were arguing, accusing each other of leaving the freezer door open, completely unbothered by the screams of their victim. I could hear him being tossed to the ground and I peered around the corner of the machine cautiously.

"No, please, please don't kill me! My dad has money, okay? You can demand a ransom, he'll pay it! Anything you want, just please don't kill me," the boy cried. He had sandy-red hair, lots of freckles, and a bright red face covered in tears. He couldn't have been more than 16. The male owner handcuffed him to a table near the trough then turned back to the woman. He barked at her that she was a horrible wife that couldn't do anything right, and she roared back that she swore she never left the door open. Then she turned to the boy who was still begging for his life and told him to 'shut the hell up' and slapped him in the face. He cried harder but stopped speaking.

I nearly jumped out of my crouched position, but Hunter held me back. He noticed that the couple turned around and started walking back through the freezer.

We waited for a moment and then jumped into action. We ran over to the boy and asked him if he was okay while Hunter pulled out a pick and began trying to get him out of the cuffs.

"Were you attacked too?" He asked.

I shook my head, "not exactly, but we *are* going to

get you out of here, I promise."

He looked around and saw all the dead bodies and began to have a panic attack. His breathing became labored and his whole-body shook. Amity held his head in her hands and tried to hold him still. At first it scared him more, but as she shushed him, he began to calm down.

"Close your eyes," she told him, "everything's going to be okay, just don't look, alright? Tell me your name."

"Tyler."

"It's nice to meet you, Tyler. I'm Amity. Now what happened, how did you end up here?"

Tyler took a few deep breaths, still trying to stay calm, "I just… came in to get a job application. They seemed nice at first, said they'd hire me on the spot and took me to the back, but then they shoved me in the freezer and dragged me here from there. What do they want with me?"

"Not money," I scoffed.

He glanced up at the corpses hanging from the ceiling and started crying again. Hunter was able to release him from the cuffs then and we helped him to stand up.

"We need to be quick, and cautious," Hunter stated, "we may not have much time before they come back.

"Are they murders?" Tyler asked.

"Yes, but they're also worse than that." I responded.

"What do you mean?"

Hunter shook his head.

"Sorry Hunter, but I think he's in too deep to keep

it a secret. If we want to get out of here, he may have to help fight our way out."

His eyes grew wide.

"Tyler, those people aren't really people at all. They're vampires."

"For real?"

I nodded.

Hunter grabbed the weapons off the rack and handed one to each of us. A cleaver for Tyler, a machete for Amity, a katana for me, and a small scythe for himself.

"Go for the neck?" Amity asked.

"Go for the neck, be swift, and go deep. The deeper, the better. Either way though, we will still have to go back and carve out the hearts so make your swings count. You get all of that, kiddo?"

Tyler gulped and nodded, sweat beading up on his forehead.

We all got into a single-file line behind Hunter and followed him to the door. Into the freezer we went with sadness in our hearts. We needed to get out of there and regroup, get Tyler home to his family, and figure out what to do about these awful vampires. Was there any hope for rehabilitation? Could we even try? I didn't want to kill them if we didn't have to, but even if we could convince them to get their fix without harming anyone, who's to say the moment we were out of their hair they wouldn't go back to doing what they're doing now?

Before I even had time to finish my thoughts, the door to the freezer opened. We had nowhere to hide. *Shit.*

"What the-" The male owner shouted upon seeing

us. Hearing his bellows, the female owner and two employees followed him into the freezer. We had two choices, we could scatter and try to run, but they were blocking the door and had the advantage, or we could fight. So, we had to fight. It was four against four, but I wasn't sure you could really count Tyler, so I pushed him behind us. He didn't have the experience and skill set that we had acquired for this exact scenario.

For a moment it was a stare-down.

"Wait, I know you two," the woman pointed.

"You came into the shop yesterday," The man added, "what are you doing in here?"

"I don't think we need to answer that," I frowned.

"You know what this means, don't you?" he asked, looking at Tyler and lowering his eyebrows even further.

"No, what does it mean?" Amity wondered.

"It means you can't leave this building alive now. You've seen too much."

"You don't scare us!" Hunter threatened.

"I think you should reconsider."

The man ordered the employees to grab us, and they sure tried, but we fought back hard. We all stood our ground and flexed our muscles; it was an even match, and when the owners saw that their employees were struggling to do what they were told, they jumped in too, and soon it became a brawl.

They had their own knives and stakes, so the brawl became more of a sword fight. I swung my katana every-which way, but the vampires struck back. Our blades clashed together with a metallic *clink,* until the blade on his snapped right off the handle. I made the split-second decision to use the opportunity to go for the kill.

Metaphorically speaking. I really wanted to see if I could knock some sense into these people, so I held him up against me, the blade to his throat.

"You know that won't kill me," he laughed.

"Not this alone, but I will kill you. Unless you agree to some terms."

"Hah, you think you're in charge here? Absolutely not." He knocked the katana out of my hand and spun me around so that he had my wrist pinned to my back. I stomped my foot onto his then kicked back into his groin and he let go to crouch down. Amity was near my knife and was able to kick it up into her hand and toss it to me while holding off her own attacker. Sadly, I didn't wait this time. I took the opportunity to go for the kill this time, and I sliced the katana through the air.

Blood poured from his neck, and he collapsed to the ground. He would be out for a while, but since he was a vampire, it wouldn't truly have killed him. One down… I suppose.

Tyler was trying his best to jump in, but Hunter kept pushing him back, worried he would get hurt. As we circled the vampires, I noticed the doorway was clear. I jumped in front of Amity's attacker and held him off with my sword, then told her to take Tyler out of the building and get him to safety. She agreed and pulled on Tyler, running out the door.

Sighing in relief for not only Tyler's safety, but Amity's too, I regained my focus. Now it was Hunter and I against three.

The owners went after Hunter and the other person came after me. The young-looking man raised his stake in the air, and I raised my katana. My weapon easily overtook his, chopping off the sharp end of the stick. The man looked shocked as I swiftly swung my feet around, knocking him to the ground.

On the other side of the room, Hunter was also knocked to the ground by the owners. He hit his head so hard on the way down that he was out cold.

The male owner grabbed a chef's knife, preparing to stab. There was no way I was about to let them kill one of my best friends, so I did what I had to do. I took my katana, and I sliced through every one of them. With the roar of a vampire's vengeance, I recalled how upset I was the last time Hunter had been hurt, and the last time Amity had been hurt, and the last time I had been hurt, and I took that pain out on the slaughterhouse owners. Before they could even see it coming, before they could even bring their own weapons down upon Hunter, I swung my katana through the air, cutting each of their throats and torsos.

The woman screeched as her husband went down, but quickly they were both bleeding out on the floor. Their blood splattered all over my clothing and soaked my hair. It merged into a puddle on the ground and swam down into the drain. It was almost morbidly ironic that they would die in almost the same way that they killed many of their victims. Just like Elijah.

Four bodies lay on the ground, and many more hung from the ceiling. The deaths in this building would finally end for good. Hunter started to come-to then, and I reached down to help him sit up.

"Are you okay?" I asked.

"That's gunna be a nasty headache," he grunted and looked around, noticing the family of vampires and my blood-stained clothes.

"You did it."

"Don't seem so surprised," I rolled my eyes.

"I mean, one yea, but you killed all three of them... technically all 4 of them... just like that."

"I didn't want to, but they were going to kill you if I hadn't."

"Thank you."

I nodded and helped him to his feet. We went out back then to find Amity comforting Tyler, who was still in weeping from everything he had just experienced. We talked for a bit and made sure that everyone was okay before deciding it was time to go in and finish the job. Hunter stayed with Tyler, deciding what to do about his new secret and how to move on, while Amity and I were going to take care of the bodies.

We went back through the broom closet and into the kitchen, and I could hear a bell ringing from the front room.

"Oh crap, the shop is still open," Amity reminded.

We looked down at my clothes versus Amity's and knew that she would have to go be the one to tell the customer to leave, and to then shut down the shop while I got started.

The bell dinged again, and Amity hollered that she would be right there, and then she took off. I slumped back into the freezer, looking around for my knife so I could carve out the hearts. One, two, three... the fourth body was missing. It was the male owner.

"Damn it," I snarled. He was still alive. Even with a slit through his throat and a slashed ribcage, the vampire still walked.

A sharp pain shot through my chest, and I screamed. I glanced down, my eyes widening in horror at the sight of a knife protruding from my chest. It was the worst pain I had ever felt in my life. Much worse than when Tony snapped my neck. At least that was quick. This was a lingering and stinging pain, and I could feel my head going numb and my vision going dark. I slumped onto the floor thinking that this was it, this is where I would die for good. I wasn't ready, I had just found purpose in this new life. I had just found my soulmate, and my best friend, and a reason to stay alive, and now it was going to end just as quickly. I thought about Amity, about how much I loved and cared for her, and I wondered how much she would miss me. We hadn't known each other for long, but I knew that she was truly something special. She was magic to me, and I couldn't imagine the rest of my life without her.

I could hear her calling my name as I passed out on the cold, wet ground.

CHAPTER 24

Back To Kansas

I awoke to the sound of Amity's voice, soothing and gentle; her soft hand resting on mine. I felt so stiff I could barely move, so I looked around with just my eyes and noticed a makeshift hospital bed, with an IV pumping blood into my arm. Then I noticed Amity's beautiful face red from a flustered sadness. She gasped and I could tell she was relieved to see my eyes open.

"You're going to be okay!" She cheered. She gave me a gentle hug and asked if anything hurt.

"Everything does," I replied, "where are we?"

It didn't look like a hospital, it looked like someone's room, but with fancy medical equipment.

"We're at Oliver's house. M has been taking care of you."

"How long have I been out?"

"About a day."

M came in then with a smile. She sat down in a chair next to me, as Amity was on the other side, and explained to me what happened.

"Amity called me as soon as she could, we rushed you here and did some serious heart surgery. Luckly, he missed the major parts, and we were able to stitch you back up and give you a blood transfusion. Then we noticed this morning that you were starting to heal, and we knew that it had worked."

"You all saved my life, thank you so much," I cried.

M patted my head gently, "of course, now stay still for a while, you're probably gunna need another day or so before you can start walking around. This was a bad injury, and it will take a bit longer to heal than any of your previous wounds."

I nodded in response.

"I'm going to get you some blood to drink, I know you've got the transfusion, but now that you're awake it would be good to fill your tummy up too."

She left and it was just Amity and I again, and I thanked her profusely and told her that I loved her. Then I wondered what happened.

"I heard you scream, and I came running. I found you passed out with a knife in your back and that man was about to do much worse to you, so I finished him off."

"What do you mean?"

"I took that katana to the back of his neck and his head fell completely off his body."

"Holy shit, you did that?"

"Yeah, I did. After that I called Hunter back in and we decided what to do. I called M and she told me to bring you here. So, I did, and then we went back and burned the whole place down. Really took a page out of your book."

I laughed weakly and asked how Hunter was doing.

"He's okay, he would be here, but he hit his head pretty good, so he'll probably be out all week, resting and healing. He's in a real hospital."

"I'm just glad he'll be okay."

"Thanks to you. He told me you saved his life."

"I tried," I shrugged.

"I love you," Amity grinned.

"I love you too," I replied. She leaned in and kissed me on the forehead, then let me get some rest.

The next day I was feeling much better, enough to get out of bed and head back home. I thanked M and Oli for coming to my rescue and for sparing extra blood for me and they replied that they were just glad that I was okay. Amity took me home and for the rest of the evening we relaxed, watched movies, and played board games together.

The following night I received a call from my boss at the bookstore. They asked if Amity was with me, so I said yes and put it on speaker. We were then put on blast for not showing up to work for three days with no-call-no-show and promptly fired. We tried to explain the situation, but they didn't want to hear us out; instead, they hung up on us and wouldn't answer when we tried to call back.

"Well, that's just great," I sighed.

"Now what are we gunna do?"

"How are we going to pay our bills until we can find new jobs? And it's not like there's many night-time friendly jobs out in the mountains."

"I don't know," Amity sighed too, "I'm almost thinking we should move to New York City or Las Vegas or something where there is always something going on at night."

"Moving's not a bad idea. To be honest, after what happened... I'm not sure I want to do this anymore," I stated.

"Do what?" she asked.

"I don't think I want to live like Hunter. I mean, I'm glad I know how to kill a vampire now, but it's just so dangerous and I don't want you getting hurt."

"Don't worry about me, I can handle it."

"I know you can I just… I don't know. I just want to kill Tony and be done with it."

"Well, why not?"

"Why not what?"

"Why don't we go find Tony and make sure he's gone for good?"

"You mean move back home?"

"Maybe. Or we could just go back home for a bit, and then we could move somewhere exotic or fun and just… be vampires."

"Be together."

"Forever."

I smiled from ear to ear, "I love that."

"Then let's do it!"

She hugged me tightly and I squeezed her back. Finally, something positive to look forward to. Not that I didn't love our life here in Colorado, but I didn't love that we were constantly killing other vampires, even if we felt like it was for the right reasons. It totally went against my original beliefs, and I still felt the guilt of that every day. I just wanted to be done with it.

Explaining to Hunter why we wanted to leave was hard. He didn't understand why we would want to stop "helping curb the vampire population" and why we would want to leave the beautiful mountains. We told him that we would really miss him and wanted to stay in touch, and he was devastated. I think he thought of us as best friends, just like we did him, and part of me felt bad about leaving.

"I really enjoyed having partners in crime," he said.

"Hey, maybe you could recruit Tyler," Amity suggested.

"You know, that's not a bad idea."

"Oh no, don't ruin his innocence," I teased.

"Yeah, I think it's too late for that, he's seen way more than any teen should," Hunter added.

"He seemed very anxious... but not incapable, he really tried to be prepared and help us fight, it was us that stopped him from fighting," Amity reminded.

"You know, we kinda talked about it a bit before things got worse at the butcher shop, he said he felt bad that he hadn't helped more, and that he wanted to."

"Did you get his contact information?"

"I did, just to check in on him and make sure he was okay. I also told him if he needed to talk about what happened or to vent, that he could always call me, since this was something he couldn't tell anyone else about."

"Poor kid, that's such a big secret to keep from everyone."

I nodded in agreement, and we gave Hunter goodbye hugs. After that we headed back to the house and started packing our things. I thought it would be best not to tell anyone, especially my mom, that we were coming back, just in case someone would be 'listening'. Plus, I figured it would also be a nice surprise for my mom. She hadn't really heard from me a lot in the last month or two since we had been so busy working, training, going on missions, and volunteering. There wasn't a whole lot to pack, and we got most of it done in one night.

The following night was blood-truck night with the Peaceful Vampires, and we figured it was a good night to get a fresh stash and say our final goodbyes, so once the blood drive was over, we let everyone know the sad news.

"I'm so sorry to see you go," Sasha sighed with a heavy heart, "but I hope your next adventure is amazing."

The others agreed and said similar responses, and then there were hugs all around. We would really miss these guys. I had never met another group of people so utterly amazing. They were respectful, kind, and generous, and I was sad that I may not ever get to see them again.

"Hey, don't worry," Amity told me later, "we're vampires remember? We have hundreds, if not thousands of years, to come back and visit them."

I smiled, "yeah, you're right."

We finished packing, piling up all our belongings into two cars, my mom's that she let us borrow, and our new Hummer (thank you Elijah). Unfortunately, that meant we would not be able to drive back home together, but throughout the trip we kept each other on speakerphone and listened to the radio together so we could keep each other company. We did have more night-time to travel, since it was winter, but the trip would be over 10 hours, so we decided to split it into two nights and get a hotel in Oakley, Kansas.

Oakley is a small town on the west side of Kansas. It has somewhere around 2,000 residents, which is less than just the number of kids that I went to high school with, but it was a cute little town. We stopped at the Annie Oakley Motel and spent some time stretching out our legs before going in. It was about 2 am and there was absolutely no one around.

The night went smoothly and the following night we finished our journey to the suburbs of KC. Assuming that my mother would let us stay with her, we first went straight home to my house. Amity and I held hands up to the front porch and I rang the doorbell. I knew that in the early hours of the morning, a knock would not have woken either of my parents up. The doorbell did. Both of my parents were at the door quickly, peeking through the curtains, probably wondering who the hell was at their door in the middle of the night. When they saw it was me, the door swung open, and we were both pulled in for big hugs.

"It's my baby!" my mom squealed and sobbed, and she refused to let go of me. I laughed and told her it was good to see her too.

She then looked over at Amity and pulled her into a group hug. Amity grinned and said she was happy to see her. Once the tears finally subsided and my mom finally let go of us, she led us over to the couch and demanded we sit down.

"Oh my gosh we have missed you so much," She cried.

"We really have, how are you doing?" my dad asked.

"We're good, a lot has happened, but we're good."

"How long will you be staying? Please say forever," my mom pleaded.

"We're not totally sure yet, but at least a few days."

We took some time to catch up. Things had been going well for my parents, but they missed us (including my brother) terribly. They said they were having bad empty nest syndrome but were overjoyed that we were both off living our best lives. I kept quiet about a lot of the things Amity and I had been through, wanting to keep the little reunion light-hearted, so I mostly just told her all the good stuff, like the friends we had made and the adventures we had had. Intentionally, I left out the parts about killing people and almost dying.

They asked what our next move was, and we said we weren't entirely sure, that we were thinking about moving to Vegas or New York, and they were sad about that. They didn't want us moving that far away because of how much they would miss us.

"We are so excited for you guys! We just want you to be happy," my mom insisted.

"I know, we really appreciate that, but I think we need to go somewhere with more of a nightlife."

"We totally understand," my dad nodded.

We spent a few more hours talking and watching a movie together before the sun rose, and Amity and I were yawning every few seconds.

"You girls must be exhausted; let's all go get some sleep."

We nodded and headed off to my room, which looked exactly the way I left it, and my parents went back to their room. It was a Saturday, so they had all day to sleep in and catch up from what they missed.

My bed was small, but Amity and I squeezed in, cuddling up tightly. Something about cozy-ing up with her made me so elated. Her skin was soft, and her hair smelled sweet, like bubble gum or cotton candy. It brought me a sense of peace when the world was so uncertain. We drifted off easily and woke up with arms and legs hanging off the edge of the bed. I laughed off the stiffness in my neck and went to take a shower.

"Uh, can I come? I don't know if I want to be alone in this house just yet," Amity said nervously.

"You know my parents are awesome, you can totally just make yourself at home," I replied, "but I'm also not going to say no to that, so follow me."

I led my girlfriend to the bathroom, and we undressed and got into the shower. The water was so hot that the room quickly filled up with steam. We kept the room dark for reasons I hope are obvious, and Amity offered to help wash my hair. I nodded and handed her the shampoo. I really enjoyed having scents match, so my shampoo, conditioner, and body wash were all lavender scented. It usually helped me relax and stay calm, but the feeling of Amity gently massaging my scalp and running her fingers down my back brought me more serenity than anything else. I turned around and brought my hand up to Amity's collarbone, feeling her soft skin with the tip of my thumb. She looked into my eyes and blushed. We leaned in for a kiss, her hands around my waist and mine around her neck. Her lips were super soft, and we melted into one another. It was liberating. I think we both felt much better after our relaxing shower.

Since I was home, I raided my own closet and found some clothes I hadn't brought with me to Colorado. Skinny jeans, ballet flats, and a blue top with a sunflower on it was going to be my outfit for the night. Amity found black leggings, matching wedge heels, and a burgundy sweater.

"You look beautiful," I told her.

"Awe, so do you," She blushed.

We applied our makeup together and fixed our hair, then went downstairs to greet my parents, who were having a late dinner.

"You girls look nice," my mom grinned.

"Thanks," I responded, "whatcha having?"

"Ah we just wanted to do something simple, so we made a pizza, I'd offer some but-"

"No worries," I waved.

"So, what will you guys be doing today, or tonight I guess?"

I looked at Amity and shrugged, "I don't know, we might go downtown or something."

"That sounds fun."

I wasn't sure if I should tell her about how we were probably going to go looking for Tony, so I didn't. We conversed for a while before my parents said they were going to bed, and then we took the hummer over to Amity's house. The visit there went very differently. Her parents were mad that we knocked on the door so late. Even though they were pleased to see Amity, they were mostly cold to us. They also had completely taken apart her bedroom and turned it into a home gym.

"Where is all my stuff?" Amity asked.

"In storage bins in the basement. We had to get rid of the furniture though, sorry." Her mom responded.

Amity sighed and led me to the basement, where an organized collection of tote boxes resided. She found ones that were labeled Amity and dug through them. She found a few things that were sentimental and took the tote, then we left the house without even saying goodbye because Amity was so mad.

In the car we had a discussion regarding her feelings about how her parents treated her belongings and I told her that at least they were put into boxes instead of just thrown away.

"Yeah, I guess you're right. I just don't understand why they didn't ask me first, it's not like they couldn't."

"How much had they even contacted you while we were away? I never heard you on the phone with them."

"We texted a bit, but that's it."

"I'm sorry."

"It's okay, let's just forget about it. Where are we headed next?"

"Let's go meander downtown for a bit like I told my mom, then we can decide if we want to go to Tony's house or not."

"Sounds like a great idea."

Amity drove us up to the city, where we parked in a big garage then walked a mile or two around the block to get to PNL (the Power and Light district). It was a Saturday night, so it was packed. There were people everywhere, flooding out into the streets and alleyways. We went around a line of people and followed them up a staircase to the Mosaic Ultra Lounge. It was a bar and lounge with an ivy wall, lit with neon signs. A portion of the lounge was outside, and a portion was inside, the inside had sparkly-dangling lights hanging from the ceiling that were mesmerizing, and they were changing color with the music that the local DJ was spinning. Amity and I decided to dance and joined the crowd of people.

After a while I was feeling short of breath, so we went out of the balcony to get some air. You could see the district down below and it was so heavily crowded with people they could barely move. Up on the top was a bit less crowded, and we ran into someone I knew.

"Oh, I'm so sorry," I said as I bumped into them.

"It's okay- oh hey there miss Miller," They replied. We looked up at each other and I realized it was one of my old teachers.

"Mrs. Johnson, wow I haven't seen you in forever! You haven't aged a day!"

Mrs. Johnson was my 8th grade English teacher. I had always really liked her, but there were a lot of students that really hated her. I think she picked on the students she wasn't fond of and had a very two-faced personality. She was always nice to me though.

"Oh, thank you! Gosh has it already been like 8 years since I've seen you?"

"Ah… no, it's been about 5 years."

She frowned, "well, I'm going to pretend I didn't just hear you say that you are here, at a bar, underage."

"Anyways… this is my girlfriend, Amity." At first it felt strange to introduce people to 'my girlfriend' but the good thing about being girls is that homophobic people usually just assumed you meant girl-*friend*, like best friend. Whereas in a male scenario, straight men don't usually call they're best friend 'boyfriend', so there wasn't usually doubt. So, I found that it became easy to tell people she was my girlfriend because they were either supportive and happy for me, or they assumed that I meant she was my bestie. Little did they know she was both.

Mrs. Johnson and Amity exchanged pleasantries and something in my vampire brain was telling me she was acting strange, so I asked Amity to 'get us some drinks' so that she could talk to me more openly.

"So how have you been?" I asked her.

"I'm great, thank you. I hear you have had quite

the adventure lately."

"You've heard? Who have you heard from?"

Her smile grew cold, "let's just say a friend of a friend told me you joined team V."

I could feel the blood drain from my face as I studied hers. How could she be a vampire? She's a teacher! Who teaches during the day!

"Who told you that?"

"Like I said, a friend of a friend. Word travels when you burn down someone's home."

It was my turn to frown, "I would say I didn't mean for that to happen, but I did. Tony is a horrible person and I do not feel sorry for what I did."

"Well, last I heard, he's pissed."

"He made it out?"

"Of course he made it out. You think he's that weak to just die in a measly house fire?" she laughed, "ah, but he did loose almost all of his belongings, including all of his staff."

A wave of sadness overcame me, I never meant to harm his 'staff'. They were human, and even though some of them were on his side, it's not like they were the ones draining people of their blood and burying them in the backyard. They didn't deserve to die, especially not like that.

"I'm so sorry, I had no idea."

"He's coming for you, girlie."

"What do you mean?"

"I mean he's looking for you, and he's going to kill you. You and your little girlfriend."

"Well, lucky for me, I'm looking for him too. Because *I'm* going to kill *him*."

Johnson laughed again, "good luck. If you don't

already sleep in a coffin, you will soon."

She almost walked away then, but I stopped her, "wait, how do you teach?"

"You mean how do I go about things during the day? I'm an energy vampire."

Before I could ask her to elaborate, she walked away, and I lost her to the crowd. A moment later Amity came back, empty handed, and asked what happened. It was probably the weirdest encounter I had had yet.

CHAPTER 25

Arrival

After explaining to Amity what Johnson had told me, we decided it was best to leave. If Tony was looking for me, he could be anywhere. Heck, he could even be in Colorado, not realizing that we had come back yet. Or he could even be in the very lounge that we were in then. Amity suggested we go check out the house to see if he was there, what was going on, or if there were any clues. I agreed so we walked back to the car and drove all the way to Tony's house.

It was quite a bittersweet moment. I had so many bad memories of the place, but there were some parts that weren't totally unpleasant. It was where I met Amity after all.

We pulled up to the gated drive and Amity got out to raise up the caution tape so we could drive under it. From afar we could see that a good portion of the house was gone. Most of the middle of the house had collapsed in and was completely black. In that section there was nothing left but charcoaled wood. The portion that was left was mostly covered in soot and completely unusable. The house would need to be torn down and completely rebuilt in order to continue to live in it. Although technically a vampire could still live in those conditions, and I wondered if Tony still occupied the house. Something in my gut said probably not, he probably would've already started reconstructing the house if he really wanted to stay here. It looked completely abandoned. There were no cars in the garage, and no staff working in the yard.

We drove through the grass directly up to the house and got out. Approaching cautiously, we stepped into the house, heading towards the area that survived. It was mostly the South Wing of the mansion that wasn't burnt to a crisp, so we tiptoed up the stairs to see what we could find. That section of the house consisted of the guest-beds, home-office, and home-gym. We glanced through the rooms, but really searched through the office. It was a nice room, with a dark carpet and mahogany furniture. There were lots of books and filing cabinets, along with binders and a safe. Amity looked over at me when we noticed the safe. If there was anything juicy in this house, it would be in there, but it could take years to figure out the lock combination.

"He's an idiot," I reminded myself.

Together we searched through loose paperwork, trinkets, and everything surrounding his desk and computer to see if he left any information behind. We found out what company he owns, and how he earns his money, and it was surprisingly not surprising. He just owned some large tech company that was making millions. It wasn't one I had heard of before, but it must have been under the wing of Google, because there was a lot of Google paperwork. We also found paperwork containing large purchases, such as the mansion itself, and his many cars.

After a while I began to lose hope that we would

find anything of interest, but finally we found a piece of paper taped under his desk, with all his main passwords and his safe combination.

"Finally!" Amity cheered. She read off the combination to me as I rotated the lock. After three turns the lock clicked and the safe was open. Inside was another filing cabinet beneath a big box. We opened the box first and found a large wad of cash. Most of it was American currency, but some of it appeared to be German, European, and Japanese. We set that aside then looked at the file folders. The first file shocked me more than it probably should have. I pulled out a manilla folder and opened it up to find photos and papers containing information about ME.

The photos were of me before we even met. One was of me protesting, where I first had felt Tony's presence. Another was of me on the bus, another place where I had felt his presence. Also, there were a few more photos of me at places I had never noticed him. He had been stalking me for a lot longer than I had thought.

I felt the blood drain from my face as I dropped the folder. Amity picked it back up and gasped, seeing what I had seen. She looked at the pictures of me shopping with my friends, going to Worlds of Fun, studying at a coffee shop, eating dinner with my parents at a restaurant, and even coming out of class at school.

How had I only noticed him a couple of times before he approached me? How could I have allowed myself to-

"Are you okay?" Amity asked, a hand on my shoulder.

I shook my head no, my throat burning with a

dry rage. She hugged me for a moment before looking further into the folder. Some loose paper behind the photos contained a handwritten paragraph. In it, Tony describes my appearance, and everything he had learned about me, highlighting my veganism, age, and hobbies. He described how he planned to lure me in and turn me into a vampire to see how I would react to needing blood to survive. The worst bit of all was a little baggy at the bottom of the folder, which contained a lock of my hair. It was blonde, so it had to have been before I cut and dyed it. Which meant he either got it before he turned me into a vampire, or while I was living with him. Either way, I was mortified.

"How would he have gotten this?" I cried.

Amity shook her head, "maybe while you were sleeping? I don't know, I'm so sorry Hazel."

"I knew he had followed me at least twice, but I didn't know his stalking was to this degree."

"He's a horrible man."

"I should've guessed."

"There's nothing you could have done differently."

"I know, but still. If he stalked me that much though, he must've known where I lived. He could've kidnapped me at any time. Or worse, he could've killed my whole family. He still hasn't, which I'm glad about obviously, but like, why? If he has killed so many people, and has no remorse, why would he bother to care about whether he killed my family or not?"

"Maybe he didn't care, maybe it was more work than was worth it to him. I wonder though…"

Amity flipped through more files and pulled another one out. Just like mine, there was a manilla folder containing photos and a description of her.

"He's stalking everyone," I gasped.

Amity seemed less shocked to see her photos than I was with mine, but it was still disheartening to see. We both felt violated and depressed, but mostly angry.

"Yeah, how many people has he done this to?" She asked, fingering through more files, and finding more and more photos of young women.

"A lot, it looks like," I sighed.

"What a sick, sick man."

"This can't be his end," I stammered.

Amity looked over at me, my face probably flushed red with anger.

"We have to find him," she agreed.

"I would think it won't be too hard, seeing as he is waiting for me. This time though, I'm prepared."

"You know, he might not know that I'll be there with you too."

"You're right. Just because we escaped together doesn't mean that we stayed together. He may think we went our separate ways."

"Where do you think we should look for him?"

"Tony kept saying he was going to take me away to Florida, where he usually spends his winters. I'd say he's most likely going to be there."

"Oo, okay but if we're going to Florida, we have to take at least a one-day break to enjoy the beach."

I smiled through the anger. A day off did sound amazing, especially with Amity. I imagined cuddling on the beach with her, maybe building a sandcastle or surfing or just reading a book and sunbathing... but then I remembered we couldn't sunbathe anymore, and I was depressed again. I tried to remain positive though, a night at the beach could be just as fun as a day at the beach.

I took Amity's hand and squeezed it tightly, "of course."

She smiled back but I could see the sadness in her eyes. She was just as upset with Tony as I was. Maybe once the whole thing was over, we could just relax and try to move on with our lives.

"So where in Florida does he live?" she asked.

"I'm not exactly sure, maybe some of the paperwork will tell us."

We went back through the files in his desk and found the information about all his houses. The one in Florida was in Pensacola. I looked up the address on my phone and discovered it was right on the beach. We could see the outside of the property from Google Street View and it looked nothing like his mansion. It was genuinely surprising because it didn't seem like the type of house that Tony would be interested in. It was a large house compared to the others around it, but I wouldn't say it was large enough to be considered a mansion. It was blue, three stories tall, with a wrap-around porch. I really liked it and was kind of excited to go investigate it.

To get there by car, it would take 15 hours.

"That's a really long drive."

"Maybe we could fly?" Amity suggested. We looked up flights but there were no flights in the next two weeks flying late enough for it to be dark out. Not to mention it would be difficult to take our weapons through security.

"Road trip?"

"I'm always down for a road trip. Especially since this time we'll be in the same car."

"Yeah at least there's that."

Amity could tell I was still upset, and she gave me a tight hug. We then heard something crashing and jumped out of our embrace.

"The hell was that?" I wondered.

We quickly gathered some of the things from his office and tiptoed down the stairs. Looking around the main floor I discovered an area where all the dust and debris was flying everywhere. Signaling a disturbance. I looked up and noticed the floor of the room above had given way, the furniture and decorations scattered all over the ground.

"We should probably get out of here before the whole house collapses." I suggested.

Amity nodded and led us back to the car.

We went back to my mom's house and packed our things, then stayed the rest of the night there to get a fresh start the next night.

My parents gave us both big hugs and wished us good luck on our journey, and we were off. Most of the night went smoothly, until we stopped at a gas station in the middle of nowhere.

I went into the restroom to freshen up and a big, rough-looking man followed me into the room.

"Uh, I think you're in the wrong room," I said, trying not to judge.

The man attempted to attack me, I assumed for a sexual assault, but my instincts kicked in and I punched the guy square in the jaw. He spat onto the floor and reached for my neck, but I was quicker than him. I pushed him into the wall, trying hard not to use too much of my vampire strength, with my hand around his throat. He coughed a bit as he struggled under my grip.

"How dare you?" I shouted.

He tried to speak but I wouldn't let him.

"You have the audacity to try to attack a woman in what should be a safe place?"

I loosened my grip and allowed his feet to touch the ground so he could respond, "I'm sorry."

"You should be. You should be arrested and much worse, but I'm gunna let you off with a warning because I feel like this is a teachable moment, ok? Some women... are stronger than *you*, got it? Try this again and not only will I find you, I will *end* you."

I barred my little fangs, lowered my brows, tightened my grip, and the man's eyes grew wide. He nodded and ripped out of my hand, running out of the bathroom. I really must've put the fear in him. Good, he'll never do that again. If situations were reversed and I was human again, I would've been terrified.

I exited the building and saw the man running down the street, his pants sagging so low he had to hold them up with one hand.

"She's crazy!" he screamed, "a mad woman!"

Amity looked at me from the gas pump with a bewildered yet endearing expression and called out to me, "you okay?"

"Oh yeah, just a lil late-night gas-station attack."

"Well, you certainly scared him straight," she laughed.

"That I did."

The rest of the trip went well, and we reached the beach a couple hours before sunrise. We knew where Tony's house was, but we weren't quite ready to run into him just yet, so we picked out a hotel that had an opening nearby and checked in first, then went down to the beach to hang out until sunrise. The breeze was cool and there was a thick mist blowing in from the ocean. It wasn't uncomfortable, but we were getting wet even though we weren't in the water, so we stripped down to our bathing suits and laid out some towels to relax on.

Amity was wearing a black one-piece with a gold corset-lace over the cleavage, and I was in a dark green bikini. I told Amity how amazing she looked, and she blushed.

Together we took some time to relax and meditate, focusing on our breathing and our goals for ourselves. Then we communicated about how we wanted things to go when the time came to approach Tony. I was nervous, she was more excited. I was just ready for the whole thing to be over. I was tired of thinking about how I would end a man's life. I was tired of pretending I was okay. I was tired of how emotionally back and forth I was. One minute I feel fine, and ready to take on life and new experiences, and the next minute I'm sobbing about how much I regret the things that I've done, even if they were for the greater good. It was a vicious cycle.

Amity was an angel. She was there for me though all of it, even though she was dealing with the same issues. She held my hand, she brushed my hair, she worked me through my struggles while also dealing with her own. I couldn't be more grateful to have her in my life. I think things would've turned out very differently for me if I hadn't met her. Maybe I would have turned out more like Tony myself, or maybe I would've stayed with my parents and accidentally gotten them hurt, or worse. All I knew was that I was a better person because of her.

I looked up to my girlfriend because she always knew how to stay positive even when things were going badly. She's sweet and loving and protective and I think I'm falling in love with her.

She snapped me back out of my daydream with a tickle to the stomach. I playfully pushed her off and piled sand up at her feet. She laughed and wiggled her toes out, her ocean-blue toenails exposed from the sand. We both received an alert on our phone then that a storm was on its way, and almost as if the sky could read our minds, lightning flashed on the horizon. I pulled up the weather alert to read more about it, and it said that the storm would be bringing in a cold front, but even with the cold front, it still wasn't cold enough to snow. Nothing like Colorado. The mountains would probably be getting a few feet of snow. That was the one thing I didn't miss.

Amity sighed, "I love seeing lightning. It's almost like getting to see daylight again, just for a split second."

"Yeah, I agree, and I love all the colors too, its beautiful." I rested my head on her shoulder, and she rested hers back on mine.

"We should probably head back to the hotel then since it's about to rain. What do you want to do for the rest of the night?"

"I'm kinda missing training, maybe we could hit the gym?"

"Yeah, that sounds great."

Helping Amity to her feet, I yanked her up from the ground. She jumped up with a pop and gathered her things. We ran back to the hotel and changed into sports bras and leggings and found our way to the hotel gym. Surprisingly, the beach had been nearly empty, but the gym had quite a few people in it. Most of them were younger-looking men and women with similar workout gear and a similar passion for fitness. They were each just focused on their workout, all except one who was taking selfies in the corner.

Grabbing my gear, Amity and I headed to the mats to stretch and spar for a while before getting to weights and cardio. Altogether we were there for maybe two hours, and meanwhile all the other gym-goers were there too. Made sense that the only people in the gym at that time of night were people who are hardcore about their health and fitness. Unless they were vampires too. I kind of chuckled at that thought, but then realized it could be true. Who knows how many vampires we'd come across without even knowing it. Any one of these seemingly random strangers could be a bloodsucking monster. But I digress.

Once Amity and I finished our workout, we hit the showers then went back to our elegant hotel room. We read for a bit as the sun started to rise then passed out. I awoke to the sound of someone knocking on our door and I jumped out of bed, ready to fight. Amity yawned and stretched but woke right up when the knock could be heard again. It was definitely our door they were knocking on, but who and why?

I went over to the door and stood on my toes to look through the peephole. There was no one there. I raised my eyebrows at Amity and slowly unlocked and opened the door. No one was there but there was a piece of paper on the ground. I picked it up and quickly shut the door. Holding the paper out so Amity could see it, I read the note.

I know you're here. Meet me behind Crabs at 9.

I was shocked. He knew we were here, and not only did he know we were here in Florida, but he also knew exactly which room we were staying in. Maybe he was still stalking us to this day. He probably knew we were in Colorado that whole time.

Amity looked at me with just as much surprise as I felt. I looked at the clock and it was 6pm. That gave us three hours to prepare for the worst.

"What does he want from us?" Amity asked.

I shook my head, "who knows. I really, genuinely, have no idea what this man wants from us. Back home he always said I was his 'little experiment', I guess maybe he's just not done with me."

"And hasn't even started with me."

I frowned.

"But hey, I mean, at least his basement wasn't cages and torture devices, right?" she said, trying to remain positive.

"I guess you're right, he may be a sick, evil man, but he can't be as bad as Elijah, right? We can totally handle him, especially between the two of us."

"Exactly. We got this."

"Then again, we never know what's in the basement of this house."

"This house doesn't have a basement, it technically doesn't even have a main floor, remember? It's lifted."

"I know, but you get my point."

"Yeah, I do. We don't know what's in that house of his. We also don't know why he wants to meet us in public either. Maybe *he* fears *us*."

I doubted it, but hoped she was right. My mind and heart were racing. My anxiety was making me tremble. Maybe a shower would help me relax. I grabbed some clothes out of my suitcase and headed for the bathroom. The steam and hot water really did help calm my nerves, as did some deep breathing exercises. Once I felt level-headed, I retreated from the water and stood in front of the mirror. It took a moment for the fog to clear up, but once it did, I observed my appearance. I looked quite a bit different from when I last saw Tony. No longer did I have long blonde hair, it was shorter and brown now. I also had paler skin and sharper teeth, but most importantly, I now had muscles that can't even compare to what I had before. Before I couldn't even bench my own weight, now I was up to almost double my weight. Tony would be surprised. Or would he? If he is stalking me as closely as I think he may be, then maybe he already knows about my new appearance. We would find out once we see him in person.

For some reason I felt the need to put on makeup, so I did. I wasn't sure if it was for myself, for Amity, or for Tony. A part of me still remembered the moments when I did briefly enjoy his company, and it would be a bit awkward since I have slept with him, and now I'll be seeing him with my girlfriend in tow. Regardless, I was amping my anxiety back up by thinking about it, so I took a few more deep breaths and put my clothes on.

This time I wore athletic shorts, a sports bra, and a breathable top, along with combat boots. I braided my hair into two French braids and topped it off with bright blue hairbands. Then as Amity took her turn to get ready, I opened our weapons case and decided to bring a few things with me. I hid a stake in each boot, a knife in my pants, and a pocketknife in my bra. I just hoped I wouldn't need any of it. If it came down to it, I would have to fight Tony, but with him wanting to meet us in public, in a place where a lot of people would still be that early in the night, it would be difficult. No wonder he wanted to meet us there. He probably knew we were on a mission to kill.

Amity came out of the bathroom wearing a similar outfit and added her weapons of choice. One hour to go.

We decided it would be best to arrive early and scope the location out and make sure he didn't have any employees waiting for us, or other 'little experiments' tagging along, or anything hidden in the sand like weapons. Upon arrival, all seemed normal. It had rained all day while we were sleeping but had cleared off since. The Crab restaurant was popping, with many humans enjoying their meals outside under bright red umbrellas. Next door was an open bar, and in the sand between the two was a volleyball net, which was being used by a group of boozed-up young adults. It was times like this I wished I could just drink straight alcohol, just to take the edge off. I was feeling a bit hungry; the supply we brought would only last so long. We had maybe a week left, two if we stretched it out.

It was almost time, so we stood behind the crowd of people eating their crabs and waited for his arrival. It felt awkward to wait for someone like we were meeting up with an old friend when the reality was much worse. Amity stood strong and brushed my baby hairs away from my face as needed. She could tell how anxious I was, but I just didn't understand why she wasn't.

A few minutes later I heard my name called out

from behind. This was it. I turned around and saw the man that ended my life.

Tony.

CHAPTER 26

The Red Carpet

Tony looked as dark, business-casual as usual, with thick boots underneath black jeans and a dark blue button-up, his sleeves rolled up like usual. He grinned at Amity and I as we let go of each other's hands. His perfectly straight teeth gleamed in the moonlight and his hair was elegantly swooped back as much as the few inches could. He was different, but not really.

"What? You aren't excited to see me?" he asked with raised arms, as if he was about to come in for a hug.

I took a step back and frowned, "why would I be?"

"Because you missed me, you know you did."

"I did not actually."

"Then why did you come all the way to Florida to see me?"

I couldn't say the real reason, because, if he already knew the reason, I didn't want him to know that I knew that he knew, but if he didn't know, I didn't want him to find out. So, I kept silent.

"It's also nice to see you again too, Amity, I like the pink hair."

"Whatever, creep," she responded. "What do you want with us?"

"Wow you don't play around, do you? Why can't

we just hit the bar and catch up for a bit?"

"Here's a better idea, why don't we just go somewhere more private?"

"If you mean for a threesome, then sure, I'm down."

Amity rolled her eyes, "you wish."

"I do, but alas, follow me."

Tony walked up the beach and over to the bar, and for some reason we followed him. I kept my eyes peeled for anything extra-suspicious. We sat down on a few stools at the end of the bar, where there were fewer people, with Amity on my left and Tony on my right. I also made sure to keep an empty seat between us. A bartender greeted us then and Tony rudely told them to get him a scotch on the rocks. They sighed and turned around to start making the drink. When they came back, Tony took the glass and inched it closer to himself, then pulled out a flask and added its contents to the drink. The brown liquid turned red as he stirred it with his finger. Then he took a sip and swallowed it loudly.

He offered us some, but we shook our heads. We didn't even know that we could do that.

"Oh, that's right, you're on your 'ethical' diet," he laughed.

A woman came up to him then and whispered in his ear. She looked around 30, with black curly hair and a margarita in hand. She was only wearing a bikini with a cover, and sandals. They laughed together and then she took the empty seat between Tony and me. She looked over at us and introduced herself as Evelyn. She was a strikingly gorgeous woman, way out of Tony's league, with medium-dark skin and a busty figure. I wondered what her deal was. She took a drink from the light green margarita, and I realized she was human. My eyes lowered at Tony, and he grinned.

"Oh, I'm so glad you all could meet miss Evelyn here, she is truly phenomenal."

"I'm sure," I frowned.

The four of us made pleasantries and chatted for a bit. Evelyn seemed like a genuinely sweet person. Tony on the other hand was a very phony nice guy.

"Oh! You guys must come with us to the winter formal!" Evelyn cheered.

"I don't know about that-"

"No, that's a great idea, you should come," Tony agreed.

"We didn't bring any formal gowns," Amity stated.

"Oh, that's okay, I have tons you could borrow."

"Uh, when is it?" I asked.

"Tomorrow night, it's a vampire-themed winter ball, black tie event. Tony told me all about the one he went to last year and it sounds so fun."

"Vampire theme?"

"Oh, you know, like the décor will be red, people will be wearing fangs, you know the drill."

I looked over at Amity and she nodded, "sounds fun."

"Great! Let's just all meet at Tony's house tomorrow and I'll bring some dresses I think will look good."

"Sure."

"Hey Ev, be a dear and let me have a moment to catch up with these young ladies please."

"Sure thing!" She kissed each of us on the cheek like we were the best of friends and then went over to the other side of the bar to talk to a group of guys.

"Does she not know?" I asked.

"I'm trying something new this time."

"What's that supposed to mean?"

"I'm dating her for a while before I... tell her my secret."

"You have some serious explaining to do."

"All in good time."

"You can't keep doing this to people."

"Doing what?"

"What you did to Amity and me. You can't just make women fall for you and then hurt them!"

"Well to be fair, Amity never did fall for me."

"That's because with all you're stalking you did you still never figured out that I'm lesbian, you psycho!" Amity was fuming. I put my hand on her leg like she does for me, and she took a deep breath.

"Woah, no need for such hostility. I see that now, you two are a very cute couple."

"What matters is that you are still out here, hurting people and getting away with it."

He shrugged, "a man's gotta live somehow. You don't get as far in life as I have without shaking things up a bit."

"You are a cruel, evil man."

"Aw, thanks," he put a hand to his heart and stuck out his bottom lip. He truly did not care what we thought of him.

"Why did you tell us to meet you here? Why have you been stalking us? What is your game?"

"Yeah, and if you knew where we've been and what we've been doing, how come this is the first we've heard from you?" I added.

"Slow down, I can only answer one question at a

time. How about I answer those questions tomorrow."

"Now, answer them now."

"No one likes an impatient woman."

I crossed my arms and stood to leave but he gripped my arm and told me to sit back down. I reluctantly did so.

"I'll answer a little bit, and then the rest tomorrow. I told you to meet me here because I know what your plans are. You want to try to kill me."

I began to protest but he pressed a finger to my lips and told me to shut up.

"You are angry with me, and I get that. What I did to you must have not been fun, but you can't kill me, you need me."

"Why on earth would we need you?" Amity asked.

"Because you are horribly misguided. That Hunter guy you were hanging out with? Terrible influence. He told you to hurt your own people! If there is any rule in the vampire world, it's that you do not hurt one of your own kind! Well, at least not in a fatal way."

"I thought the rule was don't suck another vampire's blood," I stammered.

"That's another good rule, yes. Anyways, I think you both should stay here with me in Florida, and we can continue our journey together."

"What? You're asking us to move in with you? After we burned down your last house?"

"Well, no one is forcing you to. There will be no handcuffs this time, I promise, but I think it would be a good idea for the two of you to see the way that real vampire's live."

"No way, we have seen way more than enough of vampires like you."

"Mhm, yes I heard that you've had a few… nasty… encounters."

"And we'll do the same to you if you try anything," Amity scolded.

"I believe that you will try, and I am prepared for that."

He stood up from the bar and raised his glass at us, "don't worry, no harm shall come to you until you have attempted to harm me. Then it's fair game. I'll see you tomorrow."

With that, he walked over to Evelyn and wrapped his arm around her shoulder. She laughed and rested a hand on his chest, her golden rings glowing in the bar lights. She nodded at something he said then they waved goodbye to the group and walked out together.

"It really boils my blood that he's at it again," I said, nearly about to punch something.

"That poor woman. We need to get her away from him before he hurts her," Amity sighed.

"I agree, we'll tell her tomorrow what's going on and help her get away, and then we'll end him. We have to. He clearly will not change his ways."

She nodded, "we need to protect her and all his future potential victims and get vengeance for all his previous victims."

"We're going to have to be slick though. Anything we do he's going to see coming. He knows we want to kill him; his guard will be up at all times."

"We could go along with his plan to move in with him, act all cool and stuff and then attack him while he's sleeping."

"Maybe, but I've tried the 'act all cool' before. He will probably be expecting that too. I'm sure he already knows that nothing I say to him can be trusted."

"This is a tough one."

I nodded in agreement and sighed, really wishing I could have one of those drinks. I asked for a wine slushy to go, and the bartender put it in a foam cup. No glass on the beach so they probably did that all the time. We walked down the beach hand in hand back towards the hotel. The crowd of people started to die down as we did so, and by the time we made it to the section of the beach that was behind the hotel, we were almost alone. The air was crisp, but the storm was gone, and the skies were clear, revealing sparkling stars and a bright, nearly full, moon.

We dumped out most of the wine and added our 'ethically sourced' (as Tony called it) blood into our wine slushy and gave it a sip. I had never mixed blood with alcohol on my own before, and I hoped I had the ratio correct so we wouldn't get sick. From what I saw with Tony, you probably needed more blood than booze.

"Okay I'm not going to lie, this is pretty tasty," I announced.

Amity gave it a sip and agreed, "as much as I hate to admit it, you're right, it tastes amazing."

We drank the whole thing in just a few minutes and felt a tiny buzz. It used up a good portion of our blood supply, but it was worth it. Together we got minorly tipsy and tried to forget about what atrocities may happen tomorrow.

When tomorrow came I sauntered into the bathroom to get ready for the night, and Amity joined me a few moments later. We were both very tired and slightly nervous, but a cold shower woke us up quickly. We skipped the makeup and didn't worry too much about the clothes, other than needing to wear something to hide weapons in. So, we both left in jeans, boots, and light jackets.

I could tell that Amity was having some anxiety this time too, so we ended up both being nervous to approach Tony's door. As we climbed up the steps to Tony's front porch, I glanced around, taking in the view. The ocean was a backdrop in an otherwise normal looking neighborhood. It was different from back home because none of these houses had in-ground foundations, and the front yards were sand dunes instead of grassy plains, but overall, it was beautiful. I took the first step and knocked on the door.

Evelyn answered the door and ushered us inside.

"I'm so glad you could make it!" she sang.

She took us straight up the stairs to a bedroom on the top floor. We hardly had any time to look around the main level. Tony was nowhere to be seen, but I kept my eyes peeled for him just in case.

The master bedroom was painted the same light blue as the outside of the house, and the furniture was white. The decorations around the room were all nautical; anchors, buoys, and seashells lined the walls and shelves. I never thought of Tony as the nautical décor type. Eveyln opened the French doors to the master bathroom, and I was unsurprised to see the same type of décor in there too. She sat us down in the his-and-hers vanities and pulled out a huge makeup organizer.

Without either of us saying a word, Evelyn began doing our makeup, starting with me, and then Amity. She gave us both very emo-looking smokey eyes with thick liners and blood-red lips. She had already done her own makeup in a similar style, and had pulled her curly hair up. Amity's hair was so short that Evelyn just curled it around her face, and with me she curled all of it, then combed it out into waves. She then gave me a waterfall braid that reminded me of a crown. It was a gorgeous style that I had never tried before and will remember for the future.

The whole time she was working on us, she was telling stories about high school, and starting college, and how she met Tony, and how she loves parties and being social. I could tell. She said she met Tony while at the same bar we were at last night a few months ago and they had been dating ever since. She said it was love at first sight. I tried to hide an eyeroll. She then waved a brush in the air with a 'ta-da!'.

"Wow it looks great!" I exclaimed.

"Thank you! Now let's look at our dress options." She pulled us both into the closet, where there was an entire section dedicated to various fancy outfits including ballgowns. There were probably about 20 big dresses and many more little ones. She herself was in a getting-ready robe, but had a dress picked out and hanging up on the door. It was a floor-length golden gown that was slim and sparkly. I knew she would look absolutely fabulous in it. She pulled out many dresses for us to try on and eventually we found ones that fit and looked good on us.

For Amity, she had a black corset top with a long, poofy skirt. The top really accentuated her figure. For me she found a bright red gown with a floral tulle skirt and a top that had such a deep V-neck that it plummeted all the way down to just above my belly button. It also had a completely exposed back and cinched waist. It was honestly the most gorgeous dress I had even been in, and had it been white, it really would've looked like a wedding dress.

"Are you sure?" I asked Eveyln, "this isn't overdoing it?"

"Not for a vampire formal, no. This is perfect. You both look stunning."

"Thanks" Amity and I synchronized.

She put on her gown and finished getting ready by adding some golden jewelry. She showed us the big jewelry organizer she had and told Amity to pick anything in black or silver, and for me to pick anything in black or ruby red, so we would match our outfits. So, Amity picked out some matching earrings and bracelets, and a simple necklace, and I picked out just a black necklace with a blood-red teardrop that landed perfectly onto the center of my sternum, just slightly above the exposed cleavage.

Between the makeup, the gown, the jewelry, and the waterfall-hair, I was the prettiest I had felt in a long time. Amity was as stunning as she ever was, but something about the corset really had me.

Evelyn proposed we take selfies together, and although I wasn't too sure about that, it happened. There was your typical squeeze-into-the-shot selfie, and the typical mirror selfie, but I had to admit, we were a pretty hot trio.

Someone knocked on the door then and Evelyn said we were decent, so in waltz Tony in his tux, ready to go.

"Honey, you look great," Evelyn told him. He returned the compliment and kissed her on the cheek. *What a snake.*

I frowned at Tony, and he stuck his tongue out like a child. He knew what he was doing. I wasn't even sure why we were going along with this plan when we could just be killing him right now, getting it over with, then moving on with our lives. Maybe it was just an excuse to go to a fancy ball with Amity.

"So Tony, I didn't pick you to be such a... nautical... fan."

He shrugged, "eh, I just left the house as the previous owner had it. Bought it with the furniture and everything. The owners were some elderly couple that went to go live in a nursing home so they couldn't really take much with them anyways."

I nodded, "gotcha."

"Babe, will you take our picture?" Evelyn asked him.

She led us out to the balcony, and he stayed inside to get the wide shot. The beach was behind us down below, and it was a stunning view. The breeze blew our hair back from our faces and Evelyn wrapped her arms around our waists. Tony took a couple shots then handed the phone back to Evelyn, asking if we were ready to go. She said we were, and we followed the couple down back through the house and out to the driveway. On the curb was a stretch limo that seemed to go on forever, but I'd be lying if I said I wasn't excited to ride in a limo for the first time.

The ball was at a very old, converted church with a horseshoe drive up. The architecture was very gothic styled, with stones and steeples and stained-glass windows. It was no longer a church, but now a convention center, and there was a big banner for tonight's event out front. We were dropped off in the middle of the drive and there was a red carpet leading up to the doors. There were ropes on the sides and people taking pictures like paparazzi.

"Oo, I knew it was going to be fancy, but this is just phenomenal!" Evelyn told Tony. She thanked him for taking her as he helped her out of the limo.

"Some of the world's most famous vampires are here tonight," he winked at her then grinned at us. She still didn't know most, if not all, of these people were real, genuine vampires.

My anxiety grew.

It was cool to have our photos taken on the red carpet, I felt very important, but even if the photographers knew Tony, there was no way they knew us.

Once inside the building I was taken aback by how cool the building looked. There were statues and decorations and candles everywhere. The red carpet covered all the hallways and large walking areas but was left open with stone tiles for the dance floor, which I believe used to be the area where the church would have their services. There was an alter at the back of the room, which looked like it was still in use. There were candles, bowls, and a little book on a stand and it reminded me of the one singular time my parents took my family to church. I had loved the look of everything, but we decided as a family it was not for us. To be perfectly honest, I had been bored out of my mind and so had my brother.

As more partygoers filled the room, I was glad that Evelyn let us borrow dresses, because everyone else was just as formal, if not more, than we were. The men were all wearing their finest tuxedos, and the women were all wearing floor length evening gowns. Most of the gowns were black or red, like ours, but some were wearing more colorful dresses. There was one woman wearing a bright pink asymmetrical gown, and another woman in a light blue dress that reminded me of Cinderella, and then there was a few more golden gowns and even some white, wedding-looking dresses. Everyone was wearing their best, and it was a refreshing break from the parties Tony took me to back home and the raves I've attended over the years. Instead of everyone being hyped up on cocaine and half-naked, these people were much classier and more sophisticated. People were chatting and laughing, and drinking out of their champagne flutes like there wasn't a care in the world. Tony handed each of us a flute and took a large gulp of his own. I held onto mine for show, but wouldn't take a sip, as did Amity. Evelyn also took one and gulped it down so fast I didn't even have the chance to tell her not to drink it.

"Ew," she whispered, "that didn't taste like punch, what was that?"

"Blood," Tony smiled at her, and she thought he was joking.

"Oh right," she laughed.

There was a live orchestra off to the side playing traditional orchestral music, and in the middle of the dancefloor was a group of fine men and women ballroom dancing to the music. We four decided to join them at the edge, but I had never danced like that before, so Amity and I had to watch Tony and Evelyn for a bit before we tried it. It was a bit awkward, with both of us having large, poofy dresses, but we made it work and it was fun to get to try something new with Amity. The orchestra played Moonlight Sonata next, and I squeezed Amity's hand, trying to hold in my excitement. It was really the only classical song that had always stuck with me, and I never thought that I'd be at a ball, dancing to the song.

After a while a man got up on stage with a microphone and made an announcement.

"Hey! Alright everyone, thank you so much for being here. It has been another amazing year for us, and we couldn't have done it without you. First, we're going to have our best-dressed contest, and then we'll really get into the good stuff. If you are team V and you have brought your team H, please bring them up to the front and well get them prepared. Meanwhile if I could have a drumroll, please!"

"Team V?" Evelyn asked.

"You'll see," Tony replied.

Something in my gut was telling me something bad was about to happen, but I couldn't say what.

"And the winner is... Mrs. Sydney Sullivan!"

A woman with incredibly long, naturally red hair, stepped up to the alter to receive a small trophy. Her dress was black lace, the top part was see-through, revealing large, obviously fake boobs. It was tight, and shaped like a corset, but had no backing. The skirt was fluffy, and the train was so long that I didn't know how she didn't trip in it.

I turned to look at Evelyn and noticed she was gone, as was Tony. I asked Amity if she knew where they went, and she shrugged. Glancing around the room, I finally found them up front near the Alter. They were in line for something, guys on the left, and girls on the right. I pointed them out to Amity and told her I felt like something was off. She looked at me and saw the concerned expression on my face, then looked at the alter, then back to me and her eyes grew wide.

"You're right, something doesn't feel right, maybe we should get the human out of here."

I nodded and we started to make our way to the front. By that time, the crowd had gathered to watch the speaker and were not letting us through. The announcer came back to the center of the stage after letting everyone applaud the winner and shushed the crowd.

"And now... the moment you've all been waiting for."

The crowd cheered again but settled back down quickly.

The man raised an empty bowl above his head, "The sacrifice!"

My blood ran cold, and the room started to spin. I pinched myself as hard as I could as tried my best to stay focused. Someone was about to die.

CHAPTER 27

A Sacrifice

The crowd went wild, cheering for that damned bowl. Once it was set down, the man brought up the first two people in line. A man that looked a lot like James Bond, and a frail looking blonde woman. They brought the woman up to the alter and James Bond stood to the side, watching. The announcer went up to the altar and fidgeted with some tools, putting his own body in front so that the crowd below couldn't see. He then went around and brushed the woman's hair back, exposing more of her neck, and whispered in her ear. She smiled with excitement, but I couldn't understand why. Meanwhile we were still inching our way towards the front.

The announcer said something, but I was too dazed yet focused on getting to the front to comprehend exactly what he was saying. He then held the bowl on the edge of the table, just under the woman's chest. It occurred to me then just what that bowl would be used for. More quickly than I could even process, the man raised a knife from the alter and slit the woman's throat. It happened so fast the woman never even screamed, but she gargled and groaned as the blood poured down her chest and into the bowl.

I shrieked as loudly as I could, and the crowd turned towards me. I received daggers from every direction. The other man that escorted her to the alter, went behind her to catch her limp body after the blood ceased to fall. He dragged her off and the next couple were pulled up onto the stage. After that it was Evelyn and Tony. The same thing happened to the next girl as I finally made it to the front. The crowd was cheering but I was seething. I yanked Eveyln out of line, and she yelled at me.

"Why would you do that? I'm next!"

"You want to be next? You do understand what's happening, right?"

"Yeah, it's like improv, right? We're pretending to do a vampire ritual, and I get to be a sacrifice!"

"NO! These people are REAL vampires, and that woman really did just die. Tony, tell her!"

"She can believe what she wants," Tony looked to me then back to Evelyn, "you'd look beautiful up on that stage, milady."

She blushed like she really had no idea what was about to happen. Was she clueless or stupid?

"It's true, Evelyn, we need to get you out of here, now! You are a mouse in a lion's den!" Amity hollered.

She waved her hand, "you guys are overreacting, it's just part of the event!"

"How can you be so stupid?"

The announcer was ready for the next couple then and waved at Tony and Evelyn to join him on stage.

"Don't you dare!" I yelled at Tony. He ignored me and raised Evelen's hand up to steady her as she stepped up to the altar. This time I didn't hesitate to follow her up onto the stage and push Tony away from her.

The crowd gasped.

Amity and I stood in front of Evelyn and took our stakes out of our hidden locations.

"Touch her and die!" I shrieked. Both Tony and the announcer laughed at us like we were telling the funniest joke.

"Who are you exactly?" The man asked.

"I... am gunna be your worst nightmare if you don't end this little 'show' right now."

He took a step closer to me and sniffed, then looked at me up and down and scoffed. Then he did the same with Amity.

"You're vampires. Why do you do this?" he asked.

"Because what you're doing is wrong!"

"It is in our nature to kill, you know."

"It's not though. Especially not in a sacrificial way!"

"This is just a straight up cult!" Amity added.

Evelyn picked up the bloody knife from the alter and checked its sharpness.

"It's real," she gulped.

She looked over at the other human women and repeated herself. The color drained from her face as she realized what was happening. She looked down at the blood-soaked floor and held back vomit.

"Keep that knife," I told her, "you're going to need it."

All hell broke loose then, the humans started screaming as their dates attacked them. More vampires from the audience jumped on them and started biting down, soaking their gowns and tuxes in blood.

As much as I wanted to save all of them, it was already too late. They were either going to die or going to turn now. I was sure most of them had probably taken a sip of the 'punch' too.

"We gotta get out of here," Amity pushed.

"You ruined our ritual!" the announcer roared.

He reached out to us with daggers for eyes and claws for hands, and I braced myself for impact. He shoved me into Evelyn, but I shoved back even harder. He underestimated me and stumbled but caught himself.

Everything was happening in a blur. People were shouting all around me, the vaulted ceiling just echoing back every harrowing sound. The smell of blood was strong, and the sight of it was somehow stronger, but my peripherals were struggling to keep up. The place was in total chaos as more vampires approached the stage, ready to attack us. I couldn't help but notice Tony had slipped away, and we would need to too. Amity and I would not be able to take on hundreds of vampires by ourselves. I decided as much as I wanted to stop what was happening, I wouldn't be able to. So, we decided it was best to retreat and flee. We ran towards the door behind the stage which led to what used to be the room where they would keep all the church's alter supplies. We slammed the door shut and barricaded it with a shelf.

"That's not going to last long. Vampires are strong." Amity stammered.

"I know, we gotta find a way out of here."

Evelyn was obviously distressed, but she was staying strong and followed right behind. There another door on the other side of the room, and we ran towards it. As soon as we opened the door, we were ambushed by a group of angry vampires. They came at us with barred fangs and reddened eyes. There had to be at least ten of them, men and women. We backed up into a corner with Evelyn behind us and Amity on my left.

It would be the most difficult and ridiculous fight we had ever gone through. We had little help and few weapons, a recipe for disaster. I wished Hunter were there to help us. Fighting in a ballgown was a lot harder than I thought it would be.

I would kick, the dress would get in the way, I would dodge, and feel like I couldn't breathe because the dress was so tight, and don't even get me started on the heels. I felt overwhelmed and looked for another way out. Between punches I noticed a side door not too far away, I told the girls the plan and waited for the right opportunity. An arm extended out towards me and as I ducked, I hollered, "now!"

We three dropped to the ground and crawled out from their legs. Amity and Evelyn were fast, and they made it to the door, but just as I was about to stand up, I felt a group of feet stomp on my skirt then hands grabbing my leg and yanking me hard.

I yelped as they nearly broke my shin and ripped my limbs. I was bitten and beaten until gunfire could be heard. The vampires looked up as one of them dropped to the ground, his scull in pieces. Another shot went off and another one dropped. The group turned their attention over to Amity, who had found herself a nifty weapon. They raced towards her, and she shot the first three, and then the rest ran the other way. Amity had shot them all in the head. One went straight through their eye, one had blown to pieces, and another had a hole in their cheek. None of them would be completely dead, but it would give us enough time to get the hell out.

Amity helped me stand up, but I was not in good shape. I would live, but for the moment I was in a lot of pain. They had beaten me to a pulp, and I was bleeding heavily from all the bite marks and scratches. My face, neck, chest, and arms were covered in blood. My dress was ruined and some of my hair had even been ripped out, but I was alive. We ran out the side door and ended up in a garden. We passed by lots of large agave plants below some palm trees and a planted flower garden. There was a huge fountain to the right with a sculpture of a naked woman holding a bowl above her head, and the water pouring from it was dyed red. At least, I hoped it was water.

We ran as fast as our tired bodies could handle; all three of us had ditched the heels and ran barefoot. Eventually we got to the next business down the road and waited for help. Evelyn called a friend of hers that said they would come and pick us up. It was the most stressful situation I had been in a long time, every second I was checking the exits and wondering what things I could grab in self-defense. We hid in the bathroom until the friend arrived. Evelyn told the friend not to ask any questions, but of course they did.

"OMG what happened to you?" She asked.

We shook our heads and shouted to just get in the car and drive. She rushed back into the car and didn't wait for us to put on seatbelts before she sped off, leaving skid marks on the ground from how quickly she tried to accelerate. Once we were a safe distance away, we noticed that she was heading towards the hospital.

"No, no, no, we can't go there," I told her.

"Why not? You're covered in blood! Should I go to the police station instead?"

"No not there either, just somewhere safe."

I looked over at Evelyn and she asked how much she could tell her. I said it was up to her, however much she thought she could handle.

"Look, girl, it's a secret, okay? But what happened... it was vampires. Like real ones, but you can't tell anyone."

"They wouldn't believe me anyways!" She pulled the car over and took some deep breaths then asked Evelyn if she was okay.

She nodded, "thanks to these guys, I am, but there were a lot of people that didn't make it out of there."

Evelyn started crying then and her friend reached over to hug her. We sat in the car for a long time until we were all calm, and then we went to the friend's house, where we would hopefully be safe.

It was a small apartment, but it was up high in a building not too far away from the beach. It had a great view, but even with it being as small as it was, I'm sure the location made it very expensive.

"I love your place," I told her.

"Thank you," she replied, getting water out of the fridge. She offered some to all of us, but Evelyn was the only person that took one.

"I'm sorry, I just realized I still haven't caught your name," Amity said.

"Maggie," she smiled.

"Amity."

"Hazel."

"Please, make yourselves at home. If you... need to shower, I can show you how to turn the faucet on."

Maggie looked at me when talking about the shower and I nodded gratefully. Eveyln and Amity weren't covered in blood the way I was, and even though I was wounded from head to toe, it wasn't so bad that I couldn't walk or bathe myself. So, I followed her to the bathroom and once she was gone, I stepped in and let the water rinse the blood off of me.

I looked down at the shower-tub-combo floor and it was splattered red. I felt a bit lightheaded, so I sat down and let the water rain down on me while I scrubbed at the dried blood on my chest. After scrubbing for a good 20 minutes, I finally felt clean enough to get out. I wrapped a towel around myself and took a few deep breaths.

The problem was that Tony probably knew where we were, and if he didn't, he would figure it out quickly. We couldn't stay here and endanger Evelyn and Maggie's lives. We needed to leave before sunrise and Evelyn probably needed to leave the state altogether. No, we needed to end this thing with Tony once and for all. We needed to make sure he would never do something like this ever again. *Then* we could worry about the rest of those vampires from the ball. That was a whole other thing. The thing with Tony needed to happen quickly so that Evelyn would be safe. She had been nothing but kind and generous to us and I wanted to make sure she was protected at all costs.

There was a knock on the door. I cracked it open to find Amity in nothing but an extra-large T-shirt. I pulled her into the bathroom with me and shut the door behind her.

"Here, Maggie said we could have these," Amity handed me a long T-shirt and I nodded.

"How are you doing?" she asked. She looked at me with puppy dog eyes and rested her hand on my wet hair.

"Okay, I guess. Sore. How about you?" I asked. I dropped the towel and pulled the shirt down over my head. Then I picked the towel back up and patted my hair.

"I'm okay, just worried about you. You got the worst of the three of us for sure."

I looked down at my wounds that were no longer bleeding, but still alarming, and sighed, "just another day as a vampire slayer, right?"

She gave me a small smile and a quick kiss. We discussed what the next move was and decided it was best to go back to our hotel, get some rest, then go find Tony and do what we should have done already. After deciding that, we went back out to talk it through with Maggie and Evelyn.

"Maggie, I think you'll be okay, because he knew where we both lived and never once tried to touch our parents, but just in case, you may want to stay with friends or family for tomorrow." I warned.

"Okay, I can do that," she nodded.

"Evelyn... I have to say that I am so sorry Tony wasn't who you thought he was; and I'm so sorry that he put you through all of this."

"You know, I always thought he was too good to be true. He was always so sweet to me, not to mention utterly handsome and rich too. Despite what we just went through, I don't regret anything. I'm glad I got to meet the two of you." She teared up and wiped it away with the sleeve of a hoodie.

"I'm glad to have met you too."

"So, what do we do now?"

"Well, you are going to need to get away from here. Right now. After this conversation is over you need to go somewhere. Somewhere where Tony would never think to find you, a secret place that only you know about. Can you do that?"

She nodded, "for how long?"

"Just give us two days. Two days and this will all be over." I frowned, frustrated with everything, but then Evelyn reached over and gave me a huge hug and it did make me feel a bit better.

"How will you do it?" She asked.

"I'm not sure you want to know, but just know that we will make sure that he can't hurt anyone ever again."

"You don't need to worry about a thing. Hazel is amazing, and we'll be okay, and so will you," Amity added. Evelyn gave her a hug then too. Maggie offered to drive us to our locations, and we agreed. Once she dropped us off at the hotel, we waved a crestfallen goodbye. It would probably be the last time we would see either of them ever again.

In our hotel room, we dropped down onto the bed and promptly fell asleep. When we woke up the next night, we prepared ourselves for battle. We dressed in what we would normally wear to a mission and put our high ponytails in gear. Then we stashed our stakes and knives and mentally prepared for what was to come.

"Should we go over the plan one more time?" Amity asked.

"Sneak in, put him in a headlock, kill him dead."

"You make it sound so simple."

"It should be, but I know it's not."

"What do you think he's doing right now?"

"I don't know, either plotting or wallowing. Maybe both."

"What if he's not there?"

"We'll find him. Just like he found us."

She nodded and we kissed for a moment. Slow at first but then more like a kiss when you're scared of losing the person. Even though I knew she would be fine. I would make sure of that. Tony wasn't going to come close to getting his hands on her.

We realized that our car was still at Tony's house, and Evelyn's probably was too, since we all carpooled in the limo. So, it was either Uber, or walk. Since it wasn't a terrible walk, just a few miles down the beach, we decided to do that. Amity took her shoes off and walked along the water's edge, and I joined her. She took her free hand and held onto mine, and we tried to make the best of a bad situation.

"I know things may be a bit different after this..." she started, "but I want you to know that I don't regret anything. From the moment I met you I didn't regret anything. I want a life with you, Hazel. I'm sorry if it's too soon to say that; we haven't even been together for a year yet, but it's my truth. I'm glad I have you in my life and I love you. No, I don't just love you, I'm *in* love with you. And if I must spend eternity on this retched planet, I'm glad it's with you."

"I'm *in* love with you too. Whatever happens in there, just know that I want to spend the rest of eternity with you too."

"Whatever happens? You sound like there's a predetermined fate at hand."

I shook my head, "no, we'll be okay, I'll be okay. I'm

just nervous is all."

"I am too, but hey, we are together, and we are doing what's best for not just us, but sooo many women in the world that could have been his next victim. Besides, we've done this like how many times now? We've totally got this, no problem. We're gunna get it done, then call Hunter and let him know, and he'll be so proud of us."

"Whatever happens, we're together."

"Together."

She wrapped her arms around me in a tight embrace. The light of the full moon was bright and reflected off the water in shimmers. Amity pulled back from the hug and her face was radiating with beauty. We kissed until we couldn't anymore, then continued our walk to Tony's house.

A while later, Tony's house came into view, and we immediately started trying to conceal ourselves. Crawling behind tallgrass, sneaking along buildings, and hiding behind cars, until we made it to Tony's yard.

It had a partial fence that we hopped over and lots of tall plants that we crept behind. Our cars were still on the lot, as were Tony's. There was a staircase up to the back portion of the porch, much like the one in the front, so we took that up as silently as we could. Tony had good hearing as a vampire, and we did not want to risk him seeing us. We needed the element of surprise.

Luckily for us, Tony didn't have any curtains on the main floor, so we could see perfectly into the house from our perched position on the porch. The tv was on, playing Kitchen Nightmares, and Tony was pacing back and forth. He was on the phone with someone, and whoever he was on the phone with was getting an earful.

"I don't care, just do it!" he roared.

He hung up the phone then and threw it across the room. It hit a vase and it shattered. He then mumbled something and went upstairs, not even bothering to shut the tv off. We took the opportunity to sneak in the back door and hide in the kitchen. Tony's footsteps led all the way up to the top floor and a door slammed shut. We ran up the staircase as silently as we could and observed our surroundings.

There were three rooms, one door open, one door closed, and one door that was locked with three different types of locks. We crept behind the door of the room that was open. Amity listened for him as I looked around the room. It wasn't the same one that we were in when Evelyn did our makeup, it was a guest room, the one next door. I hadn't even noticed the room with the locks when we were there the other day. I wondered what Eveyln had thought about the mysterious room, because I'm guessing Tony probably never let her in there. One could only imagine.

We could hear Tony in the master bedroom loudly going through his closet, then rummaging through drawers. Then the shower turned on.

"He's in the bathroom, so we should sneak into the bedroom and take him in there," Amity whispered.

I nodded in agreement, and we crept over to the bedroom door. Amity cracked the door open and when she saw that the bathroom door was closed, we went in and found a spot behind a large dresser so that he wouldn't see us. When he came out of the bathroom, we would grab him, and stab him. Then we would tear him apart and burn the pieces.

I figured we would have to wait until he got out of the shower before he came out of the bathroom, but he must've forgotten something, because the door swung open, and out he came. He was shirtless and shoeless but still had on athletic shorts, like he had just finished a workout. He went for his bedside table and while he leaned over to pick something up, we went for him. I jumped onto his back and gripped his neck tightly while Amity pulled her stake out.

Tony groaned and gripped his fingers around my arm, trying to get me off, but I was stronger than I used to be. The last time we had fought, it was almost like an adult fighting a child. I had no chance. This time though, I had the advantage. Amity raised her stake and as her arms swung down, he kicked her away. She fell back onto the bed as he bent down and threw me over his shoulder so that we were both on top of it.

He smirked, "normally I'd love to have two pretty ladies in my bed."

I couldn't help but roll my eyes. Amity and I jumped up to a standing position, then I flipped off and stood my ground.

"Wow, you've made some improvements," he smiled.

He reached for me then with lightning speed, crouching down to hit me with his shoulder and grab me from behind. I twisted out of the way just in time and he nearly fell forward. Amity tried again to get him with the stake, but he dodged it. I pulled out one of my knives and threw it at him. He dodged it too and the knife went into the wall behind him. He was fast. Faster than I remembered.

Amity jumped down from the bed and pulled his

arms back behind him, opening his chest up to me. It was much easier like this, without the clothing, to get an accurate placement of the knife. So, I pulled out my backup and went for him again.

Tony elbowed Amity in the ribs and lowered himself, making me almost hit Amity with my knife.

"I'm so sorry!" I cried.

"It's okay, I'm fine!"

Tony popped back up then, socking me under my chin with the top of his head. I could feel my teeth smash against each other, and the edge of my tongue get bit down on. It stung so badly I had to take a step back. Amity stabbed him with her stake through his back and he winced in pain.

"And you said we needed you," Amity scoffed.

"You do," he grunted.

"We do not. We left Kansas so we could get away from you. We thrived in Colorado. We have transformed ourselves into people who can and will defeat you," I added.

He laughed weakly, "this is what I wanted."

I stood up straight and lowered my eyebrows, "what do you mean?"

"I wanted to see you thrive. I wanted to see you live; and I don't mind the challenge."

"Why?"

"Do you guys think I'm that stupid?"

"Yeah," Amity stammered.

He looked over at her then back to me, "I let you leave. I let you live. I also let your parents live but that's unrelated. I mean, I knew it was you the whole time."

"Again, I ask, what do you mean?" I reiterated.

"Did you really think that I wouldn't figure out

that it was you who released my prisoners? I showed you the basement for the first time and the *very next day* they're both gone. I put two and two together. Actually, I thought it was quite admirable. That's when I decided to find Amity for you."

"For me?"

"Yes, I knew you would help her escape too, and I knew you would bond well. Although, I will admit that I didn't think you'd end up a couple."

He looked down at the ground for a moment when the pain of his stab wound worsened. Amity gave me a quick glance and mouthed, "now!" and while he wasn't looking, I went for his throat. He moved just as the blade touched his skin, reaching out and pushing forward with his legs so that he knocked me down. Blood dripped from his throat as he hung over me, his hair just inches from my forehead. I pushed back and we rolled over a few times until we hit the back door. It was a sliding glass door that led out to the balcony, and it was open, letting in the fresh, salty air.

Amity yanked on his back, trying to pull him off of me, but he threw his arm back and she fell onto her butt. Tony then grabbed me by the collar of my shirt and dragged me out to the balcony. He pushed me up against the railing, my hair hanging over the edge. Then he dropped down and gripped my feet, throwing my feet up in the air and flipping me backwards. I felt myself falling over the edge. A fall three stories up wouldn't kill me, but I was so scared in the moment I thought it would. A scream escaped my lungs before I could react logically.

In a split second my reflexes kicked in and I reached out, grabbing the edge of the balcony just in time. I hung there, trying not to let go, as I heard Amity yell my name. I looked up, the sea breeze pushing hair into my face and making it harder for me to see. All I could see was the railing and Tony's bare feet at its edge.

Tony and Amity were grunting, as if wrestling, while I tried my hardest to pull myself up, but it wasn't like the bars at the gym, and my fear of falling had me gripping so tight I could barely think of letting go of one hand to grab anything. Amity knocked Tony into the railing so hard that it split in half, and he fell over the edge. It was too quick for him to grab on. The railing swung over my head then snapped and fell towards the ground. I yelped out of shock and dodged it on its way down.

Suddenly Amity's hands were on mine, trying to pull me up. I didn't dare look down. With both of our strengths combined we were able to get me back up to the balcony, where we collapsed onto the ground, breathing heavily. I flipped over to my stomach and crawled to the edge to look down. Tony was lying on the ground face down, blood pooling from the wound on his back and from a fresh wound on his face. He must've hit the fencepost that he was lying next to. All I could think about was that it wasn't over. Until we cut out his heart or separated his head from his shoulders, he would still be alive.

From our position on the third floor, I could see someone walking down the beach, and if they came much closer, they could potentially see his body lying there. Then the cops would be involved. We had to work quickly before someone saw us. Amity and I ran back into the house and down the three flights of stairs to the ground outside. By the time we got around to where

Tony had been lying, he was gone. There were footsteps and blood droplets leading back towards the house and disappearing where the sand stopped.

We ran back into the house and searched for the bleeding man. In the living room, we stopped to look around, and my instincts told me we weren't alone, I turned around and hollered at Amity just as Tony was coming at her with a wet rag. He bashed her head with his fist, and as she fell, he caught her with the rag and wrapped it around her head. She passed out in his arms until he dropped her to the ground.

Now I was furious.

"She'll be out for a while."

I lunged at Tony with all I had left in me, but I had no weapons anymore, and no advantage. He blocked my punches and kicks and wrapped his arms around my neck. He squeezed my neck tightly as he dragged me into the kitchen. He was just tall enough that I was touching the ground with only my toes, and I smacked at his arms to try to get him to let go of me, but it was useless. He grabbed another wet rag and wrapped it around my face. I smelled something weird, and after a minute, my kicking and scratching turned into limp limbs, and I too, passed out.

CHAPTER 28

Lonely

I awoke somewhere dank, dark, and damp. My hands were tied behind my back with chains and my feet were bound together with rope. I was chained to a stone wall and the ground below me was mud. I could hear a dripping sound above my head and waves crashing nearby. It was so dark that if I had been human, it would've been impossible to see anything; but I could tell that I was in some kind of tunnel. There was nothing in the tunnel but the stone walls and puddles in the mud. The smell of mold was strong, but the smell of chloroform was stronger. The rag was still wrapped around me, but now it was down around my neck instead of over my face.

I thought about Amity and wondered where she was. I called out to her, but there was no response other than my own echo.

"Tony!" I screeched. I shook the chains around my wrists as aggressively as I could, but they didn't budge. Wondering what Tony's plan was, I started contemplating my escape. He either wants to drown me in a tide, or leave me to starve, or maybe even worse.

I sat there for hours, but it felt like days, trying to free myself. The chains were thick, and even with my vampire strength I couldn't break them. So, I started rubbing one spot of the chains on the stone wall. If I had to spend two weeks wearing the chain down so I could free myself and find Amity, I would. When my arms would tire, I focused on the rope around my ankles. My boots had been removed and so had my socks. I was bare foot, and the rope was creating burn rings around my skin. No amount of maneuvering my legs would loosen the rope, it had some fancy knot that without hands, I never be able to untie. I had to focus on breaking the chain first.

The tunnel was slowly becoming less dark, and I realized the end of the tunnel was exposed to the outdoors on one side. The sun was starting to rise, and I had no cover from it. It was just one problem on top of the next. I scratched at the wall even more vigorously, trying to get the damn chain to break, but I had barely made a dent.

I shouted again for Amity and Tony, and again got no response. Amity must have been so scared. I tried to remind myself that she was a strong woman, and that she would be okay. Maybe she would even be able to rescue herself and then me... wherever she was. Knowing Tony, she was probably somewhere nearby. If he was smart, she would be somewhere far away. Tony wasn't smart. She was probably just out of hearing range. Probably even somewhere in the same seemingly abandoned building that I was in.

The sun got a little brighter and now it was light enough for me to see the way a human would see at noon. Moss covered large portions of the wall around me, and there was a stone pathway towards the end of the tunnel. I was somewhere in the middle, with an abrupt end on one side, and exposure to the beach on the other side. There was a half wall and above that was some tall grass. Sand piled up in the corner where it had blown in from the wind. The sun exposure was minimal, but it was enough to begin to cause me pain. Once the sun had fully touched the sky, it was too much for me to handle. My eyes stung as if I was looking into the sun directly, and I winced in pain. I was still in the shadow of the tunnel, so my skin was safe, but my eyes were a different story.

Closing my eyes as tightly as I could barely helped. My inner eyelids turned bright red and sparkled like colorful static on an old tv. The headache emerged next, then that turned into a migraine so bad all I wanted to do was scream, and I did. My screech echoed through the tunnel and back to me. The worst part though... I could have sworn I heard someone else's cries for help too. Someone nearby, but far away at the same time. Was it Amity?

Oh Amity, please be okay.

If he hurt her, I would make him suffer. I wouldn't just end his life; I'd make him immobile by cutting off all his limbs and making him watch as he bled out until he couldn't anymore. Then I'd take his head off AND carve out his heart.

The violent thoughts continued as all I could do was sit and wait for the sun to go back down. The hours ticked by slowly, and every minute was more torture than the last. I understand now more than ever why vampires live their lives throughout the night. It was like someone turning on the light while you're looking through night vision goggles... only worse.

While squeezing my eyes shut all day, I tried to

sleep, but the pain was so strong that I just couldn't shut my brain off. So I was stuck, thinking about all my regrets in life, and being alone with my thoughts. I thought about how I could have done things differently, so I wouldn't be in this situation in the first place. I also thought about how all I wanted to do was rip Tony's head off, which got me thinking about how the me before vampirism would have never thought about killing someone, even someone who was evil and probably deserved it. The new me barely flinched at murder. Was I the bad guy? I probably deserved the torture I was receiving, but Amity didn't. She was the sweetest, most thoughtful person I had ever met, and even though she had done things that old me would've shunned, she was still the most considerate, passionate, and loving person, and she deserved only the best. She did was she did because she had to, and I tried to remind myself that I did what I had to do too, and when it comes down to it, Tony has to die.

Any person that was willing to go through these lengths to torture someone deserved what he was getting. Like Elijah.

I also thought about Amity and her sweet face. I wondered where she was, if she was okay, and if she was tied up the same way I was. I tried once again to call out to her, but like before, there was nothing.

Finally, after hours and hours of searing pain, the sun touched the horizon, and the tunnel grew dark. The stones turned an orange hue as the sun set and I squinted my eyes open. I was still in pain, but I knew it was almost over. It wasn't long before the sun was completely down, and I could finally see normally again. The headache persisted, but my eyes eventually stopped stinging, and adjusted to the dark. I turned around as much as I was able and began scraping the chain against the wall again.

Exhaustion didn't even begin to describe how tired and sore I felt, but I powered through. After another few hours I had to take a break. It felt like my arms were going to fall off. I sat in silence for a few minutes before I heard footsteps in the distance.

"Amity?" no reply.

"Tony!" I roared his name as loudly and angerly as I could, frustrated with him for everything he had done. He must've left me here to die, but why I couldn't even begin to wonder.

The footsteps grew closer, and a head popped out from a hole in the wall. On the outside, I frowned, but on the inside, I grinned a bit. There was hope. I just had to time it right, and maybe I could save myself.

"Why?" the first and only thing I could say to my captor.

"Because you pissed me off." Tony crouched down in front of me, far enough away that I couldn't reach him with my feet. He was in rain boots and a matching coat and hat. As he leaned closer to me, a strong gust of wind blew in from the opening of the tunnel and whipped my hair around my neck. Tony closed his eyes and took a deep breath, then opened his eyes and stared at me with hunger.

"What are you going to do with me?" I asked, "and where's Amity?"

"Don't worry about that," he said.

He leaned closer to me and brushed my hair back behind my shoulder, hesitating to return to his previous position.

"You're going to be in here for a while, there's a storm coming in and there is no one for miles. No one can hear you scream, and no one can save you. So, get comfortable."

"Comfortable? Do you know how awful it was in here during the daytime?"

"I can imagine it was pretty bad, maybe next time you won't disobey me, and I won't have to chain you back up here again."

"What makes you think there will be a next time?"

"Because I'm done treating you nicely. From now on you will always be chained up. You live by *my* command now. If you even so much as *breathe* the wrong way, you'll come right back here, and I will wait so long that you starve and wither away, and then I'll cut you up into little pieces and throw you into the ocean. Do you know how long it takes a vampire to die of starvation?"

"A while," I mumbled.

He nodded, "a long while. And while you wait, you can spend your days hiding from the sun as best you can."

"Where am I?"

"Doesn't matter, all that matters is that you are all alone."

He leaned in closer and put his hand on my shoulder. I leaned away so that my hands were touching the ground, and my head was against the wall. It was slow, but I could see he was coming in for a kiss, and I avoided it in any way I could. I turned my head, and he smooched my cheek, then took his hand and turned my face back towards his. I all but growled back at him. As he went in again, my chin locked into his grip, I pulled my knees up to my chest and pushed against his. It got him off me, but only for a moment. He pressed my legs down into the ground, my heels digging into the mud, and forced his lips on mine. He tried to stick his tongue in my mouth, but I took the opportunity to bite down. Hard.

My fangs punctured his tongue to a point of almost ripping it off. Tony yelped and jumped back in pain. I spat at him as he wiped blood from his chin.

"You bitch!" He groaned. He raised his arm and smacked me so hard the clap echoed through the tunnel. My cheek stung, my ears rang, and my vision went fuzzy for a few seconds. Any harder and my jaw surely would've broken.

"How dare you touch me!"

"I can do whatever I want!" He mumbled. He tried to say more but his tongue was swelling up. He yelled to no one and threw his arms down like a toddler having a fit. Then he stomped off and I was left alone again.

Part of me wondered what he would have done to me had I not bitten him. I knew now that he was not going to let me go anytime soon, so I either had to save myself, or starve.

The wind picked up again and I could smell the sea in the air. He was right, a storm was coming. I wondered what would happen to the tunnel if the waves got too big. Starvation might not even be my main problem if this tunnel floods, but who knows. I'm a vampire, surely I could survive a little flooding, right?

Amity. I hoped Tony hadn't tried to do to her what he tried to do to me. She would fight back, I know that, but even just the thought of him trying to force himself on her made my blood boil. He would never the see dark of the night again. Of course, if he did *anything* to her, I would kill him.

By the end of the night, I was more exhausted than I had ever been in my life. I had been scraping at my chains and ropes all night trying to set myself free, but they just wouldn't give.

As the tunnel began to lighten for the morning, I thought about the pain I would endure for another day, but now it was for multiple reasons. I had gone almost two days with no sleep or blood to drink. I was beginning to feel hungry. It wasn't too bad yet, just felt like I had skipped a meal, but I'd be okay. In the days to come though, I knew it would grow into hunger pains, and eventually starvation. The longest I had gone without blood was maybe around a week. It felt like the longest week of my life, and it's been a while since then. I knew as a vampire, I wouldn't ever technically *die* of starvation. I would just get so hungry that I would feel like I was being eaten from the inside out. Then eventually, I would grow weaker and weaker until I became comatose. At least, that's what I've been told.

The hunger I could handle, but that on top of no sleep, and surviving through the daylight, was going to be difficult.

In my chained-up state, I was only able to move about 2 feet in any direction. Just enough for me to stand up, sit down, and change positions. With the exhaustion I felt from trying to get the chains broken, I slumped down to the ground and leaned my head against the wall, taking some deep breaths. I was covered in sweat, mud, and blood, and my hair was a tangled-up mess. At some point the ponytail had shaken out and my loose hair was all over. My clothes were soaking wet, and my feet were pruney, but the worst part was still my fear for Amity. No matter how awful I was feeling, or how scared I was, I would always worry more for Amity than myself.

I knew the sun was about to rise, so I fell onto my side and rolled onto my stomach up against the wall. I put my forehead into the mud and shielded my eyes with my body, hoping that would help. It reminded me of tornado drills from grade school. I thought maybe if I could just protect myself enough that I didn't have a migraine, I could sleep through the day, then have enough energy to free myself the next night. The tunnel lit slowly, but never got as bright as it had the day before.

A strong gust of wind came in then, along with the sound of rain. It was cloudy! The clouds were thick enough that the sun wasn't giving me a severe migraine. It was still uncomfortable for me to have my eyes open, but it wasn't so bad that I couldn't sleep, so that's exactly what I did.

Against the cold stone walls, and with mud for a mattress, I fell asleep to the sound of a thunderstorm.

The next night it was still raining, and I was sore as hell, but I had made it through the day, and I had slightly more energy. I could do this. I sat upright and stretched my legs. When I did so, I realized I had stuck my feet into a puddle that wasn't there before. I looked around and noticed that the center of the tunnel had flooded. It looked to only be maybe a few inches deep, but any more rain and that flooding would probably come up to where I was sitting.

The edge of the tunnel where the wall was exposed to the elements had a small but steady stream of water pouring in from the corner. The grass was flattened and hanging over the wall, and the smell of mold grew stronger.

I told myself I had to get out of here. If I couldn't within the next day or two, and the storm persisted, who knows what would happen to me. I thought maybe I could chew my way out of my ankle ropes, but getting my feet up to my mouth with my hands behind my back was the problem. With all my training, I had gotten extra flexible, but I was no contortionist. I attempted multiple times, but it just wasn't happening, so I needed to think of something else.

The water was slowly creeping towards me and unless I stood up, it was now unavoidable. So, I stretched my legs out and dunked my feet in the puddle, completely submerging them. I kept them in there for maybe an hour, then brought my knees up to my chest. My feet were wrinkled and purple, but the ropes were soaked and feeling a bit looser. Arching my left foot, I attempted to peel out of the rope with my right foot. It took a lot of maneuvering and wiggling, but eventually I got one foot free which freed the other as well. I breathed a sigh of relief, stretched my toes, and rolled my ankles in all directions. There were bright red rings all around the bottoms of my legs, but that was the least of my worries. That would heal quickly.

Standing up, I leaned away from the wall as much as I could. I tried every which way to bend and contort so I could get my wrists flipped from back to front but I just couldn't figure out how to do it. It made me wonder why 'how to get out of handcuffs' wasn't a lesson we learned in Hunter school. I spent all night twisting and turning and stretching, but to no avail. Eventually, I just went back to scraping at the metal to wear it down. As I did the next night too. All the while yelling occasionally to see if anyone was around to hear it.

At the beginning of the night on the fourth night, the rain had finally stopped. Luckily the water hadn't gotten much higher, only a few inches. It did soak me but at least it didn't grow 6 feet and swallow me whole. I was starting to feel famished and sore from days of sleeping on the ground in a puddle with my hands tied behind my back. My feet were swelling, and my teeth and gums were aching. More than any of that though, I missed my best friend. I hoped she was okay. I missed how it felt with her arms around me in a tight embrace, and I missed the smell of her hair just after she refreshed the color, but over everything, I missed the sound of her voice when she says, 'I love you'. I felt horrible that I had allowed Tonny's lips to touch mine. I should have bitten him long before he got that close to my face, but that's in the past. I would just have to be honest with Amity and hope that she wouldn't be furious. In this situation, and knowing Amity, I didn't think she would be.

Footsteps echoed through the tunnel again and I prepared myself to see Tony. I brought my feet up and hid them under my butt so he wouldn't see that I had gotten them out of the ropes. Then I braced myself in case he tried anything stupid. Tony poked his head around the corner then marched his way over to me. He stood a few feet away and sighed.

"You look horrible," he said.

"Gee, wonder why," I huffed.

"Are you starting to get hungry?"

I stayed silent.

Tony pulled out a blood bag from inside his raincoat and waved it in front of me. He brought it close enough for me to smell and I craved it. I knew that bag didn't come from a willing donor, and I just hoped it wasn't Evelyn's blood. I shook my head and leaned back against the wall.

"Rain's not over yet, you know," he added while shrugging and putting the blood back in his pocket. "There's a second wave coming. This one is supposed to last even longer than the last. It would be a shame for you to have to stay down here any longer."

I stood up and leaned towards him. I knew I just gave away the rope situation, but I just couldn't stand there any longer without trying everything I could to escape.

"I'm guessing you're not going to tell me where Amity is?" I asked.

He looked down at my bloodied feet then looked back up, expressionless. "Nope."

I reached out to kick him, but he was expecting it, and he grabbed my foot and pulled me up so that I was in midair. I could feel the tug all over my body, as if he would rip me in pieces if he pulled any harder. Then he let go and I fell back to the ground, hitting my head on the stone wall. I took a few deep breaths, then stood back up. I ran at him as far as the chains would allow, then back, and again, then back, and again. He dodged me every time except on the fourth go. Gathering up all the energy I could muster and thinking of how badly I wanted to rescue Amity, I pulled myself forward so hard, that the wall cracked, and the chains gave. There was a loud *clink*! and the area of the chain that I had been carving at, had finally snapped, and I was free.

Without even thinking, I lunged for Tony. This time, he wasn't expecting it, and I saw his eyes grow wide as I went for his throat.

My fangs dug into his neck. I wanted to just rip his skin apart, but as soon as my teeth touched blood, I couldn't stop myself from taking a sip. It only lasted a few seconds before I felt a surge of energy. I was no longer hungry for blood; I was hungry for vengeance. A groan escaped my lips as I tugged at Tony's neck. I punched him in the face as hard as I could and knocked him out, then I searched his person for anything useful. He had a wallet, car keys, and a pocketknife. I took the latter two. Just as I was about to use the knife on Tony, I heard something that both terrified me, and relieved me.

In the distance, I heard the ghostly sound of someone calling my name. Maybe I was imagining it. It sounded like it was coming from my own head. I listened for a few minutes to see if I heard it again, and I did. It had to be Amity. It sounded just like her, but strained, and scared. She was screaming. Then I didn't hear it again, and without blinking, I sprinted.

CHAPTER 29

Vengeance

Who cared about tony? I had to find Amity. With difficulty, I trudged through the water until I got to the hole in the wall. I turned the corner and entered another tunnel. This one had a singular light at the other end, and handlebars all the way across. The water didn't reach this area, and there was no mud, it was all stone or concrete. My wet, bare feet felt a stinging pain each time they met the concrete, but I pushed forward. I didn't care, I couldn't care. I needed Amity.

The adrenaline was still pumping through my body along with Tony's blood. I knew he wasn't dead, not yet, but he was about to be. I was going to find Amity, and we were going to go back, take the damned pocketknife, and end his life. I ran to the end of the tunnel, where the light was, and paused when I noticed a sign. A historical sign of... no I didn't have time to read a stupid sign. I had to find Amity. The only way I could go was another tunnel. This one was opened to a mass of sandy grass. I could tell the tunnels were part of a building structure, one that was very old. The edges were arched with red brick, while the rest was grey stone. There were black ropes along the edges like it was some tourist attraction. There were also more signs, but something told me I couldn't go out into that grass yet. I had to go into the next tunnel.

My heart beating fast, I ran into the next tunnel. All the way down was another hole in the wall. It looked just like the one I came out from. As I got closer to it, I noticed a hand sticking out of the hole. It was on the ground and still. The adrenaline hit even harder, and I felt my heart fall from my chest.

Amity.

I turned the corner and there she was, lying on the concrete with her head on her arm. She was out cold.

"Amity!" I gasped and dropped down beside her. There were bruises up and down her arms and legs and her pink hair was stained red with blood. I turned her over and laid her head in my lap and checked to see if she was still breathing. She was, but it was labored.

"Amity, Amity, please wake up!" I cried. I thought about picking her up and carrying her out, but I had barely made it through the tunnels myself. While I waited for her to awaken, I anticipated Tony's return. It was only a few minutes until Amity woke up, saw it was me, and jumped up with a huge grin on her face. I jumped too, in shock that she felt good enough to do that.

Her arms swung around my neck, and she squeezed tightly. I returned the hug and sighed in relief.

"I'm so glad you're okay!" we said in unison.

I backed up from the hug and kissed her deeply. It was brief, but I needed that, I missed her so much and I was ecstatic to see that she would be okay. Then I remembered Tony and released myself from her grip.

"We have to go. Tony is still alive, and who knows where he snuck off to."

She nodded and followed me through the tunnel. It seemed she had some of her energy back; you could tell she was in pain, but she was going to be brave and power through. When we reached the tunnel that led outside Amity paused to look at the scenery.

"Where are we?" she asked.

"No idea."

There was nothing around but the building. Everything else was grass and sand, leading down a small hill to the beach, and then the ocean. We were surrounded by nothingness. The only place we had to go was in the building near (but separate from) the tunnels. Amity pointed towards it, and we headed that way, staying near the wall so we wouldn't be visible in *all* directions.

A path led up to a door on the side facing away from the tunnels. A tourist sign told us we were at a historical monument. I looked up and saw old cannons on top of the building aiming at the ocean. We went inside the building and saw a little gift shop, which sold a lot of Civil War relics. There was a bathroom and employee room in the back so we decided to hide out there until we could catch our breath. We sat in some chairs next to a little kitchen area and just held each other for a moment.

Again, I noticed the bruises all over Amity's body and the closed-up gash on her head, and I lost my breath. I lowered my head and tilted Amity's chin up gently.

"What did he do to you?" I cried.

She shook her head like it was too painful to talk about.

"Amity, please."

She looked at me with puppy dog eyes and a quivering lip, "well he had me tied up, I've lost count how many days... it was so dark in there. I screamed and screamed but no one could hear me, and then one of the nights he came in and just started yelling at me, muttering something about you, I don't know what. I was sitting on the ground, kinda laying up against the wall, and he came over and..."

"And?"

"He tried to... he was going for my shorts... so I kicked him like a kangaroo," she paused like she was waiting for a reaction from me, but I needed her to tell me the rest. I was furious.

She continued, "he kinda snapped then and started beating on me. He knocked my head into the wall until I lost consciousness, and then I guess he left. He came back about 2 hours ago, and I knew he was going to try again so I instantly tried to fight back, but I was so tired and in so much pain. The bruises from that were just finally starting to heal, but I just kept thinking the whole time I was down there actually, about how I needed to get to you. Whatever happened to me, all that mattered was that you were okay. So, I tried to kill him right there. I used every bit of strength I had in me. He ran then, I don't know why. I broke free of my chains and untied my feet. I went to go look for you, shouting your name, but I didn't make it very far, and that's when you found me."

I didn't know how to console her, I felt so bad for her; and I was so mad at Tony all I wanted to do was throw and break everything in this room and then ring his neck. My arms pulled Amity in for a hug, and I rested my head on hers, softly rubbing her back.

"I'm just… I'm so sorry," I told her.

"I'll be okay," she mumbled into my chest. I couldn't let her go. We held onto each other for what felt like a long time until Amity asked about Tony, what happened to him, and what happened to me.

"Um… not too dissimilar to your story, only less bruises. He tried to kiss me. Well, he did kiss me, and I'm so sorry I let that happen, I was just so scared and in shock, but as soon as he tried to put his tongue in my mouth, I bit it as hard as I could. The next time I was ready, I got free and knocked him out. I stole his pocketknife, and I was gunna… well then I heard you and I just started running."

"I'm so sorry. You didn't think that would upset me, did you?"

"The kiss part? Maybe."

"Of course not, that was not your fault. Tony is an evil man that will take what he wants when he wants. I could never be mad at you for something you couldn't control. I'm actually very proud of you for doing what you did in response. Biting his tongue, I'm guessing hard enough for it to come off? That takes major courage."

"Well, it didn't come all the way off… I'm sure it would heal if we weren't about to go finish him off."

"Still."

We heard a door slam shut then and we knew it was go-time. A second wave of energy hit us as we ran out to greet Tony. He stood in the doorway of the shop, and we stood at the back.

"Hazel. Amity."

"You know how this has to end," I stated.

"One or two of us is going to die," he replied.

I saw some iconic Civil War weapons hanging on the wall with price tags at the bottom. They were extremely expensive, so I imagined they had to be the real deal. Amity and Tony both had the same idea though, and the three of us all jumped up onto the glass shop counter. Amity grabbed a bayonet, I got a sword, and Tony picked up a musket. I flipped off the counter and took a defensive stance. Amity did the same, but Tony just stepped off and somehow landed like he was just taking a casual step. His hat was gone, but he still had the raincoat on, and it flipped up at the ends as he came down. He pointed the musket at us and fired without hesitation. I almost went into flight mode, but I realized nothing had come out. The gun was no longer functionable. I smiled then because the gun may be useless, but the melees were just fine. A sword is still a sword even if it's old.

Tony raged with anger, he raised his arms above his head and swung the musket down, smashing the glass cabinets and most of the items inside them. Then he turned back around and started marching towards me. I ran towards him, raising my weapon. He lowered his shoulder at the last second and body checked me, wrapping his arms around my legs and flipping me over his back. Amity went after him and he tried to do the same to her but she crouched down, slashed his shins and slid over to me.

I had landed not so gracefully on my ass, nodded at Amity, then reached out and grabbed Tony by the ankles. I yanked him back and he fell flat onto his face. We went to hold him down, but he kicked the air in between us, causing us to lose grip. We all three stood back up and I tossed Amity her blade back.

"I just need to know one thing," I said, breathing heavily.

"What's that?" he frowned.

"Why me? All those people that came before me, what made me different?"

He shrugged, "you are just… different. You had something that they didn't. I don't know, a youthful, optimistic glow maybe. Something sweet and noble."

"Did you have genuine feelings for me, or was it all just for show?"

"For a brief time, I did think that maybe I was starting to feel something, but I was wrong."

"You wanted to crush my spirit."

He shrugged again.

"It was all just a game to you."

"I called you my little experiment for a reason. I wanted to know how strong you could be. Guess I didn't realize that a human could make you stronger than any vampire."

"You got that right."

I raised my sword and jumped into the air. As I came down, Tony reached up and grabbed the handle. It was an arm wrestle for who could get the sword. I pushed and pulled and pushed and pulled. Between a generally strong man who wasn't all about body building, and a woman who was all about strength gain, the match was almost even.

Amity disappeared from my view and reappeared behind Tony. She slashed him with her bayonet, which led to him dropping his grip on the sword. Then, almost instinctively, I brought down my wrath in the form of that sword. I sliced him from shoulder to waist, going down the right side of his chest.

Tony collapsed to the ground and blood pooled beneath him. I held him down as tightly as I could and gestured to Amity.

"Hurry, drink from him. Before he passes out, Amity, you need to get your strength back. It will be okay."

She nodded and tugged on Tony's left shoulder. She pulled his head back with his hair and bit into the crevasse of his neck. Tony squirmed below me for a few seconds until he passed out from severe blood loss. Amity sat up and wiped her chin with her arm. Her eyes shun with the relief she must have felt. I told her to swap blades with me and she tossed me hers as I tossed her mine. I kneeled over Tony's chest as Amity stood by his head.

We counted to three and brought down the blades with a swift motion. Amity sliced it through his neck, then slid it out, making sure the cut went all the way through. This was while I dug my knife into his chest. I carved a hole above his heart, then pulled it out with the knife and tossed it to the ground.

Amity and I both sighed in relief. I laid my head on the cold tile for a moment and gathered my thoughts. It was finally over. We had done it. Tony was finally dead. For good this time. So why did I feel so remorseful? Was it because a small part of me enjoyed it?

After taking some time to catch our breath, we knew we needed to either do something with the body or get the heck out of dodge. There was nothing around to safely make a fire. It was a historical site so we really didn't want to start a fire in the building, but also if we made a little campfire just outside of the building, either the rain would put it out, or Tony's bones would still remain, and the cops would find that. However, we also weren't sure about putting him in the ocean, because without any weights and a boat, he would just float back in with the waves. So getting out of dodge it was.

First, we had to get rid of the evidence. We left the weapons, but found cleaning supplies in the employee lounge, so we took that and got rid of any fingerprints. Then we covered up the body with some tarp that we found in the back. Someone would still find him like that, but at least the blood and gore wouldn't be so abrupt. The only thing we did take was his heart. We left the building and observed our surroundings. It seemed we were on the front side of the landmark, so we walked around and saw the ocean meet the beach slightly downhill from where we were. The beach was small and beyond that it was a bit grassy near the building. We went down to the beach, and I gave the heart to Amity. She took it and chucked it into the ocean as far as she could, and with her strength, that was a good distance. We hoped it would get eaten by sea creatures before it ever got the chance to wash up on shore.

Together we fell back onto the sand and looked up at the night sky. It was still early in the night, but the moon was still mostly full, and the stars were bright. The sky was predominantly clear, but there was a wall cloud near the horizon that I presumed was the second wave Tony had been talking about.

"How are you feeling?" I asked Amity.

She laid her head on my shoulder and wrapped her arm around my waist, "much better."

"I'm just glad this whole thing is over."

"Me too. That was probably the most scared I've

ever been."

"More scared than when we fought Elijah?"

"Well, that came close, but I think not knowing if you were okay... or even alive... was worse. That tunnel was dark, even for us, and I almost lost my sanity. I don't even know, how long were we in there?"

I sat up and looked at Amity with concern. "Did you not have a hole in wall?"

She shook her head.

"I did. Right now is the 4th night we've been here."

"So, we were in there for four days? Wait, you had a hole in the wall?"

"Kinda, it looked like it was supposed to be there, there was like a half-wall sort of thing, but the rain was coming in and flooding the ground."

"Doesn't that mean the sunlight was coming in too?"

I nodded and sighed. Then it was her turn to look concerned. She asked how I handled that I told her that I didn't really. I told her about the migraine and trying to curl up in a tight ball and sleep it off. It wasn't fun, but it wasn't the worst part about being down there.

"I'm sorry. I wish we could've been tied up together so we at least could have communicated. That sounds a lot worse than my dark tunnel."

"I'm not the one who got hit the way you did, so *I'm* sorry."

"Don't be. It's over now. I'm alive. You're alive. Tony's not. It is all going to be okay now."

I rested my head on her shoulder as the breeze blew my hair back from mine. We relaxed for another half hour or so before we figured we should probably get back to... somewhere. Anywhere far away from the body. Amity helped me up from the sand and we walked back around the building to the front. There was a small parking lot that was completely empty, and the entrance to it was barricaded with caution signs.

'Closed for tropical storm' it said.

There was one singular road, barely big enough for both directions of traffic, surrounded by small mounds of sand. I wasn't sure where we were, maybe a small island of sorts, you could see the ocean in all directions. The stone building was at the edge, where the island ended, and the other direction went on as far as the eye could see. The beach itself was like a long road, with the ocean on either side of it and a path down the middle.

Since there were no cars, we would have to go on foot. With no idea how far the beach went on for, we began our journey. After an hour or so we passed by a large hill in the middle. The road went around it, so we followed the road. A few minutes later there was a fork in the road, one leading to the hill, and one leading straight on. We decided to take a closer look at the hill, as the road didn't go very far, but it did lead to a collection of palm trees and other tropical plants. At the end of the road was a giant garage door. It appeared to be an abandoned military weapons bunker. We poked our head around, but decided it was probably safest to stay low and not risk getting in trouble with the military, so on we moved.

Another hour later and the clouds were rolling in. As we walked along the beach, dipping our toes in the water, a large wall cloud roared above us. In seconds the temperature dropped at least ten degrees. The gentle breeze had turned into strong winds, and then hard rain poured down onto us. We looked around for some type of shelter, just to sit in for a few minutes until the wall passed, but there was absolutely nothing but ocean and sand. So, we ran a while to see if we could get back out of the storm, and it wasn't long before the wall had passed and the skies began to clear again. I joked with Amity that the weather was as fickle in Florida as it was back home in Kansas.

After another hour we still hadn't gotten anywhere, but off in the distance, we began to see the tippy tops of tall buildings, and we had hope that it wouldn't take much longer to get to civilization. However, we were becoming fatigued quickly after all we had been through, and who knows how many miles we had walked at that point. We decided to follow the road in the middle to give our bare feet a break from the harsh sand. The road was dipped into the sand just enough that it had flooded from the storm, and what started out as some puddles here and there turned into 2-foot-deep pools of crystal-clear water. That didn't help the exhaustion.

All the while we passed by crabs and birds and forgotten beach toys. By the time the buildings were in clear enough view to see their details, we felt like we were about to pass out. Our feet and calves were so sore and heavy feeling it was hard to continue walking, but we pushed ourselves to our limits.

We had walked the night away, and the sun was slowly approaching. We feared that we wouldn't make it to civilization before the sun came up, but we were so close, we had to keep going.

Finally, we were within sight of some early birds surfing the last waves before the sun came up. Still following the road, we passed by a tourist sign that contained a map. The map stated how long the distance was from the hotels and other businesses, down to the fort. We had walked around 15 miles. At that point the road was blocked off due to the flooding, and we decided to take the beach the rest of the way. Only about 10 minutes later we had finally made it to the "public" beach area, and there were a few people hanging out, looking for shells and listening to music. Amity and I were breathing heavily. After 4 days without food, sleep, shoes, and proper shelter, on top of fighting with Tony and almost not winning, on top of walking 15 miles, we just could not take it anymore.

I gave Amity a weary look and she returned it with the same. I collapsed to my knees, my vision becoming fuzzy.

CHAPTER 30

A New Beginning

A few months later it was summer again. Amity and I had both turned 19... well... 18 for a second time, and we were ecstatic to be living it up in Florida.

Things had really looked up after what happened with Tony. When we passed out at the beach, some kind tourists took us in and helped us recover, as we told them we 'couldn't afford' to go to the hospital. We tried to go back to the hotel, but it was swarming with cops, looking for Tony's killer. So, we had to abandon our stuff and flee the city. We headed back home and stayed with my parents for a while. My mom had been worried sick since I hadn't called or texted her in a week. I reassured her that we were okay, but that I didn't really want to talk about it.

I made sure to keep an eye on the news to see if they talked about Tony and if the cops had figured anything out, but so many states away, they weren't really talking about him. We never got any calls, and no cops ever broke down our doors, so for the time being, we were safe.

The change came when we did get a call from someone else. Someone who worked for Tony, his 'second in command' as he called himself. He set up a meeting with us at a local coffee shop and wearily, we accepted. The man's name was Saul, and he claimed to be Tony's attorney, a very secretive attorney. He said he couldn't give us too many details, but that Tony had left a lot behind for me. I was his number one priority in his will. But I was surprised he even had a will, since he expected to live forever. However, I guess when you make a lot of enemies, you must expect that there may be one that wants to kill you.

"Don't worry," he told us quietly, "it has been arranged so that you will never be questioned about Tony's 'disappearance'."

I asked what he meant, but he again said he couldn't give us many details, just that Tony's body had been dealt with and no humans would ever know what happened. I had so many questions, but the one I had to know first was 'why were cops at the hotel then?'. Apparently, they weren't looking for Tony's killer, they just had some drunken customers fighting.

The next thing he told us about was what was left for me. There was a lot, but mainly, he left me the Florida house, and two cars, along with one million dollars to do whatever I wanted with. I had to know what he did with the rest, because I knew he had many other houses and cars and a lot more money too. Saul said that they were given to other people but wouldn't say who. I asked how we knew we could trust him, and he shook his head and told us 'you never know'. Then he slyly handed over a large wad of cash as a down payment for my million, along with a bunch of paperwork and his business card, then he took his coffee and walked out.

Then came the decision of what to do with all of it.

I could sell the house and get my own place, or I could keep the house. It was a nice location, and we loved the beach, so Amity and I decided to keep it, but donate all the furniture and decorations so that we could purchase things that fit us better. So, after a couple months we moved in, and slowly started working on repainting and redecorating the house, as well as fixing up some things that needed work. Most recently, that was the broken railing on the third-floor balcony. My parents had come to visit and absolutely loved the place, and I told them to come visit anytime they wanted, that I would pay for their flights and anything they needed. Overall, they were proud of both of us. I thought maybe they shouldn't be, because they didn't know the worst of the details, but I also didn't want to burden them with certain details.

Now that it's summer again, the neighborhood was getting busy with renters and tourists, and Amity and I had a cozy little spot on the first-floor balcony, where we could watch people having fun at the beach, or read, or just enjoy a relaxing joint. The only true struggle of moving to Florida was finding food. At first Evelyn was our savior. Before we went back home after what happened, we found Evelyn and made sure that she was okay. Luckily, Tony hadn't bothered her while we were stuck in the tunnels, as she had left town for the whole week, just to be safe. Of course, that ended up being the right move. We told her what happened and the three of us decided to remain friends. After all, she and Maggie were the only two humans in Florida that knew who we really were, and they both were kind enough to be our volunteers.

Our friends in Colorado kept in touch via snail

mail, with polaroid photos and hand-written letters. It was nice to get to hear about their achievements and how things were going in the mountains. Hunter kept in touch through text, and he was doing great too. He had actually recruited Tyler to be his next apprentice, and even though Tyler was young, he was a quick learner and a swift kicker.

"Hey, let's go catch some waves when I finish this," Amity hollered from another room of the house. I sat my book down and followed her voice into the master bedroom. Long gone were the nautical themed decorations. Now there was a nice collection of fairy lights, pictures, and artwork. We painted the walls a deep green and hung leaves and tapestries all over the ceiling. Most of the house was like this now. One of the guest bedrooms had turned into a library, and the living room was now a calming oasis.

Amity was sitting on the floor with one foot underneath her and the other stretched out. She was working on organizing photos into memory boxes. I sat across from her and picked up a stack. Looking through the photos was like looking into another lifetime. Colorado seemed so long ago, even though it had been less than a year. I stopped at a photo that made my heart melt. It was the two of us at the top of a mountain on a hiking trip. We were smiling and my arm was around Amity's shoulder. A deep valley view could be seen in the background. It was the same night we confessed our feelings for each other. I stared at the picture for a long time until Amity leaned over to see what I saw, then she scooted closer to me and leaned her head on my shoulder.

"So much has changed since then," she sighed.

"Yeah, but in a good way," I added.

I sat that photo to the side and looked at the next one, it was a selfie Amity sneakily took while Hunter and I were sparring. She was in the corner of the photo, grinning, and we were in the background. Hunter never liked photos and never let us take any with him in it, but that one he never found out about. There were a few more photos of us in Colorado, and then the stack switched to Florida, until we were up to date.

Amity stood up then and pulled me up with her. We changed into our bathing suits and got ready for the beach. After moving back to Florida, we both felt it was time for a change, so I went back to blonde, but a few shades lighter than my natural. Amity went from her cute cotton candy colored hair to a vibrant, neon yellow, which she said reminded her of the sun. I think she missed the sun sometimes, and I did too. I missed the warmth of the sun while tanning on a trampoline with a sprinkler underneath. A part of me missed the joys of my childhood, but with the money that Tony gave me, I didn't have to worry about much. If I spent the money wisely, we would have enough to keep us going for a while. However, considering the possibility of living for more than a hundred years, Amity and I invested heavily, and have already seen some return.

It only took a few minutes to walk down to the beach and set up a spot. The good thing about being out at night was we almost always had the beach to ourselves. We could pretty much do whatever we wanted and not worry about judgement, or 'Karens', or sketchy people. That night I was wearing a pink two-piece suit with a white polka dot pattern, and Amity was wearing a skimpy, stringy suit that was the same color as her hair. It didn't leave much to the imagination, but I loved it. I didn't really know her before she became a vampire, but I got the feeling that it had given her a lot of confidence. She was stronger, faster, and happier, according to her. I was just lucky to be graced with her beauty. I reminded her then just how good she looked and that I loved her, and she blushed.

We sat out some lounge chairs and laid our surfboards next to them. We had a bag of supplies in the middle and our wetsuits laid out on top. For a while we just relaxed, watching the stars and looking for comets. The moon was almost full that night, and it lit up the whole beach. The sand almost glistened when you looked at it just right. It was all incredibly peaceful.

A group of people came into view then as they walked along the water's edge. They were laughing and smoking what smelled like weed, and when the boys of the group noticed us, they waved us down. We shrugged our shoulders and walked over to the group.

"What're you ladies up to?" one man said.

"Just chillin," Amity responded.

They asked if we wanted to join them, using a very seductive tone. Even the women of the group beckoned us. Something seemed very familiar about them. There were 5 people in the group, 3 boys and 2 girls, all of various ages, but all seemed the same age mentally. They reminded me of the Peaceful Vampires. They reminded me of vampires. They each had that look in their eyes, like they were hungry. So, I told a joke and as a few of them laughed, I noticed fangs.

It made since; it was nighttime after all. They were probably looking for someone to eat.

I frowned, "I'm not sure we would be very good

company."

Amity figured it out too, "we wouldn't taste very good either."

The group stopped laughing and murmuring then. I showed them my own pointy teeth and their silence switched to cheers.

"Team V!" a couple of them shouted.

"But the question is," one of the women lowered her eyes, "are you a benevolent being, or are you malicious?"

I looked at Amity questioningly.

"Uh, benevolent I guess, what are *you*?" she asked them.

"We are most definitely benevolent."

"Yeah, we're part of a rehabilitation program," someone else added.

"Rehabilitation? From what?"

"Mostly blood addiction and abuse."

I looked around at the group and tried to see what kind of vibes I got from them. At first, I had thought they were bad vibes, but now they seemed kind of nice.

"I'm sorry, could you elaborate?" I asked. "Addiction?"

"The group we're with believes that we should ask permission before taking someone's blood. Most of us are recovering from being... well more like Jack the Ripper."

"Wait, so you guys' only drink blood from willing doners?" Amity grinned.

"Yeah, now we do," one of the girls smiled back, "oh, but we're not here to judge. If you guys aren't like that."

"We are! Actually, right now we're struggling just a

bit because we had a hookup a while back when we lived in Colorado, but right now we just have two people that rotate for us."

"You should absolutely join us tomorrow then. Have you been in Florida long? The vampire scene here is huge."

"Not super long. Sorry, maybe we should introduce ourselves. I'm Amity, and this is Hazel."

We all shook hands and the group introduced themselves. The new friend that spoke the most and stood out the most was a woman named Mina. She was a beautiful Korean woman who appeared to be in her mid-20s. She was thin, with long legs and even longer, silky black hair. Her demeanor was confident but humble, and she greeted us with the gentlest handshake of the group. Mina would be the one to guide us to wherever we would be going the next night. She separated from the group to continue talking to us while the rest of the group went ahead to splash each other in the water.

We exchanged origin stories, hers involved a Korean war, and ours was mostly extended to information about Tony. We told her about the vampire ball fiasco and about the tunnels. She was just as shocked as we were.

"That's awesome that you guys have been good from the start. Most vampires aren't like that," she smiled.

"I think things could have turned out very differently if we didn't have each other, and if we hadn't had such good support systems," I agreed.

"Well, the Tony part isn't such a surprise. Like I said earlier, the vampire scene in Florida, especially this area, is huge. I think a lot of them came from New Orleans. The problem is, we're very divided. Theres the vampires like us, who organize nonprofit events and we have schools and families and just overall are much more inclusive. Then you have the vampires like Tony, who organize sacrificial rituals and blood raves."

"Well… I can't hate on the rave part," I teased, "but yeah, everything else is awful. So where are we're going tomorrow?"

"Well, I'll tell you more when we get there, but it's basically a nonprofit organization for awareness and the funds go to helping lost or new vampires find their way."

"That's amazing," Amity grinned.

So, the next night we met up about 30 minutes inland at a brand-new-looking building in a very nice area. The building reminded me of a school, and there was a building across the street from it that *was* a school. The sign out front said, 'Blackwood Family Rehabilitation and Reintegration Center'. It looked like a very normal rehab center that any human could just walk into. The difference being that this one was lit up and functioning at night instead of day. The parking lot was full and there were a few people walking in and out. One couple was wearing very traditional Victorian apparel. Yellow light glowed from every curtained window, and the front doors where dimly lit with a purple bulb.

Mina ushered us in, the front doors automatically opening, then closing behind us. The front desk had two older women in black scrubs. One of them was on the phone, and the other was shuffling some paperwork. It all looked so… human. I looked around and most of the area was white and very sterile looking, with the addition of some plants. Behind the desk on the right-hand side was a sign that read 'volunteer sign in here'. On the left-hand side there was an informative poster that said the center was operative by invite only.

The woman shuffling papers looked up and greeted us with a smile. She knew Mina personally.

"Hi Heather!" Mina waved, "these are some new friends of mine, I was hoping they could have a tour? I don't think they are in-need of our services, but they are new in town, and I thought they might enjoy seeing the place."

"Of course! Let me just go get Mr. Blackwood."

"The owner," Mina informed.

We sat in the waiting room for around 15 minutes and people watched. The place was busy for a rehab center. All of the employees were wearing black scrubs, and the visitors wore clothing of all different eras. I saw a lot of modern outfits, but I also saw a lot of old-timey dresses and suits as well.

Mr. Blackwood came out from the back and greeted us. He was a tall and dignified looking man. He had a very Jane Austen appearance with black pants, a black tailcoat with a gilded trim, and a white shirt underneath. His hair was short, his eyes were a deep green, and he spoke with a soft voice and a slightly Old English dialect.

We introduced ourselves and he gestured for us to follow him. He first led us down a long hallway, everything seemed modern except for the lighting, which was very dim for a vampire's sensitive eyes. It simulated a torch in a dungeon as far as color and brightness went. A male employee passed by us pushing a very old woman in a wheelchair and he paused to nod at Mr. Blackwood, who nodded back with a smile.

As Mr. Blackwood took us down the hallway, he began describing the building. He said that it was new. His company had been around for a very long time, but they had just been completely renovated as the group and client needs were increasing rapidly. He first stopped in the cafeteria.

"This cafeteria is used for visitors. We sell blood obtained from ethically sourced resources. Mainly human donors."

"How do you get enough doners to feed everyone?" I asked.

"Our referrals. The vampires here have lots of human friends and family that generously give what they can."

He led us through a few more rooms then. One was a crafting room, one was a small theatre, another was a meeting room. We made our next stop in a meditation room.

"Here is where we reflect on everything we are grateful for. We try to find peace in this world that we will be in indefinitely. There are certified meditation experts, and we also do yoga in here as well."

The meditation room was absolutely the most calming room in the whole place, with fairy lights, tapestries, books, and pillows everywhere. I would happily join this place just for that alone. Next, we crossed over to a wing with many small therapy rooms. I had been to therapy once; it looked a lot like the one I went to.

"What kind of therapy do people need here?" Amity asked.

"Most of our patients have struggled with abuse and blood addiction. Meaning they were -more or less- raised to be ruthless, cold-blooded killers. Where they once thrived off stalking and mutilating humans for their blood, they now thrive in just enjoying eternal life to the fullest capacity."

"So, the rehab is basically because mean vampires decided they wanted to be good?"

"Precisely."

"How did this whole thing get started? Why is it growing so rapidly?"

"Wonderful questions," Mr. Blackwood gestured to us to sit on the couch in the therapy waiting area and we did.

"I was born in Europe in the late 15th century."

I had to stop him there, "I'm sorry, I'm just curious, if you're from the medieval times, why are you dressed more like the Georgian Era?"

"How long have you been in existence?" he asked in return.

"19 years."

"Ah, so young. Tell me, is there a style from your childhood that you still enjoy and wear to this day?"

"Um… I think ballet flats would count."

"Well, it's a bit like that. I've been around for a very long time, which means I've seen many different fashion trends come and go. What was 'trendy' when I was a kid, I will always be fond of, but my favorite fashion era was the Georgian. I suppose I just like the way I look in tailcoats," he laughed.

"Gotcha," I giggled along with him then let him continue.

"Well, there isn't much to tell of my human life.

By the time I became a vampire, I was very old. 45 was considered to have been a full life back then, unlike today's humans who live much longer. I won't bore you with the details of how I came to be a vampire, but like most of the patients here, I was very cruel in the beginning. Whenever I was hungry, I swiped a woman off the street and ended her life. It wasn't until the industrial age that I began to realize the damage I was doing. I had made my riches by then, and that's when I moved to the states to start anew.

"After a while in Louisiana I moved to Florida, and after a while here I started this company. It was slow at first. Many vampires were closed off to the idea of being kind to humans, but eventually I got people to realize that humans are just like us. There was no reason to kill them when we didn't have to, and thus, the company grew.

"Today we have 3 locations across Florida, and we have helped hundreds of vampires find the light."

"That's amazing," I gawked.

"We also now have the addition of the school, and that has been going well too."

"A school? A school for vampires?"

He nodded, "vampire children. There is a public school across the street, and we use their facilities at night for the same purpose."

"I've never even heard of vampire children," Amity stated, crossing her legs and leaning forward with curiosity.

"They are just like you, either turned too young, or birthed by a vampire couple."

"We can do that?"

"Yes, in the same way a human does, a vampire is

born and raised. They age more slowly than a human and stop aging at the equivalent of 24."

"How long does it take them to get to 24?"

"About 40 human years. So, the children take classes for 20 years. They learn everything from mathematics, world studies, science, all different kinds of languages, and the older kids have different programs for their personal studies. We hope to one day create a university. Right now, the students are getting ready for a break. We like to take summers off too, just like the humans, so they only have one week left until they're out for the season, and the eldest kids will graduate and have their own night ceremony."

"That all sounds so cool. I never knew that there were people born as vampires. I would love to visit the school too."

"Mina, would you like to take them to the school once we wrap up our tour?"

She grinned, "it would be my pleasure."

We followed Mr. Blackwood's lead and exited the room. He showed us the rest of the building which included a pool and spa area, a gym, and a hospital ward. Then we said our goodbyes and Mina walked us over to the school. Classes were in session, but the principal was willing to meet with us and show us around. He let us observe a few different classes of different age groups and it was interesting to get to see vampires that were so young. Before this, the youngest I had met was M, and she was '15'. Here they were as young as 4 looking, but they seemed as smart as 8/9-year-olds, as they were already learning multiplication.

At the end of the night, we thanked the principal for showing us around and went on our way. Amity and

I made plans to see Mina again and she gave us both hugs before getting into her car and driving off. We mentioned to each other how much we liked her and how nice she was. I told Amity how excited I was that there were so many people like us, and they were all right here in Florida.

Maybe, just maybe, we could build a life here.

EPILOGUE

A year and three months later

"Okay class! It's 4:30 am, what does that mean? That's right, it's time to go home! Everyone grab your backpacks and start loading up. Oh, and remember to tell your guardians that the Blackwood blood drive is tomorrow night!"

"Goodbye Miss Miller!"

My students waved goodbye as they filed out the door, I waved back with a warm smile and wished them well. Then I packed my own things and headed home for the day. Amity arrived home only a few minutes after me, but I was already relaxing on the couch. She joined me in relaxation and asked how my day went.

"Oh great! There were no biting accidents at school today."

"Wow! That's a first!" she laughed.

"How about you?"

Amity rolled her eyes but kept her grin. She crossed her legs and fiddled with her now-long hair. The professional extensions looked amazing with her figure; they went all the way down past her waist. She had dyed it again, of course, and now it was black on the top and blue underneath.

"Eh, it was okay, psych was good, but I don't understand why I have to take all these other classes that aren't anything to do with my major."

"I never understood that either, like why should I have to take public speaking when I will never once speak on a soap box platform."

"Who knows. I have a ton of homework for the weekend, but my grades are good so far."

"Well, that's good, if you can just finish out this semester, then you only have one more semester of hard work and then you'll be all done with your bachelors! It'll be worth it, you'll see!"

Amity yawned and pulled me off the couch to go get ready for bed. She had been taking night classes at a local community college to get a degree in psychology. With that degree she was hoping to go work for Mr. Blackwood at his facility.

I was also going to school, but for a very different reason. Back when we had first taken a tour of Blackwood's School for Vampires, the principal had mentioned that they didn't have quite enough teachers to keep up with their growing number of students. That led to me getting a job teaching the youngest group in the school. My students were all 3-4 'earth' years old, which was about the equivalent of 6-7-year-old humans. So basically, I was teaching 1st grade. It was so amazing to get to work with these kids and help them learn and grow into kind and intelligent little vampires. It was all I could have ever dreamed of.

Before I had become a vampire, I had always wanted to teach, but mainly I wanted to teach in areas where teachers were really needed. The route I took to get there was a lot different than I had anticipated, but I had finally made it. I was exactly where I needed to be in life, and I hoped to stay there forever.

After getting ready for bed, I closed all the curtains in the house. With our customized blackout curtains and low-light lamps and candles, the daytime turned into more nighttime, and we could stay up as late as we wanted. I told Amity I wanted to work on one quick project before going to bed, and she said she would help me so we could get it done quicker.

I wanted to reorganize the books. I wasn't sure why I randomly decided to do so, but reorganizing things was something that made both of us feel satisfied and fulfilled. So, our house was almost always looking neat and organized, but with lots of little trinkets and things that made us smile.

The books were currently organized by size, but I decided they might look better to be filed by color. Together, we started taking everything off the shelves and onto the floor behind us. We had kept all the books that Tony had in the house; it was probably the only thing that we had kept of his. He has a surprisingly vast collection including a few informative books about vampires. I wondered if the human world just viewed it as a satirical novel pretending to be non-fiction. We knew better though. Amity and I read through them together and it answered all our questions, like what an energy vampire was for example. So far, the only one I had ever met was Mrs. Johnson and boy was she an enigma. Apparently, they (energy vampires) are very rare. Most of them associate with humans, not vampires, because that's how they get their fuel source. Rather than draining a person's blood, they drain a person's energy. They are also the only vampires that can walk around in the daytime with no issues.

The book also revealed to us what happened to the

very first vampire. It was so old that it was only legend; but that's a long story.

Shaking my head, I regained focus on the task in front of me. I grabbed a large stack of books off the shelf and as I went to lay them down, they slipped from my hands and scattered on the ground. As they fell, a random envelope escaped one of the books and landed next to it.

"Are you okay?" Amity asked, coming over to help gather the books.

I picked up the envelope and noticed it had my name on it. Gently, I ripped the envelope open and unfolded a piece of paper.

Dear Hazel,

I know you may not believe me, but I needed to tell you something very important. I know when you read this, I will be gone, and I know why I'll be gone. However, you must know that there is just something about you... or maybe something about me, that makes me have feelings for you that I have never felt before. You did make me want to be better, but it's in my nature to be naive and reckless. That week you tried to get me to be a better person, to only drink from willing volunteers, I truly did my best to oblige. Alas, I was too stubborn. I wanted to be good for you, but by the end of that week, I realized that just wasn't me. Vampires aren't supposed to be the good guys, that's just not how we operate. Part of me wishes I could just get you to be more like me, but the other part of me wants to be more like you. All this time on the earth and not one person has made me feel that conflicted. I know you don't love me. In fact, I know that you hate me, and I sympathize. I'm a difficult man to love. I'm writing this while you are trying to survive the fortress; and putting you in there is making me hate myself even more. Especially for what I did to Amity, and for that, I'm sorry. You are the strongest, most capable woman I have ever encountered, and I know that tonight, I will die.

You will kill me tonight, and... I am okay with that. It's funny though, when I first began my experiment with you, I had a lot of theories about how it would play out, but I never thought that the pacifist would end up killing me. I will still do everything I can to fight and stay alive, and if I succeed, I will be on my way, and I will let you live your life, but shall I be defeated, just know that it was because you bested me. Also, after hundreds of years of this life, I am tired, I am bored, and I am full of hatred for myself. So, I welcome death.

You will be both my murderer and my savior. For that, I am leaving you the house, the cars, and enough money to keep you going for hundreds of years if spent correctly. Thank you for trying your best to better the world, both vampires and humans, and I hope you find peace in your existence.

Best Wishes,
Tony

I wasn't sure if I should vomit or cry. While the sentiment was sweet, I had almost wished I had never seen it. Till the very end, Tony was a nightmare, and only at the end did he realize his wrongdoings. However, it did ease the burden of guilt for killing him. All my life I had been so anti-violence and pacifistic, that to be who I was today was scary. Younger me would hear about what I did to him, and to so many others, and be terrified. But things had changed. I had changed. My goals in life were still similar though; I wanted to make the world a better place for everyone. Finally, I was getting to live that dream.

My amazing, wonderful, sweet, beautiful girlfriend put her gentle hand on my shoulder and waited for my response. When I stayed silent, so did she. She kissed my cheek and wrapped her arms around mine. She was there to support me through and through, and I couldn't be more grateful to have her in my life.

After a weekend of reflection on the beach, I went back to my students gratified and relaxed. They deserved my full attention, and I was going to give them every tool they needed to succeed in life. I thought about everything that made my life amazing, my supportive family, great friends, amazing girlfriend, rewarding job, secure house, and financial stability. All of this was reason to smile. Reason to see another night. Reason to live. I could spend the rest of eternity like this. I was finally doing what I felt like was my purpose in life. I was creating change. I was fulfilling goals. I was making life better for others, and I felt good about that.

Never again would I kill. Never again would I go against my own moral code for someone else.

I finally found peace in the world. I found...

happiness.

ABOUT THE AUTHOR

Ella Kindred

Ella Kindred is a dreamer, storyteller, and artist at heart. With a degree in liberal arts as her compass, she has been navigating the realms of imagination since she could hold a pencil. Her greatest inspiration comes from her daughter Raven, who reminds her daily of the wonder and magic in the world. When she's not  lost in the pages of her own creation, Ella can be found immersed in the vibrant hues of her paintings. 'A Vampire's Vengeance' is the culmination of her lifelong love affair with words and colors, a journey she invites you to embark on with her.

Made in the USA
Monee, IL
13 June 2025

19027909R00252